U0084675

序　言

唸研究所是一種趨勢。隨著職場競爭日趨激烈，沒有一定學術背景與實力的人，最後只能隨波逐流，永遠得不到出人頭地的機會。在這種情況下，當然要唸研究所。

在過去二十多年來，大學畢業證書，就像是鐵飯碗保證書。只要你有一張大學文憑，就代表你有勝任工作的實力，企業在徵選人才時，也常常優先錄用大學畢業生。但是，時代變了，現在大學生滿街跑。沒有研究所文憑，怎麼跟別人競爭？

參加研究所考試時，**英文是決定勝負的關鍵**。因爲其他專業科目，每個人都有唸過，分數差異不大，但是英文實力要靠平常慢慢累積，才能在考試時發揮出來。

如何準備研究所考試？準備研究所英文有三部曲。**首先，你必須熟背「研究所必考 1000 字」**，那是從歷屆考試中擷選出來的精華，要是連單字都看不懂，想猜答案也沒方向。**第二，每天做一回歷屆英文考題，「研究所英文試題詳解①～④」**就是你最好的幫手。研究所考試，各校難易度差距很大，多做考古題，可以幫助你熟悉該校的考試題型。**第三，閱讀英文報紙**，現在有許多研究所，在出閱讀測驗的考題時，喜歡和時事做連結，如果你根本不知道世界上發生了什麼事，怎麼可能得高分。

「研究所英文試題詳解④」蒐集了 93 年度最新考題，是幫助你順利考上研究所的利器。全書的完成經過審慎的校對，若有任何疏漏之處，誠盼各界先進不吝指正。如果讀者認爲應補充任何相關資料，歡迎來函指教（E-mail: learnbook@learnbook.com.tw）。

編者　謹識

目 錄

國立台灣大學九十三學年度
碩士班研究生入學考試英文試題

Directions: Choose the best answer for each question. To indicate your choice, use a 2B pencil to blacken the appropriate space on your computer card for each question.

Example : It was Joan's first visit to the country, and everything was fresh and ________ to her.

(A) dull (B) quickly
(C) new (D) excited

Answer : A B C D (C blackened)

I. Vocabulary/Usage—Instructions: Please choose the answer that best completes the sentence.

1. The boss went through the ________ when her secretary arrived late for the fourth day in a row.
(A) door (B) floor (C) window (D) roof

2. The company needs to consider how to ________ more money for its stockholders.
(A) give (B) cause (C) generate (D) induce

3. His view ________ with the general opinion of biologists on this issue.
(A) concurs (B) approves
(C) accordance (D) opposes

4. Sally didn't take long to ________ his idea in the bud.
(A) nip (B) cut (C) squeeze (D) grow

5. That action-adventure film was just too ________ for me to believe.
(A) persecuted (B) far-fetched
(C) disjointed (D) overrated

6. The assistant was so ________ that I had to copy and staple the entire report myself.
(A) impersonal (B) uncooperative
(C) implausible (D) menial

7. Going on someone else's property without permission is considered ________ and is punishable by law.
(A) harassment (B) trespassing
(C) embezzlement (D) insider trading

8. I would like to ______ my remarks by first relating a true story.
(A) preface (B) prelude
(C) present (D) prepare

9. Not giving Tom that promotion was a real ________.
(A) kick in the bucket (B) kick in the basket
(C) kick in the teeth (D) kick in the foot

10. Sam couldn't believe Tom didn't want to ________ after all the meetings they had had on this project.
(A) hammer out a deal
(B) hammer his way
(C) swallow the hammer
(D) come under the hammer

II. Vocabulary—Vocabulary in Context—Instructions: Choose the answer that best explains the meaning of the capitalized word or words in each sentence as used in that particular context.

11. After you are done with your reading, please decide on the main idea the author is trying to CONVEY.
(A) move (B) get across
(C) pretend (D) summarize

12. Americans live with a legal system that FOSTERS predatory trial lawyers.
(A) releases (B) honors
(C) condones (D) encourages

13. Over the New Year, Sam promised his wife he would TURN OVER A NEW LEAF.
(A) give her a present
(B) take a walk in the woods
(C) clean up the leaves in the yard
(D) become a better person

14. Sam was so fed up with just sitting around all day TWIDDLING HIS THUMBS that he turned in his resignation.
(A) gambling (B) typing very quickly
(C) doing nothing (D) biting his fingernails

15. How often do you come down to this BANK to fish?
(A) skating rink (B) side of the river
(C) financial institution (D) stock market

III. Error Recognition—Instructions: Identify the one underlined word or phrase that should be changed in order for the sentence to be correct.

16. When he saw the traffic accident near the circle (A), he called his mother right (B) away and tell (C) her not to wait dinner for (D) him.

17. The recent restructuring (A) of the educational system means that student (B) must get used to a new set of evaluation methods (C) in order to attain their goal of studying (D) at a university.

18. Fliers touting (A) various candidates covered bulletin boards, students discussing (B) and debated hot topics (C) and a week without (D) some sort of political rally was a rarity.

19. This is an especially (A) competitive year for the women, too, because the defending (B) champion, UCONN, did not turn (C) out to be the juggernaut it was advertise (D) to be.

20. Scientists say an enzyme in the brain that monitors (A) energy in cells (B) also appears to regulate appetite and weights (C), a discovery that could lead (D) to new treatments for obesity.

IV. Cloze Test—Instructions: Choose the best answer to fill in each blank.

Would you like to create art on your doorstep every morning? If you live with the Tamil Nadu people in southeastern India, you __(21)__! The Tamil Nadu culture teaches girls to create geometrical designs as part of their daily housekeeping __(22)__.

Traditionally, the girls and women of Tamil Nadu __(23)__ their doorsteps to start the new day. They sprinkle the ground with cow dung and water. Then they create the __(24)__ designs by letting rice powder fall __(25)__ their hands. The designs are called "Kolam" and are a unique part of the Tamil __(26)__ heritage.

The Kolam tradition serves __(27)__ purposes. Sprinkling the doorstep with cow dung and water is thought to clean the ground because the dung has purifying properties. Using rice powder is seen as an act of kindness towards ants. Drawing the figure each morning on the doorstep is done to both guard the house from evil spirits and to welcome visitors.

The Kolam is made first by creating a grid of dots, such as five dots across and five dots down. Then, the dots are either all __(28)__, or a line is drawn around the dots. It is important to the Tamils that the lines begin and end in the same place. This creates a figure that represents the never-ending __(29)__ of birth, life, and death.

Previously, only anthropologists were interested in studying this ancient cultural tradition. However, recently these Kolam figures have also drawn the attention of computer scientists who are interested in the mathematical ideas contained in these ___(30)___.

21. (A) can (B) could (C) shouldn't (D) are
22. (A) dutiful (B) duty-free (C) duties (D) duty
23. (A) sweep (B) sweeping (C) swept (D) sweeps
24. (A) complicated (B) complicating (C) complicit (D) complicates
25. (A) of (B) from (C) on (D) into
26. (A) cultured (B) cultural (C) cultures (D) culture
27. (A) few (B) four (C) much (D) little
28. (A) connections (B) connectors (C) connected (D) connects
29. (A) cycle (B) circles (C) series (D) set
30. (A) designers (B) designs (C) designates (D) decisions

V. Reading Comprehension—Instructions: Read each of the following passages and choose the best answer to each question.

Scientists may have discovered the solar system's most distant object, more than three times farther away from Earth than Pluto. "The sun appears so small from that distance that you could completely block it out with the head of a pin," said Dr. Mike Brown of the California Institute of Technology, who helped in the discovery. The object—about 8 billion miles (12.8 billion kilometers) from Earth—has been given the provisional name of Sedna, after the Inuit goddess who created the sea creatures of the Arctic. Brown and his team of astronomers, using Caltech's Palomar Observatory, found Sedna in November as part of an on-going three-year outer solar system project. Days later, the high-power Spitzer Space Telescope focused on the object. Initial details indicated Sedna to be made of ice and rock, with temperatures never rising above -400 degrees Fahrenheit (-240 degrees Celsius), according to researchers. Sedna is likely the largest object to be found circling the sun since the discovery of Pluto in 1930. It is still smaller than the ninth planet, though, with a diameter of about 1,000 miles (1,700 kilometers). The finding has sparked debate over what constitutes a planet. Many astronomers say Pluto, with a diameter of just under 1,500 miles (2,300 kilometers), is too small to be termed a planet and is just one of many minor objects in the outer reaches of the solar system. But those who argue Pluto is a planet are likely to push the assertion for Sedna to become the 10th planet in the solar system.

31. The new planet is named after a ____________
    (A) mythical figure. (B) powerful prophet.
    (C) telescope. (D) sea creature.

32. The planet is ____________
    (A) the size of a pin.
    (B) 8 billion miles.
    (C) 2,300 kilometers in diameter.
    (D) 1,700 kilometers in diameter.

33. There is disagreement as to ______________
   (A) whether Pluto and Sedna have suns.
   (B) whether Pluto and Sedna have moons.
   (C) whether Pluto and Sedna are planets.
   (D) whether Pluto and Sedna have water on their surface.

34. The best title for the above passage is ______________
   (A) New Moon Rocks the Solar System.
   (B) Sedna Rises from the Deep.
   (C) New Planet Found in Solar System.
   (D) Ice and Rock Discovered on Sedna.

35. Which of the following sentences is NOT true?
   (A) Pluto is closer to the Earth than Sedna.
   (B) Pluto was discovered in 1930.
   (C) Sedna was first sighted at the Palomar Observatory.
   (D) Temperatures on Sedna range from -400 degrees to -240 degrees.

James Baldwin was born on 2 August, 1924, in Harlem, New York. He was the oldest child in a family of nine. He saw himself as ugly, and he was small for his age. His intelligence and shyness as a child and the harshness of his relationship with his father (Baldwin found out in his teens that the man was really his step-father) made reading very attractive to him, and his bookishness later nurtured him as a writer. He followed his stepfather into the ministry when he was still a teenager, serving as a junior minister in the Fireside Pentecostal Assembly between the ages of 14 and 16.

Baldwin graduated from high school in 1942 and moved to Elle Meade, New Jersey, to help to support his family with a series of menial jobs. When his stepfather died in 1943, however, James Baldwin gave up the ministry for the life of the writer. He realized while he was still in New Jersey the depth of his rage resulting from the racism any black person confronted constantly, and he decided that either he could live "with it consciously or [surrender] to it."

He moved to Greenwich Village, New York, to be back in the greater freedom of New York City and to be in touch with other writers. In 1948, to escape American racism and homophobia, he moved to Paris, France, where he lived for the next eight years. In Paris, he joined the circle of Richard Wright, another black American expatriate, whom he had already met in Brooklyn years before. He traveled in social circles frequented by Jean-Paul Sartre, Simone de Beauvoir, Jean Genet, Saul Bellow, and Truman Capote, among others. He said he saw himself as an American writer first and foremost, not as a "black" or a "gay" writer. Although his writings of the 1960s and 1970s are so vividly about racism and the black American experience that he will always be considered one of America's foremost African-American writers, he is also a writer about the human condition, especially the destruction wrought on individuals by their hatred and crimes against each other. He wrote about the relation between polarized opposites, black and white, men and women, gays and straights.

36. The essay above is an example of a(n) ______________

(A) personal narrative. (B) argumentative essay.

(C) informative essay. (D) causal analysis.

37. Baldwin is primarily known for ______________

(A) writing about religion.

(B) writing about being an expatriate.

(C) writing on homosexuality.

(D) writing about contrasts between people.

38. The voice the author uses in this essay is ______________.

(A) angry (B) impersonal

(C) mocking (D) creative

39. One place where Baldwin did NOT live was ______________

(A) Paris. (B) Harlem.

(C) Elle Meade. (D) Brooklyn.

40. It can be surmised from the third paragraph that Baldwin decided to ______________

(A) live with racism consciously.

(B) surrender to racism.

(C) ignore racism in his writing.

(D) live without fear of racism.

SARS is not the first viral disease to burst out of China or Hong Kong. The southern Chinese region was the source of influenza pandemics in 1957 and 1968, as well as the source of novel strains of avian flu in 1997 and 2001. Why does this region keep throwing up viruses that have the potential to threaten the lives of people around the world?

Southern China's status as the world's primary breeding ground for new strains of flu is explained by the fact that its people, pigs and domestic fowl, which all harbour influenza viruses, live cheek-by-jowl, increasing the likelihood that two strains will recombine genetically to produce a deadly new variant. Preliminary evidence suggests that SARS followed a different model, apparently crossing over to people from wild animals, rather than livestock. But this, too, is not terribly surprising, given that the southern Chinese make widespread use of wild species for food and traditional medicine—practices that Chinese health officials are now trying to discourage.

Another dietary issue—specific nutritional deficiency—has also been <u>tentatively</u> linked to the emergence of new viral strains in rural China. For instance, in many parts of the country, the diet is lacking in the trace element selenium. A team led by Melinda Beck of the University of North Carolina at Chapel Hill found that when the coxsackievirus B3 infects mice deficient in selenium, it mutates at a much higher rate and can become more virulent. She has also observed increased mutation rates in flu viruses infecting selenium-deficient mice. "The fact that China has widespread selenium-deficient areas may play a role in the emergence of new viral strains," Beck claims. Other scientists regard Beck's findings as speculative, and doubt whether they offer a general explanation for the emergence of viral diseases in China. When you have the world's largest population interacting closely with livestock and wild animals, say experts, it's hardly surprising that China seems to be the origin of so many viral outbreaks. "It's a matter of exposure probability," suggests Mei-Shang Ho, an epidemiologist with Academia Sinica's Institute of Biomedical Sciences in Taipei, Taiwan.

41. One reason for the high incidence of viral diseases in China is ______
    (A) influenza occurred in 1957 and 1968.
    (B) the close proximity of people to animals.
    (C) transmission of the avian flu occurs biannually.
    (D) people don't get immunized when they are told to.

42. The word "tentatively" in the second line in the third paragraph means ______
    (A) slowly. (B) possibly.
    (C) creatively. (D) necessarily.

43. A working hypothesis is that ______
    (A) SARS is a mutated form of the avian flu.
    (B) SARS jumped from livestock to people.
    (C) SARS jumped from non-domesticated animals to people.
    (D) SARS lacks the ability to jump to wild animals from people.

44. The best title for this essay is ______.
    (A) Dietary Deficiencies Lead to SARS
    (B) Avian Flu Threatens China
    (C) China's Role in Viral Epidemics
    (D) Speculative Finding on SARS

45. It can be inferred from this passage that Dr. Mei-shang Ho thinks ________
    (A) the vitamin deficiency hypothesis is plausible.
    (B) selenium should be given to children.
    (C) people and animals living closely together is dangerous.
    (D) infected fowl should be exterminated.

Ever so slowly, some sectors of the U.S. economy are starting to bring more people aboard. In many cases, the ones doing the most hiring are relatively small, nimble, fast-growing outfits and the skills they're looking for reflect that. "There's a real shift in what the most successful companies now want," says Lin Stiles, head of executive-search firm Linford Stiles & Associates. "We're not hearing as much about traditional credentials like MBAs and CPAs. Instead, they're looking for agility, innovation, and a nontraditional approach to problem solving. So job seekers need to emphasize those skills now more than ever." In our recent conversation, Stiles offered some other tips on getting hired:

What are the "hot" industries these days? One is computer chips. A new generation of chips will inspire a fresh round of new consumer products and advances. Cisco, Intel, and Solectron are among the leaders in this field, and they need developers. Microsoft, Apple, Dell and other innovative companies are looking for chip designers, electronic engineers, and marketing people. Consumer products generally are "hot," too. The leaders have suffered less from the recession than almost anyone else. I don't mean just food and cosmetics, but furniture, upscale clothing, appliances. Companies like Nike and Victoria's Secret are growing and doing very well by getting more efficient, with low inventories and great customer service. It's paying off. And those companies need designers and talent in marketing and manufacturing.

No doubt some tech companies are "hot," but isn't outsourcing an issue? First, product design and marketing really have to stay in the U.S. But, you know, outsourcing may turn out to be a temporary phenomenon anyway, especially in (high-tech) customer service, where there is already a backlash brewing because of language differences and other problems. One thing outsourcing does is, it distances you from your customer, and that is never smart in the long run. There have also been problems with piracy by overseas contractors. And the current vast wage differential is likely to be short-lived. When you add all this together, my view is that more companies are going to realize, "Hey, we don't have to ship operations overseas. We can get a lot more efficient at doing the work here in the U.S., and keep our customers happy, too."

46. "Credentials" in line seven of the above essay is closest in meaning to ____________

(A) believability. (B) resumes.

(C) qualifications. (D) traditions.

47. Stiles does NOT include the following job type on the list of popular industries ____________
    (A) product designers.
    (B) chip developers.
    (C) marketing representatives.
    (D) customer service representatives.

48. The overall tone of this article is ____________
    (A) glum.
    (B) upbeat.
    (C) cautious.
    (D) placating.

49. Which type of companies are LESS likely to outsource?
    (A) Ones that need 24-hour customer service.
    (B) Ones that have stagnant growth.
    (C) Ones that are worried about piracy.
    (D) Ones that make cosmetics.

50. Stiles feels that outsourcing ____________
    (A) will not last long.
    (B) is a serious problem.
    (C) is efficient.
    (D) is suitable for customer service.

國立台灣大學九十三學年度
碩士班研究生入學考試英文試題詳解

I. 字彙：

1. (**D**) (B) floor (flor) *n.* 地板
(D) ***roof*** (ruf) *n.* 屋頂　***go through the roof*** 勃然大怒
boss (bɔs) *n.* 老闆　secretary (ˈsɛkrə,tɛrɪ) *n.* 秘書
in a row 連續地

2. (**C**) (B) cause (kɔz) *v.* 引起
(C) ***generate*** (ˈdʒɛnə,ret) *v.* 產生
(D) induce (ɪnˈdjus) *v.* 引起
stockholder (ˈstɑk,holdɚ) *n.* 股東

3. (**A**) (A) ***concur*** (kənˈkɝ) *v.* 與…意見一致 <*with*>
(B) approve (əˈpruv) *v.* 贊成 <*of*>
(C) accordance (əˈkɔrdn̩s) *n.* 一致
(D) oppose (əˈpoz) *v.* 反對
view (vju) *n.* 看法　general (ˈdʒɛnərəl) *adj.* 普遍的
opinion (əˈpɪnjən) *n.* 意見
biologist (baɪˈɑlədʒɪst) *n.* 生物學家
issue (ˈɪʃjʊ) *n.* 問題；議題

4. (**A**) (A) ***nip*** (nɪp) *v.* 摘取　***nip…in the bud*** 防範…於未然
(C) squeeze (skwiz) *v.* 擠壓
bud (bʌd) *n.* 芽

5. (**B**) (A) persecute (ˈpɝsɪ,kjut) *v.* 迫害
(B) ***far-fetched*** (ˈfɑrˈfɛtʃt) *adj.* 牽強的
(C) disjointed (dɪsˈdʒɔɪntɪd) *adj.* 脫節的；脫臼的
(D) overrate (ˈovɚˈret) *v.* 高估
adventure (ədˈvɛntʃɚ) *n.* 冒險

6. (**B**) (A) impersonal〔ɪm'pɝsn̩l〕*adj.* 不夾雜個人感情的
(B) ***uncooperative***〔ˌʌnko'ɑpəˌretɪv〕*adj.* 不合作的
(C) implausible〔ɪm'plɔzəbl̩〕*adj.* 難以相信的
(D) menial〔'minɪəl〕*adj.* 卑微的
assistant〔ə'sɪstənt〕*n.* 助理
staple〔'stepl̩〕*v.* 以釘書機裝訂

7. (**B**) (A) harassment〔hə'ræsmənt〕*n.* 騷擾
(B) ***trespass***〔'trɛspəs〕*v.* 侵入（他人土地、住宅）
(C) embezzlement〔ɪm'bɛzl̩mənt〕*n.* 盜用
(D) insider trading 內線交易
property〔'prɑpɚtɪ〕*n.* 財產；房地產
permission〔pɚ'mɪʃən〕*n.* 許可

8. (**A**) (A) ***preface***〔'prɛfɪs〕*v.* 以…開始 < *by* ; *with* >
(B) prelude〔'prɛljud〕*v.* 以…開始 < *with* >
(C) present〔prɪ'zɛnt〕*v.* 提出
remark〔rɪ'mɑrk〕*n.* 話
relate〔rɪ'let〕*v.* 敘述；講

9. (**C**) (A) bucket〔'bʌkɪt〕*n.* 水桶
(B) basket〔'bæskɪt〕*n.* 籃子
(C) ***kick in the teeth*** 重大挫折
teeth〔tiθ〕*n. pl.* 牙齒（單數爲 tooth）
promotion〔prə'moʃən〕*n.* 升遷

10. (**A**) (A) ***hammer out*** 詳細討論（以做出決定）
hammer〔'hæmɚ〕*n.* 鐵鎚 *v.* 鎚打；敲擊
deal〔dil〕*n.* 政策；計劃
(C) swallow〔'swɑlo〕*v.* 吞下
(D) come under 被…控制
project〔'prɑdʒɛkt〕*n.* 計劃

Ⅱ. 字彙：

11. (**B**) convey〔kən've〕*v.* 傳達
(B) ***get across*** 使瞭解
(C) pretend〔prɪ'tɛnd〕*v.* 假裝
(D) summarize〔'sʌmə,raɪz〕*v.* 總結
be done with 做完
author〔'ɔθɚ〕*n.* 作家

12. (**D**) foster〔'fɔstɚ〕*v.* 培養；助長
(A) release〔rɪ'lis〕*v.* 釋放
(B) honor〔'ɑnɚ〕*v.* 尊敬
(C) condone〔kən'don〕*v.* 原諒
(D) ***encourage***〔ɪn'kɜɪdʒ〕*v.* 鼓勵；助長
legal〔'ligḷ〕*adj.* 法律的
predatory〔'prɛdə,torɪ〕*adj.* 損人利己的
trial〔'traɪəl〕*adj.* 審判的
trial lawyer 法庭律師

13. (**D**) ***turn over a new leaf*** 改過自新
leaf〔lif〕*n.*（書籍的）一張；兩頁
(A) present〔'prɛznṭ〕*n.* 禮物
(B) woods〔wʊdz〕*n. pl.* 森林
(C) leaves〔livz〕*n. pl.* 葉子 yard〔jɑrd〕*n.* 庭院
promise〔'prɑmɪs〕*v.* 答應

14. (**C**) ***twiddle*** *one's* ***thumbs*** 旋弄兩手的大拇指；閒著沒事
twiddle〔'twɪdḷ〕*v.* 擺弄 thumb〔θʌm〕*n.* 大拇指
(A) gamble〔'gæmbḷ〕*v.* 賭博
(D) bite〔baɪt〕*v.* 咬 fingernail〔'fɪŋgɚ,nel〕*n.* 手指甲
be fed up with 對～厭煩 ***turn in*** 提出
resignation〔,rɛzɪg'neʃən〕*n.* 辭呈

15.（ **B** ） bank〔 bæŋk 〕*n.* 河岸
(A) skating〔 'sketɪŋ 〕*n.* 溜冰
rink〔 rɪŋk 〕*n.*（室內）溜冰場　***skating rink*** 溜冰場
(B) ***side of the river*** 河岸
(C) financial〔 fə'nænʃəl 〕*adj.* 金融的
institution〔 ˌɪnstə'tjuʃən 〕*n.* 機構
(D) stock〔 stɑk 〕*n.* 股票
fish〔 fɪʃ 〕*v.* 釣魚

Ⅲ. 改錯：

16.（ **C** ） *tell* → ***told***
circle〔 'sɝkḷ 〕*n.* 環狀道路
wait dinner for *sb.* 爲了等某人而延緩吃晚飯

17.（ **B** ） *student* → ***students***
recent〔 'risṇt 〕*adj.* 最近的
restructuring〔 ri'strʌktʃərɪŋ 〕*n.* 重建；重新調整
get used to 逐漸習慣　set〔 sɛt 〕*n.* 一套；一系列
evaluation〔 ɪˌvælju'eʃən 〕*n.* 評價
attain〔 ə'ten 〕*v.* 達成　university〔 ˌjunə'vɝsətɪ 〕*n.* 大學

18.（ **B** ） *discussing* → ***discussed***
flier〔 'flaɪɚ 〕*n.* 傳單
tout〔 taʊt 〕*v.* 拉生意（或選票等）
candidate〔 'kændəˌdet 〕*n.* 候選人
bulletin〔 'bʊlətɪn 〕*n.* 告示　board〔 bord 〕*n.* 木板
bulletin board 佈告欄　debate〔 dɪ'bet 〕*v.* 討論
hot〔 hɑt 〕*adj.* 熱門的
rally〔 'rælɪ 〕*n.* 集會；示威活動
rarity〔 'rɛrətɪ 〕*n.* 罕見；稀有

19. (**D**) *advertise* → ***advertised***

competitive (kəmˈpɛtətɪv) *adj.* 競爭激烈的
defending (dɪˈfɛndɪŋ) *adj.* 衛冕的；保衛的
champion (ˈtʃæmpɪən) *n.* 冠軍
UCONN 康乃狄克大學 ***turn out*** （結果）成為
juggernaut (ˈdʒʌgɚˌnɔt) *n.*【印度神話】札格納特（Krishna 神像，印度教主神之一，Vishnu 的化身，每年車節即用車載此神像遊行市中，許多人相信若能被此車輾死，即可升天，因此有人甘願投身死於輪下）；不可抗拒的力量；令人敬畏的巨大事物
advertise (ˈædvɚˌtaɪz) *v.* 廣告；宣傳

20. (**C**) *weights* → ***weight***

enzyme (ˈɛnzɪm) *n.* 酵素
monitor (ˈmɑnətɚ) *v.* 監控 cell (sɛl) *n.* 細胞
regulate (ˈrɛgjəˌlet) *v.* 管理；控制
appetite (ˈæpəˌtaɪt) *n.* 食慾
discovery (dɪˈskʌvərɪ) *n.* 發現 ***lead to*** 導致
treatment (ˈtritmənt) *n.* 治療法
obesity (oˈbisətɪ) *n.* 肥胖

IV. 克漏字：

【譯文】

你想不想要每天早上在你的門階上創作？如果你和印度東南部的坦米爾人住在一起，你就可以這樣做！坦米爾人的文化教導女孩子，要把每天創作幾何圖案，視為日常家務的一部份。

依照傳統，坦米爾的女孩和婦女，都是以打掃門階來開始新的一天。她們會在地上灑牛糞和水。然後讓米做的粉末從手中灑落，來創作複雜的圖案。這些圖案被稱為 Kolam，那是坦米爾人的文化傳統中，獨特的一部份。

Kolam 這項傳統有幾個用途。把牛糞和水灑在門階上，被認爲具有清潔地面的作用，因爲糞便具有清潔的特性。使用米做的粉末，則被視爲是對螞蟻的一種慈悲行爲。每天早上在門階上畫圖，既可以保護房子不受邪靈侵擾，還可以用來歡迎訪客。

Kolam 一開始是由棋盤狀的點所構成的，像是橫的五個點，和直的五個點。然後這些點不是全部連在一起，就是被一條線框起來。對坦米爾人來說，這些線的開始和結束要在同一個地方，是非常重要的。這樣所創造出來的圖案，才能代表誕生、生命和死亡，這種永無止境的循環。

以前，只有人類學家對研究這個古老的文化傳統有興趣。但是，現在這些 Kolam 圖案也吸引了電腦科學家的注意，他們對於這些圖案裡所包含的數學概念很有興趣。

【註】

create〔krɪ'et〕*v.* 創造；創作　doorstep〔'dor,stɛp〕*n.* 門階
geometrical〔,dʒiə'mɛtrɪkḷ〕*adj.* 幾何的
design〔dɪ'zaɪn〕*n.* 圖案
housekeeping〔'haus,kipɪŋ〕*n.* 料理家務
traditionally〔trə'dɪʃənḷɪ〕*adv.* 傳統上
sprinkle〔'sprɪŋkḷ〕*v.* 灑　cow〔kaʊ〕*n.* 母牛
dung〔dʌŋ〕*n.* 糞便　powder〔'paʊdɚ〕*n.* 粉末

unique〔ju'nik〕*adj.* 獨特的
heritage〔'hɛrətɪdʒ〕*n.* 遺產；傳統
serve～purpose 有～用途　purifying〔'pjʊrə,faɪɪŋ〕*adj.* 淨化的
property〔'prɑpɚtɪ〕*n.* 特性　ant〔ænt〕*n.* 螞蟻
figure〔'fɪgɚ〕*n.* 圖案　guard〔gɑrd〕*v.* 守護
evil spirits 惡靈　grid〔grɪd〕*n.* 棋盤格；網格
represent〔,rɛprɪ'zɛnt〕*v.* 代表

never-ending〔ˈnɛvɚ,ɛndɪŋ〕*adj.* 永無止境的
previously〔ˈpriviəslɪ〕*adv.* 以前
anthropologist〔,ænθrəˈpɑlədʒɪst〕*n.* 人類學家
ancient〔ˈenʃənt〕*adj.* 古老的
draw〔drɔ〕*v.* 吸引　　attention〔əˈtɛnʃən〕*n.* 注意力
mathematical〔,mæθəˈmætɪkḷ〕*adj.* 數學的
contain〔kənˈten〕*v.* 包含

21.（**A**）依句意，選(A) ***can***，代替 can create art on your doorstep every morning。

22.（**C**）(A) dutiful〔ˈdjutɪfəl〕*adj.* 守本份的
(B) duty-free *adj.* 免稅的
(C) ***duties***〔ˈdjutɪz〕*n. pl.* 職責
(D) duty〔ˈdjutɪ〕*n.* 關稅；本份

23.（**A**）空格應塡一動詞，依句意爲現在式，故選(A) ***sweep***〔swip〕*v.* 掃。

24.（**A**）(A) ***complicated***〔ˈkɑmplə,ketɪd〕*adj.* 複雜的
(B) complicate〔ˈkɑmplə,ket〕*v.* 使複雜
(C) complicit〔kəmˈplɪsɪt〕*adj.* 有同謀關係的

25.（**B**）依句意，「從」手中掉落，選(B) ***from***。

26.（**B**）***cultural heritage*** 文化遺產；文化傳統

27.（**B**）有「四個」用途，選(B) ***four***。

28.（**C**）(A) connection〔kəˈnɛkʃən〕*n.* 連接
(B) connector〔kəˈnɛktɚ〕*n.* 連接者（物）
(C) ***connected***〔kəˈnɛktɪd〕*adj.* 連接的
(D) connect〔kəˈnɛkt〕*v.* 連接

29. (**A**) (A) ***cycle*** (′saɪkl̩) *n.* 循環
(B) circle (′sɝkl̩) *n.* 圓圈
(C) series (′sɪrɪz) *n.* 一系列；一連串
(D) set (sɛt) *n.* 一套；一組

30. (**B**) (A) designer (dɪ′zaɪnɚ) *n.* 設計師
(B) ***design*** (dɪ′zaɪn) *n.* 圖案
(C) designate (′dɛzɪg͵net) *v.* 指定
(D) decision (dɪ′sɪʒən) *n.* 決定

V. 閱讀測驗：

A.

【譯文】

科學家可能已經發現太陽系中最遙遠的星體，它和地球的距離，比冥王星和地球之間的三倍還要遠。促使這項發現的是加州理工學院的麥克．布朗博士，他說：「從這麼遠的距離來看，太陽會顯得十分渺小，你用一根大頭針的針頭，就可以把它完全遮住。」這個星體──距離地球大約80億英哩(即128億公里)─已經有了一個暫時的名稱，叫做賽德娜，源自於伊努族（愛斯基摩人）神話中，創造北極海洋生物的女神。布朗和他的天文學家小組，利用加州理工學院位於帕勒摩山的天文台，進行為期三年的太陽系外圍觀測計劃時，在十一月發現了賽德娜。幾天過後，高倍率的史拜哲太空望遠鏡也把焦點集中在這顆星體上。根據研究員最初所發現的細節指出，賽德娜是由冰和岩石所組成的，而且溫度從來不超過華氏零下400度（攝氏零下240度）。自從1930年發現冥王星之後，賽德娜可能是繞太陽運行的星體中，最大的一顆。雖然它的直徑大約1000英哩（即1700公里），但還是比第九行星小。這個發現引起了對於行星組成要件的爭論。許多天文學家說，冥王星的直徑不到1500英哩（即2300公里），這麼小的星體不該被稱作行星，它應該只是太陽系外圍，衆多小型星體之一。但是那些主張冥王星是行星的人，可能會極力主張賽德娜是太陽系中的第十顆行星。

【答案】

31.(**A**) 32.(**D**) 33.(**C**) 34.(**C**) 35.(**D**)

【註】

solar〔'solɚ〕*adj.* 太陽的 ***solar system*** 太陽系
distant〔'dɪstənt〕*adj.* 遙遠的 object〔'ɑbdʒɪkt〕*n.* 物體；星體
farther〔'fɑrðɚ〕*adj.* 較遠的 Pluto〔'pluto〕*n.* 冥王星
appear〔ə'pɪr〕*v.* 顯得 block〔blɑk〕*v.* 遮擋
pin〔pɪn〕*n.* 大頭針；圖釘 institute〔'ɪnstə,tjut〕*n.* 學院
technology〔tɛk'nɑlədʒɪ〕*n.* 工業技術
billion〔'bɪljən〕*n.* 十億
mile〔maɪl〕*n.* 英哩（1 英哩約等於 1.6 公里）
kilometer〔'kɪlə,mitɚ〕*n.* 公里
provisional〔prə'vɪʒənl̩〕*adj.* 暫時的
Inuit〔'ɪnjuɪt〕*n.* 伊努族；愛斯基摩人
goddess〔'gɑdɪs〕*n.* 女神
creature〔'kritʃɚ〕*n.* 生物 Arctic〔'ɑrktɪk〕*n.* 北極
astronomer〔ə'strɑnəmɚ〕*n.* 天文學家
observatory〔əb'zɝvə,torɪ〕*n.* 天文台
on-going〔'ɑn,goɪŋ〕*adj.* 進行中的
project〔'prɑdʒɛkt〕*n.* 計劃 power〔'pauɚ〕*n.* 倍率
telescope〔'tɛlə,skop〕*n.* 望遠鏡
focus〔'fokəs〕*v.* 對準焦點 initial〔ɪ'nɪʃəl〕*adj.* 最初的
detail〔'ditel〕*n.* 細節 indicate〔'ɪndə,ket〕*v.* 指出
temperature〔'tɛmprətʃɚ〕*n.* 溫度 degree〔dɪ'gri〕*n.* 度
Fahrenheit〔'færən,haɪt〕*n.* 華氏 Celsius〔'sɛlsɪəs〕*n.* 攝氏
researcher〔rɪ'sɝtʃɚ〕*n.* 研究員 circle〔'sɝkl̩〕*v.* 繞著…旋轉
planet〔'plænɪt〕*n.* 行星 diameter〔daɪ'æmətɚ〕*n.* 直徑

spark〔spɑrk〕*v.* 引起　debate〔dɪ'bet〕*n.* 爭論
constitute〔'kɑnstə,tjut〕*v.* 構成　term〔tɝm〕*v.* 稱爲
minor〔'maɪnɚ〕*adj.* 較小的　reaches〔'ritʃɪz〕*n. pl.* 區域；範圍
argue〔'ɑrgjʊ〕*v.* 主張　push〔pʊʃ〕*v.* 支持
assertion〔ə'sɝʃən〕*n.* 斷定；主張
mythical〔'mɪθɪkl̩〕*adj.* 神話的　figure〔'fɪgjɚ〕*n.* 人物
prophet〔'prɑfɪt〕*n.* 先知
disagreement〔,dɪsə'grimənt〕*n.* 不一致
surface〔'sɝfɪs〕*n.* 表面　***the deep*** 大海
close〔kloz〕*adj.* 接近的　sight〔saɪt〕*v.* 看見
range from A ***to*** B （範圍）從 A 到 B

B.

【譯文】

詹姆士・鮑德溫於一九二四年八月二日，出生於紐約哈林區。他是家中九個小孩裡的老大。他覺得自己很醜，而且以他的年齡來說，他的身材顯得矮小。他在童年時的智慧與靦腆，加上和父親的惡劣關係（他在十幾歲的時候發現，那個男人眞的是他的繼父），使得閱讀對他非常具有吸引力，而且他愛讀書的習慣，後來還使他成爲一名作家。在他還只是個十幾歲的孩子時，就跟繼父一樣成爲牧師，並在十四歲到十六歲之間，擔任爐邊五旬節派教會的助理牧師。

鮑德溫於一九四二年從高中畢業，並搬到紐澤西州的 Elle Meade，然後從事一連串卑微的工作，來幫忙養家。但是當他繼父在一九四三年過世時，詹姆士・鮑德溫就爲了作家的生涯，放棄了牧師這份工作。他待在紐澤西時，就已經知道自己的強烈憤怒，要歸咎於不論哪個黑人都要經常面對的種族歧視，所以他決定，自己要不是「有意識地忍受它，就是向它屈服。」

他搬到紐約的格林威治村，回到比較自由的紐約市，並和其他作家保持聯繫。在一九四八年時，爲了逃離美國的種族歧視和對同性戀的憎惡，他搬到法國巴黎，而且之後八年都住在那裡。他在巴黎加入了另一個美國黑人移民理查·萊特的生活圈，他幾年前就在布魯克林認識了這個人。當他穿梭於社交圈中時，特別親近 Jean-Paul Sartre、Simone de Beauvoir、Jean Genet、Saul Bellow 和 Truman Capote。他說他第一次覺得自己是個美國作家，而不是個黑人作家，或同性戀作家。儘管他在一九六〇年代和一九七〇年代的著作，是如此鮮明地描述關於種族歧視和美國黑人的經歷，以致於他永遠都會被視爲美國的主要非裔美國作家，他還是個描寫人類處境的作家，尤其是那些藉著對彼此的仇恨與罪惡，而毀滅對方的情節。他還寫過關於完全對立者之間的關係，像是黑人與白人、男人和女人、同性戀者和異性戀者。

【答案】

36.（C）　37.（D）　38.（B）　39.（D）　40.（A）

【註】

see A ***as*** B 認爲 A 是 B　ugly〔ˈʌglɪ〕*adj.* 醜的
intelligence〔ɪnˈtɛlədʒəns〕*n.* 聰明；才智
shyness〔ˈʃaɪnɪs〕*n.* 害羞　harshness〔ˈhɑrʃnɪs〕*n.* 惡劣
in one's teens 在某人十幾歲時　stepfather〔ˈstɛpˌfɑðɚ〕*n.* 繼父
attractive〔əˈtræktɪv〕*adj.* 有吸引力的
bookishness〔ˈbʊkɪʃnɪs〕*n.* 好讀書　nurture〔ˈnɜtʃɚ〕*v.* 培育
ministry〔ˈmɪnɪstrɪ〕*n.* 牧師　teenager〔ˈtinˌedʒɚ〕*n.* 青少年
serve as 擔任　***junior minister*** 助理牧師
fireside〔ˈfaɪrˌsaɪd〕*n.* 爐邊　assembly〔əˈsɛmblɪ〕*n.* 集會；聚會
support〔səˈport〕*v.* 幫助；支持　series〔ˈsɪrɪz〕*n.* 一連串
menial〔ˈminɪəl〕*adj.* 低賤的；卑微的　***give up*** 放棄；停止
depth〔dɛpθ〕*n.* 深度；嚴重性　rage〔redʒ〕*n.* 憤怒

result from 起源於　racism〔'resɪzəm〕*n.* 種族歧視
black〔blæk〕*adj.* 黑人的　*n.* 黑人　confront〔kən'frʌnt〕*v.* 面對
constantly〔'kɑnstəntlɪ〕*adv.* 不斷地　***live with*** 忍受
consciously〔'kɑnʃəslɪ〕*adv.* 有意識地
surrender〔sə'rɛndɚ〕*v.* 屈服
be in touch with 和～保持聯絡　escape〔ə'skep〕*v.* 逃離；躲避
homophobia〔,homə'fobɪə〕*n.* 對同性戀的恐懼症
expatriate〔ɛks'petrɪ,et〕*n.* 移民者　***social circle*** 社交圈
frequent〔frɪ'kwɛnt〕*v.* 與…時常來往；親近
among others 其中；尤其
foremost〔'for,most〕*adj.* 第一的；主要的
first and foremost 首先；第一

gay〔ge〕*adj.* 同性戀的　*n.* 同性戀
vividly〔'vɪvɪdlɪ〕*adv.* 鮮明地；生動地
condition〔kən'dɪʃən〕*n.* 情況；處境
destruction〔dɪ'strʌkʃən〕*n.* 毀滅
wrought〔rɔt〕*v.* 起作用；產生影響（是 work 的過去式與過去分詞）
individual〔,ɪndə'vɪdʒuəl〕*n.* 個人　hatred〔'hetrɪd〕*n.* 憎恨
crime〔kraɪm〕*n.* 罪　relation〔rɪ'leʃən〕*n.* 關係
polarized〔'polə,raɪzd〕*adj.* 極端的
opposite〔'ɑpəzɪt〕*n.* 相反的人、事、物　white〔hwaɪt〕*n.* 白人

straight〔stret〕*n.* 異性戀者　essay〔'ɛse〕*n.* 文章
narrative〔'nærətɪv〕*n.* 故事
argumentative〔,ɑrgjə'mɛntətɪv〕*adj.* 似爭論的
informative〔ɪn'fɔrmətɪv〕*adj.* 提供知識或情報的
causal〔'kɔzl̩〕*adj.* 關於因果的
primarily〔'praɪ,mɛrəlɪ〕*adv.* 主要地
contrast〔'kɑntræst〕*n.* 對比　voice〔vɔɪs〕*n.* 語態
impersonal〔ɪm'pɝsn̩l〕*adj.* 非個人的；客觀的
mocking〔'mɑkɪŋ〕*adj.* 嘲笑的　surmise〔sɚ'maɪz〕*v.* 推測

C.

【譯文】

SARS 並不是第一個在中國或香港爆發的病毒性疾病。中國南方地區在 1957 年和 1968 年時，曾經是流行性感冒的發源地，而且在 1997 年和 2001 年時，還是新型禽流感的發源地。為什麼這個區域會不斷產生病毒，而且這些病毒還具有威脅全人類性命的潛力？

中國南方具有世界主要新型流感病毒繁殖地的地位，有人解釋說，那是因為藏有流感病毒的人類、豬隻和家禽住得太接近，因此提高兩種病毒的基因重新結合，並產生新型致命病毒的可能性。初步的證據顯示，SARS 是依循一種新的模式，它似乎是從野生動物傳給人們的，而不是從家畜身上。但是這也不太令人感到驚訝，因為考慮到中國南方的人，廣泛利用野生物種來做菜和傳統藥材——實際上，中國的衛生官員現在正試著阻止他們這樣做。

另一個與飲食相關的議題——缺乏特定營養——和中國鄉村所產生的新型病毒可能有關聯。舉例來說，在鄉下的許多地方，飲食中都缺乏硒這種微量元素。由美國北卡羅萊納大學教堂山分校的梅琳達・貝克所帶領的小組發現，B3 型的柯沙奇病毒會侵入缺乏硒的老鼠，並以非常快的速度突變，然後變得更具致命性。她還發現，流感病毒侵入缺硒的老鼠體內後，突變速度會加快。貝克宣稱：「中國有廣大區域的人民缺硒，而這可能是造成那裡不斷出現新型病毒的原因。」其他科學家認為貝克的發現只是一種推論，並且質疑它們能否針對中國出現病毒性疾病這件事，提出概括性的解釋。專家說，當你擁有世界上最多的人口，而且這些人和家畜、野生動物又密切地互動，那麼中國可能是這麼多病毒爆發的源頭，一點都不令人驚訝。「這只是接觸機率的問題」，在台灣台北的一位流行病學研究員，暨中研院生醫所員何美鄉指出。

【答案】

41.（**B**）　42.（**B**）　43.（**C**）　44.（**C**）　45.（**C**）

【註】

SARS〔sɑrs〕*n.* 嚴重急性呼吸道症候群（= *Severe Acute Respiratory Syndrome*）
viral〔ˈvaɪrəl〕*adj.* 病毒的　***burst out*** 爆發
southern〔ˈsʌðɚn〕*adj.* 南方的
region〔ˈridʒən〕*n.* 區域　source〔sors〕*n.* 發源地；來源
influenza〔ˌɪnfluˈɛnzə〕*n.* 流行性感冒（= *flu*）
pandemic〔pænˈdɛmɪk〕*n.* 全國（世界）性的流行病
as well as 以及　novel〔ˈnɑvl̩〕*adj.* 新的
strain〔stren〕*n.* 類型

avian〔ˈevɪən〕*adj.* 鳥的　***avian flu*** 禽流感
throw up 急速建造　virus〔ˈvaɪrəs〕*n.* 病毒
potential〔pəˈtɛnʃəl〕*n.* 潛力　threaten〔ˈθrɛtn̩〕*v.* 威脅
status〔ˈstetəs〕*n.* 地位　primary〔ˈpraɪˌmɛrɪ〕*adj.* 主要的
breeding ground 繁殖地；溫床
domestic〔dəˈmɛstɪk〕*adj.* 家庭的；馴服的
fowl〔faʊl〕*n.* 家禽　harbour〔ˈhɑrbɚ〕*v.* 窩藏
cheek-by-jowl 與…緊貼著　likelihood〔ˈlaɪklɪˌhʊd〕*n.* 可能性
recombine〔ˌrikəmˈbaɪn〕*v.* 再結合
genetically〔dʒəˈnɛtɪklɪ〕*adv.* 在基因上

deadly〔ˈdɛdlɪ〕*adj.* 致命的　variant〔ˈvɛrɪənt〕*n.* 變體
preliminary〔prɪˈlɪməˌnɛrɪ〕*adj.* 初步的
evidence〔ˈɛvədəns〕*n.* 證據；跡象　suggest〔səˈdʒɛst〕*v.* 顯示
model〔ˈmɑdl̩〕*n.* 模式　apparently〔əˈpɛrəntlɪ〕*adv.* 似乎
cross over 傳送　wild〔waɪld〕*adj.* 野生的
rather than 而不是　livestock〔ˈlaɪvˌstɑk〕*n.* 家畜
terribly〔ˈtɛrəblɪ〕*adv.* 非常地　***given that*** 假使
widespread〔ˈwaɪdˈsprɛd〕*adj.* 普遍的　species〔ˈspiʃɪz〕*n.* 物種

traditional〔trə'dɪʃənḷ〕*adj.* 傳統的
practice〔'præktɪs〕*n.* 習俗；慣例
health official 衛生官員　discourage〔dɪs'kɝɪdʒ〕*v.* 阻止
dietary〔'daɪə,tɛrɪ〕*adj.* 飲食的　issue〔'ɪʃjʊ〕*n.* 議題
nutritional〔nju'trɪʃənḷ〕*adj.* 營養的
deficiency〔dɪ'fɪʃənsɪ〕*n.* 缺乏
tentatively〔'tɛntətɪvlɪ〕*adv.* 暫時地；推測地
link〔lɪŋk〕*v.* 連接；關聯
emergence〔ɪ'mɝdʒəns〕*n.* 現出；露出

rural〔'rʊrəl〕*adj.* 鄉村的　diet〔'daɪət〕*n.* 飲食
lacking〔'lækɪŋ〕*adj.* 缺乏的　***trace element*** 微量元素
selenium〔sə'linɪəm〕*n.* 硒　chapel〔'tʃæpḷ〕*n.* 小教堂
coxsackievirus *n.* 柯沙奇病毒
infect〔ɪn'fɛkt〕*v.* 感染；（病毒）侵入
mice〔maɪs〕*n. pl.* 老鼠　deficient〔dɪ'fɪʃənt〕*adj.* 缺乏的
mutate〔'mjutet〕*v.* 變化；突變　rate〔ret〕*n.* 速度
virulent〔'vɪrulənt〕*adj.* 含毒的　observe〔əb'zɝv〕*v.* 發覺
mutation〔mju'teʃən〕*n.* 變化；突變
role〔rol〕*n.* 角色　claim〔klem〕*v.* 宣稱

regard A ***as*** B 認爲 A 是 B　finding〔'faɪndɪŋ〕*n.* 發現
speculative〔'spɛkjə,letɪv〕*adj.* 推測的
general〔'dʒɛnərəl〕*adj.* 總括的
population〔,pɑpjə'leʃən〕*n.* 人口
interact〔,ɪntɚ'ækt〕*v.* 互相影響　closely〔'kloslɪ〕*adv.* 密切地
origin〔'ɔrədʒɪn〕*n.* 起源　outbreak〔'aʊt,brek〕*n.* 爆發
exposure〔ɪk'spoʒɚ〕*n.* 暴露；接觸
probability〔,prɑbə'bɪlətɪ〕*n.* 機率
epidemiologist〔,ɛpɪ,dimɪ'ɑlədʒɪst〕*n.* 流行病學研究員
Academia Sinica 中央研究院　institute〔'ɪnstə,tjut〕*n.* 學院

biomedical〔ˌbaɪəˈmɛdɪkl〕*adj.* 生物醫學的
incidence〔ˈɪnsədəns〕*n.* 發生率
proximity〔prɑkˈsɪmətɪ〕*n.* 鄰近
transmission〔trænsˈmɪʃən〕*n.* 傳染
biannually〔baɪˈænjuəlɪ〕*adv.* 半年一次地
immunize〔ˈɪmjəˌnaɪz〕*v.* 免疫
creatively〔krɪˈetɪvlɪ〕*adv.* 創作地
necessarily〔ˈnɛsəˌsɛrəlɪ〕*adv.* 必然

working〔ˈwɝkɪŋ〕*adj.* 有用的
hypothesis〔haɪˈpɑθəsɪs〕*n.* 假設
mutated〔ˈmjutetɪd〕*adj.* 變化的；突變的
non-domesticated〔ˈnʌndəˈmɛstəˌketɪd〕*adj.* 野生的
lack〔læk〕*v.* 缺乏　　essay〔ˈɛse〕*n.* 文章
epidemics〔ˌɛpəˈdɛmɪks〕*n.* 傳染病的發生　　infer〔ɪnˈfɝ〕*v.* 推論
vitamin〔ˈvaɪtəmɪn〕*n.* 維他命
plausible〔ˈplɔzəbl〕*adj.* 有道理的
exterminate〔ɪkˈstɝməˌnet〕*v.* 滅絕

D.

【譯文】

在美國的經濟結構中，有些產業部門正開始以非常緩慢的速度，讓更多人加入它們。在許多案例中，那些僱用最多人的，都是相對來說比較小、反應比較迅速、成長比較快的公司，而且從它們所尋找的技術人員中，也反映了這一點。「現在最成功的企業所需求的人才有很大的轉變，」Linford Stiles & Associates 主管人才仲介公司的總經理，Lin Stiles 說：「我們不再常聽到像是要求 MBA 和 CPA 這種傳統的資格證明。相反地，它們要找的是敏捷、創新，還有懂得使用非傳統的方式來解決問題的人。所以，想找工作的人，要比以往任何時候還注重這些技能。」在我們最近的談話中，Stiles 還提供了其他有助於被錄取的訣竅：

最近有哪些「熱門」產業呢？電腦晶片是其中之一。新一代的晶片將導致新一輪的消費品產生和改良。Cisco, Intel, 和 Solectron 都是這個領域的領導者，而它們需要的是研發人員。Microsoft, Apple, Dell 和其他具有革新精神的公司，正在尋找晶片設計者、電子工程師和行銷人員。消費品通常也很「熱門」。這些領導業者因爲不景氣所遭受的損失，幾乎比其他任何行業都少。我指的不僅是食品業、化妝品業，還有家具業、高級成衣業、家電業。像 Nike 及 Victoria's Secret 則因爲採用較有效率的方式，而不斷成長，並經營得非常出色，它們的存貨少，而且有完善的顧客服務。這樣的經營方式是很成功的。而那些公司需要的是設計師，還有行銷和製造方面的人才。

無疑地，有些科技公司也很「熱門」，但外包不也是問題所在？首先，產品設計和行銷必須留在美國。但是，你也知道，無論如何外包終究只是暫時的現象，特別是（高科技公司的）顧客服務，在這個部分已經因爲語言差異和其他問題，而醞釀出反彈。外包的另一個問題是，它使你和消費者疏遠，就長期來看，這絕對不是聰明的做法。而海外承包商也會帶來很多盜版問題。再加上目前的龐大薪資差異，可能只是短暫的現象。當你把這些事加在一起，我的看法是，有越來越多的公司開始了解到「嘿，我們並不需要把業務移到海外去。我們在美國本土做這些事會更加有效率，而且還會讓我們的顧客更開心。」

【答案】

46.（**C**）　47.（**D**）　48.（**B**）　49.（**C**）　50.（**A**）

【註】

ever so 非常地　　sector〔ˈsɛktɚ〕*n.*（產業）部門
aboard〔əˈbɔrd〕*adv.* 入夥；參加
relatively〔ˈrɛlətɪvlɪ〕*adv.* 相對地；比較上
nimble〔ˈnɪmbl̩〕*adj.* 敏捷的；反應快的　outfit〔ˈaʊtˌfɪt〕*n.* 公司
skill〔skɪl〕*n.* 技能　　reflect〔rɪˈflɛkt〕*v.* 反應

look for 尋找　real〔ˈriəl〕*adj.* 十足的；完全的
shift〔ʃɪft〕*n.* 轉移；轉變　head〔hɛd〕*n.* 總經理
executive〔ɪgˈzɛkjutɪv〕*n.* 主管　search〔sɝtʃ〕*n.* 尋找
credential〔krɪˈdɛnʃəl〕*n.* 資格證明書
MBA 工商管理碩士（= *Master of Business Administration*）
CPA 政府檢定合格會計師（= *Certified Public Accountant*）
instead〔ɪnˈstɛd〕*adv.* 相反地　agility〔əˈdʒɪlətɪ〕*n.* 敏捷
innovation〔ˌɪnəˈveʃən〕*n.* 創新
nontraditional〔ˌnɑntrəˈdɪʃənḷ〕*adj.* 非傳統的
approach〔əˈprotʃ〕*n.* 方法　solve〔sɑlv〕*v.* 解決

seeker〔ˈsikɚ〕*n.* 尋找者　emphasize〔ˈɛmfəˌsaɪz〕*v.* 注重；強調
recent〔ˈrisṇt〕*adj.* 最近的　tip〔tɪp〕*n.* 訣竅
industry〔ˈɪndəstrɪ〕*n.* 產業　chip〔tʃɪp〕*n.* 晶片
generation〔ˌdʒɛnəˈreʃən〕*n.* 代
inspire〔ɪnˈspaɪr〕*v.* 激勵；導致　fresh〔frɛʃ〕*adj.* 新的
round〔raʊnd〕*n.* 一輪　consumer〔kənˈsumɚ〕*n.* 消費者
advance〔ədˈvæns〕*n.* 進展　developer〔dɪˈvɛləpɚ〕*n.* 研發人員
innovative〔ˈɪnəˌvetɪv〕*adj.* 具有革新精神的
designer〔dɪˈzaɪnɚ〕*n.* 設計者
electronic〔ɪˌlɛkˈtrɑnɪk〕*adj.* 電子的
engineer〔ˌɛndʒəˈnɪr〕*n.* 工程師　marketing〔ˈmɑrkɪtɪŋ〕*n.* 行銷

generally〔ˈdʒɛnərəlɪ〕*adv.* 通常
suffer〔ˈsʌfɚ〕*v.* 蒙受損害；遭受　recession〔rɪˈsɛʃən〕*n.* 不景氣
cosmetics〔kɑzˈmɛtɪks〕*n. pl.* 化妝品
furniture〔ˈfɝnɪtʃɚ〕*n.* 家具
upscale〔ˈʌpˈskel〕*adj.* 高級的；質優價高的
appliance〔əˈplaɪəns〕*n.* 家電用品
efficient〔əˈfɪʃənt〕*adj.* 有效率的
inventory〔ˈɪnvənˌtorɪ〕*n.* 存貨
pay off 成功　talent〔ˈtælənt〕*n.* 人才

manufacturing〔,mænjə'fæktʃərɪŋ〕*n.* 製造　***no doubt*** 無疑地
tech〔tɛk〕*n.* 科技（= ***technology***）
outsourcing〔'aʊt'sɔrsɪŋ〕*n.* 外包　issue〔'ɪʃju〕*n.* 問題
design〔dɪ'zaɪn〕*n.* 設計　***turn out*** 結果成為
temporary〔'tɛmpə,rɛrɪ〕*adj.* 暫時的；臨時的
phenomenon〔fə'nɑmə,nɑn〕*n.* 現象
backlash〔'bæk,læʃ〕*n.* 激烈的反應
brewing〔'bruɪŋ〕*n.* 釀造；醞釀　difference〔'dɪfərəns〕*n.* 差異
distance〔'dɪstəns〕*v.* 使疏遠
in the long run 就長遠的觀點來看；最後

piracy〔'paɪrəsɪ〕*n.* 盜版；侵害著作權
overseas〔'ovə'siz〕*adj.* 海外的　〔,ovə'siz〕*adv.* 向海外；在海外
contractor〔kən'træktə〕*n.* 承包商　current〔'kɝənt〕*adj.* 目前的
vast〔væst〕*adj.* 巨大的　wage〔wedʒ〕*n.* 工資；薪資
differential〔,dɪfə'rɛnʃəl〕*n.* 差異
short-lived〔'ʃɔrt'laɪvd〕*adj.* 持續不久的；短暫的
view〔vju〕*n.* 看法　ship〔ʃɪp〕*v.* 以船送達；移動
operation〔,ɑpə'reʃən〕*n.* 業務；營業　essay〔'ɛse〕*n.* 文章
believability〔bɪ,livə'bɪlətɪ〕*n.* 可信任的事
resume〔,rɛzu'me〕*n.* 履歷表

qualification〔,kwɑləfə'keʃən〕*n.* 資格
include〔ɪn'klud〕*v.* 包含　list〔lɪst〕*n.* 名單；清單
representative〔,rɛprɪ'zɛntətɪv〕*n.* 代表
overall〔'ovə,ɔl〕*adj.* 整體的　tone〔ton〕*n.* 語氣
article〔'ɑrtɪkl̩〕*n.* 文章　glum〔glʌm〕*adj.* 陰鬱的；沉默的
upbeat〔'ʌp,bit〕*adj.* 令人愉快的
cautious〔'kɔʃəs〕*adj.* 小心的；謹慎的
placating〔'pleketɪŋ〕*adj.* 安撫的；撫慰的
stagnant〔'stægnənt〕*adj.* 停滯的
last〔læst〕*v.* 持續　suitable〔'sutəbl̩〕*adj.* 適合的

國立政治大學九十三學年度
碩士班研究生入學考試英文試題

I. Structure: 30%

A. Identifying sentence errors. 16%

Directions: The following sentences test your knowledge of grammar, usage, and idioms. Some sentences are correct, and no sentence contains more than one error. You will find some elements are underlined and given a letter. Elements of the sentence that are not underlined are correct and cannot be changed. If the underlined portion is an error, select the letter of that underlined part. If there is no error, select answer E.

Example : The other members (A) of the team and her (B) suddenly (C) appealed to the jury formed (D) to handle the negotiation. No error (E).

Answer : B

1. Even when having (A) a dream, you must have a basic understanding (B) of reality if one hopes (C) to survive (D). No error (E).

2. Although science offers the hope of reducing the use of
A
pesticides and prevent plants from being eaten by insects,
B
there are difficult environmental questions raised by the
C　D
genetically modified plants. No error.
E

3. The man, was claiming to have seen the flying saucer arrived
A　B　C
at the press conference last night to describe what he had
D
seen. No error.
E

4. Even a careful listener could scarcely distinguish facts from
A　B
opinions, for the issue had become a highly emotional one.
C　D
No error.
E

5. To learn more about Hakka culture, the department invited
A
a speaker who had conducted research regard to the customs
B　C　D
of Hakka people in early times. No error.
E

6. Each academic discipline has its own practices, or
A
conventions, that people writing in the discipline follow
B　C
when engaged in a scholar dialogue. No error.
D　E

7. The maintain of peace and stability in the Taiwan Strait
(A: maintain; B: Taiwan Strait)
and the welfare of the people of Taiwan remain of
(C: remain)
profound importance to the United States. No error.
(D: profound importance; E: No error)

8. To fight and conquer in all your battles are not supreme
(A: To fight and conquer; B: are)
excellence; supreme excellence consists of breaking the
(C: breaking)
enemy's resistance without fighting. No error.
(D: without fighting; E: No error)

B. Cloze: Read the following text and choose the best answer to fill in the blank. 14%

Just as a language may develop varieties in the form of dialects, languages as a whole may change. Sometimes rapid language change occurs as a result of __(9)__ between peoples who each speak a different language. In such circumstances a pidgin language may __(10)__. Pidgins are grammatically __(11)__ on one language but are also influenced, especially in vocabulary, __(12)__ the others; they have relatively small sound systems, reduced vocabularies and simplified and altered grammars, and they rely __(13)__ on context in order to be understood.

Pidgins are often the result of traders meeting island and coastal peoples. A pidgin has no native speakers: when speakers of a pidgin have children who learn the pidgin as their first language, that language is then called a Creole. __(14)__ the Creole has enough native speakers to form a speech community, it may __(15)__ into a fuller language.

9. (A) link (B) acquaintance
   (C) contact (D) connection

10. (A) stem (B) spring (C) arise (D) rise

11. (A) based (B) built (C) derived (D) hinged

12. (A) to (B) from (C) in (D) by

13. (A) closely (B) communicatively
    (C) heavily (D) derisively

14. (A) Whereas (B) Promptly
    (C) Presently (D) Once

15. (A) enlarge (B) develop
    (C) swell (D) increase

Ⅱ. Reading (Vocabulary and Comprehension): 40%

Passages 1 and 2

For each blank in passage 1 and 2, choose among the four possible vocabulary items the most appropriate one and mark its corresponding letter on your answer card.

Passage 1

We naturally choose to write about subjects that ___(16)___ us. Historians should not, however, let their own concerns and ___(17)___ direct the way they interpret the ___(18)___. A student of early modern Europe, for example, might be ___(19)___ by the legal, social, and economic limitations placed on women in that period. ___(20)___ sixteenth-century men for being "selfish and chauvinistic" might forcefully express such a student's sense of

__(21)__ about what appears to modern eyes as unjust, but it is not a useful approach for the historian, who tries to understand the viewpoints of people in earlier times in the social __(22)__ of the period under study.

16. (A) appeal (B) bestow (C) dismiss (D) interest
17. (A) biases (B) fears (C) problems (D) quests
18. (A) pass (B) passed (C) past (D) pastime
19. (A) assured (B) dismayed (C) encouraged (D) satisfied
20. (A) Approaching (B) Assuming (C) Requiring (D) Reproaching
21. (A) independence (B) indifference (C) indignation (D) individuality
22. (A) context (B) content (C) conference (D) confederation

Passage 2

The red wolf is __(23)__ species. Its numbers have declined __(24)__, both because of willful slaughter __(25)__ by government bounties and because of the wolf's __(26)__ to the deadly destruction of intestinal __(27)__. And now the species may face total __(28)__ because of its ability to breed with a closely related but far more numerous cousin, the coyote. Thus, having survived the worst that humans and worms can do, the red wolf is now endangered by the loss of its own __(29)__ genes.

23. (A) a dangerous (B) an endangered
(C) a depreciated (D) an enchanting

24. (A) perfectly (B) permanently
(C) precisely (D) perilously

25. (A) subsidized (B) substantiated
(C) subscribed (D) succeeded

26. (A) suspension (B) suspicion
(C) susceptibility (D) sustaining

27. (A) projects (B) pressure
(C) poisons (D) parasites

28. (A) extinction (B) exception
(C) exemption (D) exhaustion

29. (A) disinherit (B) distinguishing
(C) distorting (D) dislocated

Passage 3

This passage is followed by questions based on its content. After reading the passage, choose the best answer to each question. Answer all questions on the basis of what is stated or implied in that passage.

Globalization is not a benign force. It creates a world of winners and losers. Indeed the statistics are daunting. The share of the poorest fifth of the world's population in global income has dropped from 2.3 percent to 1.4 percent over the past 10 years. The proportion taken by the richest fifth, on the other hand, has risen. In many less developed countries, safety and environmental regulations are low or virtually non-existent. Some transnational companies sell goods **there** that are controlled or banned in the industrial countries—poor quality medical drugs, destructive pesticides or high tar-and-nicotine content cigarettes.

Along with health risk, expanding inequality is the most serious problem facing world society. It will not do merely to blame it on the wealthy. Globalization today is only partly Westernization. Globalization is becoming increasingly decentralized. Its effects are felt as much in Western countries as elsewhere.

This is true of the global financial system and of changes affecting the nature of government itself. What one could call "reverse colonization" is becoming more and more common. Reverse colonization means that non-Western countries influence developments in the West. Examples abound, such as the Latinizing of Los Angeles, the emergence of a globally oriented hi-tech sector in India, or the selling of Brazilian TV programs to Portugal.

30. What evidence does the speaker have for the negative effect of globalization?
    (A) Rich countries are controlling statistics.
    (B) Many goods produced in the Third World are unsafe.
    (C) Less developed countries are a dumping ground for certain goods.
    (D) We blame the rich countries for all the problems facing society.

31. One effect of globalization mentioned in the text is that
 (A) only Western culture is beginning to dominate the world.
 (B) former colonies are beginning to play a greater international role.
 (C) the West is at greater risk of pollution.
 (D) less developed countries have almost no environmental regulations.

32. What does "there" in line 8 refer to in the text?
 (A) industrial countries
 (B) the less developed countries
 (C) the richest fifth
 (D) high-tech sectors

33. Which of the following best describes the term "decentralized"?
 (A) not under the control of any one group
 (B) in the center of Western countries
 (C) not in the hands of a central government
 (D) in the management of a large corporation

34. Which of the following best describes the relationship of sentence 1 to the rest of the paragraph?
 (A) It establishes the organization of the paragraph as a whole.
 (B) It establishes the basis for comparison between the poorest fifth and the richest fifth.
 (C) It shows the writer's authority on the subject.
 (D) It presents the idea that is to be further demonstrated later.

35. In the second paragraph, the function of using the expression "along with health risk" is to
    (A) summarize what has been discussed.
    (B) prepare the reader for other dangers globalization might bring.
    (C) suggest globalization is not a benign force.
    (D) emphasize the selling of goods mentioned previously.

Ⅲ. Essay Writing: 30 %

Studies have shown that because of a competitive job market, diplomas do pay off. Write an essay of around 500 words discussing whether it pays to receive higher education and diplomas. Be sure to give reasons for your opinion and to support those reasons with specific examples from your reading (information in the following tables is for you to cite) or your own experiences.

Median wages for full-time workers:

Education level	Men	Women
High school graduate	$26,218	$18,042
College graduate	$39,894	$27,654
Master's degree	$47,002	$33,122

Source: The National Committee on Pay Equity, based on the U.S. Census Bureau.

Average cost of education (tuition, books and room and board) for four years:

Education cost	Private university	Public university
1990	$22,200	$19,880
2000	$27,400	$23,000

Source: Survey by the College Board

Average monthly salary for college graduates with degrees:

Degree	Salary
Engineering	$2,953
Social sciences	$1,841
Humanities	$1,592
Law and medicine	$4,961

Source: U.S. Census Bureau

國立政治大學九十三學年度
碩士班研究生入學考試英文試題詳解

I. 結構：30 %

A.

1. (**C**) *one hopes* → ***you hope***
   understanding〔,ʌndɚ'stændɪŋ〕*n.* 理解
   reality〔rɪ'ælətɪ〕*n.* 現實
   survive〔sɚ'vaɪv〕*v.* 存活
   error〔'ɛrɚ〕*n.* 錯誤

2. (**B**) *prevent* → ***preventing***
   pesticide〔'pɛstɪsaɪd〕*n.* 殺蟲劑
   prevent〔prɪ'vɛnt〕*v.* 防止　　plant〔plænt〕*n.* 植物
   insect〔'ɪnsɛkt〕*n.* 昆蟲
   environmental〔ɪn,vaɪrən'mɛntḷ〕*adj.* 環境的
   raise〔rez〕*v.* 引起；產生
   genetically〔dʒə'nɛtɪkḷɪ〕*adv.* 在基因上
   modify〔'mɑdə,faɪ〕*v.* 改造
   genetically modified 基因改造的

3. (**A**) *was claiming* → ***who claimed***
   claim〔klem〕*v.* 聲稱　　***flying saucer*** 飛碟
   press conference 記者會　　describe〔dɪ'skraɪb〕*v.* 描述

4. (**E**) scarcely〔'skɛrslɪ〕*adv.* 幾乎不
   distinguish〔dɪ'stɪŋgwɪʃ〕*v.* 區別
   opinion〔ə'pɪnjən〕*n.* 意見
   issue〔'ɪʃju〕*n.* 議題　　highly〔'haɪlɪ〕*adv.* 非常
   emotional〔ɪ'moʃənḷ〕*adj.* 訴諸情感的；情緒激動的

5. (**C**) *regard to* → ***with regard to***
Hakka ('hak'ka) *adj.* 客家的
department (dɪ'partmənt) *n.* 部門
conduct (kən'dʌkt) *v.* 進行；做
research ('risɝtʃ) *n.* 研究
with regard to 關於　custom ('kʌstəm) *n.* 習俗

6. (**D**) *scholar dialogue* → ***scholarly dialogue***
academic (ˌækə'dɛmɪk) *adj.* 學術的
discipline ('dɪsəplɪn) *n.* 學問（的領域）；學科
practice ('præktɪs) *n.* 習俗；慣例
convention (kən'vɛnʃən) *n.* 傳統；慣例
follow ('falo) *v.* 遵守　engage (ɪn'gedʒ) *v.* 從事
scholarly ('skaləlɪ) *adj.* 學術上的

7. (**A**) *maintain* → ***maintenance***
maintenance ('mentənəns) *n.* 維持
peace (pis) *n.* 和平　stability (stə'bɪlətɪ) *n.* 穩定
Taiwan Strait 台灣海峽　welfare ('wɛlˌfɛr) *n.* 福利
remain (rɪ'men) *v.* 依然
profound (prə'faʊnd) *adj.* 重大的

8. (**B**) *are* → ***is***
conquer ('kaŋkɚ) *v.* 征服；擊敗
battle ('bætl̩) *n.* 戰爭
supreme (sə'prim) *adj.* 最高的
excellence ('ɛksl̩əns) *n.* 卓越；優秀
consist of 由～組成
enemy ('ɛnəmɪ) *n.* 敵人
resistance (rɪ'zɪstəns) *n.* 反抗

B.

【譯文】

由於語言可能會發展出各種不同形式的方言，所以，語言整體而言，可能是會改變的。由於說著不同語言的人互相接觸，有時候會產生快速的語言變革。在這種情況下，可能就會產生洋涇濱語。洋涇濱語的文法是根據一種語言，但也同時受到其他語言的影響，尤其是在字彙方面；洋涇濱語的發音方式比較少，字彙也較少，而且文法被簡化和改變，所以爲了要讓對方瞭解，它們非常依賴前後文的關聯。

洋涇濱語常常都是由於貿易商和島上、沿海的居民接觸，所產生的結果。沒有人是以洋涇濱語爲母語：當說洋涇濱語的人的孩子學洋涇濱語，作爲他們的母語時，那種語言就會被稱爲混合語。一旦有夠多人以混合語爲母語，他們就會形成一個語言團體，而這個語言可能也會發展成一個更完整的語言。

【註】

variety〔vəˈraɪətɪ〕*n.* 變化；多樣性
in the form of 以～形式　　dialect〔ˈdaɪəˌlɛkt〕*n.* 方言
as a whole 整體而言　　rapid〔ˈræpɪd〕*adj.* 迅速的
circumstance〔ˈsɝkəmˌstæns〕*n.* 情形；情況
pidgin〔ˈpɪdʒɪn〕*n.* 洋涇濱語；混合語
grammatically〔grəˈmætɪklɪ〕*adv.* 在文法上
influence〔ˈɪnfluəns〕*v.* 影響

especially〔əˈspɛʃəlɪ〕*adv.* 特別是
vocabulary〔vəˈkæbjəˌlɛrɪ〕*n.* 字彙
relatively〔ˈrɛlətɪvlɪ〕*adv.* 相對地；比較上而言
reduced〔rɪˈdjust〕*adj.* 減少的；簡化的
simplified〔ˈsɪmpləˌfaɪd〕*adj.* 簡化的
altered〔ˈɔltɚd〕*adj.* 改變的；更改的

grammar〔'græmɚ〕*n.* 文法；文法規則　　***rely on*** 依賴
context〔'kɑntɛkst〕*n.* 上下文；情況
trader〔'tredɚ〕*n.* 商人；貿易者　　island〔'aɪlənd〕*adj.* 島的
coastal〔'kostḷ〕*adj.* 海岸的；沿岸的
native〔'netɪv〕*adj.* 本地的；本國的
native speaker 以某語言爲母語的人
first language 第一語言；母語
Creole〔'kriol〕*n.* 克里奧爾語；混合語
community〔kə'mjunətɪ〕*n.* 社區
speech community 語言社區　　full〔fʊl〕*adj.* 完整的

9.（**C**）(A) link〔lɪŋk〕*n.* 連結
(B) acquaintance〔ə'kwentəns〕*n.* 認識的人
(C) ***contact***〔'kɑntækt〕*n.* 接觸
(D) connection〔kə'nɛkʃən〕*n.* 連接；聯繫

10.（**C**）(A) stem〔stɛm〕*v.* 源自 <*from*>
(B) spring〔sprɪŋ〕*v.* 跳躍；發源 <*from*>
(C) ***arise***〔ə'raɪz〕*v.* 出現；產生
(D) rise〔raɪz〕*v.* 升起；上升

11.（**A**）(A) ***be based on*** 以～爲基礎；根據
(C) derive〔də'raɪv〕*v.* 起源於 <*from*>
(D) ***hinge on*** 取決於

12.（**D**）表「受～」的影響，介系詞用 ***by***。

13.（**C**）(A) closely〔'kloslɪ〕*adv.* 接近地；密切地
(B) communicatively〔kə'mjunə,ketɪvlɪ〕*adv.* 愛說話地
(C) ***heavily***〔'hɛvɪlɪ〕*adv.* 很；極；大大地
(D) derisively〔dɪ'raɪsɪvlɪ〕*adv.* 嘲笑地

14. (**D**) (A) whereas〔hwɛr'æz〕*conj.* 然而；雖然
(B) promptly〔'prɑmptlɪ〕*adv.* 立刻地
(C) presently〔'prɛzn̩tlɪ〕*adv.* 目前
(D) ***once***〔wʌns〕*conj.* 一旦；一當

15. (**B**) (A) enlarge〔ɪn'lɑrdʒ〕*v.* 放大
(B) ***develop into*** 發展成
(C) swell〔swɛl〕*v.* 膨脹
(D) increase〔ɪn'kris〕*v.* 增加

Ⅱ. 閱讀（字彙與理解）：40 %

Passage 1

【譯文】

我們很自然地會選擇自己有興趣的主題來寫。但是，歷史學家不該讓他們自己所關心的事和偏見，來主導他們詮釋過去的方法。就以一個歐洲近代初期的學生爲例，他可能會因那個時期加諸於女性身上的法律、社會和經濟限制，而感到驚訝。對於那些以現代的眼光看來，似乎十分不公平的事，可能會使這名學生強烈地表達出自己的憤怒，責怪十六世紀的男性，「既自私又沙文主義」，但這對歷史學家來說，並不是一種有用的方法，他們要試著去了解自己所研究的時期，處於當時那種社會情況中的早期人們的看法。

【註】

naturally〔'nætʃərəlɪ〕*adv.* 自然地　subject〔'sʌbdʒɪkt〕*n.* 主題
historian〔hɪs'torɪən〕*n.* 歷史學家
concern〔kən'sɝn〕*n.* 關心的事　direct〔də'rɛkt〕*v.* 指引；主導
interpret〔ɪn'tɝprɪt〕*v.* 詮釋　legal〔'lig!〕*adj.* 法律的
economic〔,ikə'nɑmɪk〕*adj.* 經濟的
limitation〔,lɪmə'teʃən〕*n.* 限制

place〔 ples 〕*v.* 加諸於　period〔 ˈpɪrɪəd 〕*n.* 時期
century〔 ˈsɛntʃərɪ 〕*n.* 世紀　selfish〔 ˈsɛlfɪʃ 〕*adj.* 自私的
chauvinistic〔 ˌʃovɪˈnɪstɪk 〕*adj.* 沙文主義的
forcefully〔 ˈforsfəlɪ 〕*adv.* 強烈地
express〔 ɪkˈsprɛs 〕*v.* 表達　sense〔 sɛns 〕*n.* 感覺
appear〔 əˈpɪr 〕*v.* 似乎　eyes〔 aɪz 〕*n. pl.* 看法
unjust〔 ʌnˈdʒʌst 〕*adj.* 不公平的
approach〔 əˈprotʃ 〕*n.* 方法　***earlier times*** 早期
under study 研究中

16.（ **D** ）(A) appeal〔 əˈpil 〕*v.* 吸引 <*to*>
(B) bestow〔 bɪˈsto 〕*v.* 賦予
(C) dismiss〔 dɪsˈmɪs 〕*v.* 解散；下（課）
(D) ***interest***〔 ˈɪntrɪst 〕*v.* 使…感興趣

17.（ **A** ）(A) ***bias***〔 ˈbaɪəs 〕*n.* 偏見
(D) quest〔 kwɛst 〕*n.* 追求

18.（ **C** ）(A) pass〔 pæs 〕*v.* 走過；經過
(C) ***past***〔 pæst 〕*n.* 過去的事
(D) pastime〔 ˈpæsˌtaɪm 〕*n.* 消遣

19.（ **B** ）(A) assure〔 əˈʃur 〕*v.* 保證
(B) ***dismay***〔 dɪsˈme 〕*v.* 使驚慌
(C) encourage〔 ɪnˈkɝɪdʒ 〕*v.* 鼓勵
(D) satisfy〔 ˈsætɪsˌfaɪ 〕*v.* 使滿意；使滿足

20.（ **D** ）(A) approach〔 əˈprotʃ 〕*v.* 接近
(B) assume〔 əˈsjum 〕*v.* 假定
(C) require〔 rɪˈkwaɪr 〕*v.* 需要
(D) ***reproach***〔 rɪˈprotʃ 〕*v.* 譴責

21. (C) (A) independence [,ɪndɪ'pɛndəns] *n.* 獨立
(B) indifference [ɪn'dɪfərəns] *n.* 漠不關心
(C) ***indignation*** [,ɪndɪg'neʃən] *n.* 憤怒
(D) individuality [,ɪndə,vɪdʒʊ'ælətɪ] *n.* 個性；個人

22. (A) (A) ***context*** ['kɑntɛkst] *n.* 上下文；情況
(B) content [kən'tɛnt] *n.* 內容
(C) conference ['kɑnfərəns] *n.* 會議
(D) confederation [kən,fɛdə'reʃən] *n.* 聯盟

Passage 2

【譯文】

紅狼是一種瀕臨絕種的動物。牠的數量已經減少到快滅絕的地步，那是因爲政府的獎勵，使得任意宰殺的情況更嚴重，還有因爲這種狼很容易感染具有致命破壞力的腸道寄生蟲。而現在這個物種可能面臨完全性的滅絕，因爲牠能和血緣關係相近的郊狼共同繁殖，但是郊狼的數量比紅狼多很多。因此，在從人類和蟲所造成的最糟情況中生存下來之後，紅狼現在瀕臨絕種，是因爲牠喪失了自己本身的獨特基因。

【註】

wolf [wʊlf] *n.* 狼　species ['spiʃɪz] *n.* 物種
decline [dɪ'klaɪn] *v.* 減少　willful ['wɪlfəl] *adj.* 任意的
slaughter ['slɔtɚ] *n.* 宰殺　bounty ['baʊntɪ] *n.* 獎勵
deadly ['dɛdlɪ] *adj.* 致命的
destruction [dɪ'strʌkʃən] *n.* 破壞
intestinal [ɪn'tɛstɪnḷ] *adj.* 腸的　face [fes] *v.* 面臨
breed [brid] *v.* 繁殖　closely ['kloslɪ] *adv.* 密切地

relate〔rɪ'let〕*v.* 與…有關係　***closely related*** 有近親關係的
numerous〔'njumərəs〕*adj.* 許多的
cousin〔'kʌzn̩〕*n.* 同種；同類　coyote〔kaɪ'ot〕*n.* 郊狼
thus〔ðʌs〕*adv.* 因此　survive〔sə'vaɪv〕*v.* 經歷…後還活著
worm〔wɜm〕*n.* 蟲　endanger〔ɪn'dendʒə〕*v.* 危及
loss〔lɔs〕*n.* 喪失　gene〔dʒin〕*n.* 基因

23.（**B**）(A) dangerous〔'dendʒərəs〕*adj.* 危險的
(B) ***endangered***〔ɪn'dendʒəd〕*adj.* 瀕臨絕種的
(C) depreciate〔dɪ'priʃɪ,et〕*v.* 輕視；瞧不起；貶值
(D) enchanting〔ɪn'tʃæntɪŋ〕*adj.* 迷人的

24.（**D**）(A) perfectly〔'pɜfɪktlɪ〕*adv.* 完全地；完美地
(B) permanently〔'pɜmənəntlɪ〕*adv.* 永久地
(C) precisely〔prɪ'saɪslɪ〕*adv.* 精密地；準確地
(D) ***perilously***〔'pɛrələslɪ〕*adv.* 危險地

25.（**A**）(A) ***subsidize***〔'sʌbsə,daɪz〕*v.* 補助
(B) substantiate〔səb'stænʃɪ,et〕*v.* 使具體化
(C) subscribe〔səb'skraɪb〕*v.* 訂閱
(D) succeed〔sək'sid〕*v.* 成功

26.（**C**）(A) suspension〔sə'spɛnʃən〕*n.* 懸吊
(B) suspicion〔sə'spɪʃən〕*n.* 嫌疑；疑心
(C) ***susceptibility***〔sə,sɛptə'bɪlətɪ〕*n.* 容易感染
(D) sustain〔sə'sten〕*v.* 維持

27.（**D**）(A) project〔'prɑdʒɛkt〕*n.* 計畫
(B) pressure〔'prɛʃə〕*n.* 壓力
(C) poison〔'pɔɪzn̩〕*n.* 毒藥
(D) ***parasite***〔'pærə,saɪt〕*n.* 寄生蟲

28.（**A**）(A) ***extinction***〔ɪk'stɪŋkʃən〕*n.* 滅絕；絕種
(B) exception〔ɪk'sɛpʃən〕*n.* 例外
(C) exemption〔ɪg'zɛmpʃən〕*n.*（課稅、義務等的）免除
(D) exhaustion〔ɪg'zɔstʃən〕*n.* 耗盡

29.（**B**）(A) disinherit〔,dɪsɪn'hɛrɪt〕*v.* 剝奪（孩子）的繼承權
(B) ***distinguishing***〔dɪ'stɪŋgwɪʃɪŋ〕*adj.* 特殊的
(C) distort〔dɪs'tɔrt〕*v.* 扭曲
(D) dislocate〔'dɪslo,ket〕*v.* 使脫臼

Passage 3

【譯文】

全球化並不是一種好的力量。它創造了贏家和輸家的世界。事實上，統計數字會令人感到氣餒。全球最窮的那五分之一的人口，在過去十年裡，佔全球收入的比例，從 2.3%降到 1.4%。另一方面，全球最富有的那五分之一的人口，佔全球收入的比例，卻上升了。在許多低度開發國家中，對於安全和環境的限制都很少，或是根本不存在。有些跨國企業，會將在高度發展國家受到管制或禁止的產品──品質不佳的藥品、有害的殺蟲劑，或含大量焦油與尼古丁的香煙，賣到那裡去。

危害健康的事物和不平等現象的擴張，都是這個世界所面臨的最嚴重問題。只將這件事怪罪在有錢人身上是不行的。現今的全球化只不過是部分西化。全球化正變得愈來愈分散。它對西方國家和其他地方的影響是一樣的。

它的影響對全球的金融體制，和政府本質的改變來說，都是非常確切的。你可以稱這種愈來愈普遍的現象為「逆殖民化」。逆殖民化意味著非西方國家影響西方的發展。這樣的例子大量存在，像是洛杉磯的拉丁化、以全球為取向的高科技企業在印度出現，或是巴西的電視節目賣到葡萄牙去。

【答案】

30. (C)　31. (B)　32. (B)　33. (A)
34. (D)　35. (A)

【註】

globalization (,globəlaɪ'zeʃən) *n.* 全球化
benign (bɪ'naɪn) *adj.* 良性的　force (fors) *n.* 力量
create (krɪ'et) *v.* 創造；產生
indeed (ɪn'did) *adv.* 的確；眞正地
statistics (stə'tɪstɪks) *n. pl.* 統計數字
daunt (dɔnt) *v.* 令人氣餒　fifth (fɪfθ) *n.* 五分之一
population (,pɑpjə'leʃən) *n.* 人口數
global ('globḷ) *adj.* 全球的　income ('ɪn,kʌm) *n.* 收入
drop (drɑp) *v.* 下降　proportion (prə'porʃən) *n.* 比例
developed (dɪ'vɛləpt) *adj.* 已開發的
regulation (,rɛgjə'leʃən) *n.* 管制；限制
virtually ('vɜtʃuəlɪ) *adv.* 事實上；幾乎
non-existent (,nɑnɪg'zɪstənt) *adj.* 不存在的
transnational (træns'næʃənəl) *adj.* 跨國的
goods (gʊdz) *n. pl.* 商品　control (kən'trol) *v.* 管制
ban (bæn) *v.* 禁止
industrial (ɪn'dʌstrɪəl) *adj.* 工業高度發展的
poor (pʊr) *adj.* 差勁的　quality ('kwɑlətɪ) *n.* 品質
medical ('mɛdɪkḷ) *adj.* 醫療的；醫學的
drug (drʌg) *n.* 藥品　destructive (dɪ'strʌktɪv) *adj.* 有害的
pesticide ('pɛstɪsaɪd) *n.* 殺蟲劑
tar-and-nicotine ('tɑrɛnd'nɪkə,tin) *n.* 焦油與尼古丁

cigarette〔'sɪgə,rɛt〕*n.* 香煙 ***along with*** 連同
risk〔rɪsk〕*n.* 危險；風險 expand〔ɪk'spænd〕*v.* 擴張
inequality〔,ɪnɪ'kwɑlətɪ〕*n.* 不平等；不公平
face〔fes〕*v.* 使面對 do〔du〕*v.* 行得通
merely〔'mɪrlɪ〕*adv.* 單單；僅僅 blame〔blem〕*v.* 責備
wealthy〔'wɛlθɪ〕*adj.* 富有的
Westernization〔,wɛstənaɪ'zeʃən〕*n.* 西化
increasingly〔ɪn'krisɪŋlɪ〕*adv.* 逐漸地
decentralized〔di'sɛntrəl,aɪzd〕*adj.* 分散的

elsewhere〔'ɛls,hwɛr〕*adv.* 在別處 ***be true of*** 適用於
financial〔faɪ'nænʃəl〕*adj.* 金融的 affect〔ə'fɛkt〕*v.* 影響
nature〔'netʃɚ〕*n.* 本質
reverse〔rɪ'vɝs〕*adj.* 相反的；顚倒的
colonization〔,kɑlənaɪ'zeʃən〕*n.* 殖民化
common〔'kɑmən〕*adj.* 普遍的；常見的
abound〔ə'baʊnd〕*v.* 大量存在
Latinizing〔'lætɪn,aɪzɪŋ〕*n.* 拉丁化
emergence〔ɪ'mɝdʒəns〕*n.* 露出；出現
globally〔'globḷɪ〕*adv.* 全球地

oriented〔'orɪ,ɛntɪd〕*adj.* 以…爲取向的
hi-tech〔haɪ'tɛk〕*n.* 高科技
sector〔'sɛktɚ〕*n.*（產業、經濟等的）部門
evidence〔'ɛvədəns〕*n.* 證據
negative〔'nɛgətɪv〕*adj.* 負面的
the Third World 第三世界（尤指亞洲、非洲的不結盟中立國家；開發中國家）
dumping〔'dʌmpɪŋ〕*n.*（垃圾等的）傾倒
ground〔graʊnd〕*n.* 地面；地 certain〔'sɝtṇ〕*adj.* 某些

mention〔ˈmɛnʃən〕*v.* 提到　text〔tɛkst〕*n.* 內文
dominate〔ˈdɑmə,net〕*v.* 支配；控制
former〔ˈfɔrmɚ〕*adj.* 從前的　colony〔ˈkɑlənɪ〕*n.* 殖民地
role〔rol〕*n.* 角色　pollution〔pəˈluʃən〕*n.* 污染
refer to 是指　describe〔dɪˈskraɪb〕*v.* 描述
term〔tɝm〕*n.* 名詞；用語　central〔ˈsɛntrəl〕*adj.* 中央的
management〔ˈmænɪdʒmənt〕*n.* 經營；管理

corporation〔,kɔrpəˈreʃən〕*n.* 公司
establish〔əˈstæblɪʃ〕*v.* 建立；確立
organization〔,ɔrgənəˈzeʃən〕*n.* 組織；構造
as a whole 整體而言
comparison〔kəmˈpærəsn̩〕*n.* 對照；比較
authority〔əˈθɔrətɪ〕*n.* 權威
subject〔ˈsʌbdʒɪkt〕*n.* 主題；題目

present〔prɪˈzɛnt〕*v.* 表達；提出
further〔ˈfɝðɚ〕*adv.* 更進一步地
demonstrate〔ˈdɛmən,stret〕*v.* 證明；說明
function〔ˈfʌŋkʃən〕*n.* 目的；作用
summarize〔ˈsʌmə,raɪz〕*v.* 概括地說
suggest〔səˈdʒɛst〕*v.* 暗示　emphasize〔ˈɛmfə,saɪz〕*v.* 強調
previously〔ˈprivɪəslɪ〕*adj.* 先前地

Ⅲ. 寫作：30 %

研究顯示，因爲就業市場競爭激烈，所以學位眞的有用。請寫一篇約五百字的文章，來討論接受高等教育和取得文憑是否有用。一定要針對你的意見提出理由，而且要從你的文章（下表中的資訊，就是你可以引證的來源）或自身經驗中，找到具體的例子來支持這些理由。

專職勞動者的平均薪資：

教育程度	男性	女性
高中畢業	$26,218	$18,042
大學畢業	$39,894	$27,654
碩士學位	$47,002	$33,122

來源：國家薪資公平委員會，以美國人口普查局爲依據。

四年的平均教育成本（學費、書籍、住宿和膳食）

教育成本	私立大學	公立大學
1990 年	$22,200	$19,880
2000 年	$27,400	$23,000

來源：大學理事會的調查

大學畢業生的平均月薪：

學　位	薪　資
工　程　學	$2,958
社 會 科 學	$1,841
人 類 科 學	$1,592
法律與醫學	$4,961

來源：美國人口普查局

【作文範例】

In considering the emphasis placed on getting an education, you need to look no further than your monthly paycheck the next time payday comes around. Everybody goes to school so they can get a diploma certifying them as being qualified for higher paying jobs. Working for minimum wage at a McDonald's is anything but comparable to working for a law firm.

Many people still question the economic benefits and payoffs of getting a higher education. According to the U.S. Census Bureau, the median wage for workers that are college graduates is nearly a third greater than that of those who only make it past high school. The fact is, while educational costs are skyrocketing year after year, so are the related benefits that come with a degree. It is a trade-off. You pay ridiculous amounts of money for an education so you can make it all back once you have entered the workforce.

With today's highly inflated cost of living, one cannot afford to ignore the monetary incentives that a college education offers. Further statistics from the U.S. Census Bureau reveal that college graduates with degrees in fields of engineering, social sciences, law or medicine make on average $3000 a month. After mortgage, rent or car payments have been deducted from this amount, there remains a small margin of disposable income for households to enjoy. And that is with a college degree! There is little wonder that our parents push us to get a good education. They realize the economic hardships that life can dish out. It is hard enough to scrape by working on a janitor's wage or a convenience store clerk's salary alone; it becomes nearly impossible if you have a family.

A higher education leads to higher pay. It is rightly so that one is compensated more for being able to do more. And nothing says you are qualified to do more than a college diploma. In today's highly competitive job market, it is ever important to present yourself well so to attract recruiters. Workers are demanded to do much more for companies today than they were twenty and even ten years ago. A college education can properly train a person to perform well in today's workforce. Although longer hours are being spent at the office, workers will be greatly rewarded monetarily.

The statistics on pay equity collected by the U.S. Census should be telling enough. College graduates do earn considerably more than people who only attended high school. College graduates who go on to earn their master's degree continue to make even more money. While money is a poor motivation to get a higher education, those that toil away at menial jobs cleaning toilets or those that fail to make their mortgage payments and as a result get evicted might think otherwise.

國立台灣師範大學九十三學年度 碩士班研究生入學考試英文試題

I. Vocabulary: (20 points)

Choose the most appropriate word to complete each of the following sentences.

1. General Motors ________ reluctantly that there were defects in its new Buicks.
(A) preceded (B) revealed
(C) innovated (D) threatened

2. The ________ became a tragedy for those who attempted it because they were all killed.
(A) ambush (B) devastation
(C) colleague (D) ventilation

3. A sign in the elevator stated that its ________ was 1100 pounds.
(A) document (B) capacity
(C) possession (D) revelation

4. Being a good author, he is always ________ not to exaggerate when he writes.
(A) fertile (B) bulky
(C) diminished (D) cautious

5. The ________ thief was able to enter the apartment through the narrow window.
   (A) massive (B) enormous
   (C) slender (D) gigantic

6. Everyone who lived in the ________ of the bomb test site was in peril.
   (A) pioneer (B) vicinity
   (C) detection (D) authority

7. The boys felt that ________ things were starting to happen when they entered the haunted house.
   (A) weird (B) jealous
   (C) expensive (D) thrifty

8. If we could eliminate losses caused by people who ________ the government, tax rates could be lowered.
   (A) excel (B) absorb
   (C) defraud (D) revive

9. The criminal found it hard to ________ the truth when he was questioned by the keen lawyer.
   (A) surpass (B) conceal
   (C) perish (D) emerge

10. The stories John told people about his adventures turned out to be merely ________.
   (A) fiction (B) cinema
   (C) glance (D) obesity

Ⅱ. Cloze: (20 points)

Choose the most appropriate word to complete each blank in the following passages.

Passage A:

Today's technology has not only changed the way we work and play, it has also changed the way we receive information and communicate with others. From the 1920s ___(11)___, first radio and then television have brought the outside world into the living rooms of America. Today, by enabling us to ___(12)___ the Net for news and send e-mail and faxes via modem, the computer has introduced us to a whole new ___(13)___ of communication: cyberspace. Sato Kenji, a Japanese author, wrote that cyberspace "has become the ultimate ___(14)___ of the American dream. Free from the restraints of reality, cyberspace surpasses any earthly nation in promising an ___(15)___ right to pursue freedom and prosperity."

11. (A) on　　(B) into
    (C) about　　(D) through

12. (A) acquiring　　(B) surf
    (C) commuting　　(D) harassing

13. (A) realm　　(B) fluency
    (C) duration　　(D) council

14. (A) fatigue (B) vacancy
    (C) prohibition (D) embodiment

15. (A) indifferent (B) unfettered
    (C) ambitious (D) experimental

Passage B:

There are two systems of health care in the United States today. The first is ___(16)___ Western medicine, with its well-known web of preferred and secondary providers, insurance forms, expensive drugs and testing, and limited office hours and ___(17)___ to information.

___(18)___, less well-known, but gaining in acceptance, is the domain of alternative medicine, ___(19)___ includes a diversity of specialties such as homeopathy, acupuncture, herbal medicine, energy medicine and naturopathic medicine, ___(20)___ just a few.

16. (A) hoarse (B) exterior
    (C) irritable (D) conventional

17. (A) access (B) biography
    (C) inflation (D) sanitation

18. (A) Other (B) Another
    (C) Others (D) The other

19. (A) that (B) where
    (C) which (D) though

20. (A) name (B) named
(C) names (D) to name

Ⅲ. Reading Comprehension:(20 points)
Choose the best answer for each question.

Passage A:

The causes of headaches, whether they are the common kind of tension headache or migraine headaches, or any other kind, are usually the same. During periods of stress, muscles in the neck, head and face are contracted so tightly that they exert tremendous pressure on the nerves beneath them; headaches, taking many forms from a constant, dull pain to an insistent hammering, result.

Although at least 50% of American adults are estimated to suffer one or more headaches per week, it is the 20 million migraine sufferers who are in special difficulties. Migraines, which are mostly suffered by women, can involve tremendous, unrelieved pain.

Migraines, which may also be caused by stress, can occur in people who bottle up their emotions and who are very conscientious in their performance. Escaping from stressful situations, being open with one's feelings, and lowering one's expectations can help reduce the stress and so cut down on those headaches which cannot be helped by aspirin and other non-prescription painkillers.

21. It can be inferred from the passage that ____________.
    (A) headaches can have a variety of symptoms
    (B) headaches always produce the same result
    (C) tension or migraine headaches are common to all people
    (D) migraine headaches are suffered by at least 50% of American adults

22. According to the passage, during periods of stress, ________.
    (A) a constant dull pain always results
    (B) the neck, hand and face are contracted
    (C) some nerves have great pressure put on them
    (D) some important muscles experience hammering

23. From the passage, we learn that in America, ____________.
    (A) only women suffer migraines
    (B) over 20 million men suffer migraines
    (C) a majority of adults have at least one headache a week
    (D) a majority of the headaches suffered are migraine headaches

24. According to the author, migraines can be caused by ____________.
    (A) releasing stress
    (B) expressing one's emotions
    (C) lowering your expectations in life
    (D) being too worried about doing a good job

25. From the passage, we learn that headaches can be avoided by ________________.
(A) taking aspirin
(B) being very emotional
(C) avoiding stressful situations
(D) taking painkillers which do not require a prescription

Passage B:

One theory that integrates diverse findings on hunger, eating, and weight argues that body weight is governed by a set-point, a homeostatic mechanism that keeps people at roughly the weight they are genetically designed to be. Set-point theories claim that everyone has a genetically programmed basal metabolism rate, the rate at which the body burns calories for energy, and a fixed number of fat cells, which are cells that store fat for energy. These cells may change in size (the amount of fat they contain), but never in number. After weight loss, they just lurk around the body, waiting for the chance to puff up again. According to set-point theory, there is no single area in the brain that keeps track of weight. Rather, an interaction of metabolism, fat cells, and hormones keeps people at the weight their bodies are designed to be. When a heavy person diets, the body slows down to conserve energy (and its fat reserves). When a thin person overeats, the body speeds up to burn energy.

26. This passage is most likely found in a textbook on the topic of ___________.
    (A) biology (B) chemistry
    (C) psychology (D) social studies

27. This passage is most likely followed by a passage that focuses on ______________.
    (A) the importance of a proper diet
    (B) a different theory on body weight
    (C) how to keep fat cells from enlarging
    (D) the relation between activity and weight

28. It can be concluded from the passage that __________.
    (A) a genetically thin person can easily gain weight
    (B) humans are genetically designed to be overweight
    (C) it is impossible for genetically predisposed overweight people to lose weight
    (D) people don't have as much control over their body weight as they might think

29. The author's attitude toward the subject of weight could best be described as ____________.
    (A) emotional (B) scientific
    (C) depressing (D) disbelieving

30. The author's purpose in writing this passage is to _________.
    (A) inform (B) criticize
    (C) compare (D) illustrate

IV. Fill in each of the following blanks with ONE word to complete the passage.(20 points)

Oscar-winning films started talking 75 years ago and never looked back. Sunday's Academy Awards ceremony, ___(31)___ silence was most definitely not golden, was no exception.

___(32)___ are four of the more memorable jokes and comments from the stars ___(33)___ on-stage and off at the 76th annual Oscars:

"___(34)___ am I wearing tonight? Boxers." (Bill Murray, before the show's start, answering the ubiquitous ___(35)___ asked of every arriving female star.)

"I think I'll have a few sips ___(36)___ champagne, then I'm going to crash out." (Annie Lennox, best song winner, backstage, on ___(37)___ she was planning to celebrate.)

"It's now official. ___(38)___ is nobody left in New Zealand to thank." (Billy Crystal, after *Lord of the Rings* won its first five Oscars, ___(39)___ of a total of eleven on the night.)

"I can't wait for his tax audit—scary times." (Crystal, after Errol Morris' remarks, ___(40)___ drew loud applause from the audience.)

V. English Composition:(20 points)

Write an English composition of no less than 200 words which begins with: "If I were the President of National Taiwan Normal University..."

國立台灣師範大學九十三學年度
碩士班研究生入學考試英文試題詳解

I. 字彙：20 %

1. (**B**) (A) precede〔priˈsid〕*v.* 在～之前
(B) ***reveal***〔rɪˈvil〕*v.* 透露
(C) innovate〔ˈɪnə͵vet〕*v.* 革新
(D) threaten〔ˈθrɛtn̩〕*v.* 威脅
General Motors 通用汽車公司
reluctantly〔rɪˈlʌktəntlɪ〕*adv.* 不情願地
defect〔dɪˈfɛkt, ˈdifɛkt〕*n.* 缺點；瑕疵

2. (**A**) (A) ***ambush***〔ˈæmbuʃ〕*n.* 埋伏
(B) devastation〔͵dɛvəsˈteʃən〕*n.* 毀壞；荒廢
(C) colleague〔ˈkɑlig〕*n.* 同事
(D) ventilation〔͵vɛntl̩ˈeʃən〕*n.* 通風
tragedy〔ˈtrædʒədɪ〕*n.* 悲劇
attempt〔əˈtɛmpt〕*v.* 嘗試
be killed （因意外而）死亡

3. (**B**) (A) document〔ˈdɑkjəmənt〕*n.* 文件
(B) ***capacity***〔kəˈpæsətɪ〕*n.* 容量
(C) possession〔pəˈzɛʃən〕*n.* 擁有；財產
(D) revelation〔͵rɛvl̩ˈeʃən〕*n.* 揭露
sign〔saɪn〕*n.* 告示
elevator〔ˈɛlə͵vetɚ〕*n.* 電梯
state〔stet〕*v.* 敘述；說明
pound〔paʊnd〕*n.* 磅

4. (**D**) (A) fertile〔ˈfɝtḷ〕*adj.* 肥沃的
(B) bulky〔ˈbʌlkɪ〕*adj.* 笨重的
(C) diminish〔dəˈmɪnɪʃ〕*v.* 減少
(D) ***cautious***〔ˈkɔʃəs〕*adj.* 小心的；謹慎的
author〔ˈɔθɚ〕*n.* 作家
exaggerate〔ɪgˈzædʒəˌret〕*v.* 誇大

5. (**C**) (A) massive〔ˈmæsɪv〕*adj.* 大量的
(B) enormous〔ɪˈnɔrməs〕*adj.* 巨大的
(C) ***slender***〔ˈslɛndɚ〕*adj.* 苗條的
(D) gigantic〔dʒaɪˈgæntɪk〕*adj.* 巨大的
thief〔θif〕*n.* 小偷
narrow〔ˈnæro〕*adj.* 窄的

6. (**B**) (A) pioneer〔ˌpaɪəˈnɪr〕*n.* 開拓者；先驅
(B) ***vicinity***〔vəˈsɪnətɪ〕*n.* 附近
(C) detection〔dɪˈtɛkʃən〕*n.* 發覺
(D) authority〔əˈθɔrətɪ〕*n.* 權力；權威
bomb〔bɑm〕*n.* 炸彈　　test〔tɛst〕*n.* 測試
site〔saɪt〕*n.* 地點　　peril〔ˈpɛrəl〕*n.* 危險

7. (**A**) (A) ***weird***〔wɪrd〕*adj.* 怪異的
(B) jealous〔ˈdʒɛləs〕*adj.* 嫉妒的
(D) thrifty〔ˈθrɪftɪ〕*adj.* 節省的
haunted〔ˈhɔntɪd〕*adj.* 鬼魂出沒的

8. (**C**) (A) excel〔ɪkˈsɛl〕*v.*（以…）擅長；（在…）勝過
(C) ***defraud***〔dɪˈfrɔd〕*v.* 向～騙取（東西）
(D) revive〔rɪˈvaɪv〕*v.* 復活
eliminate〔ɪˈlɪməˌnet〕*v.* 消除
tax rate 稅率　　lower〔ˈloɚ〕*v.* 減少

9. (**B**) (A) surpass [sɚˈpæs] *v.* 超過
(B) ***conceal*** [kənˈsil] *v.* 隱藏；隱瞞
(C) perish [ˈpɛrɪʃ] *v.* 死亡；毀滅
(D) emerge [ɪˈmɝdʒ] *v.* 出現
criminal [ˈkrɪmənl̩] *n.* 罪犯
question [ˈkwɛstʃən] *v.* 質問；詢問
keen [kin] *adj.* 敏銳的；精明的
lawyer [ˈlɔjɚ] *n.* 律師

10. (**A**) (A) ***fiction*** [ˈfɪkʃən] *n.* 虛構的事
(B) cinema [ˈsɪnəmə] *n.* 電影
(C) glance [glæns] *n.* 一瞥；看一眼
(D) obesity [oˈbisətɪ] *n.* 肥胖
adventure [ədˈvɛntʃɚ] *n.* 冒險故事
turn out to be 結果是　　merely [ˈmɪrlɪ] *adv.* 僅；只

Ⅱ. 克漏字：20 %

A.

【譯文】

現今的科技不只改變了我們工作與玩樂的方式，也改變了我們接收資訊還有和彼此溝通的方式。從 1920 年代開始，第一部收音機和電視機，已經把外面的世界帶到美國人的客廳裡。現在，從我們能上網看新聞，還有透過數據機來寄電子郵件和傳真，電腦已經把我們帶入一個全新的通訊領域：網際空間。一位日本作家 Sato Kenji 寫到，網際空間「已經變成美國夢的最具體呈現。擺脫現實的束縛，網際空間能超越地球上任何一個國家，因爲它保證你有不受拘束地追求自由與成功的權利。」

【註】

technology〔tɛkˈnɑlɪdʒ〕*n.* 科技
receive〔rɪˈsiv〕*v.* 接收
communicate〔kəˈmjunəˌket〕*v.* 溝通；通訊
Net〔nɛt〕*n.* 網路（= *Internet*）　fax〔fæks〕*n.* 傳眞
via〔ˈvaɪə〕*prep.* 經由　modem〔ˈmodɛm〕*n.* 數據機
introduce sb. to 帶領某人進入　whole〔hol〕*adj.* 完全的
cyberspace〔ˈsaɪbɚˌspes〕*n.* 網際空間
author〔ˈɔθɚ〕*n.* 作家

ultimate〔ˈʌltəmɪt〕*adj.* 最終的；最好的
restraint〔rɪˈstrent〕*n.* 束縛　reality〔rɪˈælətɪ〕*n.* 現實
surpass〔sɚˈpæs〕*v.* 超越　earthly〔ˈɝθlɪ〕*adj.* 地球上的
promise〔ˈprɑmɪs〕*v.* 保證（給予）
pursue〔pɚˈsu〕*v.* 追求
prosperity〔prɑsˈpɛrətɪ〕*n.* 繁榮；成功

11.（**A**）表「從…（時候）以來」，須用 from…on，故選(A)。

12.（**B**）(A) acquire〔əˈkwaɪr〕*v.* 獲得
(B) ***surf***〔sɝf〕*v.* 瀏覽
(C) commute〔kəˈmjut〕*v.* 通勤
(D) harass〔həˈræs〕*v.* 騷擾

13.（**A**）(A) ***realm***〔rɛlm〕*n.* 領域（= *field*）
(B) fluency〔ˈfluənsɪ〕*n.* 流利
(C) duration〔djʊˈreʃən〕*n.* 期間
(D) council〔ˈkaʊnsḷ〕*n.* 會議；議會

14. (**D**) (A) fatigue〔fə'tig〕*n.* 疲勞
(B) vacancy〔'vekənsɪ〕*n.*（旅館等的）空房間
(C) prohibition〔,proə'bɪʃən〕*n.* 禁止
(D) ***embodiment***〔ɪm'bɑdɪmənt〕*n.* 化身；具體表現

15. (**B**) (A) indifferent〔ɪn'dɪfərənt〕*adj.* 漠不關心的
(B) ***unfettered***〔ʌn'fɛtɚd〕*adj.* 不受拘束的
(C) ambitious〔æm'bɪʃəs〕*adj.* 有抱負的
(D) experimental〔ɪk,spɛrə'mɛntḷ〕*adj.* 實驗的

B.

【譯文】

美國現在有兩種醫療系統。第一種是傳統的西醫，它有著名的網絡，包括首選和第二的醫療提供者、保險種類、昂貴的藥品和檢查，有限的營業時間和取得資訊的管道。

另一種醫療系統比較不有名，但逐漸被大家所接受，那是另一種醫學領域，它包含許多專門研究，像是順勢療法、針灸、中藥、能量醫學和自然療法，以上只是舉出了其中一些而已。

【註】

health care 醫療保健　　medicine〔'mɛdəsṇ〕*n.* 醫學
well-known〔'wɛl'non〕*adj.* 著名的
web〔wɛb〕*n.* 網絡；組織
preferred〔prɪ'fɝd〕*adj.* 優先選取的；更好的
secondary〔'sɛkənd,ɛrɪ〕*adj.* 第二位的；次要的
provider〔prə'vaɪdɚ〕*n.* 提供者
insurance〔ɪn'ʃurəns〕*n.* 保險　　drug〔drʌg〕*n.* 藥品
testing〔'tɛstɪŋ〕*n.* 檢查　　limited〔'lɪmɪtɪd〕*adj.* 有限的
office hours 辦公時間；營業時間　　gain〔gen〕*v.* 增加

acceptance〔ək'sɛptəns〕*n.* 接受
domain〔do'men〕*n.* 領域
alternative〔ɔl'tɝnətɪv〕*adj.* 另一可供選擇的；可用以替換的
diversity〔daɪ'vɝsətɪ〕*n.* 多種；多樣性
specialty〔'spɛʃəltɪ〕*n.* 專門研究
homeopathy〔,homɪ'ɑpəθɪ〕*n.* 順勢療法
acupuncture〔'ækju,pʌŋktʃɚ〕*n.* 針灸
herbal〔'hɝbḷ〕*adj.* 草藥的　energy〔'ɛnɚdʒɪ〕*n.* 能量
naturopathic〔,netʃərə'pæθɪk〕*adj.* 自然療法的

16.（**D**）(A) hoarse〔hors〕*adj.* 沙啞的
(B) exterior〔ɪk'stɪrɪɚ〕*adj.* 外部的
(C) irritable〔'ɪrətəbḷ〕*adj.* 暴躁的
(D) ***conventional***〔kən'vɛnʃənḷ〕*adj.* 傳統的

17.（**A**）(A) ***access***〔'æksɛs〕*n.* 接近或使用權
(B) biography〔baɪ'ɑgrəfɪ〕*n.* 傳記
(C) inflation〔ɪn'fleʃən〕*n.* 通貨膨脹
(D) sanitation〔,sænə'teʃən〕*n.*（公共）衛生

18.（**D**）兩者中的「另一個」，須用 ***The other***，選 (D)。

19.（**C**）空格應填一關代，引導形容詞子句，又前有逗點，關代不可用 that，故選 (C) ***which***。

20.（**D**）***to name just a few*** 僅列舉幾個

Ⅲ. 閱讀測驗：20%

A.

【譯文】

無論是一般的緊張性頭痛，或偏頭痛，頭痛的原因通常都是一樣的。在有壓力的時候，頸部、頭部和臉部的肌肉都會繃得很緊，以致於對這些部位下方的神經，施加了相當大的壓力；頭痛發作時有很多種類型，從持續性的隱隱作痛到頭痛欲裂都有。

儘管據估計至少有百分之五十的美國人，每週會發生一次或一次以上的頭痛，但是會特別痛的只有那兩千萬名偏頭痛患者。患有偏頭痛的大多都是女性，它會引起極大而且無法緩和的痛苦。

偏頭痛也有可能是由壓力所引起的，它可能會發生在常常隱藏情緒的人身上，還有很在意自己表現的人身上。要從充滿壓力的環境中跳脫出來，就要坦白說出自己的感覺，降低對自己的期望，這樣才有助於減輕壓力，也可以減輕那些連阿斯匹靈和其他非處方止痛藥，都無效的頭痛。

【答案】

21.（**A**）　22.（**C**）　23.（**C**）　24.（**D**）　25.（**C**）

【註】

cause〔kɔz〕*n.* 原因　headache〔ˈhɛdˌek〕*n.* 頭痛
common〔ˈkɑmən〕*adj.* 一般的　tension〔ˈtɛnʃən〕*n.* 緊張
migraine〔ˈmaɪgren〕*n.* 偏頭痛
period〔ˈpɪrɪəd〕*n.* 時期　stress〔strɛs〕*n.* 壓力
muscle〔ˈmʌsl̩〕*n.* 肌肉　neck〔nɛk〕*n.* 頸部
contracted〔kənˈtræktɪd〕*adj.* 收縮的　exert〔ɪgˈzɝt〕*v.* 施加
tremendous〔trɪˈmɛndəs〕*adj.* 巨大的

pressure〔'prɛʃɚ〕n. 壓力　nerve〔nɜv〕n. 神經
beneath〔bɪ'niθ〕prep. 在…之下　***take～form*** 以～形式出現
constant〔'kɑnstənt〕adj. 持續的　dull〔dʌl〕adj. 隱約的
insistent〔ɪn'sɪstənt〕adj. 強烈的
hammering〔'hæmərɪŋ〕adj. 錘擊般的
result〔rɪ'zʌlt〕v. 發生　***at least*** 至少
adult〔ə'dʌlt〕n. 成人　estimate〔'ɛstə,met〕v. 估計
suffer〔'sʌfɚ〕v. 經歷；遭受　per〔pɚ〕prep. 每一
sufferer〔'sʌfərɚ〕n. 受害者；患者

involve〔ɪn'vɑlv〕v.（必然）伴有
unrelieved〔,ʌnrɪ'livd〕adj. 無法緩和的
bottle up 隱藏；抑制　emotion〔ɪ'moʃən〕n. 情緒
conscientious〔,kɑnʃɪ'ɛnʃəs〕adj. 認眞的；小心謹慎的
performance〔pɚ'fɔrməns〕n. 表現　escape〔ə'skep〕v. 逃脫
stressful〔'strɛsfəl〕adj. 充滿壓力的
situation〔,sɪtʃʊ'eʃən〕n. 情況
open〔'opən〕adj. 不隱瞞的；坦白的
expectation〔,ɛkspɛk'teʃən〕n. 期望
reduce〔rɪ'djus〕v. 減輕　***cut down on*** 減少

aspirin〔'æsprɪn〕n. 阿斯匹靈
prescription〔prɪ'skrɪpʃən〕n. 處方
painkiller〔'pen,kɪlɚ〕n. 止痛藥
infer〔ɪn'fɜ〕v. 推論　variety〔və'raɪətɪ〕n. 多樣性
a variety of 各式各樣的　symptom〔'sɪmptəm〕n. 症狀
experience〔ɪk'spɪrɪəns〕v. 經歷
majority〔mə'dʒɔrətɪ〕n. 大多數　author〔'ɔθɚ〕n. 作者
release〔rɪ'lis〕v. 釋放　express〔ɪk'sprɛs〕v. 表達
emotional〔ɪ'moʃənl̩〕adj. 情緒化的

B.

【譯文】

有一個理論整合了關於飢餓、食物和體重的許多發現，這個理論主張，體重是被一個定點所主宰，那是一種體內平衡機制，它可以使人們大約維持在遺傳所預定的體重上。固定體重理論主張，每個人都有由基因所決定的基礎代謝率，也就是身體燃燒卡路里以產生能量的速率，而且每個人都有固定數量的脂肪細胞，它們是用來儲存可以轉換成能量的脂肪。這些細胞的大小（它們所含有的脂肪量）可能會改變，但是數量絕對不會變。在減重之後，它們會隱藏在身體的各部位，等待機會再度膨脹。根據固定體重理論，大腦裡面沒有任何一個區域會注意體重。說得更確切一點，代謝作用、脂肪細胞和賀爾蒙的交互作用，會使身體維持在本來預定要有的體重。當一個胖子節食，身體會爲了節省能量而減緩代謝速度（這樣就能保留脂肪）。當一個瘦子吃太多時，身體就會加速燃燒能量。

【答案】

26.（**A**） 27.（**B**） 28.（**D**） 29.（**B**） 30.（**A**）

【註】

theory〔ˈθiərɪ〕*n.* 理論 integrate〔ˈɪntəˌgret〕*v.* 整合
diverse〔daɪˈvɝs〕*adj.* 多種的 findings〔ˈfaɪndɪŋz〕*n. pl.* 發現
argue〔ˈɑrgjʊ〕*v.* 主張 govern〔ˈgʌvən〕*v.* 主宰
set-point〔ˈsɛtˈpɔɪnt〕*n.* 定點
homeostatic〔ˌhomɪəˈstætɪk〕*adj.* 體內平衡的
mechanism〔ˈmɛkəˌnɪzəm〕*n.* 機制
roughly〔ˈrʌflɪ〕*adv.* 概略地；大約
genetically〔dʒəˈnɛtɪklɪ〕*adv.* 遺傳上
design〔dɪˈzaɪn〕*v.* 預定 claim〔klem〕*v.* 主張；宣稱
programmed〔ˈprogræmd〕*adj.* 按規劃的；有計劃的

basal〔ˈbesl̩〕*adj.* 基礎的
metabolism〔məˈtæbl̩ˌɪzəm〕*n.* 代謝作用
calorie〔ˈkælərɪ〕*n.* 卡路里 energy〔ˈɛnɚdʒɪ〕*n.* 能量
fixed〔fɪkst〕*adj.* 固定的 fat〔fæt〕*n.* 脂肪
fat cell 脂肪細胞 store〔stor〕*v.* 儲存
contain〔kənˈten〕*v.* 包含 lurk〔lɝk〕*v.* 隱藏
puff up 膨脹 single〔ˈsɪŋgl〕*adj.* 單一的
area〔ˈɛrɪə〕*n.* 區域 ***keep track of*** 不斷地注意
rather〔ˈræðɚ〕*adv.* 說得更確切一點

interaction〔ˌɪntɚˈækʃən〕*n.* 交互作用
hormone〔ˈhɔrmon〕*n.* 賀爾蒙 diet〔ˈdaɪət〕*v. n.* 節食
conserve〔kənˈzɝv〕*v.* 節省 reserve〔rɪˈzɝv〕*v.* 保留
overeat〔ˈovɚˈit〕*v.* 吃得過量 ***speed up*** 加速
textbook〔ˈtɛkstˌbʊk〕*n.* 教科書
biology〔baɪˈɑlədʒɪ〕*n.* 生物學 chemistry〔ˈkɛmɪstrɪ〕*n.* 化學
psychology〔saɪˈkɑlədʒɪ〕*n.* 心理學
focus〔ˈfokəs〕*v.* 集中；著重< *on* >
proper〔ˈprɑpɚ〕*adj.* 適當的 enlarge〔ɪnˈlɑrdʒ〕*v.* 增大
relation〔rɪˈleʃən〕*n.* 關係 activity〔ækˈtɪvətɪ〕*n.* 活動

conclude〔kənˈklud〕*v.* 斷定
overweight〔ˈovɚˈwet〕*adj.* 超重的；太胖的
predisposed〔ˌpridɪsˈpozd〕*adj.* 天生的
attitude〔ˈætəˌtjud〕*n.* 看法；態度
scientific〔ˌsaɪənˈtɪfɪk〕*adj.* 科學的；有系統的
depressing〔dɪˈprɛsɪŋ〕*adj.* 令人沮喪的
disbelieving〔ˌdɪsbɪˈlivɪŋ〕*adj.* 不相信的
inform〔ɪnˈfɔrm〕*v.* 告知 criticize〔ˈkrɪtəˌsaɪz〕*v.* 批評
compare〔kəmˈpɛr〕*v.* 比較 illustrate〔ˈɪləstret〕*v.* 說明

IV. 填充：20％

【譯文】

奥斯卡得獎影片從七十五年前開始有音效，而且從此不再開倒車。在星期天的奥斯卡頒獎典禮上，毫無例外地，沉默絕對不是金。

在第七十六屆的奥斯卡典禮上，有四個比較令人難忘笑話和評論，它們是由台上和台下的明星所說出的：

「我今晚穿的是什麼？是四角褲。」（Bill Murray在節目開始之前，回答每位抵達會場的女明星都會被問到的問題。）

「我想我會喝幾口香檳，然後就睡著。」（最佳歌曲獎得主Annie Lennox，在後台談到她打算如何慶祝時這樣說。）

「大家目前公認。現在在紐西蘭已經沒有尚未感謝的人了。」（Billy Crystal，在「魔戒」贏得當晚十一座奥斯卡獎項的前五項時。）

「我等不及要看到他被查稅──恐怖的時刻。」（Crystal在Errol Morris說完話之後這樣說，並贏得了觀衆的熱烈掌聲。）

【答案】

31. where	32. Here	33. both	34. What	35. question
36. of	37. how	38. There	39. out	40. which

【註】

Oscar〔ˈɔskɚ〕*n.* 奥斯卡金像獎（= *the Academy Awards*）
look back 開倒車　　academy〔əˈkædəmɪ〕*n.* 協會
award〔əˈwɔrd〕*n.* 獎　　ceremony〔ˈsɛrə͵monɪ〕*n.* 典禮
silence〔ˈsaɪləns〕*n.* 沉默
definitely〔ˈdɛfənɪtlɪ〕*adv.* 一定；絕對

golden〔ˈgoldn̩〕*adj.* 金的　　exception〔ɪkˈsɛpʃən〕*n.* 例外
memorable〔ˈmɛmərəbl̩〕*adj.* 難忘的
comment〔ˈkɑmɛnt〕*n.* 評論　　stage〔stedʒ〕*n.* 舞台
annual〔ˈænjuəl〕*adj.* 年度的
boxers〔ˈbɑksɚ〕*n. pl.* 四角褲　　show〔ʃo〕*n.* 表演；節目
ubiquitous〔juˈbɪkwətəs〕*adj.* 無所不在的
female〔ˈfimel〕*adj.* 女性的　　sip〔sɪp〕*n.* 一啜；一口
champagne〔ʃæmˈpen〕*n.* 香檳　　***crash out*** 睡著
backstage〔ˈbækˌstedʒ〕*adv.* 在後台

celebrate〔ˈsɛləˌbret〕*v.* 慶祝
official〔əˈfɪʃəl〕*adj.* 正式的；公認的
lord〔lɔrd〕*n.* 主人　　tax〔tæks〕*n.* 稅
audit〔ˈɔdɪt〕*n.* 查帳；審計　　scary〔ˈskɛrɪ〕*adj.* 恐怖的
remark〔rɪˈmɑrk〕*n.* 話；評論
draw〔drɔ〕*v.* 贏得　　loud〔laʊd〕*adj.* 熱烈的
applause〔əˈplɔz〕*n.* 鼓掌　　audience〔ˈɔdɪəns〕*n.* 觀衆

V. 寫作：20％

寫一篇200字以上的英文作文，並以：If I were the President of National Taiwan Normal University（如果我是國立台灣師範大的校長）開頭。

If I were the President of National Taiwan Normal University, I would create a student educational forum day every year. The forum will be a day of discussions held between the professors, the students and myself. The purpose for the dialogue is to foster an environment where students can have more of a say in their education.

I think communication is key in today's society. Sometimes, professors can lag behind the changing times and may not realize what subjects are no longer relevant today. Giving students a chance to address their concerns or grievances can help the school better tailor the curriculum to the student's discourse. College, after all, is a proving ground for tomorrow's Bill Gates.

I think a more open atmosphere like the one I'm proposing will also help the students to be more vocal. Chinese people are notorious for being too polite and quiet. I think these forums will help the students become more assertive and in the process better prepare them for tomorrow's challenges. Because if you realize something is wrong but you don't say anything about it, then how can you bring about a change?

I think students will embrace and appreciate the chance to meet with their professors out of a class setting. I think the professors, myself included, will learn a lot just by listening to what the students have to say and that will help us become more effective educators.

國立台北大學九十三學年度 碩士班研究生入學考試英文試題

第壹部份：測驗題

一、詞彙與慣用語法（20 %）

說明：第 1 至 20 題，每題選出最適當的一個選項，標示在答案卷之「選擇題答案區」。每題答對得 1 分，答錯不倒扣。

1. Making ________ remarks about others may hurt them emotionally for a long time.
   (A) vulgar (B) eloquent
   (C) uncertain (D) humorous

2. Our government decided to increase rewards to police officers who contribute to cracking cases of copyright ________.
   (A) excitement (B) infringement
   (C) supplement (D) complement

3. The free flow of information and a sincere respect for ________ political and religious beliefs will lead a nation to strength and stability.
   (A) apparent (B) chaotic
   (C) divergent (D) struggling

4. Certain universal rights, which are the birthright of people everywhere, are now ________ in the United Nations Declaration on Human Rights.
   (A) to enshrine (B) being enshrine
   (C) to be enshrine (D) enshrined

5. Even if no violation of law is discovered, the issue ________ troubling questions of political ethics in this country.
   (A) is risen (B) raises
   (C) rises (D) arises

6. ________ there yesterday, I could have prevented that woman from being killed.
   (A) If I would be (B) If I have been
   (C) Have I had been (D) Had I been

7. His failure to ________ the agreement leaves everyone frustrated.
   (A) honor (B) depart
   (C) doing (D) do

8. Taiwan is one of the most ________ places on earth with a population density of about 600 persons per square kilometer.
   (A) homogeneous (B) exciting
   (C) crowded (D) unpleasant

9. He said he had done nothing to ________ a criminal investigation.
   (A) receive (B) cost
   (C) merit (D) marry

10. Parents should teach their children to ________ their money at an early age. Otherwise, they may never know how to manage money properly.
   (A) borrow (B) budget
   (C) lend (D) collect

11. Two roads ______ in a yellow wood. And I was sorry I could not travel both.
    (A) diverge (B) diverged
    (C) grew (D) grow

12. Those who appreciate the arts often gain a broader ______ on the world.
    (A) perspective (B) persistent
    (C) motivation (D) ambition

13. Keeping up with the computer, Internet and telecommunication revolutions requires layers of ________, such as financial institutions and equipment, and a culture of technological know-how.
    (A) skills (B) studies
    (C) structures (D) infrastructure

14. DPP Lawmaker Shen Fu-hsiung has come under ________ for his recent proposal that the DPP should avoid using "loving Taiwan" in election campaigns.
    (A) critic (B) criticize
    (C) criticism (D) critical

15. The world economy ________ to grow by 3.7% this year, with the U.S. still the main locomotive.
    (A) expects (B) will expect
    (C) is expecting (D) is expected

16. World-famous ________ expert Dr. Henry Lee came to Taiwan to investigate the March 19 shooting incident.
    (A) forensic (B) foreign
    (C) shooting (D) figurative

17. When it comes to ________ future trends, those in the travel industry work harder than most.
(A) being predicted (B) predicting
(C) having predicted (D) predicted

18. Beach volleyball first ________ in California in the 1920s as an offshoot of volleyball.
(A) spring out (B) skilled up
(C) sprang up (D) skill down

19. ________ thinking is comprehensive, long-term, and theoretical.
(A) Strategic (B) Sophistry
(C) Tactic (D) Tactical

20. ________ thinking is more limited. It is about the practical, concrete actions to be taken.
(A) Strategic (B) Sophistry
(C) Tactic (D) Tactical

二、文意選填 (20 %)

說明： 第 21 至 40 題，每題一個空格。請依文意在每段文章後所提供的選項中分別選出最適當者，並將其字母代號標示在答案卷之「選擇題答案區」。每題答對得 1 分，答錯不倒扣。

(21-24)

Trying foods from other countries is a great way to __(21)__ different cultures. People around the world have __(22)__ and creative ways of __(23)__ food. The __(24)__ and combinations they use may surprise you.

(A) unique (B) ingredients (C) experience (D) preparing

(25-28)

Sportsmanship means the right kind of spirit a person should have when taking part in any sport or game. Its components are ___(25)___, enthusiasm for the game, ___(26)___ to opponents, courage and the ability to take defeat well. If, when ___(27)___, he can sincerely ___(28)___ his opponent, and shows no signs of humiliation, then he has indeed demonstrated true sportsmanship.

(A) congratulate (B) defeated
(C) fair play (D) generosity

(29-32)

When you do something for someone else, you stop ___(29)___ on yourself. An even better feeling can come from doing something ___(30)___ (that is, you do something without others knowing who did it). ___(31)___ a bad mood not only makes you feel better, but a ___(32)___ outlook may also help you stay healthy.

(A) anonymously (B) Beating
(C) positive (D) focusing

(33-37)

Many karaoke places ___(33)___ music at around 115 decibels. That's ___(34)___ to a loud car horn. Even just 100 minutes of karaoke can ___(35)___ decrease one's hearing ability. Constant ___(36)___ can cause ___(37)___ damage.

(A) comparable (B) exposure
(C) temporarily (D) permanent (E) blare

(38-40)

One trick to improve your English pronunciation is to ___(38)___ yourself reading an article. Listen to yourself and try to ___(39)___ mistakes. You will also ___(40)___ sounds you need to practice.

(A) discover (B) catch (C) record (D) repeat

三、閱讀測驗（26 %）

說明：第 41 至 53 題，每題分別根據各篇文章的文意選出最適當的一個選項，標示在答案卷之「選擇題答案區」。每題答對得 2 分，答錯倒扣 1 分。

I. (41-44)

If history is like a mirror in which we see the lessons of the past, then one of the great lessons of World War II is the danger of Fascism. Yet Fascism has never completely disappeared from the face of the earth. It did not die with the defeat of Nazi Germany or Mussolini's Italy. Its embers waft in the air, waiting to be fanned by opportunistic politicians.

According to Laurence Britt, a noted historian, some of Fascism's features are:

(1) It celebrates race as a community above all other loyalties and advances a myth of rebirth.

(2) It encourages participation in politics but is elitist in that it treats the people's will as embodied in one supreme leader.

(3) It stirs up the support of the masses with displays of flags, demonstrations, and slogans which instill a feverish sense of national pride and xenophobic suspicion.

(4) It identifies scapegoats, which are ethnic minorities. A doctrine of racial superiority is used to suppress enemies and shift blame for failures.

(5) It justifies what it does in the name of national interests. Any disagreement is labeled as unpatriotic and treasonous.

(6) Artists and intellectuals who do not serve the patriotic ideal are neglected or outlawed.

(7) Leaders receive financial gifts from businessmen close to them who gain their favoritism. This corruption and cronyism goes on unconstrained and unknown to the public.

(8) Leaders manipulate elections by controlling the system, intimidating opposition voters, and destroying legal votes.

41. What is the most appropriate title for this passage?
(A) On Opportunistic Politicians
(B) On Nazi Germany (C) On Fascism
(D) On Lessons of History

42. What does "scapegoats" mean here?
(A) People fighting for themselves.
(B) People who are blamed for the fault of others.
(C) People believing in racial superiority.
(D) People longing for national interests.

43. Who in Fascism may gain leaders' favoritism?
(A) Businessmen who give financial gifts to leaders.
(B) Artists who love leaders.
(C) Intellectuals who serve the patriotic ideal.
(D) Leaders' opponents.

44. Which of the following things will a Fascist leader NOT do during an election?
    (A) control the election system
    (B) intimidate opposition voters
    (C) select a righteous candidate
    (D) destroy legal votes

II. (45-47)

"The chance of one single ancestor of ours not dying while growing up is one in several billion. Actually, *all* our ancestors have grown up and had children—even during the worst natural disasters, even when the child mortality rate was enormous. Of course, a lot of them have suffered from illness, but we've always pulled through.... Our life on this planet has been threatened by insects, wild animals, lightning, sickness, war, floods, fires, and poisonings. I am talking about one long chain of coincidences. In fact, the chain goes right back to the first living cell, which divided in two, and from there gave birth to everything growing and sprouting on this planet today. The chance of *my* chain not being broken at one time or another during three or four billion years is so little that it is almost inconceivable. But I have pulled through. In return, I appreciate how fantastically lucky I am to be able to experience and realize how lucky every single little crawling insect on this planet is."

"What about the unlucky ones?"

"They don't *exist!*" he almost shouted. "They were never born. Life is one huge lottery where only the winning tickets are visible."

45. The chance of my chain not being broken…is so little it is almost inconceivable. Here "inconceivable" means
(A) imperative.
(B) unimaginable.
(C) not impossible.
(D) very likely.

46. What does "Life is one huge lottery where only the winning tickets are visible" mean?
(A) In order to win in a big lottery, we must become gamblers.
(B) To live is to win a big lottery.
(C) All living things that we can see are winners in the process of evolution.
(D) Losers must go into hiding and never be seen.

47. Which of the following statements is NOT true according to this passage?
(A) Every one of us is extremely lucky to be alive.
(B) The chance of any single one of our ancestors dying without having offspring is great.
(C) Each one of us has inherited a long chain of coincidences from the first living cell.
(D) Since we are alive, we should all go out and buy a lot of lottery tickets.

Ⅲ. (48-49)

"The crisis of authority is one of the causes for all the atrocities we are seeing in the world today," says Vaclav Havel, Czechoslovakia's leading playwright and a writer of compelling essays on repression and dissent. "The post-Communist world presented a chance for new moral leaders. But gradually people were repressed, and much of that opportunity was lost." In 1989, he was elected president of the newly formed Czech Republic, the first non-Communist leader in more than 40 years. Havel remains one of democracy's most principled voices. "There are certain leaders one can respect, like the Dalai Lama," he says. "Although often they have no hope, they are still ready to sacrifice their lives and their freedom. They are ready to assume responsibility for the world—or the part of the world they live in. Courage means going against majority opinion in the name of truth."

48. Which of the following statements best conveys the main idea of this reading?
   (A) The world is faced with too many pains and cruelties.
   (B) Havel was elected the first non-Communist leader of the Czech Republic because he wrote well.
   (C) The Dalai Lama is admirable because he takes responsibility.
   (D) Havel thinks respectable leaders are responsible and courageous in their fight for truth.

49. The writing style of this reading passage is
   (A) artistic.
   (B) journalistic.
   (C) argumentative.
   (D) business-like.

IV. (50-53)

Tow hundred years ago, passenger pigeons were the most numerous birds in the world. A flock of them might include over two million birds. When they flew overhead, they darkened the sky for hundreds of miles. Today, not a single one of these birds exists. Incredible as it may seem, all these millions of birds were hunted down for food, feathers and sport.

The story of the passenger pigeon is just one of many sad stories about animals that have disappeared. At least 461 species of birds and mammals have become extinct in the past 400 years. And among plant species the number at risk reaches 25,000.

The cause of this terrible destruction is always the same: humankind. Sometimes people have killed off species directly by hunting them, as with the passenger pigeon. The most frequent cause of extinction, however, is the human destruction of the environment. On the Hawaiian Islands, for instance, European and American settlers cut down the forests for farmland. This killed off many of Hawaii's unique species of birds and plants. Even more dramatic, is the situation in the Amazon rain forest today. Here, each square mile of the forest contains thousands of plant and animal species. These species depend on each other and on their special environment. When the trees are cut down, the environment changes or is destroyed altogether. And many species disappear forever.

Scientists are very concerned. The loss of fellow creatures is a loss for us as well. We lose the chance to learn more about ourselves and our environment. We also lose valuable economic and scientific resources. The loss of species also means a narrower range of genetic possibilities in the world. Scientists do not know what that will mean, but they are worried.

50. This passage is about
    (A) the extinction of species due to humankind.
    (B) many kinds of plants and animals that are used by humans.
    (C) how Europeans destroyed species on the Hawaiian islands.
    (D) how hunting causes certain animals to become extinct.

51. How many pieces of evidence (including examples) are used to support the theme of the article?
    (A) one (B) two
    (C) three (D) four

52. When people cut down large areas of rain forest, they
    (A) drive endangered species out of the woods.
    (B) help many species to multiply and grow in number.
    (C) discover many useful species.
    (D) destroy many species before they have a chance to be identified or studied.

53. We can infer from this passage that people
   (A) have always been concerned about the survival of different species.
   (B) have rarely been concerned about saving different species.
   (C) have eliminated different species whenever possible.
   (D) do not like wild animals very much.

第貳部份：非測驗題

一、中譯英（15 %）

說明：1. 依提示在「答案卷」上將下列句子譯成英文。
　　　2. 請依序作答並標明題號。

一、台灣人的生命力就在那裡！

二、他在苦難的時候，並不強調苦難，

三、而是想怎樣去克服那個困境。

四、全球化是一個既讓人歡迎又讓人不安的現象。

五、誰有權力，誰就要負責任。

二、英文作文（19 %）

說明：1. 題目：What Can Be Done About Telephone Fraud?
　　　2. 文長以 120 字左右爲原則。
　　　3. 請寫在「答案卷」上。

國立台北大學九十三學年度
碩士班研究生入學考試英文試題詳解

第一部分：測驗題

一、詞彙與慣用語法：20％

1. (**A**) (A) ***vulgar*** (ˈvʌlgɚ) *adj.* 粗俗的
(B) eloquent (ˈɛləkwənt) *adj.* 善辯的；口才好的
(C) uncertain (ʌnˈsɝtn̩) *adj.* 不確定的
(D) humorous (ˈhjumərəs) *adj.* 幽默的
remark (rɪˈmɑrk) *n.* 話；評論
emotionally (ɪˈmoʃənl̩ɪ) *adv.* 情感上

2. (**B**) (B) ***infringement*** (ɪnˈfrɪndʒmənt) *n.* 侵害
(C) supplement (ˈsʌpləmənt) *n.* 補足；追加
(D) complement (ˈkɑmpləmənt) *n.* 補充
reward (rɪˈwɔrd) *n.* 獎賞；懸賞金
contribute (kənˈtrɪbjut) *v.* 貢獻；促成
crack (kræk) *v.* 破解　case (kes) *n.* 案件
copyright (ˈkɑpɪˌraɪt) *n.* 著作權；版權

3. (**C**) (A) apparent (əˈpærənt) *adj.* 明顯的
(B) chaotic (keˈɑtɪk) *adj.* 混亂的
(C) ***divergent*** (daɪˈvɝdʒənt) *adj.* 不同的
(D) struggling (ˈstrʌglɪŋ) *adj.* 掙扎的
flow (flo) *n.* 流動　sincere (sɪnˈsɪr) *adj.* 眞誠的
religious (rɪˈlɪdʒəs) *adj.* 宗教的
belief (bɪˈlif) *n.* 信念　lead (lid) *v.* 引導
strength (strɛŋθ) *n.* 力量
stability (stəˈbɪlətɪ) *n.* 穩定

4.（ **D** ）(A) enshrine〔ɪn'ʃraɪn〕*v.* 銘記
certain〔'sɝtn̩〕*adj.* 某些
universal〔,junə'vɝsl̩〕*adj.* 普遍存在的
birthright〔'bɝθ,raɪt〕*n.* 與生俱來的權利
United Nations 聯合國
declaration〔,dɛklə'reʃən〕*n.* 宣言
Declaration on Human Rights 人權宣言

5.（ **B** ）(A) rise〔raɪz〕*v.* 升起；上升
(B) ***raise***〔rez〕*v.* 提高；引起
(D) arise〔ə'raɪz〕*v.* 產生；出現
violation〔,vaɪə'leʃən〕*n.* 違反
discover〔dɪ'skʌvɚ〕*v.* 發現　　issue〔'ɪʃjʊ〕*n.* 議題
troubling〔'trʌbl̩ɪŋ〕*adj.* 令人困擾的
political〔pə'lɪtɪkl̩〕*adj.* 政治的
ethics〔'ɛθɪks〕*n. pl.* 倫理；道德規範

6.（ **D** ）prevent〔prɪ'vɛnt〕*v.* 防止；阻止

7.（ **A** ）(A) ***honor***〔'ɑnɚ〕*v.* 實踐；執行
(B) depart〔dɪ'pɑrt〕*v.* 出發
failure〔'feljɚ〕*n.* 未能
agreement〔ə'grimənt〕*n.* 協定
leave〔liv〕*v.* 使處於某種狀態
frustrated〔'frʌstretɪd〕*adj.* 感到沮喪的

8.（ **C** ）(A) homogeneous〔,homə'dʒinɪəs〕*adj.* 同質的
(C) ***crowded***〔'kraʊdɪd〕*adj.* 擁擠的
(D) unpleasant〔ʌn'plɛznt〕*adj.* 令人不愉快的
population〔,pɑpjə'leʃən〕*n.* 人口
density〔'dɛnsətɪ〕*n.* 密度
per〔pɚ〕*prep.* 每…　　square〔skwɛr〕*n.* 平方
kilometer〔'kɪlə,mitɚ〕*n.* 公里

9. (**C**) (A) receive〔rɪ'siv〕*v.* 收到
(C) ***merit***〔'mɛrɪt〕*v.* 值得
(D) marry〔'mærɪ〕*v.* 結婚
criminal〔'krɪmənḷ〕*adj.* 犯罪的
investigation〔ɪn,vɛstə'geʃən〕*n.* 調查

10. (**B**) (A) borrow〔'bɑro〕*v.* 借（入）
(B) ***budget***〔'bʌdʒɪt〕*v.* 規劃；編…的預算
(C) lend〔lɛnd〕*v.* 借（出）
(D) collect〔kə'lɛkt〕*v.* 收集
otherwise〔'ʌðɚ,waɪz〕*adv.* 否則
properly〔'prɑpɚlɪ〕*adv.* 適當地

11. (**B**) (A) diverge〔daɪ'vɝdʒ〕*v.* 分岔　travel〔'trævḷ〕*v.* 走

12. (**A**) (A) ***perspective***〔pɚ'spɛktɪv〕*n.* 眼界
(B) persistent〔pɚ'zɪstənt〕*adj.* 持續的
(C) motivation〔,motə'veʃən〕*n.* 動機
(D) ambition〔æm'bɪʃən〕*n.* 抱負
appreciate〔ə'priʃɪ,et〕*v.* 欣賞
gain〔gen〕*v.* 獲得　broad〔brɔd〕*adj.* 寬闊的

13. (**D**) (C) structure〔'strʌktʃɚ〕*n.* 結構
(D) ***infrastructure***〔'ɪnfrə,strʌktʃɚ〕*n.* 基礎
catch up with 趕上
telecommunication〔,tɛləkə,mjunə'keʃən〕*n.* 電信
revolution〔,rɛvə'luʃən〕*n.* 革命　layer〔'leɚ〕*n.* 層
financial〔faɪ'nænʃəl〕*adj.* 金融的；財務的
institution〔,ɪnstə'tjuʃən〕*n.* 機構
equipment〔ɪ'kwɪpmənt〕*n.* 設備；知識
culture〔'kʌltʃɚ〕*n.* 訓練
technological〔,tɛknə'lɑdʒɪkḷ〕*adj.* 科技的
know-how〔'no,haʊ〕*n.* 專門知識；技術

14. (**C**) (A) critic〔 'krɪtɪk 〕*n.* 批評家；評論家
(B) criticize〔 'krɪtə,saɪz 〕*v.* 批評
(C) ***criticism***〔 'krɪtə,sɪzəm 〕*n.* 批評
(D) critical〔 'krɪtɪkl 〕*adj.* 批評的；吹毛求疵的
lawmaker〔 'lɔ,mekɚ 〕*n.* 立法者
come under 受到　recent〔 'risnt 〕*adj.* 最近的
proposal〔 prə'pozl 〕*n.* 提議　avoid〔 ə'vɔɪd 〕*v.* 避免
election〔 ɪ'lɛkʃən 〕*n.* 選舉；競選
campaign〔 kæm'pen 〕*n.* 宣傳活動

15. (**D**) economy〔 ɪ'kɑnəmɪ 〕*n.* 經濟　main〔 men 〕*adj.* 主要的
locomotive〔 ,lokə'motɪv 〕*n.* 火車頭

16. (**A**) (A) ***forensic***〔 fə'rɛnsɪk 〕*adj.* 法醫的
(B) foreign〔 'fɔrɪn 〕*adj.* 外國的
(C) shooting〔 'ʃutɪŋ 〕*n.* 射擊；槍擊
(D) figurative〔 'fɪgjərətɪv 〕*adj.* 比喻的
world-famous〔 'wɝld'feməs 〕*adj.* 舉世聞名的
expert〔 'ɛkspɝt 〕*n.* 專家
investigate〔 ɪn'vɛstə,get 〕*v.* 調查
incident〔 'ɪnsədənt 〕*n.* 事件

17. (**B**) (A) predict〔 prɪ'dɪkt 〕*v.* 預測
when it comes to + V-ing 一提到
trend〔 trɛnd 〕*n.* 趨勢　industry〔 'ɪndəstrɪ 〕*n.* 產業

18. (**C**) (A) spring〔 sprɪŋ 〕*v.* 跳
(B) skill〔 skɪl 〕*n.* 技術
(C) ***spring up*** 產生；出現
beach〔 bitʃ 〕*n.* 海灘　volleyball〔 'vɑlɪ,bɔl 〕*n.* 排球
offshoot〔 'ɔf,ʃut 〕*n.* 分支

19.（**A**）(A) ***strategic***〔strə'tidʒɪk〕*adj.* 戰略上的
(B) sophistry〔'sɑfɪstrɪ〕*n.* 謬論
(C) tactic〔'tæktɪk〕*n.* 戰術
(D) tactical〔'tæktɪkḷ〕*adj.* 戰術的；足智多謀的
comprehensive〔,kɑmprɪ'hɛnsɪv〕*adj.* 廣泛的
long-term〔'lɔŋ,tɝm〕*adj.* 長期的
theoretical〔,θiə'rɛtɪkḷ〕*adj.* 理論的；推理的

20.（**D**）limited〔'lɪmɪtɪd〕*adj.* 有限的
practical〔'præktɪkḷ〕*adj.* 實際的
concrete〔'kɑnkrit〕*adj.* 具體的

二、文意選填：20％

(21-24)

【譯文】

嚐試來自其他國家的食物，是體驗不同文化的好方法。世界各地的人們，對於準備食物，都有其獨特和獨創的方法。他們所使用的原料和搭配方式，可能會讓你嚇一跳。

【註】

creative〔krɪ'etɪv〕*adj.* 獨創的；有創造力的
combination〔,kɑmbə'neʃən〕*n.* 搭配
surprise〔sə'praɪz〕*v.* 使驚訝
unique〔ju'nik〕*adj.* 獨特的
ingredient〔ɪn'gridɪənt〕*n.* 原料
experience〔ɪk'spɪrɪəns〕*v.* 體驗
prepare〔prɪ'pɛr〕*v.* 準備做（飯菜）；調製

【答案】

21.（**C**）　22.（**A**）　23.（**D**）　24.（**B**）

(25-28)

【譯文】

運動家精神是指一個人在參加任何運動或比賽時，所應具備的正確心態。它的構成要素包括公平的比賽、比賽的熱忱、對對手寬大為懷、勇氣，和坦然接受失敗的能力。如果當一個人被擊敗時，能夠衷心地祝賀他的對手，而且沒有表現出任何丟臉的樣子，那麼他的確展示出了眞正的運動家精神。

【註】

sportsmanship〔'sportsmən,ʃɪp〕*n.* 運動家精神
spirit〔'spɪrɪt〕*n.* 心態　***take part in*** 參加
component〔kəm'ponənt〕*n.* 構成要素；成份
enthusiasm〔ɪn'θjuzɪ,æzəm〕*n.* 熱忱
opponent〔ə'ponənt〕*n.* 對手　courage〔'kɝɪdʒ〕*n.* 勇氣
defeat〔dɪ'fit〕*n.* 失敗　sincerely〔sɪn'sɪrlɪ〕*adv.* 由衷地
sign〔saɪn〕*n.* 表示；跡象　humiliation〔hju,mɪlɪ'eʃən〕*n.* 丟臉
indeed〔ɪn'did〕*adv.* 眞正地
demonstrate〔'dɛmən,stret〕*v.* 表露；展示
congratulate〔kən'grætʃə,let〕*v.* 祝賀　fair〔fɛr〕*adj.* 公平的
play〔ple〕*n.* 比賽　generosity〔,dʒɛnə'rɑsətɪ〕*n.* 寬大

【答案】

25.（**C**）　26.（**D**）　27.（**B**）　28.（**A**）

(29-32)

【譯文】

當你為了其他人做某件事時，你不再將注意力集中在自己身上。更美好的感覺可能來自於匿名做一些事（也就是你做這些事，但沒有人知道是誰做的）。戰勝壞心情不只會讓你覺得更快樂，而且樂觀的看法還有助於你保持健康。

【註】

that is 也就是說　　mood〔 mud 〕*n.* 心情
not only…but (also) ~ 不僅…而且~
outlook〔 ˈaʊt,lʊk 〕*n.* 看法　　stay〔 ste 〕*v.* 保持
healthy〔 ˈhɛlθɪ 〕*adj.* 健康的
anonymously〔 əˈnɑnəməslɪ 〕*adv.* 匿名地
beat〔 bit 〕*v.* 戰勝　　positive〔 ˈpɑzətɪv 〕*adj.* 樂觀的
focus〔 ˈfokəs 〕*v.* 集中（注意力）於 <*on*>

【答案】

29.（**D**）　30.（**A**）　31.（**B**）　32.（**C**）

(33-37)

【譯文】

很多卡拉 OK 都把喇叭的聲音開在 115 分貝左右。那和汽車的喇叭一樣大聲。甚至只唱 100 分鐘的卡拉 OK，都可能會使我們的聽力減退。而持續暴露在這樣的環境下，則可能會造成永久的傷害。

【註】

karaoke〔 ,kɑrəˈoke 〕*n.* 卡拉 OK
decibel〔 ˈdɛsə,bɛl 〕*n.* 分貝　　loud〔 laʊd 〕*adj.* 大聲的
horn〔 hɔrn 〕*n.* 喇叭　　hearing〔 ˈhɪrɪŋ 〕*n.* 聽力
constant〔 ˈkɑnstənt 〕*adj.* 持續的　　damage〔 ˈdæmɪdʒ 〕*n.* 損害
comparable〔 ˈkɑmpərəbl̩ 〕*adj.* 相當的；可與~匹敵的 <*to*>
exposure〔 ɪkˈspoʒɚ 〕*n.* 暴露；接觸
temporarily〔 ˈtɛmpə,rɛrəlɪ 〕*adv.* 暫時地
permanent〔 ˈpɝmənənt 〕*adj.* 永久的
blare〔 blɛr 〕*n.*（喇叭等的）聲音

【答案】

33.（E）　34.（A）　35.（C）　36.（B）　37.（D）

(38-40)

【譯文】

有個讓你的英文發音改善的祕訣，那就是把你唸一篇文章的聲音錄下來。聽自己唸，並試著抓出錯誤。你還會發現，自己需要多練習的一些發音。

【註】

trick〔trɪk〕*n.* 訣竅　improve〔ɪm'pruv〕*v.* 改善
pronunciation〔prə,nʌnsɪ'eʃən〕*n.* 發音
article〔'ɑrtɪkḷ〕*n.* 文章　record〔rɪ'kɔrd〕*v.* 錄音
repeat〔rɪ'pit〕*v.* 重覆

【答案】

38.（C）　39.（B）　40.（A）

三、閱讀測驗：26％

I. (41-44)

【譯文】

如果歷史就像一面鏡子，能讓我們看見過去的教訓，那麼第二次世界大戰最大的教訓，就是法西斯主義的危險。但是法西斯主義並沒有完全從地球表面消失。它並沒有隨著納粹德國或義大利墨索里尼的失敗而消失。它的餘燼仍然飄蕩在空中，等待投機的政客為它煽風點火。

根據著名的歷史學家 Laurence Britt 的理論，法西斯主義有這些特色：

(1) 它歌頌種族，把它說成是超越所有其他忠誠的集團，並提出復興的神話。

(2) 它鼓勵參與政治，但是要採行菁英主義，因爲它認爲人民的意志，會在一位最高領導者的身上具體呈現。

(3) 它會以懸掛旗幟、示威遊行和口號，來煽動群衆的支持，並且灌輸強烈的民族尊嚴意識，而且它有厭惡外國人的嫌疑。

(4) 它會把少數民族視同代罪羔羊。優秀民族論被它用來鎭壓反對者，並且把失敗歸咎到他們身上。

(5) 它會以國家利益來爲自己的行爲辯護。任何意見分歧都會被說成是不愛國和叛國。

(6) 不信奉愛國理想的藝術家和知識份子，會被輕視或視爲不法之徒。

(7) 領導者會從親近他們的商人那裡收到禮金，而那些商人則會獲得他們的偏袒。這種賄賂和偏袒的現象很自然地發生，而且不爲衆人所知。

(8) 領導者靠操縱制度、威脅反對黨的選民，並破壞合法選票來操縱選舉。

【註】

mirror〔 ′mɪrɚ 〕*n.* 鏡子　lesson〔 ′lɛsn̩ 〕*n.* 教訓
past〔 pæst 〕*n.* 過去　danger〔 ′dendʒɚ 〕*n.* 危險
Fascism〔 ′fæʃ,ɪzəm 〕*n.* 法西斯主義；獨裁的社會國家主義
completely〔 kəm′plitlɪ 〕*adv.* 完全地
disappear〔 ,dɪsə′pɪr 〕*v.* 消失　face〔 fes 〕*n.* 表面
die〔 daɪ 〕*v.* 消失　defeat〔 dɪ′fit 〕*n.* 失敗
Nazi〔 ′nætsɪ 〕*n.* 納粹　Germany〔 ′dʒɝmənɪ 〕*n.* 德國
Mussolini〔 ,musl̩′inɪ 〕*n.* 墨索里尼　Italy〔 ′ɪtl̩ɪ 〕*n.* 義大利

ember〔'ɛmbɚ〕*n.* 餘燼　waft〔wæft〕*v.* 飄蕩
fan〔fæn〕*v.* 搧（火）；煽動
opportunistic〔,ɑpɚtju'nɪstɪk〕*adj.* 投機的
politician〔,pɑlə'tɪʃən〕*n.* 政客　noted〔'notɪd〕*adj.* 著名的
historian〔hɪs'torɪən〕*n.* 歷史學家　feature〔'fitʃɚ〕*n.* 特色
celebrate〔'sɛlə,bret〕*v.* 讚頌　race〔res〕*n.* 種族
community〔kə'mjunətɪ〕*n.* 集團
loyalties〔'lɔɪəltɪz〕*n. pl.* 忠誠；忠心
advance〔əd'væns〕*v.* 提出　myth〔mɪθ〕*n.* 神話
rebirth〔ri'bɝθ〕*n.* 復興；復活　encourage〔ɪn'kɝɪdʒ〕*v.* 鼓勵

participation〔pɚ,tɪsə'peʃən〕*n.* 參與
politics〔'pɑlə,tɪks〕*n.* 政治　elitist〔ɪ'litɪst〕*adj.* 精英主義的
in that 因為（= *because*）　***treat*** A ***as*** B 把A視為B
will〔wɪl〕*n.* 意志　embody〔ɪm'bɑdɪ〕*v.* 具體表現
supreme〔sə'prim〕*adj.* 最高的　stir〔stɝ〕*v.* 煽動
stir up 煽動　support〔sə'port〕*n.* 支持
mass〔mæs〕*n.* 群衆　display〔dɪ'sple〕*n.* 陳列；展示
flag〔flæg〕*n.* 旗子；國旗
demonstration〔,dɛmən'streʃən〕*n.* 示威遊行

slogan〔'slogən〕*n.* 口號　instill〔ɪn'stɪl〕*v.* 灌輸
feverish〔'fivərɪʃ〕*adj.* 強烈的　sense〔sɛns〕*n.* 意識
national〔'næʃənl̩〕*adj.* 民族的　pride〔praɪd〕*n.* 自尊
xenophobic〔,zɛnə'fobɪk〕*adj.* 厭惡外國人（事物）的
suspicion〔sə'spɪʃən〕*n.* 感覺；嫌疑
identify〔aɪ'dɛntə,faɪ〕*v.* 確認
scapegoat〔'skep,got〕*n.* 代罪羔羊　ethnic〔'ɛθnɪk〕*adj.* 民族
minority〔mə'nɔrətɪ〕*n.* 少數民族
doctrine〔'dɑktrɪn〕*n.* 教條；理論
racial〔'reʃəl〕*adj.* 種族的；民族的

superiority〔 sə,pɪrɪ'ɔrətɪ 〕*n.* 優越
suppress〔 sə'prɛs 〕*v.* 鎭壓　enemy〔 'ɛnəmɪ 〕*n.* 敵人；反對者
shift〔 ʃɪft 〕*v.* 把（責任、過失）轉嫁
blame〔 blem 〕*n.* 責備；責任
justify〔 'dʒʌstə,faɪ 〕*v.* 使成爲正當；爲～辯護
in the name of 以～名義　interest〔 'ɪntrɪst 〕*n.* 利益
disagreement〔 ,dɪsə'grimənt 〕*n.* 意見的分歧
be labeled as 被稱爲　unpatriotic〔 ,ʌnpetrɪ'ɑtɪk 〕*adj.* 不愛國的
treasonous〔 'triznəs 〕*adj.* 叛國的
intellectual〔 ,ɪntl'ɛktʃuəl 〕*n.* 知識份子　serve〔 sɝv 〕*v.* 爲～效勞
patriotic〔 ,petrɪ'ɑtɪk 〕*adj.* 愛國的　ideal〔 aɪ'diəl 〕*n.* 理想
neglect〔 nɪ'glɛkt 〕*v.* 忽視；輕視
outlaw〔 'aʊt,lɔ 〕*v.* 宣布…爲不法之徒
financial〔 fə'nænʃəl 〕*adj.* 金錢的；財政的　gain〔 gen 〕*v.* 獲得
favoritism〔 'fevərɪt,ɪzəm 〕*n.* 偏袒
corruption〔 kə'rʌpʃən 〕*n.* 貪污；賄賂
cronyism〔 'kronɪɪzəm 〕*n.* 對好朋友的偏袒　***go on*** 進行
unconstrained〔 ,ʌnkən'strend 〕*adj.* 無拘束的；自由的
unknown〔 ʌn'non 〕*adj.* 不爲…所知的 < *to* >
the public 一般大衆　manipulate〔 mə'nɪpjə,let 〕*v.* 操縱
election〔 ɪ'lɛkʃən 〕*n.* 選舉　intimidate〔 ɪn'tɪmə,det 〕*v.* 恐嚇
opposition〔 ,ɑpə'zɪʃən 〕*n.* 反對黨　voter〔 'votɚ 〕*n.* 選民
destroy〔 dɪ'strɔɪ 〕*v.* 破壞　legal〔 'ligl 〕*adj.* 合法的
vote〔 vot 〕*n.* 選票　appropriate〔 ə'proprɪɪt 〕*adj.* 適當的
fight for 爲～而戰　fault〔 fɔlt 〕*n.* 過錯
racial〔 'reʃəl 〕*adj.* 種族的　superiority〔 sə,pɪrɪ'ɔrətɪ 〕*n.* 優越
long for 渴望　opponent〔 ə'ponənt 〕*n.* 對手
righteous〔 'raɪtʃəs 〕*adj.* 正義的；有德的
candidate〔 'kændə,det 〕*n.* 候選人

【答案】

41.（C） 42.（B） 43.（A） 44.（C）

Ⅱ. (45-47)

【譯文】

我們的祖先，沒有在成長的過程中死亡的機率，是幾十億分之一。事實上，我們所有的祖先都長大了，而且還生了小孩──甚至在天災最嚴重的時期，甚至是當小孩的死亡率非常高時。當然，他們很多人都生過病，但是我們總能脫離險境…。我們在地球上的生活，曾經受到昆蟲、野生動物、閃電、疾病、戰爭、水災、火災和中毒的威脅。我講的是一長串的巧合。事實上，這一連串都要回溯到第一個活體細胞，它分裂成兩個，然後從那裡產生現在在這個地球上生長和萌芽的每樣東西。我這一條脈絡，沒有在三、四十億年間的某個時候被打斷，這種機率是小到令人無法想像的。但是我也度過那些難關了。能夠作爲回報的，就是我知道自己是如此幸運，可以經歷並了解這個星球上的每一隻爬行的昆蟲有多幸運。」

「那些不幸的傢伙怎麼了？」

「他們並不存在！」他幾乎是大喊著這樣說。「他們沒有出生過。生命就是一場大樂透，只能看到中獎的彩票。」

【註】

single〔ˈsɪŋgl̩〕*adj.* 單一的　ancestor〔ˈænsɛstɚ〕*n.* 祖先
billion〔ˈbɪljən〕*n.* 十億　actually〔ˈæktʃuəlɪ〕*adv.* 事實上
worst〔wɝst〕*adj.* 最惡劣的　natural〔ˈnætʃərəl〕*adj.* 自然界的
disaster〔dɪzˈæstɚ〕*n.* 災害　***natural disaster*** 天災
mortality〔mɔrˈtælətɪ〕*n.* 大規模死亡；死亡率
enormous〔ɪˈnɔrməs〕*adj.* 巨大的　***suffer from*** 罹患

illness〔 'ɪlnɪs 〕*n.* 疾病　***pull through*** 脫離險境
planet〔 'plænɪt 〕*n.* 行星（在此指「地球」）
threaten〔 'θrɛtṇ 〕*v.* 威脅　insect〔 'ɪnsɛkt 〕*n.* 昆蟲
wild〔 waɪld 〕*adj.* 野生的　lightning〔 'laɪtnɪŋ 〕*n.* 閃電
flood〔 flʌd 〕*n.* 水災　poisoning〔 'pɔɪzṇɪŋ 〕*n.* 中毒
chain〔 tʃen 〕*n.* 一連串　coincidence〔 ko'ɪnsədəns 〕*n.* 巧合
living〔 'lɪvɪŋ 〕*adj.* 活的　cell〔 sɛl 〕*n.* 細胞
divide〔 də'vaɪd 〕*v.* 分裂　***give birth to*** 產生
sprout〔 spraʊt 〕*v.* 萌芽　***at one time or another*** 在某個時候
inconceivable〔 ˌɪnkən'sivəbḷ 〕*adj.* 難以想像的

in return 作爲回報　appreciate〔 ə'priʃɪˌet 〕*v.* 知道
fantastically〔 fæn'tæstɪkəlɪ 〕*adj.* 難以置信地
experience〔 ɪk'spɪrɪəns 〕*v.* 經歷　realize〔 'riəˌlaɪz 〕*v.* 了解
crawling〔 'krɔlɪŋ 〕*adj.* 爬行的
unlucky〔 ʌn'lʌkɪ 〕*adj.* 不幸的　exist〔 ɪg'zɪst 〕*v.* 存在
shout〔 ʃaʊt 〕*v.* 大叫　huge〔 hjudʒ 〕*adj.* 巨大的
lottery〔 'lɑtərɪ 〕*n.* 樂透彩　winning〔 'wɪnɪŋ 〕*adj.* 中獎的
ticket〔 'tɪkɪt 〕*n.* 彩票　visible〔 'vɪzəbḷ 〕*adj.* 看得見的
imperative〔 ɪm'pɛrətɪv 〕*adj.* 非做不可的
unimaginable〔 ˌʌnɪ'mædʒɪnəbḷ 〕*adj.* 無法想像的；想像不到的

likely〔 'laɪklɪ 〕*adj.* 可能的　gambler〔 'gæmblɚ 〕*n.* 賭客
process〔 'prɑsɛs 〕*n.* 過程
evolution〔 ˌɛvə'luʃən 〕*n.* 進化；發展
loser〔 'luzɚ 〕*n.* 失敗者　***go into hiding*** 躲起來
following〔 'fɑləwɪŋ 〕*adj.* 下列的
statement〔 'stetmənt 〕*n.* 敘述
extremely〔 ɪk'strimlɪ 〕*adv.* 非常地
alive〔 ə'laɪv 〕*adj.* 活著的　offspring〔 'ɔfˌsprɪŋ 〕*n.* 子孫
inherit〔 ɪn'hɛrɪt 〕*v.* 繼承

【答案】

45.（**B**）　　46.（**C**）　　47.（**D**）

Ⅲ. (48-49)

【譯文】

「我們在現今世界所見到的所有暴行，主權危機就是原因之一，」瓦茨拉夫・哈維爾說，他是捷克的主要劇作家，也是一位專門寫些關於鎮壓與持異議者的動人評論的作家。「後共產黨世界給了新的精神領袖一個機會。但人們卻漸漸被鎮壓住，然後失去許多機會。」他在1989年時，被選爲新建立的捷克共和國總統，他是四十多年來，第一位非共產黨領袖。他也是民主政體最有原則的代言人之一。「我們可以尊敬某些領袖，像是達賴喇嘛，」他說道。「雖然他們常常沒什麼希望，但仍然願意犧牲自己的生命與自由。他們會做好爲這個世界承擔責任的準備──或是爲他們所居住的地區。勇氣就是能夠以眞理之名，違背大多數人的意見。」

【註】

crisis〔ˈkraɪsɪs〕*n.* 危機
authority〔əˈθɔrətɪ〕*n.* 權威；權力　　cause〔kɔz〕*n.* 原因
atrocity〔əˈtrɑsətɪ〕*n.* 暴行　　leading〔ˈlidɪŋ〕*adj.* 主要的
playwright〔ˈpleˌraɪt〕*n.* 劇作家
compelling〔kəmˈpɛlɪŋ〕*adj.* 動人的　　essay〔ˈɛse〕*n.* 評論
repression〔rɪˈprɛʃən〕*n.* 鎮壓
dissent〔dɪˈsɛnt〕*n.* 意見的分歧；異議
post- 表「後～的」。
Communist〔ˈkɑmjʊˌnɪst〕*adj.* 共產主義的
present〔prɪˈzɛnt〕*v.* 給；贈送

moral〔ˈmɔrəl〕*adj.* 精神上的
gradually〔ˈgrædʒuəlɪ〕*adv.* 逐漸地；漸漸地
repress〔rɪˈprɛs〕*v.* 鎮壓；壓制
opportunity〔ˌɑpɚˈtjunətɪ〕*n.* 機會　***be elected～*** 被選爲～
newly〔ˈnjulɪ〕*adv.* 新近地　form〔fɔrm〕*v.* 形成
republic〔rɪˈpʌblɪk〕*n.* 共和國　remain〔rɪˈmen〕*v.* 仍然是
democracy〔dəˈmɑkrəsɪ〕*n.* 民主政體
principled〔ˈprɪnsəpḷd〕*adj.* 有原則的
voice〔vɔɪs〕*n.* 代言人　certain〔ˈsɝtṇ〕*adj.* 某些

Dalai Lama 達賴喇嘛　***be ready to*** 願意
sacrifice〔ˈsækrəˌfaɪs〕*v.* 犧牲　assume〔əˈsjum〕*v.* 承擔
responsibility〔rɪˌspɑnsəˈbɪlətɪ〕*n.* 責任
go against 違背　majority〔məˈdʒɔrətɪ〕*n.* 大多數
opinion〔əˈpɪnjən〕*n.* 意見　truth〔truθ〕*n.* 眞理
convey〔kənˈve〕*v.* 傳達
face〔fes〕*v.* 使面對　***be faced with*** 面對
pain〔pen〕*n.* 痛苦　cruelty〔ˈkruəltɪ〕*n.* 殘酷

admirable〔ˈædmərəbḷ〕*adj.* 令人欽佩的
respectable〔rɪˈspɛktəbḷ〕*adj.* 可敬的
courageous〔kəˈredʒəs〕*adj.* 勇敢的
artistic〔ɑrˈtɪstɪk〕*adj.* 藝術的
journalistic〔ˌdʒɝnḷˈɪstɪk〕*adj.* 報章雜誌式的
argumentative〔ˌɑrgjəˈmɛntətɪv〕*adj.* 論證式的
business-like〔ˈbɪznɪsˌlaɪk〕*adj.* 商業化的

【答案】

48.（**D**）　49.（**B**）

IV. (50-53)

【譯文】

兩百年前，旅鴿是世界上數目最多的鳥。一群旅鴿可能就超過兩百萬隻。當牠們從上面飛過時，會讓好幾百英哩的天空都變暗。現在，這些鳥沒有一隻還活著。雖然這件事似乎令人難以置信，但是這些數百萬隻的鳥，全都爲了被拿來當食物、取得牠們的羽毛，或只是爲了好玩而被獵捕。

在許多關於絕種動物的悲慘故事中，旅鴿的故事只是其中之一。在過去四百年間，至少有四百六十一種鳥類和哺乳類動物絕種。而在植物當中，處於危險狀態的數目則高達兩萬五千種。

造成這種嚴重破壞的原因，一直都是同一個：人類。有時候人們是以獵捕的方式，直接消滅那些物種，就像對待旅鴿那樣。但是，最常造成絕種的原因，就是人們對環境的破壞。以夏威夷群島爲例，歐洲和美洲的移民砍伐森林，來當作農地。這樣的做法，消滅了許多夏威夷獨有的鳥類和植物。現在，在亞馬遜雨林的情況，則是更加驚人。在這裡，每平方英哩的森林，就有數千種植物和動物。這些物種彼此依存，並且依賴它們這種特殊的環境。當樹木被砍伐時，環境同時也會改變，或者被破壞。而許多物種就永遠消失了。

科學家都非常關心。失去這些動物，對我們來說也是一種損失。我們失去更加了解自己與環境的機會。而且失去珍貴的經濟與科學資源。失去這些物種，也意味著在這個世界上，基因發展的可能範圍變得更小了。科學家們不知道這將意味著什麼，但卻感到十分憂心。

【註】

passenger pigeon 旅鴿【北美產，能飛長距離，現已絕種】
numerous〔ˈnjumərəs〕*adj.* 很多的　　flock〔flɑk〕*n.*（鳥）群
overhead〔ˈovɚˌhɛd〕*adv.* 在頭頂上
darken〔ˈdɑrkən〕*v.* 使黑暗　　exist〔ɪgˈzɪst〕*v.* 生存；活著
incredible〔ɪnˈkrɛdəbl̩〕*adj.* 令人無法相信的
hunt〔hʌnt〕*v.* 獵捕　　feather〔ˈfɛðɚ〕*n.* 羽毛
sport〔sport〕*n.* 遊戲；娛樂　　disappear〔ˌdɪsəˈpɪr〕*v.* 消失
at least 至少　　species〔ˈspiʃɪz〕*n.*（動植物分類上的）種
mammal〔ˈmæml̩〕*n.* 哺乳類動物
extinct〔ɪkˈstɪŋkt〕*adj.* 絕種的

at risk 有危險　　reach〔ritʃ〕*v.*（數量）達到
terrible〔ˈtɛrəbl̩〕*adj.* 嚴重的；可怕的
destruction〔dɪˈstrʌkʃən〕*n.* 破壞
humankind〔ˈhjumənˌkaɪnd〕*n.* 人類　　***kill off*** 滅絕；殺死
directly〔dəˈrɛktlɪ〕*adv.* 直接地
frequent〔ˈfrikwənt〕*adj.* 常見的；經常的
cause〔kɔz〕*n.* 原因
extinction〔ɪkˈstɪŋkʃən〕*n.* 滅絕；滅亡
environment〔ɪnˈvaɪrənmənt〕*n.* 環境
Hawaiian〔həˈwɑjən〕*adj.* 夏威夷的

European〔ˌjurəˈpiən〕*adj.* 歐洲的
American〔əˈmɛrɪkən〕*adj.* 美洲的
settler〔ˈsɛtlɚ〕*n.* 移民者　　***cut down*** 砍伐
forest〔ˈfɔrɪst〕*n.* 森林　　farmland〔ˈfɑrmˌlænd〕*n.* 農地
unique〔juˈnik〕*adj.* 獨特的；特有的
dramatic〔drəˈmætɪk〕*adj.* 戲劇性的
Amazon〔ˈæməˌzɑn〕*n.* 亞馬遜河　　***rain forest*** 雨林
square〔skwɛr〕*adj.* 平方的　　contain〔kənˈten〕*v.* 包含

destroy〔dɪ'strɔɪ〕*v.* 毀壞；破壞
altogether〔,ɔltə'gɛðɚ〕*adv.* 一起地
concerned〔kən'sɝnd〕*adj.* 擔心的
loss〔lɔs〕*n.* 失去　***fellow creature*** 同類的動物
as well 也（= *too*）
valuable〔'væljuəbḷ〕*adj.* 珍貴的；有價值的
economic〔,ikə'nɑmɪk〕*adj.* 經濟上的
scientific〔,saɪən'tɪfɪk〕*adj.* 科學上的
resource〔rɪ'sors〕*n.* 資源

narrow〔'næro〕*adj.* 窄小的；受限制的
range〔rendʒ〕*n.* 範圍　genetic〔dʒə'nɛtɪk〕*adj.* 基因的
possibility〔,pɑsə'bɪlətɪ〕*n.* 可能性；發展的可能性
due to 由於　certain〔'sɝtn̩〕*adj.* 某些
piece〔pis〕*n.* 件；個　evidence〔'ɛvədəns〕*n.* 證據
support〔sə'port〕*v.* 支持；證實　theme〔θim〕*n.* 主題
article〔'ɑrtɪkḷ〕*n.* 文章　area〔'ɛrɪə〕*n.* 區域；範圍
drive〔draɪv〕*v.* 驅逐
endangered〔ɪn'dendʒɚd〕*adj.*（物種等）瀕臨絕種的

endangered species 瀕臨絕種的動物　woods〔wudz〕*n. pl.* 森林
multiply〔'mʌltə,plaɪ〕*v.* 繁殖　***in number*** 大量地
discover〔dɪ'skʌvɚ〕*v.* 發現　identify〔aɪ'dɛntə,faɪ〕*v.* 辨認出
infer〔ɪn'fɝ〕*v.* 推論　survival〔sɚ'vaɪvḷ〕*n.* 生存
rarely〔'rɛrlɪ〕*adv.* 很少　***be concerned about*** 關心
save〔sev〕*v.* 拯救　eliminate〔ɪ'lɪmə,net〕*v.* 除去
wild〔waɪld〕*adj.* 野生的

【答案】

50.（**A**）　51.（**C**）　52.（**D**）　53.（**B**）

第貳部分：非測驗題

一、中譯英：15％

1. That is where the life force of the Taiwanese comes from!
2. During his hardship, he never emphasized his suffering,
3. but to think about how to conquer that destitution.
4. Globalization is both a welcoming and unsettling phenomenon.
5. Whomever has power has to take responsibility.

二、英文作文：19％

What Can Be Done About Telephone Fraud?

The government should crack down on telephone fraud because it costs consumers and tax payers millions of dollars each year. The government needs to pass laws and regulations punishing individuals for using telephones to defraud people.

There are many scams through telephones being used today. There are those that send SMS messages to people's mobile phones telling about great travel deals if they call back the number and then being socked with a huge phone bill at the end of the month.

The government should create a hotline for consumers to report telephone fraud. Then the government should work with the phone companies to block out people trying to commit crimes. The government should also punish the phone companies with fees and revoke their license if they don't do so.

國立清華大學九十三學年度
碩士班研究生入學考試英文試題

Part 1 Vocabulary (20%)

Read the following sentences and select the best answer for each of the blanks.

1. I think that I committed a ________ in asking her because she seemed very upset by my question.
   (A) blunder (B) revenge
   (C) reproach (D) scandal

2. In the past 40 years skyscrapers have developed ________ in Chicago and New York City.
   (A) homogeneously (B) simultaneously
   (C) spontaneously (D) illegitimately

3. The changing image of the family on television provides ________ into changing attitudes toward the family in society.
   (A) insights (B) presentations
   (C) memories (D) specifications

4. Diamonds have little ________ value; their price depends almost entirely on their scarcity.
   (A) extinct (B) permanent
   (C) surplus (D) intrinsic

5. The goal is to make higher education available to everyone who is willing and capable, ________ his/her financial situation.
   (A) with respect to (B) in accord with
   (C) regardless of (D) in terms of

6. Although there are occasional outbreaks of gunfire, we can report that the rebellion has in the main been ________.
   (A) canceled (B) destructed
   (C) suppressed (D) maintained

7. The presidential candidate ________ his position by winning several primary elections.
   (A) enforced (B) enriched
   (C) intensified (D) consolidated

8. Frankly speaking, your article is very good except for some ________ mistakes in grammar.
   (A) obscure (B) growing
   (C) trivial (D) rarely

9. The famous scientist ________ his success to hard work.
   (A) imparted (B) granted
   (C) ascribed (D) acknowledged

10. Franklin D. Roosevelt argued that the depression stemmed from the American economy's ________ flaws.
   (A) underlining (B) vulnerable
   (C) vulgar (D) underlying

Part 2 Reading Comprehension (30%)

Read the following passages and select the best answer for each question.

Passage One

Imagine a world in which there was suddenly no emotion—a world in which human beings could feel no love or happiness, no terror or hate. Try to imagine the consequences of such a transformation. People might not be able to stay alive: knowing neither joy nor pleasure, anxiety nor fear, they would be as likely to repeat acts that hurt them as acts that were beneficial. They could not learn: they could not benefit from experience because this emotionless world would lack rewards and punishments. Society would soon disappear: people would be as likely to harm one another as to provide help and support. Human relationships would not exist: in a world without friends or enemies, there could be no marriage, affection among companions, or bonds among members of groups. Society's economic underpinnings would be destroyed: since earning $10 million would be no more pleasant than earning $10, there would be no incentive to work. In fact, there would be no incentives of any kind. For as we will see, incentives imply a capacity to enjoy them.

In such a world, the chances that the human species would survive are next to zero, because emotions are the basic instrument of our survival and adaptation. Emotions structure the world for us in important ways. As individuals, we categorize objects on the basis of our emotions. True we consider the length, shape, size or texture, but an object's physical aspects are less important than what it has done or can do to us—hurt us, surprise us, anger us or make us joyful. We also use categorizations colored by emotion in our families, communities, and overall society. Out of our emotional experiences with objects and events comes a social feeling of agreement that certain things and actions are "good" and others are "bad", and we apply these categories to every aspect of our social life—from what foods we eat and what clothes we wear to how we keep promises and which people our group will accept. In fact, society exploits our emotional reactions and attitudes, such as loyalty, morality, pride, shame, guilt, fear, and greed, in order to maintain itself. It gives high rewards to individuals who perform important tasks such as surgery, makes heroes out of individuals for unusual or dangerous achievements such as flying fighter planes in a war and uses the legal and penal systems to make people afraid to engage in antisocial acts.

11. The reason why people might not be able to stay alive in a world without emotion is that ___________.
    (A) they would not be able to tell the texture of objects
    (B) they would not know what was beneficial and what was harmful to them
    (C) they would not be happy with a life without love
    (D) they would do things that hurt each other's feelings

12. According to the passage, people's learning activities are possible because they ____________.
    (A) believe that emotions are fundamental for them to stay alive
    (B) benefit from providing help and support to one another
    (C) enjoy being rewarded for doing the right thing
    (D) know what is vital to the progress of society

13. It can be inferred from the passage that the economic foundation of society is dependent on ___________.
    (A) the ability to make money
    (B) the will to work for pleasure
    (C) the capacity to enjoy incentives
    (D) the categorization of our emotional experiences

14. Emotions are important for human being's survival and adaptation because ________.
(A) they provide the means by which people view the size or shape of object
(B) they are the basis for the social feeling of agreement by which society is maintained
(C) they encourage people to perform dangerous achievements
(D) they generate more love than hate among people

15. The emotional aspects of an object are more important than its physical aspects in that they ________.
(A) help society exploit its members for profit
(B) encourage us to perform important tasks
(C) help to perfect the legal and penal system
(D) help us adapt our behavior to the world surrounding us

Passage Two

Taking charge of yourself involves putting to rest some very prevalent myths. At the top of the list is the notion that intelligence is measured by your ability to solve complex problems; to read, write and compute at certain levels; and to resolve abstract equations quickly. This vision of intelligence asserts formal education and bookish excellence as the true measures of self-fulfillment. It encourages a kind of intellectual prejudice that has brought with it some discouraging results. We have come to believe that someone who has more educational merit badges, who is very good at some form of school discipline is "intelligent." Yet mental hospitals are filled with patients who have all of the properly lettered certificates. A truer indicator of intelligence is an effective, happy life lived each day and each present moment of every day.

If you are happy, if you live each moment for everything it is worth, then you are an intelligent person. Problem solving is a useful help to your happiness, but if you know that given your inability to resolve a particular concern you can still choose happiness for yourself, or at a minimum refuse to choose unhappiness, then you are intelligent. You are intelligent because you have the ultimate weapon against the big N.B.D.—Nervous Breakdown.

"Intelligent" people do not have N.B.D.'s because they are in charge of themselves. They know how to choose happiness over depression, because they know how to deal with the problems of their lives. You can begin to think of yourself as truly intelligent on the basis of how you choose to feel in the face of trying circumstances. The struggles of life are pretty much the same for each of us. Everyone who is involved with other human beings in any social context has similar difficulties. Disagreements, conflicts and compromises are a part of what it means to be human. Similarly, money, growing old, sickness, death, natural disasters and accidents are all events which present problems to virtually all human beings. But some people are able to make it, to avoid immobilizing depression and unhappiness despite such occurrences, while others collapse or have an N.B.D. Those who recognize problems as the human condition and don't measure happiness by absence of problems are the most intelligent kind of humans we know; also the most rare.

16. According to the author, the conventional notion of intelligence measured in terms of one's ability to read, write and compute ______________.
    (A) is a widely held but wrong concept
    (B) will help eliminate intellectual prejudice
    (C) is the root of all mental distress
    (D) will contribute to one's self fulfillment

17. It is implied in the passage that holding a university degree ______________.
    (A) may result in one's inability to solve complex real life problems
    (B) does not indicate one's ability to write properly worded documents
    (C) may make one mentally sick and physically weak
    (D) does not mean that one is highly intelligent

18. The author thinks that an intelligent person knows ________.
    (A) how to put up with some very prevalent myths
    (B) how to find the best way to achieve success
    (C) how to avoid depression and make his/her life worthwhile
    (D) how to persuade others to compromise

19. In the last paragraph, the author tells us that ___________.
    (A) difficulties are but part of everyone's life
    (B) depression and unhappiness are unavoidable in life
    (C) everybody should learn to avoid trying circumstances
    (D) good feelings can contribute to eventual academic excellence

20. According to the passage, what kind of people are rare?
    (A) Those who don't emphasize bookish excellence in their pursuit of happiness.
    (B) Those who are aware of difficulties in life but know how to avoid unhappiness.
    (C) Those who measure happiness by an absence of problems but seldom suffer from N.B.D.
    (D) Those who are able to secure happiness though having to struggle against trying circumstances.

Passage Three

Not too many decades ago it seemed "obvious" both to the general public and to sociologists that modern society has changed people's natural relations, loosened their responsibilities to kin and neighbors, and substituted in their place superficial relationships with passing acquaintances. However, in recent years a growing body of research has revealed that the "obvious" is not true. It seems that if you are a city resident, you typically know a smaller proportion of your neighbors than you do if you are a resident of a smaller community. But, for the most part, this fact has few significant consequences.

Even in very large cities, people maintain close social ties within small, private social worlds. Indeed, the number and quality of meaningful relationships do not differ between more and less urban people. Small town residents are more involved with kin than are big-city residents. Yet city dwellers compensate by developing friendships with people who share similar interests and activities. Urbanism may produce a different style of life, but the quality of life does not differ between town and city. Nor are residents of large communities any likelier to display psychological symptoms of stress or alienation, a feeling of not belonging, than are residents of smaller communities. However, city dwellers do worry more about crime, and this leads them to a distrust of strangers.

These findings do not imply that urbanism makes little or no difference. If neighbors are strangers to one another, they are less likely to sweep the sidewalk of an elderly couple living next door or keep an eye out for young troublemakers. Moreover, as Writhe suggested, there may be a link between a community's population size and its social heterogeneity. For instance, sociologists have found much evidence that the larger the size of a community the more it is associated with bad behavior, including gambling, drugs, etc. Large-city urbanites are also more likely than their small town counterparts to have a cosmopolitan outlook, to display less responsibility to traditional kinship roles, to vote for leftist political candidates, and to be tolerant of non-traditional religious groups, unpopular political groups, and so-called undesirables. Everything considered, heterogeneity and unusual behavior seem to be outcomes of large population size.

21. Which of the following statements best describes the organization of the first paragraph?
    (A) Two contrasting views are presented.
    (B) An argument is examined and possible solutions given.
    (C) Research results concerning the quality of urban life are presented in order of time.
    (D) A detailed description of the difference between urban and small town life is given.

22. According to the passage, it was once a common belief that urban residents ______________.
    (A) did not have the same interests as their neighbors
    (B) could not develop long-lasting relationship
    (C) tended to be associated with bad behavior
    (D) usually had more friends

23. One of the consequences of urban life is that impersonal relationships among neighbors ______________.
    (A) disrupt people's natural relations
    (B) make them worry about crime
    (C) cause them not to show concern for one another
    (D) cause them to be suspicious of each other

24. It can be inferred from the passage that the bigger a community is ______________.
    (A) the better its quality of life
    (B) the more similar its interests
    (C) the more tolerant and open-minded it is
    (D) the likelier it is to display psychological symptoms of stress

25. What is the passage mainly about?
    (A) Similarities in the interpersonal relationships between urbanites and small town dwellers.
    (B) Advantages of living in big cities as compared with living in small towns.
    (C) The positive role that urbanism plays in modern life.
    (D) The strong feeling of alienation of city inhabitants.

Part 3 Translation (20%)

Translate the following passages into Chinese.

1. Of course, there is nothing new about this kind of civil disobedience. It was practiced superbly by the early Christians who were willing to face hungry lions and the excruciating pain of chopping blocks before submitting to certain unjust laws of the Roman Empire....To a degree academic freedom is a reality today because Socrates practiced civil disobedience. (5%)

2. Humor, in fact, is an aspect of freedom, without which it cannot exist at all. By its nature, humor implies, when it does not state, criticism of existing institutions, beliefs, and functionaries. Absolute power means absolute solemnity, and the degree to which a society is free, and therefore civilized, may be measured by the degree to which it permits ridicule ....In King Lear's misfortunes his only faithful and true counselor was the Fool. It might be so with us. The ultimate safeguard is perhaps not atomic weapons, larger and better bases, louder radio stations, but more fools. The foolishness of man, Blake wrote, is the wisdom of God; and it may well be that those who seek to suppress or limit laughter are more dangerous than all the subversive conspiracies which the F.B.I. ever has or will uncover. Laughter, in fact, is the most effective of all subversive conspiracies, and it operates on *our* side. (15%)

Part 4 Composition (30%)

Write a 200-word composition on "Culture Shock" based on the following passage, in which Edward Hall (1959:59) describes a hypothetical example of an American living abroad for the first time:

At first, things in the cities look pretty much alike. There are taxis, hotels with hot and cold running water, theaters, neon lights, even tall buildings with elevators and a few people who can speak English. But pretty soon the American discovers that underneath the familiar exterior there are vast differences. When someone says "yes" it often doesn't mean yes at all, and when people smile it doesn't always mean they are pleased. When the American visitor makes a helpful gesture he may be rebuffed; when he tries to be friendly, nothing happens. People tell him that they will do things and don't. The longer he stays, the more enigmatic the new country looks.

國立清華大學九十三學年度
碩士班研究生入學考試英文試題詳解

Part 1 字彙：20%

1. (**A**) (A) ***blunder*** ('blʌndɚ) *n.* 錯誤
(B) revenge (rɪ'vɛndʒ) *n.* 復仇
(C) reproach (rɪ'protʃ) *n.* 責備
(D) scandal ('skændḷ) *n.* 醜聞
commit (kə'mɪt) *v.* 犯（罪、過錯等）
upset (ʌp'sɛt) *adj.* 不高興的

2. (**B**) (A) homogeneously (,homə'dʒinɪəslɪ) *adv.* 同樣地
(B) ***simultaneously*** (,saɪmḷ'tenɪəslɪ) *adv.* 同時地
(C) spontaneously (spɑn'tenɪəslɪ) *adv.* 自發性地；自動地
(D) illegitimately (,ɪlɪ'dʒɪtəmɪtlɪ) *adv.* 非法地
skyscraper ('skaɪ,skrepɚ) *n.* 摩天樓

3. (**A**) (A) ***insight*** ('ɪn,saɪt) *n.* 洞悉；深入瞭解
(B) presentation (,prɛzṇ'teʃən) *n.* 報告；演出
(C) memory ('mɛmərɪ) *n.* 記憶
(D) specification (,spɛsəfə'keʃən) *n.* 詳細說明
image ('ɪmɪdʒ) *n.* 形象　　provide (prə'vaɪd) *v.* 提供
attitude ('ætə,tjud) *n.* 態度；看法

4. (**D**) (A) extinct (ɪk'stɪŋkt) *adj.* 絕種的
(B) permanent ('pɜmənənt) *adj.* 永久的
(C) surplus ('sɜplʌs) *n.* 剩餘；盈餘
(D) ***intrinsic*** (ɪn'trɪnsɪk) *adj.* 本質的
diamond ('daɪəmənd) *n.* 鑽石　　***depend on*** 視～而定
scarcity ('skɛrsətɪ) *n.* 稀罕；缺乏

5. (**C**) (A) with respect to 關於
(B) in accord with 與…一致
(C) ***regardless of*** 不管
(D) in terms of 從…的觀點來看

available〔ə'veləbl̩〕*adj.* 可獲得的
willing〔'wɪlɪŋ〕*adj.* 樂意的
capable〔'kepəbl̩〕*adj.* 有能力的
financial〔fə'nænʃəl〕*adj.* 財務的
situation〔ˌsɪtʃʊ'eʃən〕*n.* 狀況

6. (**C**) (A) cancel〔'kænsl̩〕*v.* 取消
(B) destruct〔dɪ'strʌkt〕*v.* 使（火箭、飛彈等）自毀；爆破
(C) ***suppress***〔sə'prɛs〕*v.* 鎮壓；壓制
(D) maintain〔men'ten〕*v.* 維持

occasional〔ə'keʒənl̩〕*adj.* 偶爾的
outbreak〔'aʊtˌbrek〕*n.* 發生；爆發
gunfire〔'gʌnˌfaɪr〕*n.* 槍擊
report〔rɪ'port〕*v.* 報導
rebellion〔rɪ'bɛljən〕*n.* 叛亂；造反
in the main 大致上

7. (**D**) (A) enforce〔ɪn'fors〕*v.* 實施；強迫
(B) enrich〔ɪn'rɪtʃ〕*v.* 使豐富
(C) intensify〔ɪn'tɛnsəˌfaɪ〕*v.* 增強
(D) ***consolidate***〔kən'sɑləˌdet〕*v.* 鞏固；強化

presidential〔ˌprɛzə'dɛnʃəl〕*adj.* 總統的
candidate〔'kændəˌdet〕*n.* 候選人
position〔pə'zɪʃən〕*n.* 地位
primary〔'praɪˌmɛrɪ〕*adj.* 主要的
election〔ɪ'lɛkʃən〕*n.* 選舉

8.（ C ） (A) obscure〔əb'skjur〕*adj.* 模糊的
(B) growing〔'groɪŋ〕*adj.* 增大的；發展中的
(C) ***trivial***〔'trɪvɪəl〕*adj.* 微不足道的
(D) rarely〔'rɛrlɪ〕*adv.* 罕有地；極少地
frankly speaking 坦白說
except for 除了…之外
grammar〔'græmɚ〕*n.* 文法

9.（ C ） (A) impart〔ɪm'pɑrt〕*v.* 傳授（知識）
(B) grant〔grænt〕*v.* 答應
(C) ***ascribe***〔ə'skraɪb〕*v.* 歸因於 <*to*>
(D) acknowledge〔ək'nɑlɪdʒ〕*v.* 承認
famous〔'feməs〕*adj.* 有名的

10.（ D ） (A) underline〔ˌʌndɚ'laɪn〕*v.* 在…之下劃線
(B) vulnerable〔'vʌlnərəbl̩〕*adj.* 易受傷的；脆弱的
(C) vulgar〔'vʌlgɚ〕*adj.* 粗俗的
(D) ***underlying***〔'ʌndɚ'laɪɪŋ〕*adj.* 潛在的；根本的
argue〔'ɑrgjʊ〕*v.* 主張
depression〔dɪ'prɛʃən〕*n.* 不景氣
stem from 起源於　　economy〔ɪ'kɑnəmɪ〕*n.* 經濟
flaw〔flɔ〕*n.* 缺陷

Part 2 閱讀測驗：30％

Passage One

【譯文】

想像一個突然不具情感的世界——那是一個人們感受不到愛或幸福，恐懼或厭惡的世界。試著去想像這樣的改變，會造成什麼後果。人們可能沒辦法活下去：分辨不出歡樂或喜悅，焦慮或害怕，他們可能會像重複對自己有利的行為那樣，來重複對自己有害的行為。他們不會學習：他們無法從經驗中獲益，因爲這個無情的世界沒有賞罰。社會將迅速消失：人們可能會像提供協助和支持那樣，互相傷害對方。人際關係將不存在：在一個沒有朋友或敵人的世界，可能也沒有婚姻、友情，或群體成員之間的關係。社會經濟的支柱會遭到破壞：因爲賺一千萬不會比賺十塊錢開心，工作的誘因並不存在。事實上，做任何事的誘因都將消失。因爲就如我們所見，誘因意味著能樂於做這些事。

在這樣的世界裡，人類存活的機率近似於零，因爲情感是讓我們存活與適應的基本工具。情感在很多重要的方面，替我們建構了這個世界。我們個人會以自己的感情爲基礎，來把東西分類。我們的確會考慮長度、形狀、尺寸或質地，但是一個物品曾經或能夠對我們造成什麼影響，比它的實體形象來得重要──像是傷害我們，讓我們感到驚訝，惹我們生氣，或是逗我們開心。我們在自己的家庭、社區和整個社會，也會運用受情感影響的分類方式。我們從對物品和事件的情感經驗中，得出了一致的社會情感，並認爲某些事物和行爲是好的，而其他則是不好的，然後再把這些分類方式，應用到社交生活的各個方面──從我們吃的食物，穿的衣服，到我們如何信守承諾，還有我們的團體會接受哪些人。事實上，社會爲了繼續存在下去，會利用我們的情緒反應和態度，像是忠實、道德、驕傲、羞恥、內疚、害怕，和貪婪。它會給予執行像是動手術這種重要任務的人，很高的報酬，並從許多人之中，創造一些英雄，因爲他們有不尋常或危險的成就，像是在戰爭中駕駛戰鬥機，以及運用法律和刑法制度，來讓人不敢從事危害社會的行動。

【答案】

11. (**B**)　12. (**C**)　13. (**C**)　14. (**B**)　15. (**D**)

【註】

imagine〔ɪ'mædʒɪn〕v. 想像
suddenly〔'sʌdn̩lɪ〕adv. 突然地　emotion〔ɪ'moʃən〕n. 情緒
terror〔'tɛrɚ〕n. 恐懼　hate〔het〕n. 憎恨
consequence〔'kɑnsə,kwɛns〕n. 後果
transformation〔,trænsfɚ'meʃən〕n. 轉變
alive〔ə'laɪv〕adj. 活的　pleasure〔'plɛʒɚ〕n. 喜悅
anxiety〔æŋ'zaɪətɪ〕n. 焦慮　likely〔'laɪklɪ〕adj. 可能的
repeat〔rɪ'pit〕v. 重複
beneficial〔,bɛnə'fɪʃəl〕adj. 有利的　benefit〔'bɛnəfɪt〕v. 獲益

emotionless〔ɪ'moʃənlɪs〕adj. 不帶感情的
lack〔læk〕v. 缺乏　reward〔rɪ'wɔrd〕n. 報酬　v. 答謝
punishment〔'pʌnɪʃmənt〕n. 處罰　exist〔ɪg'zɪst〕v. 存在
enemy〔'ɛnəmɪ〕n. 敵人　affection〔ə'fɛkʃən〕n. 感情
companion〔kəm'pænjən〕n. 同伴
bond〔bɑnd〕n. 關係；關聯
economic〔,ikə'nɑmɪk〕adj. 經濟的
underpinning〔'ʌndɚ,pɪnɪŋ〕n. 支柱
destroy〔dɪ'strɔɪ〕v. 破壞；毀壞

pleasant〔'plɛzn̩t〕adj. 令人愉快的
incentive〔ɪn'sɛntɪv〕n. 誘因
imply〔ɪm'plaɪ〕v. 暗示　capacity〔kə'pæsətɪ〕n. 能力
species〔'spiʃɪz〕n. 物種　survive〔sɚ'vaɪv〕v. 存活；生存
next to 幾乎　zero〔'zɪro〕n. 零
instrument〔'ɪnstrəmənt〕n. 工具　survival〔sɚ'vaɪvl̩〕n. 存活
adaptation〔,ædəp'teʃən〕n. 適應
structure〔'strʌktʃɚ〕v. 建構
categorize〔'kætəgə,raɪz〕v. 把…分類
object〔'ɑbdʒɪkt〕n. 物體　length〔lɛŋθ〕n. 長度

shape〔ʃep〕*n.* 形狀　texture〔ˈtɛkstʃɚ〕*n.* 質地
physical〔ˈfɪzɪkl̩〕*adj.* 物質的；實體的
aspect〔ˈæspɛkt〕*n.* 形象；外觀　anger〔ˈæŋgɚ〕*v.* 使發怒
joyful〔ˈdʒɔɪfəl〕*adj.* 快樂的
categorization〔ˌkætəgəraɪˈzeʃən〕*n.* 分類方式
color〔ˈkʌlɚ〕*v.* 影響　community〔kəˈmjunətɪ〕*n.* 社區
overall〔ˈovɚˌɔl〕*adj.* 整個的　emotional〔ɪˈmoʃənl̩〕*adj.* 情感的
agreement〔əˈgrimənt〕*n.* 一致　certain〔ˈsɝtn̩〕*adj.* 某些
apply〔əˈplaɪ〕*v.* 應用　category〔ˈkætəˌgorɪ〕*n.* 分類
promise〔ˈprɑmɪs〕*n.* 承諾　exploit〔ɪkˈsplɔɪt〕*v.* 利用

reaction〔rɪˈækʃən〕*n.* 反應　attitude〔ˈætəˌtjud〕*n.* 態度
loyalty〔ˈlɔɪəltɪ〕*n.* 忠實　morality〔mɔˈrælətɪ〕*n.* 道德
pride〔praɪd〕*n.* 驕傲　shame〔ʃem〕*n.* 羞恥
guilt〔gɪlt〕*n.* 內疚　greed〔grid〕*n.* 貪婪
maintain〔menˈten〕*v.* 維持　perform〔pɚˈfɔrm〕*v.* 執行；做
task〔tæsk〕*n.* 任務；工作　surgery〔ˈsɝdʒərɪ〕*n.* 手術
achievement〔əˈtʃivmənt〕*n.* 成就
fly〔flaɪ〕*v.* 駕駛（飛機）　***fighter plane*** 戰鬥機
legal〔ˈligl̩〕*adj.* 法律的　penal〔ˈpinl̩〕*adj.* 刑法的
engage in 從事　antisocial〔ˌæntɪˈsoʃəl〕*adj.* 危害社會的

tell〔tɛl〕*v.* 分辨　***be happy with*** 對～感到滿足
fundamental〔ˌfʌndəˈmɛntl̩〕*adj.* 基本的；必須的
vital〔ˈvaɪtl̩〕*adj.* 非常重要的　progress〔ˈprɑgrɛs〕*n.* 發展
infer〔ɪnˈfɝ〕*v.* 推論　foundation〔faʊnˈdeʃən〕*n.* 基礎
be dependent on 依賴　will〔wɪl〕*n.* 意志；意願
encourage〔ɪnˈkɝɪdʒ〕*v.* 鼓勵
generate〔ˈdʒɛnəˌret〕*v.* 產生　***in that*** 因爲（＝*because*）
profit〔ˈprɑfɪt〕*n.* 利益；好處　perfect〔ˈpɝfɪkt〕*v.* 使完美
adapt〔əˈdæpt〕*v.* 使適應　surround〔səˈraʊnd〕*v.* 環繞

Passage Two

【譯文】

掌控自己就意味著忘掉一些非常普遍的迷思。其中，最荒唐的想法，就是智慧是以你解決複雜問題的能力來衡量；還有你閱讀、寫作和計算的能力達到某種程度；再加上能快速地解開抽象的方程式。在這種看法下的智力，主張正規教育和能否把書唸得很好，就是衡量自我實現的可靠標準。這種觀念會促成對智力的偏見，因而產生某些令人失望的結果。我們已經變得深信，擁有較多獎狀，和非常擅長某些學科的人是「聰明的」。可是精神病院裡，卻充滿這種擁有所有正式學問證書的病人。一個更正確的智力指標，就是每一天都能過著更有效率、更快樂的生活，而且每天的每一刻，都要過著這樣的生活。

如果你很快樂，如果你能把握每一刻，那麼你就是個聰明人。解決問題的能力，是使你快樂的好幫手，但如果你了解，假使你不能解決某件特定的事，你還是可以替自己選擇快樂，或者至少可以拒絕選擇不快樂，那麼你就是聰明的。你很聰明，因爲你擁有對抗嚴重 N.B.D.（即神經衰弱）的終極武器。

「聰明」人不會神經衰弱，因爲他們可以掌控自己。他們知道如何選擇快樂，而不是意志消沉，因爲他們知道如何處理自己的人生問題。你可以開始把自己看成眞正的聰明人，就以當你面對艱苦的情況時，你會選擇怎麼想爲基礎。對我們每個人來說，在生活中所碰到的掙扎都非常類似。在任何社交關係裡，每個和別人有關聯的人，都會碰到類似的難題。意見不合、衝突和妥協都是人生的一部份。同樣地，金錢、老化、生病、死亡、自然災害和意外，以上這些事所引起的問題，幾乎是全人類都要面對的。但是有些人會想辦法，即使發生這樣的事，他們還是會避免一直憂鬱和不開心，然而其他人卻會意志消沉或是精神衰弱。那些把問題當作人生境遇，而且不以問題是否消失來衡量快樂與否的人，是就我們所知最聰明的人，也是最少見的人。

【答案】

16.（A） 17.（D） 18.（C） 19.（A） 20.（B）

【註】

take charge of 照顧；負責管理
involve〔ɪn'vɑlv〕*v.* 意味著；和…有關聯
put to rest 忘掉（= *lay to rest*）
prevalent〔'prɛvələnt〕*adj.* 普遍的
myth〔mɪθ〕*n.* 不實的想法；迷思
list〔lɪst〕*n.* 名單 notion〔'noʃən〕*n.* 想法；觀念
intelligence〔ɪn'tɛlədʒəns〕*n.* 智慧
measure〔'mɛʒɚ〕*v.* 衡量 *n.* 標準

complex〔'kɑmplɛks〕*adj.* 複雜的
compute〔kəm'pjut〕*v.* 計算 certain〔'sɝtn̩〕*adj.* 某些
level〔'lɛvl̩〕*n.* 程度 resolve〔rɪ'zɑlv〕*v.* 解開
abstract〔æb'strækt〕*adj.* 抽象的
equation〔ɪ'kweʃən〕*n.* 方程式
vision〔'vɪʒən〕*n.* 看法 assert〔ə'sɝt〕*v.* 主張
formal〔'fɔrml̩〕*adj.* 正規的
bookish〔'bʊkɪʃ〕*adj.* 喜歡讀書的；和書籍有關的
excellence〔'ɛksl̩əns〕*n.* 卓越

self-fulfillment〔ˌsɛlfful'fɪlmənt〕*n.* 自我實現
encourage〔ɪn'kɝɪdʒ〕*v.* 促使
intellectual〔ˌɪntl̩'ɛktʃuəl〕*adj.* 智力的
prejudice〔'prɛdʒədɪs〕*n.* 偏見；損害
discouraging〔dɪs'kɝɪdʒɪŋ〕*adj.* 令人失望的
come to 變得 merit〔'mɛrɪt〕*n.* 榮譽
badge〔bædʒ〕*n.* 獎章 ***be good at*** 擅長
discipline〔'dɪsəplɪn〕*n.* 學科；訓練

intelligent 〔ɪn'tɛlədʒənt〕*adj.* 聰明的
mental 〔'mɛntḷ〕*adj.* 精神的　patient 〔'peʃənt〕*n.* 病人
properly 〔'prɑpəlɪ〕*adv.* 正式地
lettered 〔'lɛtəd〕*adj.* 印有文字的
certificate 〔sə'tɪfəkɪt〕*n.* 證書　indicator 〔'ɪndə,ketə〕*n.* 指標
effective 〔ə'fɛktɪv〕*adj.* 有效率的
present 〔'prɛzṇt〕*adj.* 現在的
given 〔'gɪvən〕*prep.* 假使；如果

inability 〔,ɪnə'bɪlətɪ〕*n.* 不能
particular 〔pə'tɪkjələ〕*adj.* 某一的
concern 〔kən'sɝn〕*n.* 關心的事；重要的事
minimum 〔'mɪnəməm〕*n.* 最小量
at a minimum 至少　refuse 〔rɪ'fjuz〕*v.* 拒絕
ultimate 〔'ʌltəmɪt〕*adj.* 終極的　weapon 〔'wɛpən〕*n.* 武器
nervous breakdown 精神衰弱
depression 〔dɪ'prɛʃən〕*n.* 沮喪；意志消沉
deal with 處理　***think of*** A ***as*** B 視 A 爲 B
on the basis of 以…爲基礎

in the face of 面臨；碰到　trying 〔'traɪɪŋ〕*adj.* 艱苦的
circumstances 〔'sɝkəm,stænsɪz〕*n. pl.* 情況
struggle 〔'strʌgḷ〕*n.* 掙扎　pretty 〔'prɪtɪ〕*adv.* 非常
be involved with 與～有牽連；與～有關係
human being 人類　context 〔'kɑntɛkst〕*n.* 關係；情況
similar 〔'sɪmələ〕*adj.* 類似的
disagreement 〔,dɪsə'grimənt〕*n.* 意見不合
conflict 〔'kɑnflɪkt〕*n.* 衝突
compromise 〔'kɑmprə,maɪz〕*n.* 妥協
similarly 〔'sɪmələlɪ〕*adv.* 同樣地
disaster 〔dɪz'æstə〕*n.* 災害

present〔prɪ'zɛnt〕*v.* 呈現；引起
virtually〔'vɝtʃʊəlɪ〕*adv.* 幾乎　***make it*** 成功；辦到
immobilizing〔ɪ'mobḷ,aɪzɪŋ〕*adj.* 不斷的
despite〔dɪ'spaɪt〕*prep.* 儘管；即使
occurrence〔ə'kɝəns〕*n.* 事件
collapse〔kə'læps〕*v.* 意志消沉
recognize〔'rɛkəg,naɪz〕*v.* 認爲；當作
condition〔kən'dɪʃən〕*n.* 境遇　absence〔'æbsṇs〕*n.* 消失
rare〔rɛr〕*adj.* 稀有的
conventional〔kən'vɛnʃənḷ〕*adj.* 傳統的
in terms of 以…的角度　widely〔'waɪdlɪ〕*adv.* 廣泛地

hold〔hold〕*v.* 持有　concept〔'kɑnsɛpt〕*n.* 觀念；想法
eliminate〔ɪ'lɪmə,net〕*v.* 消除　root〔rut〕*n.* 根源
distress〔dɪ'strɛs〕*n.* 痛苦　***contribute to*** 有助於
imply〔ɪm'plaɪ〕*v.* 暗示　degree〔dɪ'gri〕*n.* 學位
indicate〔'ɪndə,ket〕*v.* 表示　worded〔'wɝdɪd〕*adj.* 措辭…的
document〔'dɑkjəmənt〕*n.* 文件
mentally〔'mɛntḷɪ〕*adv.* 精神上；心理上
physically〔'fɪzɪkḷɪ〕*adv.* 身體上　weak〔wik〕*adj.* 虛弱的
highly〔'haɪlɪ〕*adv.* 非常地　***put up with*** 忍受
achieve〔ə'tʃiv〕*v.* 達成；獲得

worthwhile〔'wɝθ'hwaɪl〕*adj.* 有價值的；有意義的
persuade〔pɚ'swed〕*v.* 說服
unavoidable〔,ʌnə'vɔɪdəbḷ〕*adj.* 難以避免的
eventual〔ɪ'vɛntʃuəl〕*adj.* 最後的；結果的
academic〔,ækə'dɛmɪk〕*adj.* 學術上的
emphasize〔'ɛmfə,saɪz〕*v.* 強調
pursuit〔pɚ'sut〕*n.* 追求　aware〔ə'wɛr〕*adj.* 知道的
suffer from 罹患　secure〔sɪ'kjʊr〕*v.* 獲得

Passage Three

【譯文】

幾十年前，有件事對一般大衆和社會學家兩者來說，似乎是「很明顯的」，那就是現代社會改變了人們的自然關係，放鬆了他們對親戚和鄰居的責任，取而代之的，是與偶然認識的朋友之間的膚淺關係。但是，在最近幾年，愈來愈多的研究顯示，這個「明顯的事實」並不是眞的。看來如果你是住在城市裡的人，你所認識的鄰居，和如果你是住在較小的社區相比，通常比例上會較少。可是，大體上來說，這件事並不太重要。

即使是在一個非常大的城市，人們還是會在小型的私人社交圈裡，維持密切的社交關係。實際上，就有意義的關係而言，其數量和品質，在都市人和非都市人之間，並沒有什麼差異。小鎭的居民和親戚間的關係，會比大城市的居民要來得好。但是城市的居民，會和擁有相同興趣，還有從事相同活動的人發展友誼，來作爲補償。城市居民的生活方式，可能會產生一種不同的生活型態，但是就生活品質來說，城鎭和都市並沒有什麼差別。住在大型社會的人，和住在小型社會的人相比，不會比較容易顯出壓力或疏離的心理症狀，即缺乏歸屬感。可是，住在都市的人，確實比較擔心犯罪，而這使得他們不信任陌生人。

這些研究結果並不表示，城市居民的生活方式沒有差異。如果鄰居互相不認識，那他們替住在隔壁的老夫婦、打掃人行道，和密切注意年輕搗蛋鬼的可能性就比較小。而且，就像 Writhe 所提出的，一個地區的人口多寡，和其社會異質性可能有所關聯。舉例來說，社會學家已經找到許多證據，證明愈大型的社會，和不良行爲的關聯就愈多，包括賭博、毒品等。住在大城市相對於住在小鎭來說，也比較可能擁有國際觀，所承擔的傳統親戚關係職責比較少，會投票給激進派的政治候選人，而且會容忍非傳統的宗教團體、不受歡迎的政黨，還有所謂的不受歡迎的人。總而言之，異質性和不尋常的行爲，似乎是人口衆多所造成的結果。

【答案】

21.（**A**）　22.（**B**）　23.（**C**）　24.（**C**）　25.（**A**）

【註】

decade〔ˈdɛked〕*n.* 十年　seem〔sim〕*v.* 似乎
obvious〔ˈɑbvɪəs〕*adj.* 明顯的　***the general public*** 一般大衆
sociologist〔ˌsoʃɪˈɑlədʒɪst〕*n.* 社會學家
relation〔rɪˈleʃən〕*n.* 關係　loosen〔ˈlusn̩〕*v.* 放鬆
responsibility〔rɪˌspɑnsəˈbɪlətɪ〕*n.* 責任
kin〔kɪn〕*n.* 親戚　substitute〔ˈsʌbstəˌtjut〕*v.* 取代
superficial〔ˌsupɚˈfɪʃəl〕*adj.* 膚淺的

relationship〔rɪˈleʃənˌʃɪp〕*n.* 關係
passing〔ˈpæsɪŋ〕*adj.* 偶然的
acquaintance〔əˈkwentəns〕*n.* 認識的人
growing〔groɪŋ〕*adj.* 發展中的　***a body of*** 許多
research〔ˈrisɝtʃ〕*n.* 研究　reveal〔rɪˈvil〕*n.* 顯示
resident〔ˈrɛzədənt〕*n.* 居民　typically〔ˈtɪpɪkl̩ɪ〕*adv.* 通常
proportion〔prəˈporʃən〕*n.* 比例；部份

community〔kəˈmjunətɪ〕*n.* 集團；社會
for the most part 大體上
significant〔sɪgˈnɪfəkənt〕*adj.* 意義重大的
consequence〔ˈkɑnsəˌkwɛns〕*n.* 結果；後果
maintain〔menˈten〕*v.* 維持　close〔kloz〕*adj.* 密切的
ties〔taɪz〕*n. pl.* 關係　private〔ˈpraɪvɪt〕*adj.* 私人的

indeed〔ɪn'did〕*adv.* 實際上
meaningful〔'minɪŋfl̩〕*adj.* 有意義的
differ〔'dɪfɚ〕*v.* 不同　urban〔'ɝbən〕*adj.* 城市的
involved〔ɪn'vɑlvd〕*adj.* 有關係的　dweller〔'dwɛlɚ〕*n.* 居民
compensate〔'kɑmpən,set〕*v.* 補償　share〔ʃɛr〕*v.* 共有
urbanism〔'ɝbənɪzm̩〕*n.* 都市生活　display〔dɪ'sple〕*v.* 顯露
psychological〔,saɪkə'lɑdʒɪkl̩〕*adj.* 心理上的
symptom〔'sɪmptəm〕*n.* 症狀　stress〔strɛs〕*n.* 壓力
alienation〔,eljən'eʃən〕*n.* 疏離；孤獨感
belong〔bə'lɔŋ〕*v.* 屬於　crime〔kraɪm〕*n.* 犯罪

lead〔lid〕*v.* 使…　distrust〔dɪs'trʌst〕*n.* 不信任
stranger〔'strendʒɚ〕*n.* 陌生人
sweep〔swip〕*v.* 清掃　sidewalk〔'saɪd,wɔk〕*n.* 人行道
elderly〔'ɛldɚlɪ〕*adj.* 年老的　***keep an eye out*** 密切注意
troublemaker〔'trʌbl̩,mekɚ〕*n.* 惹事生非的人
suggest〔sə'dʒɛst〕*v.* 提出　link〔lɪŋk〕*n.* 關聯
population〔,pɑpjə'leʃən〕*n.* 人口　size〔saɪz〕*n.* 規模
heterogeneity〔,hɛtərədʒə'niətɪ〕*n.* 異質
for instance 舉…爲例　evidence〔'ɛvədəns〕*n.* 證據
associated〔ə'soʃɪ,etɪd〕*adj.* 有關聯的

gambling〔'gæmblɪŋ〕*n.* 賭博
drug〔drʌg〕*n.* 毒品　urbanite〔'ɝbən,aɪt〕*n.* 城市居民
counterpart〔'kaʊntɚ,pɑrt〕*n.* 對應的人或物
cosmopolitan〔,kɑzmə'pɑlətn̩〕*adj.* 國際的
outlook〔'aʊt,lʊk〕*n.* 看法
traditional〔trə'dɪʃənl̩〕*adj.* 傳統的
kinship〔'kɪnʃɪp〕*n.* 親戚關係　role〔rol〕*n.* 角色
vote for 投票給～　leftist〔'lɛftɪst〕*adj.* 激進的；左派的
political〔pə'lɪtɪkl̩〕*adj.* 政治的

candidate〔ˈkændə,det〕*n.* 候選人
tolerant〔ˈtɑlərənt〕*adj.* 容忍的
religious〔rɪˈlɪdʒəs〕*adj.* 宗教的
so-called〔ˈsoˈkɔld〕*adj.* 所謂的
undesirable〔,ʌndɪˈzaɪrəbḷ〕*n.* 不受歡迎的人
everything considered 總而言之
outcome〔ˈaʊt,kʌm〕*n.* 結果
organization〔,ɔrgənəˈzeʃən〕*n.* 組織；構造
contrasting〔kənˈtræstɪŋ〕*adj.* 對比的；對照的
view〔vju〕*n.* 看法　　present〔prɪˈzɛnt〕*v.* 提出

argument〔ˈɑrgjəmənt〕*n.* 論點
examine〔ɪgˈzæmɪn〕*v.* 檢查
solution〔səˈluʃən〕*n.* 解決之道
concerning〔kənˈsɝnɪŋ〕*prep.* 關於　　***in order of～*** 按～順序
detailed〔dɪˈteld〕*adj.* 詳細的
description〔dɪˈskrɪpʃən〕*n.* 敘述；描寫
common〔ˈkɑmən〕*adj.* 普遍的　　belief〔bɪˈlif〕*n.* 信念
long-lasting〔ˈlɔŋˈlæstɪŋ〕*adj.* 持久的
tend to V. 易於　　impersonal〔ɪmˈpɝsṇḷ〕*adj.* 非個人的
disrupt〔dɪsˈrʌpt〕*v.* 使破裂　　concern〔kənˈsɝn〕*n.* 關心

suspicious〔səˈspɪʃəs〕*adj.* 懷疑的
open-minded〔ˈopənˈmaɪndɪd〕*adj.* 沒有偏見的
mainly〔ˈmenlɪ〕*adv.* 主要地
similarity〔,sɪməˈlærətɪ〕*n.* 相似點
interpersonal〔,ɪntɚˈpɝsənḷ〕*adj.* 人與人之間的
advantage〔ədˈvæntɪdʒ〕*n.* 好處
(as) compared with 和…相比
positive〔ˈpɑzətɪv〕*adj.* 正面的
inhabitant〔ɪnˈhæbətənt〕*n.* 居民

Part 3 翻譯：20％

1. 當然，這種和平抵抗已經不新鮮了。早期的基督徒就做得很好，他們在屈服於某些不公平的羅馬帝國法律之前，願意面對飢餓的獅子和被剁成一塊一塊的劇痛…。現在學術自由在一定的程度上，是一種事實，因為蘇格拉底實行過和平抵抗。（5%）

【註】

civil disobedience 和平抵抗　practice〔ˈpræktɪs〕*v.* 實行
superbly〔sʊˈpɝblɪ〕*adv.* 極好地
Christian〔ˈkrɪstʃən〕*n.* 基督徒
willing〔ˈwɪlɪŋ〕*adj.* 願意的
excruciating〔ɪkˈskruʃɪˌetɪŋ〕*adj.* 劇烈的；難以忍受的
chop〔tʃɑp〕*v.* 剁　block〔blɑk〕*n.* 一塊
submit〔səbˈmɪt〕*v.* 服從　unjust〔ʌnˈdʒʌst〕*adj.* 不公平的
empire〔ˈɛmpaɪr〕*n.* 帝國　***to a degree*** 在某種程度上
academic freedom 學術自由
Socrates〔ˈsɑkrəˌtiz〕*n.* 蘇格拉底

2. 事實上，幽默也是一種自由的型態，沒有自由，幽默根本不可能存在。就幽默的本質來說，雖然沒有明講，但它暗示著對現行制度、信仰和官員的批評。絕對的權利意謂著絕對的嚴肅，一個社會的自由程度，還有因此而來的文明，可能要以其容忍愚蠢的程度來衡量…。在李爾王的悲劇中，他唯一忠心而忠實的顧問就是愚蠢。我們可能也是如此。最終的保衛措施可能不是原子武器、更大更好的基地，和更大聲的廣播電台，而是更多愚蠢的人。Blake 寫到，人類的愚蠢是上帝的智慧；而且也許那些試圖忍住或限制自己笑的人，比 F.B.I 已經或即將揭發的所有顛覆陰謀，還要危險。笑，其實就是所有顛覆陰謀中最有效的作法，而且它對我們很有用。（15%）

【註】

humor〔'hjumɚ〕*n.* 幽默　aspect〔'æspɛkt〕*n.* 方面
not at all 一點也不　exist〔ɪg'zɪst〕*v.* 存在
nature〔'netʃɚ〕*n.* 本質
imply〔ɪm'plaɪ〕*v.* 暗示；含有…的意思
state〔stet〕*v.* 敘述；說明
criticism〔'krɪtə,sɪzəm〕*n.* 批評
existing〔ɪg'zɪstɪŋ〕*adj.* 現行的
institution〔,ɪnstə,tjuʃən〕*n.* 制度　belief〔bɪ'lif〕*n.* 信仰
functionary〔'fʌŋkʃən,ɛrɪ〕*n.* 官員；公務員

absolute〔'æbsə,lut〕*adj.* 絕對的
solemnity〔sə'lɛmnətɪ〕*n.* 嚴肅　degree〔dɪ'gri〕*n.* 程度
civilized〔'sɪvḷ,aɪzd〕*adj.* 文明的
measure〔'mɛʒɚ〕*v.* 衡量　permit〔pɚ'mɪt〕*v.* 允許；容許
ridicule〔'rɪdɪ,kjul〕*n.* 嘲笑
misfortune〔mɪs'fɔrtʃən〕*n.* 不幸
faithful〔'feθfəl〕*adj.* 忠實的　counselor〔'kaʊnsḷɚ〕*n.* 顧問
fool〔ful〕*n.* 傻瓜；呆子　ultimate〔'ʌltəmɪt〕*adj.* 最終的
safeguard〔'sef,gɑrd〕*n.* 保護措施

atomic〔ə'tɑmɪk〕*adj.* 原子的　base〔bes〕*n.* 基地
radio station 廣播電台　foolishness〔'fulɪʃnɪs〕*n.* 愚蠢
wisdom〔'wɪzdəm〕*n.* 智慧　***may well*** 也許；很可能
seek〔sik〕*v.* 試圖　suppress〔sə'prɛs〕*v.* 抑制
subversive〔səb'vɝsɪv〕*adj.* 顛覆的
conspiracy〔kən'spɪrəsɪ〕*n.* 陰謀
uncover〔ʌn'kʌvɚ〕*v.* 揭發　effective〔ə'fɛktɪv〕*adj.* 有效的
operate〔'ɑpə,ret〕*v.* 起作用；有影響

Part 4 作文：30％

寫一篇關於“Culture Shock”「文化衝擊」的兩百字作文，並以下列這段文章爲基礎，在這段文章中，Edward Hall（1959：59）講了一個假設性的例子，那是關於一個美國人第一次到國外生活：

一開始，城市裡的事物看起來都非常類似。有計程車、供應熱水和冷水的旅館、戲院、霓虹燈，甚至是有電梯的高樓，和一些會講英語的人。但是很快地，這名美國人發現，在熟悉的外觀之下，有著非常大的差異。當某人說「好」，這個字常常意味著一點都不好，而且當人們微笑，也不一定意謂著他們很開心。當這名美國觀光客做出願意幫忙的表示時，他可能會被拒絕；當他試著表現得友善時，卻什麼事也沒發生。人們告訴他，他們是有所爲，有所不爲。他待得愈久，這個新國度看起來就愈難以捉摸。

【註】

hypothetical〔ˌhaɪpəˈθɛtɪkl̩〕*adj.* 假定的
running water 自來水　***neon light*** 霓虹燈
underneath〔ˌʌndɚˈniθ〕*prep.* 在…之下
exterior〔ɪkˈstɪrɪɚ〕*n.* 外部
vast〔væst〕*adj.* 巨大的　pleased〔plizd〕*adj.* 高興的
gesture〔ˈdʒɛstʃɚ〕*n.* 表示　rebuff〔rɪˈbʌf〕*v.* 斷然拒絕
enigmatic〔ˌɛnɪgˈmætɪk〕*adj.* 謎般的；難解的

Culture Shock

One thing that most American travelers share when they go abroad is culture shock. It's an overwhelming feeling of bewilderment at being in an unknown land with no traceable similarities to your home country.

The people do not speak English so asking for directions in an unfamiliar city is all but ruled out. Even though the city is filled with the amenities of modernity like hotels, taxis and clean running water, nothing is recognizable. From the local custom of eating dog meat and drinking snake blood to bringing your own toilet paper wherever you go, different cultures have a way of making the unsuspecting American's head spin!

But one thing all American visitors must do is to let the initial culture shock set in and then just go with the flow. But keep in mind that the American will be the stranger to the local people. So do not be offended if you offer helpful gestures and are completely ignored or people offer misleading promises and do not always greet you with a smile.

Experiencing different cultures and customs is the best and perhaps most important part of traveling. If in the end, the new country is still as mysterious and far-fetched as when the American first arrived, at least take comfort in having had a chance of visiting in the first place.

國立成功大學九十三學年度 碩士班研究生入學考試英文試題

I. Choose the word that is closest in meaning to the underlined words in the sentences. 45% (each 3%)

1. Spain mourns its terrorist victims, while others ask if it is appeasing terrorists.
   (A) irritating (B) challenging
   (C) applauding (D) placating

2. Christianity is very deeply embedded in American culture.
   (A) influenced (B) rooted
   (C) engaged (D) reminded

3. They attempt to nullify the election results.
   (A) invalidate (B) accuse
   (C) debate (D) retaliate

4. We should pay attention to the etiquette of using mobile phones.
   (A) costs (B) problems
   (C) rules (D) functions

5. The "Lord of the Rings" trilogy based on J.R.R. Tolkien's fantasy novels is a sweeping spectacle of computer-generated imagery.
   (A) montage (B) performance
   (C) mixture (D) technology

6. Changes in our environment, lifestyle and behavior all help to encourage the spread of <u>infectious</u> diseases.
(A) contagious (B) unknown
(C) new (D) deadly

7. <u>Swapping</u> music over the Internet is fun and easy.
(A) Listening to (B) Exchanging
(C) Searching (D) Purchasing

8. The film is <u>blasted</u> as an allegory of Western imperialism over Islamic countries.
(A) praised (B) regarded
(C) ignored (D) criticized

9. If you struggle with any business <u>predicament</u>, you can benefit from brainstorming.
(A) situation (B) meeting
(C) dilemma (D) deal

10. Oregon Attorney General Hardy Myers says banning same-sex marriage probably <u>violates</u> Oregon's Constitution.
(A) follows (B) revises
(C) breaks (D) fulfills

11. The recent discovery of the mineral hematite on Mars has <u>sparked</u> discussion among scientists who are trying to determine if water exists on the Red Planet.
(A) accelerated (B) caused
(C) renewed (D) invented

12. More women should <u>be involved</u> in decision-making.
    (A) excite (B) be absorbed
    (C) participate (D) separate

13. The laws require advertisers to <u>substantiate</u> their claims.
    (A) prove (B) review
    (C) explain (D) promote

14. These results have been achieved by a series of political <u>maneuvers</u>.
    (A) negotiations (B) discussions
    (C) debates (D) ploys

15. The number of people going to the cinema seems to <u>dwindle</u> steadily.
    (A) decline (B) disappear
    (C) increase (D) rise

II. Reading Comprehension : Choose the best answer to each question based on the following passage. 15% (Each 3%)

So long as the bulk of the population remains on the land as subsistence farmers, a modern industrial society cannot develop. The farmers do not produce enough extra food to feed the workers needed in nonagricultural pursuits. Nor can workers be released from the farms to the factories while so many hands are needed for traditional methods of cultivation. And farmers who are not producing for the market cannot go to the market as purchasers themselves. Local demand for consumer goods does not expand. There is thus no stimulus to local industrial production. Agriculture must, therefore, yield workers and savings to the new industrialized, urbanized sectors if a modern economy is to be achieved.

1. What is the author's main point?
   (A) Traditional farming methods can enrich civilization.
   (B) The development of an urban economy depends on the modernization of agriculture.
   (C) People who work on farms tend to eat more than people who live in cities.
   (D) The industrialization of modern society stabilizes the agricultural economy.

2. According to the passage, a characteristic of food production in a subsistence economy is that farmers
   (A) must bring in workers from urban communities.
   (B) cannot produce all their own food.
   (C) must buy some foods to achieve a balanced diet.
   (D) cannot grow enough food to support nonfarmers.

3. According to the passage, what is a disadvantage of traditional farming methods?
   (A) Workers do not enjoy their jobs.
   (B) Workers do not get enough to eat.
   (C) Too many workers are necessary.
   (D) Too many jobs are poorly paid.

4. According to the passage, why is local industrial production NOT stimulated in a subsistence economy?
   (A) No modern equipment is available to begin production.
   (B) Industry cannot develop when there are few customers for its products.
   (C) Farmers do not want to go to markets very far from where they live and work.
   (D) Locally produced consumer goods are generally not well made.

5. The paragraph following the passage most probably discusses
   (A) the difficult transition from an agricultural to an industrial economy.
   (B) the creation of a demand for more agricultural products.
   (C) guidelines for hiring greater numbers of farm workers.
   (D) the recent revival of the family farm system.

Ⅲ. Translate the following English passage into Chinese and the Chinese passage into English (10%) (5% each)

1. Anti-spam groups are trying to stem the tide of unsolicited e-mail.

2. 為了做你喜愛的工作，你可能必須學一些新的技能、磨練現有的能力或再取得另一個學位。

Ⅳ. Essay Writing 30% (Write a short essay of around 250 words)
Please discuss the question:

Do you believe that entering graduate school will help you become more competitive in the job market?

國立成功大學九十三學年度
碩士班研究生入學考試英文試題詳解

I. 選同義字：45%

1. (**D**) appease〔əˈpiz〕*v.* 安撫
   (A) irritate〔ˈɪrəˌtet〕*v.* 激怒
   (B) challenge〔ˈtʃælɪndʒ〕*v.* 挑戰
   (C) applaud〔əˈplɔd〕*v.* 鼓掌
   (D) ***placate***〔ˈpleket〕*v.* 安撫
   Spain〔spen〕*n.* 西班牙　mourn〔morn〕*v.* 哀悼
   terrorist〔ˈtɛrərɪst〕*n.* 恐怖份子　*adj.* 恐怖份子的
   victim〔ˈvɪktɪm〕*n.* 受害者

2. (**B**) embed〔ɪmˈbɛd〕*v.* 把…嵌入；使深留腦中
   (A) influence〔ˈɪnfluəns〕*v.* 影響
   (B) ***root***〔rut〕*v.* 使（思想、信仰）扎根；使根深蒂固
   (C) engage〔ɪnˈgedʒ〕*v.* 使參與
   (D) remind〔rɪˈmaɪnd〕*v.* 提醒
   Christianity〔ˌkrɪstʃɪˈænətɪ〕*n.* 基督教；基督教精神

3. (**A**) nullify〔ˈnʌləˌfaɪ〕*v.* 使無效
   (A) ***invalidate***〔ɪnˈvæləˌdet〕*v.* 使無效
   (B) accuse〔əˈkjuz〕*v.* 控告
   (C) debate〔dɪˈbet〕*v.* 辯論
   (D) retaliate〔rɪˈtælɪˌet〕*v.* 報復
   attempt〔əˈtɛmpt〕*v.* 企圖

4. (**C**) etiquette〔ˈɛtɪˌkɛt〕*n.* 禮節
   (D) function〔ˈfʌŋkʃən〕*n.* 功能
   mobile phone 手機

5. (**B**) spectacle〔ˈspɛktəkḷ〕*n.* 表演；場面
(A) montage〔mɑnˈtɑʒ〕*n.* 蒙太奇（將種種不同畫面合成一個畫面之手法）
(B) ***performance***〔pəˈfɔrməns〕*n.* 表演
(C) mixture〔ˈmɪkstʃə〕*n.* 混合
(D) technology〔tɛkˈnɑlədʒɪ〕*n.* 科技
trilogy〔ˈtrɪlədʒɪ〕*n.* 三部曲
be based on 根據；以～爲基礎
fantasy〔ˈfæntəsɪ〕*n.* 奇想；幻想
novel〔ˈnɑvḷ〕*n.* 小說
sweeping〔ˈswipɪŋ〕*adj.* 可看到廣大範圍的
generate〔ˈdʒɛnə,ret〕*v.* 產生
imagery〔ˈɪmɪdʒərɪ〕*n.* 形象；意象

6. (**A**) infectious〔ɪnˈfɛkʃəs〕*adj.* 傳染性的
(A) ***contagious***〔kənˈtedʒəs〕*adj.*（接觸）傳染性的
(D) deadly〔ˈdɛdlɪ〕*adj.* 致命的
spread〔sprɛd〕*v.* 蔓延；傳播
disease〔dɪˈziz〕*n.* 疾病

7. (**B**) swap〔swɑp〕*v.* 交換
(B) ***exchange***〔ɪksˈtʃendʒ〕*v.* 交換
(C) search〔sɜtʃ〕*v.* 搜尋
(D) purchase〔ˈpɜtʃəs〕*v.* 購買

8. (**D**) blast〔blæst〕*v.* 猛烈抨擊；譴責
(A) praise〔prez〕*v.* 稱讚
(B) regard〔rɪˈgɑrd〕*v.* 認爲
(D) ***criticize***〔ˈkrɪtə,saɪz〕*v.* 批評
allegory〔ˈælə,gorɪ〕*n.* 寓言；諷喻
imperialism〔ɪmˈpɪrɪəl,ɪzəm〕*n.* 帝國主義；領土擴張主義
Islamic〔ɪsˈlæmɪk〕*adj.* 伊斯蘭教的；回教的

9. (**C**) predicament (prɪ'dɪkəmənt) *n.* 困境
   (C) ***dilemma*** (də'lɛmə) *n.* 進退兩難；窘境
   (D) deal (dil) *n.* 交易
   struggle ('strʌgl̩) *v.* 奮鬥；搏鬥
   benefit ('bɛnəfɪt) *v.* 獲益
   brainstorming ('bren,stɔrmɪŋ) *n.* 腦力激盪

10. (**C**) violate ('vaɪə,let) *v.* 違反；違背
   (B) revise (rɪ'vaɪz) *v.* 修訂
   (C) ***break*** (brek) *v.* 違反；違背
   (D) fulfill (fʊl'fɪl) *v.* 履行；完成
   attorney general 檢察長；首席檢察官
   ban (bæn) *v.* 禁止　sex (sɛks) *n.* 性別
   marriage ('mærɪdʒ) *n.* 結婚
   constitution (,kɑnstə'tjuʃən) *n.* 憲法

11. (**B**) spark (spɑrk) *v.* 引起
   (A) accelerate (æk'sɛlə,ret) *v.* 加速
   (C) renew (rɪ'nju) *v.* 更新
   (D) invent (ɪn'vɛnt) *v.* 發明
   recent ('risn̩t) *adj.* 最近的
   mineral ('mɪnərəl) *adj.* 礦物的
   hematite ('hɛmə,taɪt) *n.* 赤鐵礦
   Mars (mɑrz) *n.* 火星（= *the Red Planet* ）
   determine (dɪ'tɝmɪn) *v.* 確定
   planet ('plænɪt) *n.* 行星

12. (**C**) ***be involved in*** 參與
   (B) absorb (əb'sɔrb) *v.* 吸收
   (C) ***participate*** (pɑr'tɪsə,pet) *v.* 參與 < *in* >
   (D) separate ('sɛpə,ret) *v.* 使分開
   decision-making (dɪ'sɪʒən,mekɪŋ) *n.* 決策

13. (**A**) substantiate〔 səb'stænʃɪ,et 〕*v.* 證實

(A) ***prove***〔 pruv 〕*v.* 證明

(B) review〔 rɪ'vju 〕*v.* 複習

(D) promote〔 prə'mot 〕*v.* 升遷

advertiser〔 'ædvə,taɪzə 〕*n.* 刊登廣告者

claim〔 klem 〕*n.* 主張；宣稱

14. (**D**) maneuver〔 mə'nuvə 〕*n.* 策略；花招

(A) negotiation〔 nɪ,goʃɪ'eʃən 〕*n.* 談判

(C) debate〔 dɪ'bet 〕*n.* 辯論

(D) ***ploy***〔 plɔɪ 〕*n.* 策略

series〔 'sɪrɪz 〕*n.* 一系列

political〔 pə'lɪtɪkḷ 〕*adj.* 政治的

15. (**A**) dwindle〔 'dwɪndḷ 〕*v.* 逐漸減少

(A) ***decline***〔 dɪ'klaɪn 〕*v.* 減少

(B) disappear〔 ,dɪsə'pɪr 〕*v.* 消失

(C) increase〔 ɪn'kris 〕*v.* 增加

(D) rise〔 raɪz 〕*v.* 上升

cinema〔 'sɪnəmə 〕*n.* 電影院

steadily〔 'stɛdəlɪ 〕*adv.* 持續地

II. 閱讀測驗：15%

【譯文】

只要大部分的人都還留在田裡，當自給自足的農民，就不可能發展出現代化的工業社會。這些農民並沒有生產出多餘的食物，來養活那些從事非農業的工人。由於傳統的耕作方式需要許多工人，所以也沒辦法從農場釋出一些人到工廠去。而且農民生產的東西不拿到市場賣，他們就沒有錢去市場買東西。當地對於消費品的需求也不會擴大。因此，如果想要有現代化的經濟，農業就必須讓出一些工人和存款，給新興的工業化和都市化部門。

【答案】

1. (**B**) 2. (**D**) 3. (**C**) 4. (**B**) 5. (**A**)

【註】

so long as 只要 bulk〔bʌlk〕*n.* 大部分
population〔ˌpɑpjəˈleʃən〕*n.* 人口；居民
remain〔rɪˈmen〕*v.* 仍然；留下 land〔lænd〕*n.* 田地
subsistence〔səbˈsɪstəns〕*n.*（最低限度的）生活；生計
industrial〔ɪnˈdʌstrɪəl〕*adj.* 工業的
extra〔ˈɛkstrə〕*adj.* 額外的 feed〔fid〕*v.* 養（活）
nonagricultural〔ˌnɑnˌægrɪˈkʌltʃərəl〕*adj.* 非農業的
pursuit〔pɚˈsut〕*n.* 從事的事；工作
release〔rɪˈlis〕*v.* 釋出 hand〔hænd〕*n.* 人手

cultivation〔ˌkʌltəˈveʃən〕*n.* 耕作
purchaser〔ˈpɝtʃəsɚ〕*n.* 購買者 local〔ˈlokḷ〕*adj.* 當地的
consumer〔kənˈsumɚ〕*n.* 消費者
consumer goods 消費品 expand〔ɪkˈspænd〕*v.* 擴大
stimulus〔ˈstɪmjələs〕*n.* 刺激
agriculture〔ˈægrɪˌkʌltʃɚ〕*n.* 農業 yield〔jild〕*v.* 放棄；讓出
savings〔ˈsevɪŋz〕*n. pl.* 存款
industrialized〔ɪnˈdʌstrɪəlˌaɪzd〕*adj.* 工業化的

urbanized〔ˈɝbənˌaɪzd〕*adj.* 都市化的
sector〔ˈsɛktɚ〕*n.*（產業的）部門
economy〔ɪˈkɑnəmɪ〕*n.* 經濟 achieve〔əˈtʃiv〕*v.* 獲得
farming〔ˈfɑrmɪŋ〕*n.* 農業 enrich〔ɪnˈrɪtʃ〕*v.* 充實；使豐富
civilization〔ˌsɪvḷaɪˈzeʃən〕*n.* 文明 urban〔ˈɝbən〕*adj.* 都市的
modernization〔ˌmɑdənəˈzeʃən〕*n.* 現代化
tend to V. 易於；傾向於
industrialization〔ɪnˌdʌstrɪəlaɪˈzeʃən〕*n.* 工業化

stabilize〔ˈstebḷˌaɪz〕v. 使穩定
characteristic〔ˌkærɪktəˈrɪstɪk〕n. 特徵　　***bring in*** 引進
community〔kəˈmjunətɪ〕n. 社區；社會
balanced〔ˈbælənst〕adj. 均衡的　　diet〔ˈdaɪət〕n. 飲食
support〔səˈport〕v. 支持；扶養
disadvantage〔ˌdɪsədˈvæntɪdʒ〕n. 缺點
be poorly paid 薪水很少
stimulate〔ˈstɪmjəˌlet〕v. 刺激

equipment〔ɪˈkwɪpmənt〕n. 配備；器材
product〔ˈprɑdʌkt〕n. 產品
locally〔ˈloklɪ〕adv. 在本地
generally〔ˈdʒɛnərəlɪ〕adv. 通常
transition〔trænˈzɪʃən〕n. 轉變；過渡期
creation〔krɪˈeʃən〕n. 創造
guideline〔ˈgaɪdˌlaɪn〕n. 指導方針　　hire〔haɪr〕v. 僱用
revival〔rɪˈvaɪvḷ〕n. 恢復；復興

Ⅲ. 翻譯：10%

1. 反垃圾郵件團體正試著阻擋那股不請自來的電子郵件潮。

【註】

anti-spam 反垃圾郵件　　stem〔stɛm〕v. 阻擋
tide〔taɪd〕n. 潮流；形勢
unsolicited〔ˌʌnsəˈlɪsɪtɪd〕adj. 未經請求的；自發的

2. In order to do the job you like, you may have to learn some new skills, cultivate original ability, or get another degree.

IV. 短文寫作：30%

提示：請寫一篇250字左右的短文，來探討這個問題：
你認爲進入研究所，會使你在就業市場上更具競爭力嗎？

Today's job market is highly charged with competition as more and more qualified applicants are graduating from university each year. An undergraduate degree is no longer sufficient and this is why I believe graduate school can help me become more distinguished when applying for a job.

Employers will naturally seek out the best candidates for their firms and having a graduate degree can give me a competitive edge in my job hunt. A graduate degree centralizes a specialty in a particular field of study and an expert understanding can be obtained as a result. This expertise then becomes a gigantic selling point to employers as the number of job-seekers that have obtained a post-undergraduate degree remains at a minimal amount.

By entering graduate school, I can also show my commitment to bettering myself which can be advantageous on my job applications. Likewise, many sophisticated jobs today require advanced degrees and there is a gap forming between jobs available and qualified applicants. Therefore, I believe that in order to place myself at a gainful position going into the job market today, I will need a graduate degree.

國立中山大學九十三學年度
碩士班研究生入學考試英文試題

This test consists of a Grammar part, a Vocabulary part, and a Reading Comprehension part. The total number of questions is 50, and you get 2 points for each correct answer.

- ➢ For the Grammar and Vocabulary parts, circle the letter of the word or phrase that fits best in the blank of the given sentence.
- ➢ For the Reading Comprehension part, circle the letter of the answer that comes closest to the meaning of the text.

I. Grammar

1. When Professor Jones lectures, all the students have a very ________ look on their faces.
   (A) bored (B) boring
   (C) boorish (D) boredom

2. Isn't it _______: Janet acts so stupidly because she loves John!
   (A) refreshing (B) obvious
   (C) obviously (D) strangely

3. George ________ privately admit that he hates his boss.
   (A) has (B) fears
   (C) would have (D) will

4. I ________ awful if he had tripped over my bike.
   (A) felt (B) would have felt
   (C) should feel (D) will feel

5. "Are you ready to go?"
   "________. Just let me check the gas."
   (A) No　　(B) Where?
   (C) Tonight　　(D) Almost

6. His watch is slow. He keeps using it, ________, and is always late.
   (A) all the time　　(B) although
   (C) therefore　　(D) though

7. "You shouldn't have screamed at her!"
   "I know, and I really regret ________ my temper."
   (A) lose　　(B) to lose
   (C) having lost　　(D) for losing

8. "Look, the key is in the lock!"
   "Thank God! I ________ forgotten to take it out and put it in my pocket!"
   (A) should have　　(B) shall have
   (C) must have　　(D) haven't

9. Please, ________ your litter in a responsible way.
   (A) dispose　　(B) dispose of
   (C) disposing　　(D) disposal

10. Can't you see that I am ________ busy?
    (A) extremely　　(B) so
    (C) how　　(D) greatly

11. It is unwise to love someone ________ your parents do not approve.
    (A) who　　(B) of whom
    (C) that　　(D) which

12. That dress really ________ her figure!

(A) shows up (B) shows to
(C) shows of (D) shows off

13. "Tea or coffee?"
"Tea, please. I really do not ________ coffee."

(A) care much about (B) care much for
(C) stand (D) like much

14. "Do you like mountain climbing?"
"Yes, I do. I like everything that ________ nature."

(A) contacts me with (B) contacts me with the
(C) gets me out in the (D) gets me in touch with

15. Fixing a car transmission is not ________ done.

(A) easy to (B) by yourself
(C) without help (D) easily

16. My room was fine, but ________ was horrible.

(A) Ernests' (B) Ernest
(C) Ernests's (D) Ernest's

17. John's mother objected to ________ to smoke.

(A) he is allowed (B) his being allowed
(C) he been allowed (D) allowing

18. "Is he a lenient teacher?"
"Yes, a little too much ________."

(A) leniency (B) that
(C) so (D) then

19. I would have phoned you ________ your number.
    (A) if I have (B) would I have
    (C) had I had (D) if you give me

20. But I do have hobbies! ________, I like fishing, reading, and mountain climbing.
    (A) For examples (B) For example
    (C) On the contrary (D) At the same time

Ⅱ. Vocabulary

21. Protesters ________ against the outcome of the election.
    (A) accused (B) demonstrated
    (C) procrastinated (D) originated

22. The pattern of that sweater he is wearing is so ________!
    (A) intricate (B) intoxicant
    (C) intrinsic (D) intolerant

23. My plane's departure was ________ by a bomb scare.
    (A) put out (B) delayed
    (C) moved on (D) depended

24. What ________ measures do you think the president should take to solve this particular crisis?
    (A) general (B) specifically
    (C) normal (D) supposed

25. She plays the piano so ________ that the glasses rattle in the cupboard.
    (A) compulsively (B) frequently
    (C) vigorously (D) intently

26. The two presidents ________ for days to hammer out a compromise.
(A) congregated (B) confabulated
(C) conferred (D) confederated

27. I sometimes wonder if there is anything at all that ________ common ground between Carla and her boyfriend.
(A) constitutes (B) compromises
(C) confers (D) entails

28. The ________ scholar of Chinese visited NSYSU on March 2nd.
(A) extinguished (B) distinct
(C) pertinent (D) distinguished

29. Don't worry: I think his advice is truly ________.
(A) disinterested (B) indifferent
(C) uninterested (D) interesting

30. Why are you crying? Is ________ OK?
(A) all (B) something
(C) everything (D) anything

31. In the ________ world, people order all sorts of things over the Internet.
(A) nowadays (B) today's
(C) of today (D) modern

32. When you write an English letter, make sure to ________ a dictionary.
(A) counsel (B) consult
(C) consider (D) concord

33. George and his wife Mary slowly drifted apart, mostly, I think, because George ________ Mary.
    (A) hit (B) omitted
    (C) neglected (D) inconsiderate of

34. My grandmother's voice grew ________ with age.
    (A) tremulous (B) sonorous
    (C) booming (D) melodious

35. Back after a week's vacation, I found my email account ________ with junk mail.
    (A) annoyed (B) inundated
    (C) aborted (D) stalled

36. He ________ that smoking is a dangerous habit, but he cannot give it up.
    (A) believes (B) denies
    (C) develops (D) lets

37. He has the ________ look of not having slept for a week.
    (A) caring (B) cheerful
    (C) charitable (D) unkempt

38. This road goes in a ________ direction all the way to Taipei.
    (A) straight (B) far
    (C) mountain (D) northerly

39. That dog had a ________ escape from being run over by that truck!
    (A) near (B) clear
    (C) narrow (D) bare

40. I don't know how foreigners ________ without eating rice at least once a day!
(A) get on (B) get by
(C) get through (D) get up

Ⅲ. Reading Comprehension

Generally speaking, humor is a quality in an event or expression of ideas which often evokes a physical response of laughter in a person. It is an evasive quality that over the centuries has been the subject of numerous theories attempting to describe its origins. There are essentially three main theories of humor, each of which has a number of variants: the superiority theory, the incongruity theory, and the relief theory. The superiority theory, which dates back to Aristotle, through Thomas Hobbes (1651) and Albert Rapp (1951), describes all humor as derisive. In other words, people laugh at the misfortunes of others or themselves. Humor is, therefore, a form of ridicule that involves the process of judging or degrading something or someone thought to be inferior.

The incongruity theory, on the other hand, maintains that humor originates from disharmony or inappropriateness. Koestler (1964), for example, argues that humor involves coexisting incompatible events. In other words, when two opposite or opposing ideas or events exist at the same time, humor exists. Finally, the relief theory rejects the notion that either superiority or incongruity are the bases for humor. Rather, proponents of this theory believe that humor is a form of release from psychological tension. Humor provides relief from anxiety, hostility, aggression, and sexual tension. Earlier psychologists, such as Freud, Dewey, and Kline, were strong proponents of this theory.

(Adapted from John M. Swales and Christine B. Feak, *Academic Writing for Graduate Students.* Ann Arbor: U of Michigan Press, 1994)

41. What is humor?
    (A) a physical response of laughter in a person
    (B) an evasive quality of laughter
    (C) some quality in words or events that makes people laugh
    (D) a form of ridicule that involves the process of judging or degrading someone or something

42. According to this passage, which of the theories of humor is the correct one?
    (A) The superiority theory.
    (B) The incongruity theory.
    (C) The relief theory.
    (D) The article doesn't judge correctness of the theories, but only describes them.

43. According to the incongruity theory of humor, __________
    (A) humor is inappropriate and creates disharmony.
    (B) humor is not superior to disharmony or inappropriateness.
    (C) humor occurs when incongruous ideas or events exist at the same time.
    (D) humor brings anxiety, hostility, aggression, and sexual tension.

44. Which of the three theories is the oldest one?
    (A) The superiority theory.
    (B) The incongruity theory.
    (C) The relief theory.
    (D) It isn't clear from the passage which is the oldest one.

45. The relief theory of humor ______________.
    (A) is based in psychology
    (B) is based in criminology
    (C) is based in sexology
    (D) incorporates the incongruity theory

As a people, we Americans have become obsessed with health. There is something fundamentally, radically unhealthy about all this. We do not seem to be seeking more exuberance in living as much as staving off failure, putting off dying. We have lost all confidence in the human body.

The new consensus is that we are badly designed, intrinsically fallible, vulnerable to a host of hostile influences inside and around us, and only precariously alive. We live in danger of falling apart at any moment, and are therefore always in need of surveillance and propping up. Without the professional attention of a health care system, we would fall in our tracks.

This is a new way of looking at things, and perhaps it can only be accounted for as a manifestation of spontaneous, undirected, societal *propaganda*. We keep telling each other this sort of thing, and back it comes on television or in the weekly news magazines, confirming all the fears, instructing us, as in the usual final paragraph of the personal advice columns in the daily papers, to "seek professional help."

It is extraordinary that we have just now become convinced of our bad health at the very time when the facts should be telling us the opposite. In a more rational world, you'd think that we would be celebrating our general good health. Despite the persisting roster of still-unsolved major diseases—cancer, heart disease, stroke, arthritis, and the rest—most of us have a clear, unimpeded run at a longer and healthier lifetime than could have been foreseen by any earlier generation.

(Adapted from Lewis Thomas, "The Health Care System." *The Medusa and the Snail.* New York: Viking, 1979.)

46. According to this passage, why is it unhealthy to be obsessed with health?
    (A) Because this obsession is too fundamental and radical.
    (B) Because this obsession cannot help us to stave off failure and put off dying.
    (C) Because this obsession makes us overeat.
    (D) Because this obsession makes us lose confidence in our bodies.

47. "The new consensus is that we are badly designed...."
    (A) The author agrees with this consensus.
    (B) The author disagrees with this consensus.
    (C) The author thinks that this consensus might be based on facts.
    (D) The author thinks that this consensus will be based on facts.

48. "In a more rational world, you'd think that we would be celebrating our general good health."
    (A) The author wishes that we would look at the facts more rationally.
    (B) The author expects that the world will become more rational.
    (C) The author knows that celebrations are good for our general good health.
    (D) The author hopes that our general good health will improve in the future.

49. What does the author remark about those major diseases that continue to plague us?
    (A) That people can become healthier if they exercise regularly.
    (B) That cures for those diseases will be found in the lifetime of most of us.
    (C) That surviving those diseases makes you stronger than you were earlier.
    (D) That in spite of those diseases, most of us can still look forward to a longer, healthier life than earlier generations.

50. According to this author, television, news magazines and newspapers ________
    (A) keep us informed about health matters.
    (B) instruct us as to when it is wise to seek professional help.
    (C) are part of the societal propaganda that confirms irrational fears about health.
    (D) warn us about our bad state of health.

國立中山大學九十三學年度
碩士班研究生入學考試英文試題詳解

I. 文法：

1. (**A**) 空格應塡一形容詞，依句意，選(A) ***bored***「覺得無聊的」。
(B) boring〔'bɔrɪŋ〕*adj.* 無聊的
(C) boorish〔'bʊrɪʃ〕*adj.* 粗野的；沒禮貌的
(D) boredom〔'bɔrdəm〕*n.* 無聊
professor〔prə'fɛsɚ〕*n.* 教授　　lecture〔'lɛktʃɚ〕*v.* 講課
look〔lʊk〕*n.* 表情

2. (**B**) be動詞後，需接形容詞，做主詞補語。
(A) refreshing〔rɪ'frɛʃɪŋ〕*adj.* 使人振奮的
(B) ***obvious***〔'ɑbvɪəs〕*adj.* 明顯的
(C) obviously〔'ɑbvɪəslɪ〕*adv.* 明顯地
(D) strangely〔'strendʒlɪ〕*adv.* 奇怪地
stupidly〔'stjupɪdlɪ〕*adv.* 愚蠢地

3. (**D**) 空格後是原形動詞admit，故選(D) ***will***。
privately〔'praɪvɪtlɪ〕*adv.* 私下地
admit〔əd'mɪt〕*v.* 承認　　hate〔het〕*v.* 討厭

4. (**B**) 依句意，爲「與過去事實相反」的假設，故主要子句須用should/would/could/might + had + p.p.，故選(B)。
awful〔'ɔfʊl〕*adj.* 難過的
trip over sth. 被某物絆倒

5. (**D**) check〔tʃɛk〕*v.* 檢查　　gas〔gæs〕*n.* 汽油

6. (**D**) 依句意，選(D) ***though***，置於句中或句尾，作「不過」解。
而(A)總是，(B)雖然，(C)因此，均不合。

7. (**C**) { ***regret* + *V-ing*** 後悔～
***regret* + *to V*.** 很遺憾要～ }
scream (skrim) *v.* 尖叫　　regret (rɪˈgrɛt) *v.* 後悔
temper (ˈtɛmpɚ) *n.* 脾氣　　***lose one's temper*** 發脾氣

8. (**C**) 「must + have + p.p.」表「當時一定～」。
lock (lɑk) *n.* 鎖　　pocket (ˈpɑkɪt) *n.* 口袋

9. (**B**) 依句意，選 (B) ***dispose of***「處理」。而 (A) dispose (dɪsˈpoz) *v.* 處置，爲不及物動詞，不可直接接受詞，(D) disposal「處置」，是名詞，在此不合。
litter (ˈlɪtɚ) *n.* 雜物；垃圾
responsible (rɪˈspɑnsəbḷ) *adj.* 負責任的

10. (**A**) (A) ***extremely*** (ɪkˈstrimlɪ) *adv.* 非常 (= *very*)

11. (**B**) ***approve of***「贊成」，在本句中，介系詞移至關代 whom 之前。　　unwise (ʌnˈwaɪz) *adj.* 不智的

12. (**D**) (A) show up 使突出；使顯眼
(D) ***show off*** 把…襯托得更好
figure (ˈfɪgɚ) *n.* 身材

13. (**B**) (A) care about 關心
(B) ***care for*** 喜歡
(C) stand (stænd) *v.* 忍受

14. (**D**) 依句意，選 (D) ***gets me in touch wit***「使我接觸」。

15. (**D**) 依句意，選 (D) ***easily***。而 (A) 須改成 easy to be 才能選。
fix (fɪks) *v.* 修理
transmission (trænsˈmɪʃən) *n.* 變速器

16. (**D**) Ernest 的所有格是 Ernest's，選 (D)。
horrible〔 'hɑrəbḷ 〕*adj.* 可怕的；恐怖的

17. (**B**) 「***object to*** + ***N./V-ing***」表「反對～」，且依句意，反對「他被允許抽煙」，故選 (B) ***his being allowed***。

18. (**C**) 依句意，選 (C) ***so***。so 可連接前述事項，作「那樣地」解。
lenient〔 'linɪənt 〕*adj.* 寬大的
(A) leniency〔 'linɪənsɪ 〕*n.* 寬大

19. (**C**) 依句意為「與過去事實相反的假設」，if 子句須用過去完成式，寫成：if I had had your number，而 if 可省略，但須將 had 移至主詞之前倒裝，寫成：had I had your number 故選 (C)。
phone〔 fon 〕*v.* 打電話給～

20. (**B**) 依句意，選 (B) ***for example***「例如」。而 (C) on the contrary「相反地」，則不合句意。
hobby〔 'hɑbɪ 〕*n.* 嗜好

Ⅱ. 字彙：

21. (**B**) (A) accuse〔 ə'kjuz 〕*v.* 控告
(B) ***demonstrate***〔 'dɛmən,stret 〕*v.* 示威
(C) procrastinate〔 pro'kræstə,net 〕*v.* 拖延
(D) originate〔 ə'rɪdʒə,net 〕*v.* 起源於
protester〔 prə'tɛstɚ 〕*n.* 抗議者
against〔 ə'gɛnst 〕*prep.* 反對
outcome〔 'aʊt,kʌm 〕*n.* 結果
election〔 ɪ'lɛkʃən 〕*n.* 選舉

22. (**A**) (A) ***intricate*** (′ɪntrəkɪt) *adj.* 複雜的
(B) intoxicant (ɪn′tɑksəkənt) *adj.* 醉人的
(C) intrinsic (ɪn′trɪnsɪk) *adj.* 本質上的；固有的
(D) intolerant (ɪn′tɑlərənt) *adj.* 不能忍受的
pattern (′pætɚn) *n.* 圖案
sweater (′swɛtɚ) *n.* 毛衣

23. (**B**) (A) put out 熄滅
(B) ***delay*** (dɪ′le) *v.* 使延誤
(C) move on 繼續前進
(D) depend (dɪ′pɛnd) *v.* 依賴
departure (dɪ′pɑrtʃɚ) *n.* 啓程；出發
bomb (bɑm) *n.* 炸彈　　scare (skɛr) *n.* 恐慌

24. (**A**) (A) ***general*** (′dʒɛnərəl) *adj.* 全面的
(B) specifically (spɪ′sɪfɪklɪ) *adv.* 具體地；明確地
(C) normal (′nɔrml̩) *adj.* 正常的
(D) supposed (sə′pozd) *adj.* 想像的；假定的
measure (′mɛʒɚ) *n.* 措施
president (′prɛzədənt) *n.* 總統
particular (pɚ′tɪkjəlɚ) *adj.* 特別的
crisis (′kraɪsɪs) *n.* 危機

25. (**C**) (A) compulsively (kəm′pʌlsɪvlɪ) *adv.* 強制地
(B) frequently (′frikwəntlɪ) *adv.* 經常
(C) ***vigorously*** (′vɪgərəslɪ) *adv.* 用力地；強烈地
(D) intently (ɪn′tɛntlɪ) *adv.* 專心地
rattle (′rætl̩) *v.* 格格作響
cupboard (′kʌbɚd) *n.* 碗櫥

26. (**C**) (A) congregate〔ˈkɑŋgrɪˌget〕*v.* 聚集（= *gather*）
(B) confabulate〔kənˈfæbjəˌlet〕*v.* 談笑；閒聊
(C) ***confer***〔kənˈfɝ〕*v.* 商議
(D) confederate〔kənˈfɛdəˌret〕*v.* 結成同盟
hammer out 苦心想出（方法）；努力打開（僵局）
compromise〔ˈkɑmprəˌmaɪz〕*n.* 妥協；折衷方案

27. (**A**) (A) ***constitute***〔ˈkɑnstəˌtjut〕*v.* 形成；構成
(B) compromise〔ˈkɑmprəˌmaɪz〕*v.* 使和解
(C) confer〔kənˈfɝ〕*v.* 商議
(D) entail〔ɪnˈtel〕*v.*（必然）伴有…；需要
wonder〔ˈwʌndɚ〕*v.* 想知道　***at all*** 到底；究竟
common ground 共同點

28. (**D**) (A) extinguish〔ɪkˈstɪŋgwɪʃ〕*v.* 使熄滅
(B) distinct〔dɪˈstɪŋkt〕*adj.* 獨特的；不同的
(C) pertinent〔ˈpɝtṇənt〕*adj.* 有關的
(D) ***distinguished***〔dɪˈstɪŋgwɪʃt〕*adj.* 著名的
scholar〔ˈskɑlɚ〕*n.* 學者
NSYSU 國立中山大學（= *National Sun Yat-sen University*）

29. (**A**) (A) ***disinterested***〔dɪsˈɪntrɪstɪd〕*adj.* 無私的；公平的
(B) indifferent〔ɪnˈdɪfərənt〕*adj.* 漠不關心的
(C) uninterested〔ʌnˈɪntərɪstɪd〕*adj.* 不感興趣的
(D) interesting〔ˈɪntrɪstɪŋ〕*adj.* 有趣的

30. (**C**) 依句意，選 (C) Is ***everything*** OK?「一切都還好嗎？」。

31. (**D**) (A) nowadays〔ˈnaʊəˌdez〕*adv.* 現今
(B) 所有格不可與 the 連用，故不選。
(D) ***modern***〔ˈmɑdɚn〕*adj.* 現代的
sort〔sɔrt〕*n.* 種類

32.（**B**）(A) counsel〔ˈkaʊnsl̩〕*v.* 勸告；建議
(B) ***consult***〔kənˈsʌlt〕*v.* 查閱
(C) consider〔kənˈsɪdɚ〕*v.* 考慮
(D) concord〔ˈkɑnkɔrd〕*n.* 協調；和諧

33.（**C**）(B) omit〔oˈmɪt〕*v.* 省略
(C) ***neglect***〔nɪˈglɛkt〕*v.* 忽視
(D) inconsiderate〔ˌɪnkənˈsɪdərɪt〕*adj.* 不體貼的
drift apart 感情變淡　　mostly〔ˈmɔstlɪ〕*adv.* 大多

34.（**A**）(A) ***tremulous***〔ˈtrɛmjələs〕*adj.* 顫抖的
(B) sonorous〔səˈnorəs〕*adj.* 宏亮的
(C) booming〔ˈbumɪŋ〕*adj.* 日漸興隆的
(D) melodious〔məˈlodɪəs〕*adj.* 曲調優美的
grow〔gro〕*v.* 變得

35.（**B**）(A) annoy〔əˈnɔɪ〕*v.* 使惱怒
(B) ***inundate***〔ɪnˈʌndet〕*v.* 塞滿 <*with*>
(C) abort〔əˈbɔrt〕*v.* 流產；墮胎
(D) stall〔stɔl〕*v.* 把（馬、牛）關進馬廄、牛舍
account〔əˈkaʊnt〕*n.* 帳戶；帳號
junk mail 垃圾郵件

36.（**A**）(B) deny〔dɪˈnaɪ〕*v.* 否認
(C) develop〔dɪˈvɛləp〕*v.* 發展
give up 放棄；戒掉

37.（**D**）(A) care〔kɛr〕*v.* 關心
(B) cheerful〔ˈtʃɪrfəl〕*adj.* 高興的
(C) charitable〔ˈtʃærətəbl̩〕*adj.* 仁慈的
(D) ***unkempt***〔ʌnˈkɛmpt〕*adj.* 邋遢的
look〔lʊk〕*n.* 樣子；外表

38. (**D**) (D) ***northerly*** ('nɔrðəlɪ) *adj.* 向北的

go (go) *v.* 延伸 ***all the way*** 一路上

39. (**C**) (C) ***narrow*** ('næro) *adj.* 勉強的；間不容髮的

have a narrow escape 死裡逃生

(D) bare (bɛr) *adj.* 赤裸的

run over 輾過 truck (trʌk) *n.* 卡車

40. (**B**) (A) get on 上（車）

(B) ***get by*** 勉強度過

(C) get through 穿過（後須接受詞）

(D) get up 起立；起床

foreigner ('fɔrɪnə) *n.* 外國人

rice (raɪs) *n.* 米飯 ***at least*** 至少

Ⅲ. 閱讀測驗：

A.

【譯文】

一般說來，幽默是在一個事件中，或在表達想法時，所表現出的一種特質，它常能在一個人身上，引起笑這種身體反應。它是一種無法捉摸的特質，所以幾世紀以來，有許多理論以幽默爲主題，並試圖說明它的起源。基本上，幽默有三個主要的理論，每個理論都有許多變異：優秀理論、失諧理論，和消遣理論。優秀理論源自亞里斯多德，和湯瑪士・霍伯斯（1651）、亞伯特・瑞普（1951），這個理論把所有的幽默都看成是嘲笑。換句話說，人們是在嘲笑其他人或是自己的不幸。因此，幽默是一種嘲笑人的方式，它包含批評的過程，或是貶低某些被認爲較差的東西或人。

可是，失諧理論則是主張幽默是源自於不和諧或不恰當。舉例來說，科斯勒（1964）主張，幽默包含共存而矛盾的事。也就是說，當兩個相反或對立的意見或事件同時存在，那麼就存在著幽默。最後，消遣理論拒絕接受以優秀或失諧的概念，來作爲幽默的理論基礎。相反地，支持這個理論的人相信，幽默是一種從精神緊張中放鬆的方式。幽默可以消除憂慮、敵意、侵略和曖昧。較早期的心理學家，像是佛洛依德、杜威和克蘭，都是這個理論的積極支持者。

（改寫自 John M. Swales 和 Christine B. Feak，的研究生論文。密西根大學出版部 Ann Arbor，1994 年）

【答案】

41.（**C**）　42.（**D**）　43.（**C**）　44.（**A**）　45.（**A**）

【註】

generally speaking 一般說來　humor〔ˈhjumɚ〕*n.* 幽默
quality〔ˈkwɑlətɪ〕*n.* 特質　expression〔ɪkˈsprɛʃen〕*n.* 表達
evoke〔ɪˈvok〕*v.* 引起；喚起　physical〔ˈfɪzɪkḷ〕*adj.* 身體的
response〔rɪˈspɑns〕*n.* 回應；反應
laughter〔ˈlæftɚ〕*n.* 笑；笑聲
evasive〔ɪˈvesɪv〕*adj.* 無法捉摸的　subject〔ˈsʌbdʒɪkt〕*n.* 主題
numerous〔ˈnjumərəs〕*adj.* 許多的　theory〔ˈθiərɪ〕*n.* 理論
attempt〔əˈtɛmpt〕*v.* 企圖　origin〔ˈɔrədʒɪn〕*n.* 來源；起源
essentially〔əˈsɛnʃəlɪ〕*adv.* 基本上；在本質上
variant〔ˈvɛrɪənt〕*n.* 變異；變體
superiority〔səˌpɪrɪˈɔrətɪ〕*n.* 優秀；卓越
incongruity〔ˌɪnkɑŋˈgruətɪ〕*n.* 不和諧　relief〔rɪˈlif〕*n.* 消遣
date back to 追溯到　derisive〔dɪˈraɪsɪv〕*adj.* 嘲笑的；嘲弄的
laugh at 嘲笑　misfortune〔mɪsˈfɔrtʃən〕*n.* 不幸

ridicule〔'rɪdɪkjul〕*n.* 嘲笑　involve〔ɪn'vɑlv〕*v.* 包含；涉及
process〔'prɑsɛs〕*n.* 過程　judge〔dʒʌdʒ〕*v.* 批評
degrade〔dɪ'gred〕*v.* 貶低　inferior〔ɪn'fɪrɪɚ〕*adj.* 較差的
maintain〔men'ten〕*v.* 主張；堅持
originate〔ə'rɪdʒə,net〕*v.* 起源於 <*from*>
disharmony〔dɪs'hɑrmənɪ〕*n.* 不和諧
inappropriateness〔,ɪnə'proprɪɪtnɪs〕*n.* 不適當
argue〔'ɑrgjʊ〕*v.* 主張　coexisting〔,ko·ɪg'zɪstɪŋ〕*adj.* 共存的
incompatible〔,ɪnkəm'pætəbḷ〕*adj.* 矛盾的；不相容的
opposite〔'ɑpəzɪt〕*adj.* 相反的　opposing〔ə'pozɪŋ〕*adj.* 對立的

exist〔ɪg'zɪst〕*v.* 存在　reject〔rɪ'dʒɛkt〕*v.* 拒絕
notion〔'noʃən〕*n.* 概念；觀念　rather〔'ræðɚ〕*adv.* 相反地
proponent〔prə'ponənt〕*n.* 支持者　release〔rɪ'lis〕*n.* 放鬆
psychological〔,saɪkə'lɑdʒɪkḷ〕*adj.* 心理上的；精神的
tension〔'tɛnʃən〕*n.* 緊張　anxiety〔æŋ'zaɪətɪ〕*n.* 憂慮
hostility〔hɑs'tɪlətɪ〕*n.* 敵意
aggression〔ə'grɛʃən〕*n.* 侵略；侵犯
sexual〔'sɛkʃʊəl〕*adj.* 性的；兩性之間的
adapt〔ə'dæpt〕*v.* 改寫；改編
academic〔,ækə'dɛmɪk〕*adj.* 學術的

graduate〔'grædʒʊ,et〕*adj.* 研究生的
press〔prɛs〕*n.* 出版社；發行機構
correctness〔kə'rɛktnɪs〕*n.* 正確性
inappropriate〔,ɪnə'proprɪɪt〕*adj.* 不適當的
create〔krɪ'et〕*v.* 製造；產生　***be superior to*** 比～優越
occur〔ə'kɝ〕*v.* 發生　incongruous〔ɪn'kɑŋgrʊəs〕*adj.* 不和諧的
criminology〔,krɪmə'nɑlədʒɪ〕*n.* 犯罪學
sexology〔sɛks'ɑlədʒɪ〕*n.* 性科學
incorporate〔ɪn'kɔrpə,ret〕*v.* 合併；結合

B.

【譯文】

就整個民族來說，我們美國人已經變得為健康所困擾。這一切從根本上來說，有著非常不健康的影響。我們尋求避免失敗、晚一點死，但似乎不再追求更豐富的生活。我們已經對人體完全失去信心了。

大家最新的共識是，我們天生有缺陷，而且本質上就容易出問題，對於內在和週遭的許多不良影響非常敏感，然後就只是不安地活著。我們每分每秒都活在崩潰的危險中，因此總是需要被監視和支持。如果沒有保健系統的專業照顧，我們就會死掉。

這是看待事物的新方向，而且或許它只能被解釋成一種無意識、盲目的社會宣傳現象。我們不斷地告訴彼此這種想法，然後電視或時事週刊的資訊，卻又提倡那個理論，並加深所有的恐懼，就像日報的個人建議專欄中，最後一段通常會教我們，去「尋求專業協助」。

奇怪的是，我們現在已經變得深信自己的身體不好，就在我們應該被告知事實上並非如此時。在一個比較理性的世界，你就會覺得我們應該要慶祝自己大體上是很健康的。儘管尚待解決的重大疾病仍然持續存在——癌症、心臟病、中風、關節炎等等——我們大多數的人都擁有較少阻礙，且較長與較健康的人生，這是之前的世代所料想不到的。

【答案】

46.（D） 47.（B） 48.（A） 49.（D） 50.（C）

【註】

people〔ˈpipḷ〕*n.* 民族　　obsess〔əbˈsɛs〕*v.* 困擾
fundamentally〔ˌfʌndəˈmɛntḷɪ〕*adv.* 基本上
radically〔ˈrædɪkḷɪ〕*adv.* 根本上
unhealthy〔ʌnˈhɛlθɪ〕*adj.* 不健康的　　seek〔sik〕*v.* 尋求
exuberance〔ɪgˈzjubərəns〕*n.* 豐富；茂盛
stave off 防止；避開　　***put off*** 延期；延後
confidence〔ˈkɑnfədəns〕*n.* 信心
consensus〔kənˈsɛnsəs〕*n.* 共識　　design〔dɪˈzaɪn〕*v.* 設計
intrinsically〔ɪnˈtrɪnsɪkḷɪ〕*adv.* 在本質上

fallible〔ˈfæləbḷ〕*adj.* 容易犯錯的
vulnerable〔ˈvʌlnərəbḷ〕*adj.* 易受傷害的
a host of 許多　　hostile〔ˈhɑstɪl〕*adj.* 不利的；不良的
influence〔ˈɪnfluəns〕*n.* 影響
precariously〔prɪˈkɛrɪəslɪ〕*adv.* 不安地　　***fall apart*** 崩潰
surveillance〔sɚˈveləns〕*n.* 監視；監督
prop〔prɑp〕*v.* 支持；支援
professional〔prəˈfɛʃənḷ〕*adj.* 專業的

attention〔əˈtɛnʃən〕*n.* 照料；照顧
health care 健康照顧；保健
track〔træk〕*n.* 路；軌道　　***fall in** one's **tracks*** 失敗；死亡
account for 作出解釋；作出說明
manifestation〔ˌmænəfɛsˈteʃən〕*n.* 現象
spontaneous〔spɑnˈtenɪəs〕*adj.* 無意識的
undirected〔ˌʌndəˈrɛktɪd〕*adj.* 盲目的
societal〔səˈsaɪətḷ〕*adj.* 社會上的
propaganda〔ˌprɑpəˈgændə〕*n.* 宣傳

weekly〔ˈwiklɪ〕*adj.* 每週的　confirm〔kənˈfɝm〕*v.* 加強
instruct〔ɪnˈstrʌkt〕*v.* 教導　column〔ˈkɑləm〕*n.* 專欄
extraordinary〔ɪkˈstrɔrdn̩,ɛrɪ〕*adj.* 異常的
convince〔kənˈvɪns〕*v.* 使確信
opposite〔ˈɑpəzɪt〕*n.* 相反的東西
rational〔ˈræʃənl̩〕*adj.* 理性的　celebrate〔ˈsɛlə,bret〕*v.* 慶祝
general〔ˈdʒɛnərəl〕*adj.* 大體的；大致的
persisting〔pɚˈzɪstɪŋ〕*adj.* 持續的
roster〔ˈrɑstɚ〕*n.* 名册；名單　disease〔dɪˈziz〕*n.* 疾病

cancer〔ˈkænsɚ〕*n.* 癌症　stroke〔strok〕*n.* 中風
arthritis〔ɑrˈθraɪtɪs〕*n.* 關節炎　***and the rest*** …等等
unimpeded〔,ʌnɪmˈpidɪd〕*adj.* 未受妨礙的　run〔rʌn〕*n.* 旅程
lifetime〔ˈlaɪf,taɪm〕*n.* 一生　foresee〔forˈsi〕*v.* 預料
generation〔,dʒɛnəˈreʃən〕*n.* 世代
obsession〔əbˈsɛʃən〕*n.* 擺脫不了的思想；著迷
overeat〔ˈovɚˈit〕*v.* 吃得過量　author〔ˈɔθɚ〕*n.* 作者
rationally〔ˈræʃənl̩ɪ〕*adv.* 理性地
celebration〔,sɛləˈbreʃən〕*n.* 慶祝

remark〔rɪˈmɑrk〕*v.* 談論　plague〔pleg〕*v.* 煩擾；折磨
regularly〔ˈrɛgjələlɪ〕*adv.* 規律地；定期地
cure〔kjʊr〕*v.* 治療
survive〔sɚˈvaɪv〕*v.* 經過～而繼續存在
look forward to 期待
informed〔ɪnˈfɔrmd〕*adj.* 了解情況的；消息靈通的
matter〔ˈmætɚ〕*n.* 問題；事情
irrational〔ɪˈræʃənl̩〕*adj.* 不理性的
warn〔wɔrn〕*v.* 警告　state〔stet〕*n.* 狀態

國立中正大學九十三學年度 碩士班研究生入學考試英文試題

PART I. Vocabulary: Choose one correct answer. (40%)

1. **post**-, as in postscript, means:
   (A) after (B) against
   (C) write (D) behind

2. **poly**-, as in polygamy, means:
   (A) little (B) normal
   (C) few (D) many

3. **bio**-, as in biology, means:
   (A) science (B) animal
   (C) life (D) two

4. **mal**-, as in malevolence, means:
   (A) best (B) good
   (C) bad (D) wrong

5. **noct**-, as in nocturnal, means:
   (A) day (B) late
   (C) night (D) fear

6. **inter**-, as in interlock, means:
   (A) nations (B) between
   (C) next (D) amid

7. **spec**-, as in retrospect, means:
   (A) examine (B) search
   (C) read (D) see

8. **retro**-, as in retrospection, means:
   (A) backward (B) previous
   (C) forward (D) against

9. **corp**-, as in corporation, means:
   (A) body (B) company
   (C) section (D) military

10. **pac**-, as in pacific or pacify, means:
    (A) cold (B) sleep
    (C) ocean (D) peace

11. **macro**-, as in macrocosm, means:
    (A) loose (B) tiny
    (C) small (D) big

12. **chrono**-, as in chronometer, means:
    (A) time (B) tempo
    (C) life (D) order

13. **manu**-, as in manufacture, means:
    (A) produce (B) make
    (C) hand (D) labor

14. **frag-**, as in fragment or fragile, means:
(A) explode (B) cut
(C) crack (D) break

15. **phon-**, as in symphony, means:
(A) hear (B) sound
(C) music (D) distance

16. **omni-**, as in omnipotent or omniscience, means:
(A) entry (B) every
(C) powerful (D) all

17. **hetero-**, as in heteronym, means:
(A) same (B) different
(C) distant (D) close

18. **-graphy**, as in biography, means:
(A) compare (B) book
(C) write (D) language

19. **-cracy**, as in bureaucracy, means:
(A) people (B) group
(C) growth (D) rule by

20. **super-**, as in superfluous, means:
(A) under (B) strong
(C) great (D) beyond

PART II. Choose the best answer. (40%)

<Reading A: Questions 21 ~ 25>

Einstein was born in Germany in 1879 of Jewish parents. He loved math and physics, but he disliked the discipline of formal German schooling. Because of his poor memory of words, his teachers believed that he was a slow learner. Einstein left school before receiving his ___(21)___ and tried to pass the exam to enter the Swiss Polytechnic Institute, but he ___(22)___ on his first attempt. On his second attempt, he passed. He graduated in 1900. He had planned to become a teacher of physics and math, but he could not find a job in this field. ___(23)___, he worked in a patent office as a third class technical expert from 1902 to 1909. While he was working at this job, he wrote in his spare time. In 1905, when he was only 26 years old, he published three papers that explained the basic structure of the universe. His theory of ___(24)___ explained the relationship of space and time. Einstein was finally ___(25)___ for his brilliant discovery. He returned to Germany to accept a research position at the University of Berlin. However, in 1920, while he was lecturing at the university, anti-Jewish groups often interrupted his lectures, saying they were "un-German."

21. (A) gift (B) intelligence
    (C) diploma (D) grade

22. (A) caught (B) missed
    (C) failed (D) went through

23. (A) Rather (B) Instead
    (C) Because (D) Despite that

24. (A) gravity (B) relativity
    (C) sensitivity (D) activity

25. (A) accused (B) suspected
    (C) capable (D) respected

<Reading B: 26～30>

Kids like to spend money. Many parents give their children an ___(26)___ each week and let their children spend it as they please. Other parents expect their kids to earn their money by babysitting for younger brothers and sisters, washing the dishes, or cleaning the house. If a child asks for money but he doesn't do his chores, he doesn't get any. This child learns that money "doesn't grow on ___(27)___" and that if he needs some, he has to do something to get it. Some parents let their kids spend all of the money they get, but others want their kids to ___(28)___ some in their own bank account. If the child wants to buy a special toy, he can pay for it himself.

Why do kids need so much money? Kids see something new and they want to buy it. Also, kids like to be just like their friends--if their friends have a new doll or game, they want one just like it. If their friends have designer blue jeans, they have to have exactly the same kind. If parents say no, kids usually respond, "All of my friends have one. I'll die if I don't get one." Parents who feel ___(29)___ for not spending enough time with their kids often ___(30)___ to their kids' demands.

26. (A) assignment (B) break
(C) allowance (D) compensation

27. (A) roofs (B) cables
(C) foot (D) trees

28. (A) check (B) lend
(C) save (D) loan

29. (A) pleased (B) guilty
(C) overwhelmed (D) accountable

30. (A) give up (B) give in
(C) give it a try (D) give nothing

<Reading C: 31 ~ 40>

Americans are concerned about their weight. Everyone knows that it's important to eat well and exercise ___(31)___. We see beautiful, thin fashion models and want to look like them. We see commercials for exercise machines showing fit, thin people exercising. Health clubs are full of people trying to get ___(32)___. Sales of diet colas and low-calorie foods indicate that Americans want to be ___(33)___. However, 50 percent of Americans are overweight. Why is this so?

First, today's lifestyle does not include enough physical activity. When the U.S. was an agricultural society, farmers ate a big, heavy meal, but they burned off the calories by doing hard physical labor. Today, most people don't get enough exercise. They don't do __(34)__ walking. Americans drive almost everywhere, even when the __(35)__ is close to home. When people get home from work, they're usually too tired to exercise. After dinner, they just watch TV. They have no chance to __(36)__ calories.

Another reason why Americans don't lose weight is that they eat __(37)__. They are influenced by commercials and ads for fatty foods, soft drinks, candy, and sugary cereals that look good. Even though most people know that these foods aren't healthy, many don't have enough time to eat a __(38)__ diet. It's easy to stop at a fast-food restaurant and __(39)__ a greasy burger and fries. These foods are high in fat, carbohydrates, sodium, and calories. People eat them quickly and in large quantities--triple burgers, extra-large colas, large orders of fries.

Eating a high-fat diet and not getting enough exercise will __(40)__ heart disease for many people.

31. (A) consequently (B) subsequently
    (C) regularly (D) sequentially

32. (A) better off (B) in shape
    (C) ready (D) rich

33. (A) thin (B) fatty
(C) strong (D) happy

34. (A) home (B) enough
(C) no (D) kind of

35. (A) tour (B) trip
(C) journey (D) travel

36. (A) burn off (B) burn down
(C) put down (D) cut off

37. (A) actively (B) pleasantly
(C) satisfactory (D) poorly

38. (A) real (B) high-fat
(C) well-balanced (D) rich

39. (A) pick on (B) pick up
(C) make up (D) give away

40. (A) result from (B) reduce
(C) result in (D) due to

PART III. Writing (20%)

Write a letter or an email (2-3 paragraphs, a total of 150～200 words) giving advice to your friend looking for a job.

國立中正大學九十三學年度 碩士班研究生入學考試英文試題詳解

PART I. 字彙：40%

1. (**A**) post- 表示「（在）後」的意思。
   postscript〔'post·skrɪpt〕*n.* 後記；附記
   (B) against〔ə'gɛnst〕*prep.* 對抗
   (D) behind〔bɪ'haɪnd〕*adv.* 在後面

2. (**D**) poly- 表示「多」的意思。
   polygamy〔pə'lɪgəmɪ〕*n.* 重婚
   (B) normal〔'nɔrml̩〕*adj.* 正常的

3. (**C**) bio- 表示「生命」的意思。
   biology〔baɪ'ɑlədʒɪ〕*n.* 生物學

4. (**C**) mal- 表示「壞；不良」的意思。
   malevolence〔mə'lɛvələns〕*n.* 惡意；壞心腸

5. (**C**) noct- 表示「夜晚」的意思。
   nocturnal〔nɑk'tɝnl̩〕*adj.* 夜間的

6. (**B**) inter- 表示「在（兩者）之間」的意思。
   interlock〔ˌɪntɚ'lɑk〕*v.* 連結
   (D) amid〔ə'mɪd〕*prep.* 在…中

7. (**D**) spec- 表示「看」的意思。
   retrospect〔'rɛtrəˌspɛkt〕*n.* 回顧；追憶
   (A) examine〔ɪg'zæmɪn〕*v.* 檢查
   (B) search〔sɝtʃ〕*v.* 搜尋

8. (**A**) retro- 表示「向後；回溯」的意思。
retrospection〔,rɛtrə'spɛkʃən〕*n.* 回顧；回想
(B) previous〔'priviəs〕*adj.* 以前的

9. (**A**) corp- 表示「公司」的意思。
corporation〔,kɔrpə'reʃən〕*n.* 公司
(C) section〔'sɛkʃən〕*n.* 部分
(D) military〔'mɪlə,tɛrɪ〕*adj.* 軍事的

10. (**D**) pac- 表示「和平」的意思。
pacific〔pə'sɪfɪk〕*adj.* 和平的
pacify〔'pæsə,faɪ〕*v.* 使平靜
(D) ***peace***〔pis〕*n.* 和平

11. (**D**) macro- 表示「大」的意思。
macrocosm〔'mækrə,kɑzəm〕*n.* 宇宙
(A) loose〔lus〕*adj.* 鬆的
(B) tiny〔'taɪnɪ〕*adj.* 微小的

12. (**A**) chrono- 表示「時間」的意思。
chronometer〔krə'nɑmətɚ〕*n.* 精密的計時器
(B) tempo〔'tɛmpo〕*n.* 節奏

13. (**C**) manu- 表示「手」的意思。
manufacture〔,mænjə'fæktʃɚ〕*v.* 製造
(A) produce〔prə'djus〕*v.* 生產；製造
(D) labor〔'lebɚ〕*n.* 勞力

14.（ **D** ） frag- 表示「打破」的意思。
fragment〔ˈfrægmənt〕*n.* 片斷；碎片
fragile〔ˈfrædʒəl〕*adj.* 易碎的
(A) explode〔ɪkˈsplod〕*v.* 爆炸
(C) crack〔kræk〕*v.* 裂開

15.（ **B** ） phon- 表示「聲音」的意思。
symphony〔ˈsɪmfənɪ〕*n.* 交響樂
(D) distance〔ˈdɪstəns〕*n.* 距離

16.（ **D** ） omni- 表示「全…」的意思。
omnipotent〔ɑmˈnɪpətənt〕*adj.* 全能的
omniscience〔ɑmˈnɪʃəns〕*n.* 無所不知
(A) entry〔ˈɛntrɪ〕*n.* 入口
(C) powerful〔ˈpaʊɚfəl〕*adj.* 強有力的

17.（ **B** ） hetero- 表示「相異的」的意思。
heteronym〔ˈhɛtərəˌnɪm〕*n.* 同拼法異音異義的字
（如 tear〔tɪr〕*n.* 眼淚 與 tear〔tɛr〕*v.* 撕裂）
(C) distant〔ˈdɪstənt〕*adj.* 遙遠的

18.（ **C** ） -graphy 表示「寫」的意思。
biography〔baɪˈɑgrəfɪ〕*n.* 傳記
(A) compare〔kəmˈpɛr〕*v.* 比較

19.（ **D** ） -cracy 表示「統治集團；政府」的意思。
bureaucracy〔bjʊˈrɑkrəsɪ〕*n.* 官僚政治；官僚制度
(D) ***rule***〔rul〕*v.* 統治

20.（ **D** ） super- 表示「超過」的意思。
superfluous〔sʊˈpɝfluəs〕*adj.* 多餘的

PART Ⅱ. 克漏字：40%

<Reading A: Questions 21-25>

【譯文】

愛因斯坦於 1879 年出生於德國，父母都是猶太人。他熱愛數學和物理，但是他不喜歡德國正規學校教育的訓練。因爲他背單字的能力不好，所以老師就認爲他學得很慢。愛因斯坦在拿到畢業證書之前，就離開學校了，之後他試著要通過瑞士工藝學院的入學考試，但他第一次嘗試時卻失敗了。他第二次才通過考試。他在 1900 年畢業。他原本打算要當物理和數學老師，但在這個領域卻找不到工作。於是他只好到專利局工作，從 1902 年到 1909 年，都在那裡擔任三級技師的工作。在他從事這份工作時，他會在空閒時間寫作。在 1905 年時，他才二十六歲，就發表了三篇論文，說明宇宙的基本結構。他的相對論可以解釋空間與時間的關係。愛因斯坦最後因爲他的卓越發現而受到尊敬。他回到德國，並接下了柏林大學的研究工作。但是，在 1920 年時，當他在大學講課時，常會有反猶太人的團體打斷他的教學，而且還說他們是「反德國的」。

【註】

Jewish〔ˈdʒuɪʃ〕*adj.* 猶太人的　　physics〔ˈfɪzɪks〕*n.* 物理
discipline〔ˈdɪsəplɪn〕*n.* 紀律；訓練
formal〔ˈfɔrml̩〕*adj.* 正規的　　schooling〔ˈskulɪŋ〕*n.* 學校教育
poor〔pur〕*adj.* 差的　　memory〔ˈmɛmərɪ〕*n.* 記憶力
polytechnic〔ˌpɑləˈtɛknɪk〕*adj.* 工藝的
institute〔ˈɪnstəˌtjut〕*n.* 學院
attempt〔əˈtɛmpt〕*n.* 嘗試　　field〔fild〕*n.* 領域
patent office 專利局　　class〔klæs〕*n.* 等級
technical〔ˈtɛknɪkl̩〕*adj.* 技術上的　　expert〔ˈɛkspɝt〕*n.* 專家

spare time 空閒時間　　publish〔ˈpʌblɪʃ〕*v.* 發表；出版
paper〔ˈpepɚ〕*n.* 論文　　structure〔ˈstrʌktʃɚ〕*n.* 結構
universe〔ˈjunəˌvɝs〕*n.* 宇宙
relationship〔rɪˈleʃənˌʃɪp〕*n.* 關係
space〔spes〕*n.* 空間　　brilliant〔ˈbrɪljənt〕*adj.* 卓越的
discovery〔dɪˈskʌvərɪ〕*n.* 發現　　research〔rɪˈsɝtʃ〕*n.* 研究
position〔pəˈzɪʃən〕*n.* 職位；工作
lecture〔ˈlɛktʃɚ〕*v. n.* 講課　　***anti-*** 反對
interrupt〔ˌɪntəˈrʌpt〕*v.* 打斷
un-German 非德國風格的；反德的

21.（**C**）(B) intelligence〔ɪnˈtɛlədʒəns〕*n.* 智力
(C) ***diploma***〔dɪˈplomə〕*n.* 文憑；畢業證書
(D) grade〔gred〕*n.* 成績

22.（**C**）(D) go through 通過

23.（**B**）(A) rather〔ˈræðɚ〕*adv.* 更確切地說
(B) ***instead***〔ɪnˈstɛd〕*adv.* 更換；作爲替代
(D) despite〔dɪˈspaɪt〕*prep.* 儘管

24.（**B**）(A) gravity〔ˈgrævətɪ〕*n.* 重力；地心引力
(B) ***relativity***〔ˌrɛləˈtɪvətɪ〕*n.* 相對論
(C) sensitivity〔ˌsɛnsəˈtɪvətɪ〕*n.* 敏感度
(D) activity〔ækˈtɪvətɪ〕*n.* 活動

25.（**D**）(A) accuse〔əˈkjuz〕*v.* 控告
(B) suspect〔səˈspɛkt〕*v.* 懷疑
(D) ***respect***〔rɪˈspɛkt〕*v.* 尊敬

<Reading B: 26-30>

【譯文】

小孩喜歡花錢。很多父母每個星期都會給孩子零用錢，而且隨便他們想要怎麼花這筆錢。有些父母則希望自己的小孩，能以當弟妹的臨時褓母、洗碗，或是打掃房子，來賺到這筆錢。如果孩子要錢，但卻不想做家事，那麼他就拿不到任何錢。這個孩子會了解錢「不是長在樹上」，所以如果他需要錢，就必須做一些事，才能得到那筆錢。有些父母會讓自己的孩子把得到的錢全部花掉，但是有些父母則會要孩子存一些在他們自己的銀行帳戶裡。如果孩子想要買一個特別的玩具，他就可以自己付錢。

爲什麼小孩子需要這麼多錢？小孩子看到新的東西就會想買。而且，小孩子喜歡和朋友一樣──如果他們的朋友有個新玩偶或新遊戲，他們就會想要一個一模一樣的。如果他們的朋友有一條設計師設計的藍色牛仔褲，他們就一定要有一條款式一樣的牛仔褲。如果父母拒絕他們，小孩子通常就會回答說：「我所有的朋友都有一條。如果我沒買，我就會死。」那些因爲沒有花足夠的時間陪伴孩子，而感到內疚的父母，常常都會順從小孩的要求。

【註】

kid (kɪd) *n.* 小孩　　please (pliz) *v.* 想做；喜歡
babysit (ˈbebɪˌsɪt) *v.* 當臨時褓母
dish (dɪʃ) *n.* 碗盤　　chores (tʃorz) *n. pl.* 家事；雜務
bank account 銀行帳戶　　doll (dɑl) *n.* 玩偶
designer (dɪˈzaɪnɚ) *adj.* 由設計師專門設計的
jeans (dʒinz) *n. pl.* 牛仔褲
exactly (ɪgˈzæktlɪ) *adv.* 正好；正是
respond (rɪˈspɑnd) *v.* 回答　　demand (dɪˈmænd) *n.* 要求

26. (**C**) (A) assignment〔əˈsaɪnmənt〕*n.*（被指定的）工作；作業
(B) break〔brek〕*n.* 休息時間
(C) ***allowance***〔əˈlaʊəns〕*n.* 零用錢
(D) compensation〔ˌkɑmpənˈseʃən〕*n.* 補償

27. (**D**) ***Money doesn't grow on trees.*** 鈔票不會長在樹上；賺錢是很辛苦的。
(A) roof〔ruf〕*n.* 屋頂
(B) cable〔ˈkebl̩〕*n.* 電纜

28. (**C**) (A) check〔tʃɛk〕*v.* 檢查
(C) ***save***〔sev〕*v.* 存（錢）
(D) loan〔lon〕*v.* 借貸

29. (**B**) (A) pleased〔plizd〕*adj.* 高興的
(B) ***guilty***〔ˈgɪltɪ〕*adj.* 有罪的；內疚的
(C) overwhelm〔ˌovɚˈhwɛlm〕*v.* 壓倒；使（人）無法對付
(D) accountable〔əˈkaʊntəbl̩〕*adj.* 應負責的

30. (**B**) (A) give up 放棄　(B) ***give in*** 屈服
(C) give it a try 試一試

<Reading B: 31-40>

【譯文】

美國人很關心自己的體重。每個人都知道，吃得好以及規律地運動是很重要的。我們看到美麗苗條的時裝模特兒，就會想跟他們一樣。我們看到運動器材的廣告裡，健康而苗條的人們正在運動。健身中心擠滿了想要變健康的人。從健怡可樂和低卡食品的銷售可以看出，美國人想要變瘦。但是卻有百分之五十的美國人超重。爲什麼會這樣？

首先，現今的生活方式並不包含充分的體能活動。當美國還是農業社會時，農夫一餐都吃很多，但是他們在從事辛苦的體力勞動時，會把卡路里消耗掉。現在，大多數的人運動量不足。他們散步的時間不夠長。美國人幾乎到哪裡都要開車，甚至是要去的地方離家很近時。當人們下班回到家時，他們通常累得無法運動。吃完晚飯後，他們就會看電視。他們沒有機會把卡路里消耗掉。

另一個美國人沒辦法減重的理由就是，他們吃得不好。他們被看起來很好吃的油膩食物、清涼飲料，糖果和含糖的穀物食品的廣告所影響。雖然大多數的人都知道這些食物有害健康，但是還是有很多人沒有足夠的時間吃均衡的飲食。把車停在速食餐館前面，然後買油膩的漢堡和薯條，這樣方便多了。這些食物含有大量的脂肪、碳水化合物、鈉和卡路里。人們迅速地吃下許多這種食物——三層漢堡、特大杯的可樂、大薯。

高脂肪的飲食，加上運動量不足，將使許多人罹患心臟病。

【註】

be concerned about 擔心；關心　　thin〔θɪn〕*adj.* 瘦的；苗條的
fashion〔ˈfæʃən〕*n.* 時尚；時裝　　model〔ˈmɑdl̩〕*n.* 模特兒
commercial〔kəˈmɝʃəl〕*n.*（電視、廣播的）商業廣告
fit〔fɪt〕*adj.* 健康的　　***health club*** 健身中心
sale〔sel〕*n.* 銷售量　　***diet cola*** 健怡可樂
calorie〔ˈkælərɪ〕*n.* 卡路里　　indicate〔ˈɪndəˌket〕*v.* 顯示

overweight〔ˈovɚˈwet〕*adj.* 超重的；太胖的
physical〔ˈfɪzɪkl̩〕*adj.* 身體的
agricultural〔ˌægrɪˈkʌltʃərəl〕*adj.* 農業的
meal〔mil〕*n.* 一餐　　***burn off*** 燃燒
labor〔ˈlebɚ〕*n.* 勞動　　walking〔ˈwɔkɪŋ〕*n.* 步行；散步

lose〔luz〕*v.* 減少　　influence〔ˈɪnfluəns〕*v.* 影響
ad〔æd〕*n.* 廣告（= *advertisement*）　　fatty〔ˈfætɪ〕*adj.* 油膩的
soft drink 清涼飲料；不含酒精的飲料
sugary〔ˈʃugərɪ〕*adj.* 甜的；含糖的　　cereal〔ˈsɪrɪəl〕*n.* 穀物食品
even though 即使；雖然　　greasy〔ˈgrisɪ〕*adj.* 油膩的
burger〔ˈbɝgɚ〕*n.* 漢堡　　fries〔fraɪz〕*n. pl.* 薯條

fat〔fæt〕*n.* 脂肪
carbohydrate〔ˈkɑrboˈhaɪdret〕*n.* 碳水化合物
sodium〔ˈsodɪəm〕*n.* 鈉　　***in large quantities*** 大量地
triple〔ˈtrɪpḷ〕*adj.* 三倍的；三重的
extra〔ˈɛkstrə〕*adj.* 特別的
order〔ˈɔrdɚ〕*n.*（食物）一份　　***heart disease*** 心臟病

31.（**C**）(A) consequently〔ˈkɑnsəˌkwɛntlɪ〕*adv.* 因此
(B) subsequently〔ˈsʌbsəkwəntlɪ〕*adv.* 後來
(C) ***regularly***〔ˈrɛgjələlɪ〕*adv.* 規律地
(D) sequentially〔sɪˈkwɛnʃəlɪ〕*adv.* 連續地

32.（**B**）***get in shape*** 變得健康
(A) better off 較富裕

33.（**A**）(A) ***thin***〔θɪn〕*adj.* 瘦的；苗條的

34.（**B**）依句意，走路走得不「夠多」，選 (B) ***enough***。

35.（**B**）(A) tour〔tur〕*n.* 旅行
(B) ***trip***〔trɪp〕*n.*（因事的）外出；走一趟
(C) journey〔ˈdʒɝnɪ〕*n.* 旅程
(D) travel〔ˈtrævḷ〕*n.* 旅行

36. (**A**) (A) ***burn off*** 燒掉
(B) burn down 燒毀
(C) put down 放下；寫下
(D) cut off 切斷

37. (**D**) (A) actively〔'æktɪvlɪ〕*adv.* 積極地
(B) pleasantly〔'plɛzn̩tlɪ〕*adv.* 愉快地
(C) satisfactory〔,sætɪs'fæktərɪ〕*adj.* 令人滿意的
(D) ***poorly***〔'purlɪ〕*adv.* 差勁地

38. (**C**) (C) ***well-balanced***〔'wɛl'bælənst〕*adj.* 均衡的

39. (**B**) (A) pick on 挑剔；責備
(B) ***pick up*** 買
(C) make up 組成；和好；化妝
(D) give away 贈送

40. (**C**) (A) result from 起因於；由於
(B) reduce〔rɪ'djus〕*v.* 減少
(C) ***result in*** 導致；引起
(D) due to 由於

PART Ⅲ. 寫作：20%

寫一封信件或電子郵件（2-3段，共150-200字），給你正在找工作的朋友一些建議。

Looking for a job is not easy. But the following is some advice that I have found to be very useful in hunting for a job. First, be patient. Looking for the right job requires time and energy and, depending on the job market, you may not see positive results for several months. Second, before going to an interview, make sure you have prepared well by researching the company, which can be done online these days. This will help you ask the right questions during the interview, and it will reduce your tension if you have an idea of the company's background. Third, before you go into the interview, take five minutes to breathe deeply outside to loosen yourself up. Fourth, during the interview always sit up straight, chest out and shoulders squared, and be confident. Make sure you give a firm handshake and always look up and smile.

The last piece of advice is do not be late! Always give yourself an extra fifteen minutes for unforeseen circumstances like traffic jams, accidents or other incidents that might make you late. Follow the above advice and you will have a successful interview. Good luck!

國立中興大學九十三學年度
碩士班研究生入學考試英文試題

I. Reading Comprehension: 20%

Article One:
DALLAS, AFP

High levels of vitamin C in the bloodstream reduce the risk of stroke by 70 percent, according to a study in the Friday edition of the publication Stroke: Journal of the U.S. American Heart Association.

Over a 20-year period beginning in 1977, researchers separated 880 men and 1,214 women in rural Japan into four groups based on the level of vitamin C in their blood. Among the study's participants, 196 suffered strokes over the 20 years.

"To my knowledge, this is the first prospective study to make the correlation between vitamin C in the bloodstream and incidence of stroke," said the study's lead author Tetsuji Yokoyama, a researcher at the Medical Research Institute of Tokyo Medical and Dental University.

"The risk of stroke was 70 percent higher among those in the lowest quarter than those in the highest," Yokoyama said, noting that those numbers were directly associated with fruit and vegetable consumption.

An increase in fruit and vegetable consumption has been associated with a lower risk of stroke in previous studies.

Even high risk factors, including high blood pressure, smoking or heavy alcohol consumption, were somewhat offset by high concentrations of vitamin C, Yokoyama said.

"Thus, we recommend healthy behavior such as eating fruits and vegetables frequently, not smoking, avoiding excess drinking, and being moderately physically active," Yokoyama said.

1. Which is the most suitable title for Article One?
   (A) Vitamins and Stroke Prevention
   (B) Annual Health Report of the American Heart Association
   (C) Vitamin C in the Bloodstream Reduces Stroke Risk

2. Which behavior is not considered to put people at a high risk for stroke?
   (A) excessive exercise
   (B) heavy drinking
   (C) smoking

3. According to Article One, we can conclude that
   (A) The Journal of the U.S. American Heart Association publishes medical studies from around the world.
   (B) There is only one specific way of getting sufficient vitamin C.
   (C) The study is an American-Japanese joint effort.

4. Which statement is clearly made in the article?
   (A) Doctors around the world have come to an agreement that this study is accurate.
   (B) Many scientists are still unsure of the effect of vitamin C.
   (C) No details are given regarding other scientists' responses.

5. Which section in the newspaper does Article One belong to?
   (A) Medicine & Health
   (B) National News
   (C) International Issues

Article Two:

DANVILLE, Kentucky, AFP

Democratic and Republican vice-presidential nominees found common ground on foreign policy in their conversational and sole political debate of the campaign Thursday, but clashed over taxes and education.

Democratic Senator for Connecticut, Joseph Lieberman, the first Jew ever to run on a presidential ticket, and former defense secretary Dick Cheney of Wyoming, sparred politely for 90 minutes over issues central to this election campaign.

The two found bipartisan agreement as they discussed foreign policy, notably events in Yugoslavia — both stating the United States should keep up pressure on President Slobodan Milosevic to ensure his departure from the political scene.

"I think the United States and its European allies ought to do everything we can to encourage the people of Serbia to do exactly what they've been doing over the last few days — to rise up and end this reign of terror," said Lieberman.

Cheney agreed Washington should do everything possible to support Milosevic's departure.

Both candidates deplored escalating violence between Israelis and Palestinians in the West Bank and Gaza, underscoring the need to get the Middle East peace process back on track.

"I hope I might, through my friendships in Israel and throughout the Arab world, play a unique role in bringing peace to this sacred region of the world," said Lieberman, who is an Orthodox Jew.

Cheney, who was defense secretary during the 1991 Gulf War, expressed the hope the violence in the Middle East would end "as soon as possible."

"My guess is that the next administration is going to be the one that's going to have to come to grips with the current state of affairs there," Cheney said.

He also argued that the United States should consider new military action against Iraq if Baghdad tries to rebuild a nuclear capability.

On domestic policies, Cheney fired one of the first salvos, saying the Democrats were going back to tax-and-spend policies and that they refused to give back to all Americans part of the US$1.8 trillion budget surplus expected over the next decade in the form of a tax cut.

Lieberman argued the Democratic ticket wanted to use the money for socially responsible programs.

"We're taking US$300 billion off the top to put into a reserve fund," he said. "The rest of it, we're going to use for middle class tax cuts and investments in programs like education."

On education, Lieberman noted achievements of the Clinton-Gore administration, arguing that, "Average test scores are up and a lot of extraordinary work is being done by tens of thousands of parents and teachers and administrators all around America."

Not to be outdone, Cheney charged that 15 million children who have graduated from high school in the last 15 years can't read at a basic level.

Dressed in similar dark suits, Lieberman and Cheney exchanged an occasional joke but refrained from the at times acerbic attacks heard during White House rivals Al Gore and George W. Bush's debate on Tuesday.

"There were no bombshells, just soft lobs," Stephen Wayne, political science professor at Georgetown University, told AFP. "There were no mistakes. It was a fine, intelligent, mature discussion."

6. Article Two does not mention
   (A) the issues Cheney and Lieberman address.
   (B) how scholars reacted to their debate.
   (C) president Clinton's comments on their debate.

7. According to Article Two, Cheney and Lieberman seemed to
   (A) show unusual politeness in their argument.
   (B) have a strong dislike for each other.
   (C) exemplify politicians of two different generations.

8. As a Democratic candidate for Vice President, Lieberman must prove that
   (A) the Clinton-Gore administration has been doing a good job.
   (B) the Clinton-Gore administration needs some improvement.
   (C) He will be a better president than Gore.

9. Which topic is NOT addressed in the debate?
   (A) education (B) international affairs
   (C) immigration

10. Which nation is NOT mentioned in Article Two?
    (A) China (B) Serbia (C) Israel

II. Sentence Completion: 50%

11. Political issues tend to be ________, so they are often avoided on social occasions.
    (A) controversial (B) convertible (C) convicted

12. We ________ the holiday sales and bought new winter jackets for the whole family.
    (A) used up
    (B) came over
    (C) took advantage of

13. Hundreds of young fans ________ outside the concert hall, hoping to catch a glimpse of their favorite movie star.
    (A) disclosed (B) lingered (C) spotted

14. The man raced after the bus, ________ of catching it while it was stopped at the light.
    (A) in the hope (B) on the track (C) by way

15. To our disappointment, the legislator refused to ________ on the foreign labor policy.
    (A) get by (B) take a stand (C) do without

16. The origin of the Mid-Autumn Festival is an ancient ________ about Chang E.
    (A) legend (B) symptom (C) taboo

17. The Internet is creating increasing social isolation, ________ people are spending more and more time communicating with others through computers.
    (A) so (B) unless (C) though

18. Requests ________ books and audio tapes should be sent to the following address.
    (A) among (B) for (C) on

19. The percentage of cell phone users in Taiwan is 55% higher now than ________ five years ago.
    (A) it was (B) they were (C) there were

20. Did the news report say ________ were working for?
    (A) the country terrorists which
    (B) which country the terrorists
    (C) the which terrorists country

21. In the middle of the discussion, one of the lawyers angrily ________ out of the room.
    (A) scaled (B) stormed (C) flamed

22. In the botanical garden, there are a total of 2,000 different kinds of plants, including both native and exotic ________.
    (A) creatures (B) species (C) livings

23. Lydia planned to finish her research last night, but she ________ a problem: an important reference book was missing from the library.
    (A) ran into (B) did away with (C) got down to

24. It's too late to return this hat: the shop ________ closed by the time we get there.
(A) had been (B) will be (C) is being

25. It ________ a disaster had we forgotten to invite the Mayor to our party.
(A) must have been
(B) would have been
(C) was

26. This is not ________ the interior of the mansion was like before the renovation.
(A) which (B) what (C) where

27. Many elderly people live alone in their houses with no one ________ care of them.
(A) takes (B) to take (C) is taken

28. In another five minutes, we ________ here for two solid hours.
(A) have been waiting
(B) have waited
(C) will have been waiting

29. The boy drew a circle for the girl's head, and put two large black dots ________ it.
(A) around (B) inside (C) through

30. ________ 13 million people are suffering from dementia worldwide.
(A) Physicians approximately report that
(B) Physicians report that approximately
(C) Approximately that report physicians

31. Cable TV revolutionized communication; ________, the very existence of that service is now threatened by satellites.
(A) consequently (B) nevertheless (C) moreover

32. Personnel has had all the references ________.
(A) checking (B) checked (C) check

33. Mr. Young will import 80,000 more cars a year if quotas ________ lifted.
(A) have been (B) be (C) are

34. The survey indicates profits are up; business ________.
(A) is good (B) is being good (C) good

35. ________ Gerald has been promoted to Manager, he rarely takes coffee breaks with the rest of the employees.
(A) In case (B) Now that (C) At the time

Ⅲ. Composition: 30 %

Write an English composition of about 150 words on the topic given below:

The Importance of Weekends

國立中興大學九十三學年度
碩士班研究生入學考試英文試題詳解

I. 閱讀測驗：20%

Article One:

【譯文】

達拉斯，法新社

根據 Stroke 雜誌星期五那一期上面的研究報告指出，血流中含有大量的維他命 C，可以減少百分之七十的中風危險：這本雜誌是由美國心臟協會所發行。

自 1977 年開始，有超過二十年的期間，研究人員將住在日本鄉村的 880 位男性和 1214 位女性，根據其血液中的維他命 C 濃度，將他們分為四組。在參與這項研究的人當中，有 196 位在這二十幾年間中風。

「據我所知，這可能是第一個要了解血液中的維他命 C 和中風發生機率是否有關聯的研究，」這項研究的主要負責人 Tetsuji Yokoyama 說，他是東京醫科齒科大學醫學研究協會的研究人員。

「血液中維他命 C 含量最低的那四分之一的人，和含量最高的那四分之一的人比起來，他們中風的危險性高出百分之七十，」Yokoyama 說，他指出那些數字和吃多少水果及蔬菜有直接關聯。

之前的研究顯示，多吃水果及蔬菜和中風機率較低有關。

Yokoyama 說，就算是那些高危險性的因素，包括血壓高、吸煙，或是酗酒，多多少少都可以藉由高濃度的維他命 C 來補救。

「因此，我們要推薦一些健康的行為，像是常吃水果及蔬菜、不要吸煙、避免飲酒過量，還有讓身體保持適度地運動，」Yokoyama 說。

【答案】

1.（C）　2.（A）　3.（A）　4.（C）　5.（A）

【註】

AFP 法國新聞社；法新社（= *Agence France Preese*）
level〔ˈlɛvl̩〕*n.* 濃度；含量　vitamin〔ˈvaɪtəmɪn〕*n.* 維他命
bloodstream〔ˈblʌdˌstrim〕*n.* 血液；血流
risk〔rɪsk〕*n.* 風險；危險　stroke〔strok〕*n.* 中風
percent〔pɚˈsɛnt〕*n.* 百分比　study〔ˈstʌdɪ〕*n.* 研究
edition〔ɪˈdɪʃən〕*n.* 版（次）；版本
publication〔ˌpʌblɪˈkeʃən〕*n.* 出版物；雜誌
journal〔ˈdʒɝnl̩〕*n.* 雜誌；期刊

association〔əˌsoʃɪˈeʃən〕*n.* 協會
researcher〔rɪˈsɝtʃɚ〕*n.* 研究人員
separate〔ˈsɛpəˌret〕*v.* 使分開
rural〔ˈrʊrəl〕*adj.* 鄉村的；鄉下的　***based on*** 根據
participant〔pɚˈtɪsəpənt〕*n.* 參與者　suffer〔ˈsʌfɚ〕*v.* 罹患
to one's knowledge 據某人所知
prospective〔prəˈspɛktɪv〕*adj.* 預期的；可能的
correlation〔ˌkɔrəˈleʃən〕*n.* 關聯；相關性

incidence〔ˈɪnsədəns〕*n.* 發生率　lead〔lid〕*adj.* 主要的
author〔ˈɔθɚ〕*n.* 作者　medical〔ˈmɛdɪkl̩〕*adj.* 醫學的
research〔rɪˈsɝtʃ〕*n.* 研究　institute〔ˈɪnstəˌtjut〕*n.* 協會
dental〔ˈdɛntl̩〕*adj.* 牙齒的　quarter〔ˈkwɔrtɚ〕*n.* 四分之一
note〔not〕*v.* 特別提到　***be associated with*** 和～有關
consumption〔kənˈsʌmpʃən〕*n.* 吃；喝
previous〔ˈprivɪəs〕*adj.* 先前的　factor〔ˈfæktɚ〕*n.* 因素

high blood pressure 高血壓　alcohol〔'ælkə,hɔl〕*n.* 酒
somewhat〔'sʌm,hwɑt〕*adv.* 多少；有幾分
offset〔ɔf'sɛt〕*v.* 彌補　concentration〔,kɑnsn̩'treʃən〕*n.* 濃度
recommend〔,rɛkə'mɛnd〕*v.* 推薦
frequently〔'frikwəntlɪ〕*adv.* 經常
excess〔ɪk'sɛs〕*adj.* 過量的　drinking〔'drɪŋkɪŋ〕*n.* 飲酒
moderately〔'mɑdərɪtlɪ〕*adv.* 適度地

physically〔'fɪzɪkl̩ɪ〕*adv.* 身體上
active〔'æktɪv〕*adj.* 活躍的　suitable〔'sutəbl̩〕*adj.* 適合的
prevention〔prɪ'vɛnʃən〕*n.* 預防
annual〔'ænjuəl〕*adj.* 一年一度的
excessive〔ɪk'sɛsɪv〕*adj.* 過度的　conclude〔kən'klud〕*v.* 斷定
publish〔'pʌblɪʃ〕*v.* 出版　specific〔spɪ'sɪfɪk〕*adj.* 特定的
sufficient〔sə'fɪʃənt〕*adj.* 充分的　joint〔dʒɔɪnt〕*adj.* 共同的
statement〔'stetmənt〕*n.* 聲明

come to an agreement 達成協議
accurate〔'ækjərɪt〕*adj.* 精確的　detail〔'ditel〕*n.* 細節
regarding〔rɪ'gɑrdɪŋ〕*prep.* 關於
response〔rɪ'spɑns〕*n.* 反應　section〔'sɛkʃən〕*n.* 部門
international〔,ɪntə'næʃənl̩〕*adj.* 國際的
issue〔'ɪʃju〕*n.* 議題

Article Two:

【譯文】

DANVILLE，肯塔基州，法新社

民主黨和共和黨的副總統提名人選，在星期四爲了競選而舉辦唯一一場座談式一對一政治辯論時，發現他們在外交政策的立場是一樣的，但在稅和教育方面卻有所衝突。

身爲民主黨在康乃迪克州的參議員，Joseph Lieberman 是至今第一個由政黨提名參加總統大選的猶太人，他和來自懷俄明州的前任國防部長 Dick Cheney，針對這次選戰的重要議題，進行了九十分鐘有禮貌的辯論。

這兩個人在討論外交政策時，發現兩黨的意見是相同的，尤其是南斯拉夫的事 ── 他們兩個都說，美國應該繼續對 Slobodan Milosevic 總統施壓，確保他離開政治舞台。

「我認爲美國和它在歐洲的盟友，應該盡我們所能，鼓勵塞爾維亞人，就是要做他們在過去幾天所做的那些事 ── 反抗，並終結恐怖統治，」Lieberman 說。

Cheney 也同意美國政府應該盡一切可能地支持 Milosevic 的離開。

兩位候選人對於在巴勒斯坦西岸和加薩走廊，以、巴之間日漸擴大的暴力行爲，都深表遺憾，他們還強調有必要使中東的和平進程回到正軌。

「我希望我能透過和以色列與整個阿拉伯世界的友好關係，來扮演一個獨特的角色，並爲這個世界聖地帶來和平，」Lieberman 說，他是正統派的猶太人。

Cheney 在 1991 年波灣戰爭時，曾任國防部長，他表示希望中東的暴力行爲能「儘快」結束。

「我猜下一任政府將必須專心處理那裡目前的形勢，」Cheney 說。

他還主張說，如果巴格達試圖重建核子作戰能力的話，美國就應該考慮採取新的軍事行動來對付伊拉克。

在國內政策方面，Cheney 激起了第一次的掌聲，他說民主黨人將回到課稅花錢的政策，而且他們拒絕將美國人未來十年預計會有的美金 1.8 兆預算盈餘，以減稅的方式還給人民。

Lieberman 則主張，民主黨的候選人是要運用這筆錢，來從事一些社會責任計劃。

「我們將從總收入中拿出美金三千億，投入準備金中，」他說。「剩下的部分，我們將爲中產階級減稅，並投資一些計劃，像是教育。」

在教育方面，Lieberman 強調柯林頓及高爾政府的成就，他主張：「數萬名的父母、老師和行政官員，使得美國各地的考試平均成績提高，而且締造了許多傑出的成果。」

爲了不輸給對方，Cheney 指控在過去十五年，有一千五百萬名高中畢業生，連基本的的東西都看不懂。

穿著同樣的深色西裝，Lieberman 和 Cheney 偶爾會互相開開玩笑，可是他們會避免像星期二時，白宮的競爭對手高爾和喬治・布希辯論時，偶爾會聽到的尖刻攻擊。

「沒有什麼令人震驚的事，雙方都很客氣，」喬治城大學的政治學教授，Stephen Wayne 跟法新社這麼說。「沒有任何錯誤。那是一場很好、很聰明，而且成熟的討論。」

【答案】

6. (**C**)　7. (**A**)　8. (**A**)　9. (**C**)　10. (**A**)

【註】

AFP 法新社（= *Agence France Preese*）
Democratic〔ˌdɛməˈkrætɪk〕*adj.* 民主黨的
Republican〔rɪˈpʌblɪkən〕*adj.* 共和黨的
vice-presidential〔ˈvaɪsˌprɛzəˈdɛnʃəl〕*adj.* 副總統的
nominee〔ˌnɑməˈni〕*n.* 被提名的人
common ground 共同立場 ***foreign policy*** 外交政策
conversational〔ˌkɑnvɚˈseʃənḷ〕*adj.* 座談式的
sole〔sol〕*adj.* 單一的 political〔ˈpəlɪtɪkḷ〕*adj.* 政治的

debate〔dɪˈbet〕*n.* 辯論 campaign〔kæmˈpen〕*n.* 競選運動
clash〔klæʃ〕*v.* 起衝突 tax〔tæks〕*n.* 稅
senator〔ˈsɛnətɚ〕*n.* 參議員 Jew〔dʒu〕*n.* 猶太人
ever〔ˈɛvɚ〕*adv.* 至今 run〔rʌn〕*v.* 參加競選
presidential〔ˌprɛzəˈdɛnʃəl〕*adj.* 總統的
ticket〔ˈtɪkɪt〕*n.* 政黨提名的候選人
former〔ˈfɔrmɚ〕*adj.* 前任的 defense〔dɪˈfɛns〕*n.* 防禦
defense secretary 國防部長 spar〔spɑr〕*v.* 辯論
politely〔pəˈlaɪtlɪ〕*adv.* 有禮貌地
central〔ˈsɛntrəl〕*adj.* 主要的 ***election campaign*** 選戰

bipartisan〔baɪˈpɑrtəzṇ〕*adj.* 兩黨的
agreement〔əˈgrimənt〕*n.* 一致；同意
notably〔ˈnotəblɪ〕*adv.* 尤其 state〔stet〕*v.* 說明；陳述
keep up 繼續；保持 pressure〔ˈprɛʃɚ〕*n.* 壓力
ensure〔ɪnˈʃur〕*v.* 確保 departure〔dɪˈpɑrtʃɚ〕*n.* 離開
scene〔sin〕*n.* 舞台 European〔ˌjurəˈpiən〕*adj.* 歐洲的
ally〔əˈlaɪ〕*n.* 盟友；同盟國 ***ought to*** 應該（= *should*）
encourage〔ɪnˈkɝɪdʒ〕*v.* 鼓勵 exactly〔ɪgˈzæktlɪ〕*adv.* 正是

rise up 反抗 ***reign of terror*** 恐怖統治
candidate〔ˈkændəˌdet〕*n.* 候選人
deplore〔dɪˈplor〕*v.* 對…深表遺憾
escalating〔ˈɛskəˌletɪŋ〕*adj.* 逐漸擴大的
violence〔ˈvaɪələns〕*n.* 暴力行爲 Israeli〔ɪzˈrelɪ〕*n.* 以色列人
Palestinian〔ˌpæləsˈtɪnɪən〕*n.* 巴勒斯坦人
the West Bank 約旦河西岸地區 Gaza〔ˈgezə〕*n.* 加薩
underscore〔ˌʌndɚˈskɔr〕*v.* 強調
process〔ˈprɑsɛs〕*n.* 進程；過程 track〔træk〕*n.* 常軌；軌道
throughout〔θruˈaʊt〕*prep.* 遍及

unique〔juˈnik〕*adj.* 獨特的 sacred〔ˈsekrɪd〕*adj.* 神聖的
region〔ˈridʒən〕*n.* 地區；地帶
Orthodox〔ˈɔrθəˌdɑks〕*adj.* 正統派的 ***Gulf War*** 波斯灣戰爭
as soon as possible 儘快 guess〔gɛs〕*v.* 猜測
administration〔ədˌmɪnəˈstreʃən〕*n.* 政府；內閣
come to grips with 專心處理 current〔ˈkɜənt〕*adj.* 目前的
the state of affairs 形勢
argue〔ˈɑrgjʊ〕*v.* 主張 military〔ˈmɪləˌtɛrɪ〕*adj.* 軍事的
against〔əˈgɛnst〕*prep.* 對抗 rebuild〔riˈbɪld〕*v.* 重建

nuclear〔ˈnjuklɪɚ〕*adj.* 核子武器的
capability〔ˌkepəˈbɪlətɪ〕*n.* 戰鬥力
domestic〔dəˈmɛstɪk〕*adj.* 國內的
fire〔faɪr〕*v.* 激起 salvo〔ˈsælvo〕*n.* 齊發的掌聲
Democrat〔ˈdɛməˌkræt〕*n.* 民主黨黨員
tax-and-spend 課稅花錢的 trillion〔ˈtrɪljən〕*n.* 一兆
budget〔ˈbʌdʒɪt〕*n.* 預算 surplus〔ˈsɜplʌs〕*n.* 盈餘
expect〔ɪkˈspɛkt〕*v.* 預計會有 decade〔ˈdɛked〕*n.* 十年
cut〔kʌt〕*n.* 縮減；降低 socially〔ˈsoʃəlɪ〕*adv.* 社會上

responsible〔rɪ'spɑnsəbḷ〕*adj.* 責任的
program〔'progræm〕*n.* 計劃　billion〔'bɪljən〕*n.* 十億
off the top 從總收入中　reserve〔rɪ'zɝv〕*adj.* 準備的
reserve fund 準備金　rest〔rɛst〕*n.* 剩餘部份
middle class 中產階級　investment〔ɪn'vɛstmənt〕*n.* 投資
note〔not〕*v.* 特別提到　achievements〔ə'tʃivmənts〕*n. pl.* 成就
score〔skor〕*n.* 分數　extraordinary〔ɪk'strɔrdṇ,ɛrɪ〕*adj.* 傑出的
work〔wɝk〕*n.* 成果　***tens of thousands of*** 數萬的
administrator〔əd'mɪnə,stretɚ〕*n.* 行政官員
outdo〔aʊt'du〕*v.* 勝過；凌駕　charge〔tʃɑrdʒ〕*v.* 指控
suit〔sut〕*n.* 西裝　exchange〔ɪks'tʃendʒ〕*v.* 相互；互換

occasional〔ə'keʒənḷ〕*adj.* 偶爾的　refrain〔rɪ'fren〕*v.* 避免
at times 偶爾；有時　acerbic〔ə'sɝbɪk〕*adj.* 尖刻的
attack〔ə'tæk〕*n.* 攻擊　***White House*** 白宮
rival〔'raɪvḷ〕*n.* 競爭對手
bombshell〔'bɑm,ʃɛl〕*n.* 令人震驚的事　lob〔lɑb〕*n.* 高球
political science 政治學　professor〔prə'fɛsɚ〕*n.* 教授
intelligent〔ɪn'tɛlədʒənt〕*adj.* 聰明的
mature〔mə'tjʊr〕*adj.* 成熟的　address〔ə'drɛs〕*v.* 提出；說
scholar〔'skɑlɚ〕*n.* 學者　react〔rɪ'ækt〕*v.* 反應

comment〔'kɑmɛnt〕*n.* 評論　politeness〔pə'laɪtnɪs〕*n.* 禮貌
argument〔'ɑrgjəmənt〕*n.* 辯論　dislike〔dɪs'laɪk〕*n.* 討厭
exemplify〔ɪg'zɛmplə,faɪ〕*v.* 是…的例證
politician〔,pɑlə'tɪʃən〕*n.* 政治人物
generation〔,dʒɛnə'reʃən〕*n.* 一代
improvement〔ɪm'pruvmənt〕*n.* 改進
immigration〔,ɪmə'greʃən〕*n.* 移民

Ⅱ. 完成句子：50%

11.（**A**）(A) ***controversial***〔ˌkɑntrəˈvɝʃəl〕*adj.* 引起爭論的
(B) convertible〔kənˈvɝtəbl〕*adj.* 可改變的；敞篷的
(C) convict〔kənˈvɪkt〕*v.* 定罪
tend to V. 易於
occasion〔əˈkeʒən〕*n.* 場合

12.（**C**）(A) use up 用完
(B) come over 過來
(C) ***take advantage of*** 利用

13.（**B**）(A) disclose〔dɪsˈkloz〕*v.* 洩露；揭發
(B) ***linger***〔ˈlɪŋgɚ〕*v.* 徘徊；逗留
(C) spot〔spɑt〕*v.* 弄髒；看出
fan〔fæn〕*n.* 狂熱支持者；迷 ***concert hall*** 音樂廳
glimpse〔glɪmps〕*n.* 瞥見；看一眼

14.（**A**）(A) ***in the hope of + V-ing*** 希望～
(B) on the track of 追蹤
(C) by way of 經由
race〔res〕*v.* 快跑

15.（**B**）(A) get by 經過
(B) ***take a stand*** 表明立場
(C) do without 免除；可以不用
disappointment〔ˌdɪsəˈpɔɪntmənt〕*n.* 失望
legislator〔ˈlɛdʒɪsˌletɚ〕*n.* 立法委員
foreign labor 外勞
policy〔ˈpɑləsɪ〕*n.* 政策

16. (**A**) (A) ***legend*** 〔'lɛdʒənd〕*n.* 傳說
(B) symptom 〔'sɪmptəm〕*n.* 徵兆
(C) taboo 〔tə'bu〕*n.* 禁忌
origin 〔'ɔrədʒɪn〕*n.* 來源
Mid-Autumn Festival 中秋節
ancient 〔'enʃənt〕*adj.* 古老的

17. (**A**) (B) unless 〔ən'lɛs〕*conj.* 除非
isolation 〔ˌaɪsl̩'eʃən〕*n.* 隔離；孤立
communicate 〔kə'mjunəˌket〕*v.* 溝通；通訊

18. (**B**) request 〔rɪ'kwɛst〕*n.* 要求；需求 <*for*>
audio tape 錄音帶　following 〔'fɑləwɪŋ〕*adj.* 以下的
address 〔ə'drɛs〕*n.* 地址

19. (**A**) percentage 〔pɚ'sɛntɪdʒ〕*n.* 百分比　***cell phone*** 手機

20. (**B**) (A) terrorist 〔'tɛrərɪst〕*n.* 恐怖份子

21. (**B**) (A) scale 〔skel〕*v.* 攀登；爬上
(B) ***storm*** 〔stɔrm〕*v.* 猛衝
(C) flame 〔flem〕*v.* 燃燒
lawyer 〔'lɔjɚ〕*n.* 律師
angrily 〔'æŋgrɪlɪ〕*adv.* 憤怒地

22. (**B**) (A) creature 〔'kritʃɚ〕*n.* 生物
(B) ***species*** 〔'spiʃɪz〕*n.* 物種
(C) living 〔'lɪvɪŋ〕*n.* 生活；生計
botanical 〔bo'tænɪkl̩〕*adj.* 植物的
botanical garden 植物園
native 〔'netɪv〕*adj.* 原產的；本地的
exotic 〔ɪg'zɑtɪk〕*adj.* 外來的

23. (**A**) (A) ***run into*** 遭遇（困難）；陷入（困境）
(B) do away with 廢除
(C) get down to 降到
research〔rɪ'sɝtʃ〕*n.* 研究
reference book 參考書

24. (**B**) 依句意爲未來式，故選 (B) ***will be***。
by the time 到了…時候

25. (**B**) 依句意爲「與過去事實相反的假設」，主要子句須用「should/would/could/might + have + p.p.」，故選 (B) ***would have been***。
disaster〔dɪz'æstɚ〕*n.* 重大的失敗；災難
mayor〔'meɚ〕*n.* 市長

26. (**B**) ***what～is like*** ～的樣子
interior〔ɪn'tɪrɪɚ〕*n.* 內部
mansion〔'mænʃən〕*n.* 豪宅
renovation〔,rɛnə'veʃən〕*n.* 整修

27. (**B**) 不定詞片語 to take care of them 做形容詞用，修飾 no one。
elderly〔'ɛldɚlɪ〕*adj.* 年老的
alone〔ə'lon〕*adv.* 獨自

28. (**C**) 依句意，爲未來式，故選 (C) ***will have been waiting***。
solid〔'sɑlɪd〕*adj.* 整整的

29. (**B**) 依句意，「在…之內」，故選 (B) ***inside***。
circle〔'sɝkḷ〕*n.* 圓
dot〔dɑt〕*n.* 點

30. (**B**) ***suffer from*** 罹患
dementia (dɪ'mɛnʃɪə) *n.* 痴呆
worldwide ('wɝld'waɪd) *adv.* 在全世界
physician (fə'zɪʃən) *n.* 內科醫師
report (rɪ'port) *v.* 報告；傳達說
approximately (ə'prɑksəmɪtlɪ) *adv.* 大約

31. (**B**) (A) consequently ('kɑnsə,kwɛntlɪ) *adv.* 因此
(B) ***nevertheless*** (,nɛvəðə'lɛs) *adv.* 儘管如此；然而
(C) moreover (mor'ovɚ) *adv.* 此外
cable TV 有線電視
revolutionize (,rɛvə'luʃən,aɪz) *v.* 徹底改革
communication (kə,mjunə'keʃen) *n.* 通訊
very ('vɛrɪ) *adj.* 正是（那個）
existence (ɪg'zɪstəns) *n.* 存在
threaten ('θrɛtn̩) *v.* 威脅
satellite ('sætl̩,aɪt) *n.* 人造衛星

32. (**B**) personnel (,pɝsn̩'ɛl) *n.* 人事室
reference ('rɛfərəns) *n.* 保證（人）；推薦信
check (tʃɛk) *v.* 檢查；核對

33. (**C**) import (ɪm'port) *v.* 進口；輸入
quota ('kwotə) *n.*（製造；輸出入的）配額
lift (lɪft) *v.* 提高

34. (**A**) survey (sɚ've) *n.* 調查
indicate ('ɪndə,ket) *v.* 指出
profit ('prɑfɪt) *n.* 利潤

35. (**B**) (A) in case 以防萬一
(B) ***now that*** 既然
promote〔prə'mot〕*v.* 升遷
rarely〔'rɛrlɪ〕*adv.* 很少
coffee break 喝咖啡的休息時間
employee〔,ɛmplɔɪ'i〕*n.* 職員

Ⅲ. 作文：30%

The Importance of Weekends

Weekends are very important. Why? We work all week from Monday to Friday and we need time off to relax and do the things we want to do. The weekends are a great opportunity for families to go out and eat together and for friends to make plans to catch a movie or go shopping. It gives us something to look forward to other than work during the week.

The weekends can help revitalize us for another long week of work. It is not healthy to be cooped up inside an office all day. Weekends give friends and families a chance to catch up with each other. With work taking up so much of our lives, its easy to forget what's really important these days. So go have fun and make the most of your next weekend!

國立彰化師範大學九十三學年度 碩士班研究生入學考試英文試題

I. Vocabulary & Grammar: Choose the best answer for each blank of the following sentences（選填句中空格之最佳答案：或 a 或 b 或 c）：50%

1. The parliament ________ the constitution to protect private property.
   (A) amended (B) demanded (C) repaired

2. Many years after the Democratic Party ________ power, the parliament added the special clause.
   (A) made (B) took (C) wrote

3. Southeast Asia is ________ the home base of the Islamic militant group.
   (A) because of (B) owing to (C) regarded as

4. The Hong Kong press reported that China has ________ heavy military equipment into the southwestern province.
   (A) moved (B) gave (C) believed

5. Can you tell them ________
   (A) how high it is? (B) how high is it?
   (C) how high it is.

6. He doesn't believe weapons of ________ will be found.
   (A) mass construction (B) mass instruction
   (C) mass destruction

7. The FBI is concerned the organization will attempt to ________ another major attack.
(A) use (B) improve (C) launch

8. The former special adviser left his ________ as the top U.S. weapons inspector.
(A) place (B) position (C) region

9. The ________ of some bloated state firms would be a slow process.
(A) trimming (B) training (C) leaving

10. I shall never forget ________ you play piano.
(A) hearing (B) to hear (C) to be heard

11. He was following ________ behind.
(A) closely (B) close (C) closed

12. I forgot ________ him books for his birthday.
(A) to buy (B) bought (C) to be bought

13. My friend is engaged ________ another line.
(A) on (B) from (C) for

14. It is nice ________ you to call back.
(A) for (B) of (C) by

15. He always buys ________, having worked for the company for a long time.
(A) cheaply (B) by cheap (C) cheap

16. The causes of the war are ________.
(A) as follows (B) as following (C) by following

17. He has been ________ for a long time.
(A) sick (B) illness (C) recovery

18. ________ a Sunday morning, he went to school.
(A) At (B) In (C) On

19. My hat blew ________.
(A) on (B) out (C) off

20. He married ________.
(A) youngly (B) young (C) youngster

21. Are cats ________ animals?
(A) cleanly (B) clean (C) cleaning

22. You are looking ________.
(A) loving (B) loved (C) lovely

23. It is beginning ________.
(A) raining (B) to rain (C) in raining

24. He is beginning ________ English.
(A) to learn (B) learning (C) to be learned

25. All my plans have gone ________.
(A) wrong (B) wrongly (C) wrongful

Ⅱ. Cloze Test: Choose the best answer for each blank. (20%; 2% for each question)

When Mr. Yoji Morita married Miss Tamiko Minemura last year, his father __(1)__ the couple's new life together __(2)__ a railroad train __(3)__ a long unknown track. "There may be curves and dark tunnels ahead," he told them, "but we wish you a safe __(4)__."

1. (A) complained (B) compared (C) competed (D) considered
2. (A) with (B) off (C) to (D) for
3. (A) on (B) to (C) of (D) under
4. (A) journey (B) month (C) company (D) stop

Most women in Ghana—the educated and illiterate, the __(5)__ and rural, the young and old—work to earn __(6)__ income in addition to maintaining their roles as housewives and mothers. Most of Ghana's working women are farmers and traders. __(7)__ one woman in five or even fewer, can be classified __(8)__ simply a housewife.

5. (A) rich (B) wild (C) urban (D) pretty
6. (A) this (B) for (C) no (D) an
7. (A) With (B) Only (C) If (D) Although
8. (A) being (B) by (C) as (D) of

Every day ___(9)___ sundown this week, the Summer Film Festival will be showing a film you should really see. A lot of adventure films were made in Hollywood ___(10)___ the 1930s and 1940s, but even in that crowd, *The Adventures of Robin Hood* stands out.

9. (A) of (B) in (C) when (D) at
10. (A) during (B) since (C) from (D) back

Ⅲ. Reading Comprehension: Answer the following questions according to the articles. Choose the best answer for each question: (30%; 3% for each question)

Americans this year will swallow 15,000 tons of aspirin, one of the safest and most effective drugs invented by man. The most popular medicine in the world today, it is an effective pain reliever. Its bad effects are relatively mild, and it is cheap.

For millions of people suffering from arthritis, it is the only thing that works. Aspirin, in short, is truly the 20th-century wonder drug. It is also the second largest suicide drug and is the leading cause of poisoning among children. It has side effects that, although relatively mild, are largely unrecognized among users.

Although aspirin was first sold by a German company in 1899, it has been around much longer than that. Hippocrates, in ancient Greece, understood the medical value of the leaves and tree bark which today are known to contain salicylates, the chemical in aspirin. During the 19th century, there was a great deal of experimentation in Europe with this chemical, and it led to the introduction of aspirin. By 1915, aspirin tablets were available in the United States.

A small quantity of aspirin (two five-grain tablets) relieves pain and inflammation. It also reduces fever by interfering with some of the body's reactions. Specifically, aspirin seems to slow down the formation of the acids involved in pain and the complex chemical reactions that cause fever. The chemistry of these acids is not fully understood, but the slowing effect of aspirin is well known.

Aspirin is very irritating to the stomach lining, and many aspirin takers complain about upset stomach. There is a right way and a wrong way to take aspirin. The best is to chew the tablets before swallowing them with water, but few people can stand the bitter taste. Some people suggest crushing the tablets in milk or orange juice and drinking that.

1. This article mainly discusses:
   (A) the history of aspirin.
   (B) only the good things about aspirin.
   (C) only the bad things about aspirin.
   (D) both the good and bad things about aspirin.

2. The information in paragraph 2 shows that:
   (A) aspirin can be dangerous.
   (B) aspirin is always safe.
   (C) aspirin has been around a long time.
   (D) aspirin is liked by children.

3. Paragraph 4 describes:
   (A) how aspirin works in the body.
   (B) the side effects of aspirin.
   (C) how to take aspirin.
   (D) the chemistry of aspirin.

4. The author of this article seems to be:
   (A) in favor of aspirin.
   (B) against the use of aspirin.
   (C) not interested in aspirin.
   (D) completely unsatisfied with aspirin.

5. In paragraph 1, "**it** is an effective pain reliever," **it** refers to
   (A) pain reliever. (B) drug.
   (C) aspirin. (D) the bad effect.

6. In the last sentence of paragraph 5, "some people suggest drinking **that**," **that** refers to:
   (A) aspirin swallowed with water.
   (B) aspirin crushed in milk or orange juice.
   (C) the right way to take aspirin.
   (D) the wrong way to take aspirin.

When children begin school in the United States, at the age of five or so, they are usually clearly either right-handed or left-handed. In schools in the United States, left-handed children are usually allowed to learn to write, cut with scissors, and work with art supplies with their preferred hand. But in the past, it was often the custom to force left-handed children to learn to write and do other work with the right hand. In some countries, this is still done today. Researchers do not agree on the effects of such a change. Some say that forcing a left-handed child to be right-handed can cause emotional and physical problems and even learning difficulties. They say such a child may start to confuse the directions left and right and reverse letters and numbers accidentally, such as writing 36 instead of 63. Other specialists laugh at such findings and say that changing children's handedness will have no such effects. Perhaps part of the disagreement is due to the fact that children differ in how strong their hand preference is. Some left-handers are so strongly left-handed that they fight any change, and if they are forced, they may indeed develop problems. Others are not so strongly left-handed and can make the change without any great difficulty.

7. According to the passage, schools in the U.S. ________
   (A) want left-handed children to write with the right hand.
   (B) let left-handed children write with the left hand.
   (C) help left-handed children learn to write with both hands.
   (D) have found that left-handed children have more difficulty in learning than do right-handed children.

8. Teaching a left-handed child to write with the right hand ________
   (A) usually causes the child to have learning difficulties.
   (B) does not cause any problems.
   (C) usually causes the child to have emotional problems.
   (D) may or may not cause problems for the child.

9. What is the "disagreement" (line 16) about?
   (A) whether left-handers are ill or not
   (B) the effects of teaching left-handers to write with the right hand
   (C) how strongly left-handed some people are
   (D) how often left-handers have fighting problems

10. How do the authors of this passage feel about teaching left-handers to use their right hands?
   (A) They think it should not be done to children who strongly prefer the left hand.
   (B) They think it prevents many serious problems.
   (C) They think it should be done to left-handers.
   (D) They think it should never be done to any left-handers.

國立彰化師範大學九十三學年度
碩士班研究生入學考試英文試題詳解

I. 字彙與文法：50％

1.（ **A** ） (A) ***amend*** ﹝ə'mɛnd﹞*v.* 修正
(B) demand ﹝dɪ'mænd﹞*v.* 要求
(C) repair ﹝rɪ'pɛr﹞*v.* 修理
parliament ﹝'pɑrləmənt﹞*n.* 國會；議會
constitution ﹝ˌkɑnstə'tjuʃən﹞*n.* 憲法
private ﹝'praɪvɪt﹞*adj.* 私人的
property ﹝'prɑpətɪ﹞*n.* 財產

2.（ **B** ） (B) ***take power*** 掌權
the Democratic Party （美國的）民主黨
add ﹝æd﹞*v.* 增加
clause ﹝klɔz﹞*n.* 條款

3.（ **C** ） (B) owing to 由於
(C) ***regard*** ﹝rɪ'gɑrd﹞*v.* 認為
southeast ﹝ˌsaʊθ'ist﹞*adj.* 東南的
home base 總部
Islamic ﹝ɪs'læmɪk﹞*adj.* 伊斯蘭教的；回教的
militant ﹝'mɪlətənt﹞*adj.* 好鬥的

4.（ **A** ） (B) move ﹝muv﹞*v.* 使移動
press ﹝prɛs﹞*n.* 新聞界
heavy ﹝'hɛvɪ﹞*adj.* 大量的；重裝備的
military ﹝'mɪləˌtɛrɪ﹞*adj.* 軍隊的；軍事的
equipment ﹝ɪ'kwɪpmənt﹞*n.* 裝備
province ﹝'prɑvɪns﹞*n.* 省

5. (**A**) 空格須填一名詞子句做 tell 的直接受詞，名詞子句中，須用直說法，主詞與動詞不須倒裝，選 (A)。

6. (**C**) (A) mass〔mæs〕*adj.* 大規模的
construction〔kən'strʌkʃən〕*n.* 建設
(B) instruction〔ɪn'strʌkʃən〕*n.* 指示
(C) ***destruction***〔dɪ'strʌkʃən〕*n.* 破壞；屠殺
weapon〔'wɛpən〕*n.* 武器

7. (**C**) (C) ***launch***〔lɔntʃ〕*v.* 發動
concerned〔kən'sɝnd〕*adj.* 擔心的
organization〔,ɔrgənə'zeʃən〕*n.* 組織
attempt〔ə'tɛmpt〕*v.* 試圖
major〔'medʒɚ〕*adj.* 重大的
attack〔ə'tæk〕*n.* 攻擊

8. (**B**) (B) ***position***〔pə'zɪʃən〕*n.* 職位
(C) region〔'ridʒən〕*n.* 地區
former〔'fɔrmɚ〕*adj.* 前任的
adviser〔əd'vaɪzɚ〕*n.* 顧問
leave〔liv〕*v.* 辭去（職務）
inspector〔ɪn'spɛktɚ〕*n.* 檢查員

9. (**A**) (A) ***trimming***〔'trɪmɪŋ〕*n.* 整頓
(B) training〔'trenɪŋ〕*n.* 訓練
bloated〔'blotɪd〕*adj.* 過大的
state〔stet〕*adj.* 國家的　　firm〔fɝm〕*n.* 公司

10. (**A**) forget + to V. 忘記去～（動作未發生）
forget + V-ing 忘記曾經～（動作已發生）
依句意，選 (A)。

11. (**B**) ***follow close behind*** 緊跟在後
而 (A) closely 「密切地」，則不合句意。

12. (**A**) ***forget to V.*** 忘記去～

13. (**A**) engaged〔ɪn'gedʒd〕*adj.* 著手於…的
be engaged on the other line 在講另外一線電話

14. (**B**) 「It is + 形容詞 + of + 人 + to V.」用以形容「某人做某事是…的」。
call back 回電話

15. (**A**) (A) ***cheaply***〔'tʃiplɪ〕*adv.* 便宜地

16. (**A**) (A) ***as follows*** 如下所述
(B) following〔'fɑləwɪŋ〕*adj.* 下述的；以下的

17. (**A**) (B) illness〔'ɪlnɪs〕*n.* 疾病
(C) recovery〔rɪ'kʌvərɪ〕*n.* 康復

18. (**C**) 指「特定日子的早、午、晚」，介系詞須用 on。

19. (**C**) blow〔blo〕*v.* 被（風）吹走
blow off 被吹掉

20. (**B**) ***marry young*** 很年輕就結婚

(A) youngly〔 'jʌŋlɪ 〕*adv.* 年輕地
(C) youngster〔 'jʌŋstɚ 〕*n.* 年輕人

21.（ **B** ） 空格應填形容詞，故選 (B) ***clean***「乾淨的」。
22.（ **C** ） (A) loving〔 'lʌvɪŋ 〕*adj.* 愛（某人）的；溫柔的
(C) ***lovely***〔 'lʌvlɪ 〕*adj.* 美麗的；可愛的

23.（ **B** ） ***begin + to V.*** 開始～

24.（ **A** ）

25.（ **A** ） ***go wrong*** 出錯
(B) wrongly〔 'rɔŋlɪ 〕*adv.* 錯誤地；非法地
(C) wrongful〔 'rɔŋfəl 〕*adj.* 壞的；邪惡的

II. 克漏字：20%

【譯文】

去年 Yoji Morita 先生和 Tamiko Minemura 小姐結婚時，他父親將這對夫婦共同的新生活，比喻成行駛在一條漫長而未知的軌道上的火車，「前方可能會有轉彎或黑暗的隧道，」他告訴他們說：「但我祝福你們有趟安全的旅程。」

【註】

couple〔 'kʌpl̩ 〕*n.* 夫婦
railroad〔 'rel,rod 〕*adj.* 鐵路的
unknown〔 ʌn'non 〕*adj.* 未知的
track〔 træk 〕*n.* 軌道　　curve〔 kɝv 〕*n.* 轉彎
tunnel〔 'tʌnl̩ 〕*n.* 隧道　　ahead〔 ə'hɛd 〕*adv.* 在前面

1. (**B**) (A) complain〔kəm'plen〕*v.* 抱怨
(B) ***compare***〔kəm'pɛr〕*v.* 比喻
(C) compete〔kəm'pit〕*v.* 競爭

2. (**C**) ***compare*** A ***to*** B 將A比喻爲B

3. (**A**)

4. (**A**) (A) ***journey***〔'dʒɝnɪ〕*n.* 旅程
(D) stop〔stɑp〕*n.* 候車站

在迦納的大多數婦女——有受過教育和目不識丁的、都市和鄉下的、年輕和老的——除了擔起家庭主婦和母親的職責之外，還會工作以賺取一份所得。迦納大多數的職業婦女都是農夫和商人。只有五分之一或更少的婦女，可以被歸類爲單純的家庭主婦。

【註】

educated〔'ɛdʒə,ketɪd〕*adj.* 受過教育的
illiterate〔ɪ'lɪtərɪt〕*adj.* 目不識丁的；文盲的
rural〔'rurəl〕*adj.* 鄉下的　***in addition to*** 除了…之外
maintain〔men'ten〕*v.* 負擔；維持
role〔rol〕*n.* 職責　working〔'wɝkɪŋ〕*adj.* 有職業的
trader〔'tredɚ〕*n.* 商人　classify〔'klæsə,faɪ〕*v.* 歸類爲
simply〔'sɪmplɪ〕*adv.* 全然；絕對地

5. (**C**) (C) ***urban***〔'ɝbən〕*adj.* 都市的
(D) pretty〔'prɪtɪ〕*adj.* 漂亮的

6. (**D**) income 是可數名詞，故空格須填冠詞，選 (D) ***an***。

7.（**B**）依句意，選 (B) ***only***「只有」。

8.（**C**）***be classified as*** 被歸類爲

這個星期每天日落之後，夏日電影節都會播放一部你眞的應該看的影片。有很多動作片都是在 1930 和 1940 年代間，在好萊塢拍攝的，但就算在那麼多部影片中，「羅賓漢」還是一部很出色的影片。

【註】

sundown〔ˈsʌn,daʊn〕*n.* 日落
festival〔ˈfɛstəvl̩〕*n.* 表演季　　***adventure film*** 動作片
Hollywood〔ˈhɑlɪ,wʊd〕*n.* 好萊塢
crowd〔kraʊd〕*n.* 許多　　***stand out*** 顯目；突出

9.（**D**）***at sundown*** 在日落時

10.（**A**）表「在～期間」，選 (A) ***during***。

Ⅲ. 閱讀測驗：30%

【譯文】

今年，美國人將呑下一萬五千噸的阿斯匹靈，那是人類所發明的藥品中，最安全，而且最有效的。它是現今世界中，最受歡迎的藥，也是最有效的止痛藥。它的不良影響相當輕微，而且它很便宜。

對患有關節炎的數百萬人來說，它是唯一有效的藥。總之，阿斯匹靈眞的是二十世紀的特效藥。它也是第二常用的自殺藥品，而且還是造成孩童藥物中毒的主要原因。雖然它的副作用比較輕微，但很多使用者都不知道它有副作用。

雖然阿斯匹靈一開始是在 1899 年時，由一家德國公司開始販賣，但它存在的時間則更為久遠。在古希臘時代，希波克拉底得知了樹葉與樹皮的醫學價值，那些東西含有我們現在所知的水楊酸，也就是阿斯匹靈裡面的化學成分。在十九世紀時，歐洲有許多關於這種化學物質的實驗，因而導致了阿斯匹靈的問世。到了 1915 年，美國已經可以買到阿斯匹靈藥片了。

少量的阿斯匹靈（兩片五喱的藥片），可以止痛和消炎。它還可以藉由干擾某些身體反應，來達到退燒的效果。具體地說，阿斯匹靈好像可以使與疼痛有關的酸性物質慢一點形成，並且緩和導致發燒的複雜化學反應。我們對這些酸性物質的化學性質不是很瞭解，但卻很清楚阿斯匹靈有減緩的效果。

阿斯匹靈對於胃壁黏膜來說非常刺激，所以許多服用阿斯匹靈的人會抱怨胃不舒服。服用阿斯匹靈有正確和錯誤的方式。最好的做法就是，在把藥片和水一起吞下去之前，先把它嚼碎，但是很少人可以忍受這種苦味。有些人建議，可以把藥片壓碎之後，倒進牛奶或柳橙汁裡，然後再喝下去。

【答案】

1.（**D**）　2.（**A**）　3.（**A**）　4.（**A**）　5.（**C**）　6.（**B**）

【註】

swallow〔ˈswɑlo〕*v.* 吞下　ton〔tʌn〕*n.* 噸
aspirin〔ˈæspərɪn〕*n.* 阿斯匹靈
effective〔əˈfɛktɪv〕*adj.* 有效的　***pain reliever*** 止痛藥
relatively〔ˈrɛlətɪvlɪ〕*adv.* 比較上；相當地
mild〔maɪld〕*adj.* 溫和的　***suffer from*** 罹患

arthritis〔ɑr'θraɪtɪs〕*n.* 關節炎
work〔wɝk〕*v.* 有效　　***in short*** 總之
wonder drug 特效藥
suicide〔'suə,saɪd〕*n.* 自殺　　leading〔'lidɪŋ〕*adj.* 主要的
poisoning〔'pɔɪzṇɪŋ〕*n.* 中毒　　***side effect*** 副作用
unrecognized〔ʌn'rɛkəg,naɪzd〕*adj.* 不知道的
ancient〔'enʃənt〕*adj.* 古代的
Greece〔gris〕*n.* 希臘
medical〔'mɛdɪkḷ〕*adj.* 醫學的
bark〔bɑrk〕*n.* 樹皮　　contain〔kən'ten〕*v.* 含有

salicylate〔sə'lɪsə,let〕*n.* 水楊酸鹽
chemical〔'kɛmɪkḷ〕*n.* 化學物質
a great deal of 許多的
experimentation〔ɪk,spɛrəmɛn'teʃən〕*n.* 實驗
lead to 導致　　introduction〔,ɪntrə'dʌkʃən〕*n.* 引進；創始
tablet〔'tæblɪt〕*n.* 藥片　　available〔ə'veləbḷ〕*adj.* 可獲得的
grain〔gren〕*n.* 喱（一喱等於 0.0648 克）
relieve〔rɪ'liv〕*v.* 減輕；緩和

inflammation〔,ɪnflə'meʃən〕*n.* 發炎
reduce〔rɪ'djus〕*v.* 降低　　fever〔'fivɚ〕*n.* 發燒
interfere〔,ɪntɚ'fɪr〕*v.* 干擾 <*with*>
reaction〔rɪ'ækʃən〕*n.* 反應
specifically〔spɪ'sɪfɪkḷɪ〕*adv.* 具體地說　　***slow down*** 減緩
formation〔fɔr'meʃən〕*n.* 形成　　acid〔'æsɪd〕*n.* 酸性物質
involved〔ɪn'vɑlvd〕*adj.* 有關的 <*in*>
complex〔kəm'plɛks；'kɑmplɛks〕*adj.* 複雜的
chemistry〔'kɛmɪstrɪ〕*n.* 化學性質

slowing〔ˈsloɪŋ〕*adj.* 減緩的
irritating〔ˈɪrəˌtetɪŋ〕*adj.* 刺激的
stomach〔ˈstʌmək〕*n.* 胃　　lining〔ˈlaɪnɪŋ〕*n.* 襯裡；黏膜
upset〔ʌpˈsɛt〕*adj.* 不舒服的　　chew〔tʃu〕*v.* 咀嚼
stand〔stænd〕*v.* 忍受　　bitter〔ˈbɪtɚ〕*adj.* 苦的
taste〔test〕*n.* 味道　　crush〔krʌʃ〕*v.* 壓碎
author〔ˈɔθɚ〕*n.* 作者　　***in favor of*** 贊成；支持
against〔əˈgɛnst〕*prep.* 反對

【譯文】

在美國，當孩子們開始上學時，大約是五歲左右，通常就能明顯分出是右撇子還是左撇子。在美國的學校，慣用左手的學生，在學寫字、拿剪刀剪東西，和使用美術用具時，通常會被允許用他們比較愛用的那隻手。但是在過去，常常有一種習俗，就是強迫慣用左手的小孩，學著用右手來寫字或做其他事。在某些國家，到現在還是這樣做。研究人員無法認同這樣的改變所帶來的影響。有些研究人員說，強迫慣用左手的小孩習慣使用右手，會造成情感上和身體上的問題，而且甚至會有學習障礙。他們指出這樣的孩子，可能會開始搞不清楚左右邊，然後還會忽然把字母和數字顛倒，像是把 63 寫成 36。其他的專家則不把這樣的發現當一回事，而且還說，改變孩子使用右手或左手的習慣，並不會造成這些影響。也許部分的意見分歧，是由於孩子們偏好使用某一隻手的程度不同。有些左撇子堅決要使用左手，以致於反對任何改變，所以如果他們被強迫改變，可能就眞的會出問題。有些就沒有這麼堅決要用左手，所以可以毫無困難地改變。

【答案】

7. (**B**)　　8. (**D**)　　9. (**B**)　　10. (**A**)

【註】

or so 大約　right-handed〔ˈraɪtˈhændɪd〕*adj.* 慣用右手的
left-handed〔ˈlɛftˈhændɪd〕*adj.* 慣用左手的
allow〔əˈlaʊ〕*v.* 允許
scissors〔ˈsɪzɚz〕*n. pl.* 剪刀
supply〔səˈplaɪ〕*n.* 日常用品　***art supplies*** 美術用品
preferred〔prɪˈfɝd〕*adj.* 比較喜歡的
custom〔ˈkʌstəm〕*n.* 習俗　force〔fɔrs〕*v.* 強迫
researcher〔rɪˈsɝtʃɚ〕*n.* 研究人員　effect〔ɪˈfɛkt〕*n.* 影響

emotional〔ɪˈmoʃənl̩〕*adj.* 情感上的
physical〔ˈfɪzɪkl̩〕*adj.* 身體上的
reverse〔rɪˈvɝs〕*v.* 顚倒　letter〔ˈlɛtɚ〕*n.* 字母
accidentally〔ˌæksəˈdɛntl̩ɪ〕*adv.* 忽然
instead of 而不是　specialist〔ˈspɛʃəlɪst〕*n.* 專家
laugh at 不把…當一回事；嘲笑
finding〔ˈfaɪndɪŋ〕*n.* 發現
handedness〔ˈhændɪdnɪs〕*n.* 偏手性；使用右手或左手的習慣
disagreement〔ˌdɪsəˈgrimənt〕*n.* 意見的分歧

due to 由於　differ〔ˈdɪfɚ〕*v.* 不同
preference〔ˈprɛfərəns〕*n.* 偏好
left-hander〔ˈlɛftˈhændɚ〕*n.* 左撇子
strongly〔ˈstrɔŋlɪ〕*adv.* 強烈地；堅決地
fight〔faɪt〕*v.* 反對　indeed〔ɪnˈdid〕*adv.* 眞正地
develop〔dɪˈvɛləp〕*v.* 逐漸顯現出
prefer〔prɪˈfɝ〕*v.* 比較喜歡　prevent〔prɪˈvɛnt〕*v.* 預防

台北市立師範學院九十三學年度 碩士班研究生入學考試英文試題

I. Vocabulary: 10%

Choose the one word or phrase that best keeps the meaning of the original sentence if it is substituted for the underlined word or phrase.

1. This poem was published anonymously.
   (A) seriously (B) without a name
   (C) in a short time (D) happily

2. We made roughly $20,000 last year.
   (A) about (B) possibly
   (C) easily (D) more than

3. I'm afraid their relationship may deteriorate in time.
   (A) develop (B) continue
   (C) grow (D) fall apart

4. Although I do not agree with the senator's policies, her hard work is laudable.
   (A) praiseworthy (B) laughable
   (C) realistic (D) helpful

5. The president hopes to avert a crisis by improving bilateral relations.
   (A) avoid (B) regulate
   (C) propagate (D) condemn

6. To read the biographies of "loners" who followed their own trail is exhilarating, not only because they beat the system, but because their system was better than the one that they beat.
   (A) arresting (B) stimulating
   (C) devastating (D) modeling

7. In the dispute the injured party has no feasible method against the judge who, in his view, has treated him ill.
   (A) compatible (B) practicable
   (C) changeable (D) flexible

8. The wing of the house must be reconstructed promptly; there is a danger, it will collapse.
   (A) resigned (B) restrained
   (C) restored (D) refund

9. Each time they amended the plan, they made it worse.
   (A) commanded (B) changed
   (C) compelled (D) clarified

10. The “two-cultures” controversy has quieted down some, but it is still with us, still unsettled because of the polarized views set out by <u>polemic</u> opinion leaders.
    (A) argumentative (B) quarrelsome
    (C) frustrating (D) hostile

II. Grammar: 10%

Choose the <u>one</u> word or phrase that best completes the sentence.

11. ________ physicist Gabriel Fahrenheit invented the mercury thermometer in 1714.
    (A) There is (B) It is
    (C) The (D) It is the

12. Deserts produce less than 0.5 grams of plant growth ________ from every square yard.
    (A) the day (B) some day
    (C) one day (D) a day

13. We weren’t very ________ about the news.
    (A) exciting (B) excited
    (C) excitement (D) excitedly

14. Before going to England, Tom already ________ English.
    (A) has learned (B) was learned
    (C) had learned (D) learns

15. That student has been to ten countries ________.

(A) until now (B) for now

(C) ever (D) so far

16. I don't know ________ in her free time.

(A) what does she do

(B) what is she doing

(C) what's she do

(D) what she does

17. Most people consider it ________ to talk on a cell phone in the theater.

(A) being rude (B) rude

(C) be rude (D) about rude

18. ________ gold, silver, copper, and platinum, nuggets of pure iron are rarely found in nature.

(A) As unlike (B) Unlike the

(C) Unlike (D) Unlikely

19. Many animals use odors for identification, ________, sexual attraction, alarm, and a variety of other purposes.

(A) the territorial marking

(B) they mark territory

(C) territorial marking

(D) mark territory

20. Temperature inversions often occur when ________ in the late afternoon.
    (A) the earth's surface cools
    (B) earth's surface is cooled
    (C) also the earth's surface is cooled
    (D) that the earth's surface is cooled

III. Reading Comprehension: 20%

Choose the best answer to each question.

Questions 21-25

"My friends call me '3M'," says Charlene Huang, forty-two, who has three master's degrees: one in seismology and one in journalism from NTU, and one in geotechnical engineering from the University of California in Berkeley. Such an educational background has allowed Huang to become an interpreter, primarily on technology-related assignments. Why is Huang's job attractive to her? She half-jokingly says that her work is great because it has three advantages by which people in Taiwan define a great job: handsome pay, a light workload and a workplace near home. Besides, an interpreter can rest well and wake up naturally.

"I used to work for a research institute in Taipei. After it moved to Hsinchu, I had to leave my home in Taipei at 6:30 in the morning and I did not get home until 7:30 in the evening. I had to spend four hours traveling between Taipei and my new workplace. At the time, my son was only seven years old, so I needed time to take care of him. As a result, I quit the job in 1991 and found another one with flexible hours."

"For me, every assignment is a new challenge because it means a new speaker, a new topic, and a new audience. You know, everyone's mental powers have a limit. And for interpreters, 20 minutes' work is rather exhausting. Many people respond with 'Wow!' when they learn how much an interpreter is paid, but they must understand that this is not an easy job. The amount of pay depends on whether the organization knows how brain-taxing this work really is."

21. In the first paragraph, *primarily* means:
    (A) most of her tasks are related to technology.
    (B) first, she did technical work and later other assignments.
    (C) her technology-related cases are basic and simple for her due to her training.
    (D) she has done only technological work.

22. Why does the author use the term *half-jokingly*?
    (A) Huang receives payment, does her job, and has a place to work. However, the pay is not attractive, the job is not easy, and the workplace is not stable.
    (B) Huang chuckles partway through her sentence.
    (C) No one really enjoys working.
    (D) It's true that her job has these three advantages, but Huang does not believe that they are the only things that make for a good job.

23. In the second paragraph, *four hours* means:
    (A) 4 hours from Taipei to Hsinchu and four more hours back from Hsinchu to Taipei.
    (B) 4 hours a week total commuting time.
    (C) 4 hours total time on the road every day.
    (D) 4 extra hours that she did not have to spend before.

24. In the second paragraph, *at the time* indicates:
    (A) when she used to work in Taipei.
    (B) when she worked in Hsinchu.
    (C) from early in the morning until late at night.
    (D) when her son needed to go to bed.

25. What does **brain-taxing** mean in the third paragraph?
    (A) The organization must consider deeply how much compensation to give her.
    (B) There is an extra, hidden cost to the company, in the form of mental anguish.
    (C) An interpreter must use a great deal of mental power.
    (D) This type of work is suitable only for intellectuals.

The influenza virus is a single molecule composed of millions of individual atoms. Although bacteria can be considered a type of plant that secretes poisonous substances into the body of the organism it attacks, viruses, like the influenza virus, are living organisms themselves. We may consider them regular chemical molecules since they have a strictly defined atomic structure; on the other hand, we must also consider them as being alive since they are able to multiply in unlimited quantities.

An attack brought on by the presence of the influenza virus in the body produces a temporary immunity, but unfortunately, the protection is against only the type of virus that caused the influenza. Because the disease can be produced by any one of three types, referred to as A, B, or C, and many strains within each type, immunity to one virus will not prevent infection by another type or strain.

Approximately every ten years, worldwide epidemics of influenza, called pandemics, occur. Thought to be caused by new strains of type-A virus, these pandemic viruses have spread rapidly, infecting millions of people. Epidemics or regional outbreaks have appeared on average every two or three years for type-A virus, and every four or five years for type B virus.

26. With what topic is the passage primarily concerned with?
    (A) The influenza virus.
    (B) Immunity to disease.
    (C) Bacteria.
    (D) Chemical molecules.

27. Why does the writer say that viruses are alive?
    (A) They have a complex atomic structure.
    (B) They move.
    (C) They multiply.
    (D) They need warmth and light.

28. The atomic structure of viruses
    (A) is variable.
    (B) is strictly defined.
    (C) cannot be analyzed chemically.
    (D) is more complex than that of bacteria.

29. How does the body react to the influenza virus?
    (A) It prevents further infection from other types and strains of the virus.
    (B) It produces immunity to the type and strain of virus that invaded it.
    (C) It becomes immune to types A, B, and C viruses, but not to various strains within the types.
    (D) After a temporary immunity, it becomes even more susceptible to the type and strain that caused the influenza.

30. The author names all of the following as characteristics of pandemics EXCEPT that
    (A) they spread very quickly.
    (B) they are caused by type-A virus.
    (C) they are regional outbreaks.
    (D) they occur once every ten years.

IV. Translation: 10%

Translate the following passage into English.

偶爾發一頓脾氣是人之常情。而且，口頭上把怒火發洩出來，可以緩和怒氣，甚至化解怒氣。有辦法的父母通常會用實例教導子女，要以直接但非激烈的方式表達忿怒，讓子女知道坦白發洩忿怒就像夏天的大雷雨，雨過天晴，可以清新空氣。

台北市立師範學院九十三學年度
碩士班研究生入學考試英文試題詳解

I. 字彙：10%

1. (**B**) anonymously〔ə'nɑnəməslɪ〕*adv.* 匿名地
   (A) seriously〔'sɪrɪəslɪ〕*adv.* 認眞地
   poem〔'po·ɪm〕*n.* 詩
   publish〔'pʌblɪʃ〕*v.* 發表；出版

2. (**A**) roughly〔'rʌflɪ〕*adv.* 大約
   (B) possibly〔'pɑsəblɪ〕*adv.* 或許

3. (**D**) deteriorate〔dɪ'tɪrɪə,ret〕*v.* 惡化
   (B) continue〔kən'tɪnjʊ〕*v.* 繼續
   (D) ***fall apart*** 瓦解；崩潰
   relationship〔rɪ'leʃən,ʃɪp〕*n.* 關係
   in time 遲早；早晚

4. (**A**) laudable〔'lɔdəbl̩〕*adj.* 值得讚美的
   (A) ***praiseworthy***〔'prez,wɝðɪ〕*adj.* 值得稱讚的
   (B) laughable〔'læfəbl̩〕*adj.* 可笑的；有趣的
   (C) realistic〔,riə'lɪstɪk〕*adj.* 現實的
   (D) helpful〔'hɛlpfəl〕*adj.* 有益的
   senator〔'sɛnətɚ〕*n.* 參議員
   policy〔'pɑləsɪ〕*n.* 政策

5.（**A**）avert〔əˈvɝt〕*v.* 避開；避免
(A) ***avoid***〔əˈvɔɪd〕*v.* 避免
(B) regulate〔ˈrɛgjə,let〕*v.* 管理
(C) propagate〔ˈprɑpə,get〕*v.* 傳播
(D) condemn〔kənˈdɛm〕*v.* 譴責
crisis〔ˈkraɪsɪs〕*n.* 危機
improve〔ɪmˈpruv〕*v.* 改善
bilateral〔baɪˈlætərəl〕*adj.* 雙方的
relation〔rɪˈleʃən〕*n.* 關係

6.（**B**）exhilarate〔ɪgˈzɪlə,ret〕*v.* 使人振奮
(A) arrest〔əˈrɛst〕*v.* 逮捕
(B) ***stimulate***〔ˈstɪmjə,let〕*v.* 刺激
(C) devastate〔ˈdɛvəs,tet〕*v.* 破壞
(D) model〔ˈmɑdl̩〕*v.* 製作模型；塑造
biography〔baɪˈɑgrəfɪ〕*n.* 傳記
loner〔ˈlonɚ〕*n.* 獨來獨往的人；獨行俠
trail〔trel〕*n.* 足跡　　beat〔bit〕*v.* 打擊

7.（**B**）feasible〔ˈfizəbl̩〕*adj.* 可行的
(A) compatible〔kəmˈpætəbl̩〕*adj.* 相容的
(B) ***practicable***〔ˈpræktɪkəbl̩〕*adj.* 可行的
(C) changeable〔ˈtʃendʒəbl̩〕*adj.* 易變的
(D) flexible〔ˈflɛksəbl̩〕*adj.* 有彈性的
dispute〔dɪˈspjut〕*n.* 爭論
injured〔ˈɪndʒɚd〕*adj.* 受傷的；受冤屈的
party〔ˈpɑrtɪ〕*n.* 當事人；一方
method〔ˈmɛθəd〕*n.* 方法　　judge〔dʒʌdʒ〕*n.* 法官
ill〔ɪl〕*adv.* 惡意地；不親切地

8. (**C**) reconstruct〔,rikən'strʌkt〕*v.* 重建

(A) resign〔rɪ'zaɪn〕*v.* 辭職

(B) restrain〔rɪ'stren〕*v.* 克制

(C) ***restore***〔rɪ'stor〕*v.* 恢復；重建

(D) refund〔rɪ'fʌnd〕*v.* 退錢

wing〔wɪŋ〕*n.* 廂房；側翼

promptly〔'prɑmptlɪ〕*adv.* 立即

danger〔'dendʒɚ〕*n.* 危險

collapse〔kə'læps〕*v.* 倒塌

9. (**B**) amend〔ə'mɛnd〕*v.* 修改

(A) command〔kə'mænd〕*v.* 命令

(C) compel〔kəm'pɛl〕*v.* 強迫

(D) clarify〔'klærə,faɪ〕*v.* 淨化；澄清

10. (**A**) polemic〔po'lɛmɪk〕*adj.* 好爭論的

(A) ***argumentative***〔,ɑrgjə'mɛntətɪv〕*adj.* 好爭論的；好辯的

(B) quarrelsome〔'kwɔrəlsəm〕*adj.* 愛爭吵的

(C) frustrating〔'frʌstretɪŋ〕*adj.* 令人沮喪的

(D) hostile〔'hɑstɪl〕*adj.* 有敵意的

controversy〔'kɑntrə,vɝsɪ〕*n.* 爭論

quiet down 使平靜下來

unsettled〔ʌn'sɛtḷd〕*adj.* 不安定的；未解決的

polarized〔'polə,raɪzd〕*adj.* 兩極化的

set out 陳述　　***opinion leaders*** 意見領袖

Ⅱ. 文法：10%

11. (**C**) 依句意，選 (C) ***The***。而 (D) 是強調句型，但在 invented 前須加 that，在此不合。
physicist〔ˈfɪzəsɪst〕*n.* 物理學家
invent〔ɪnˈvɛnt〕*v.* 發明
mercury〔ˈmɝkjərɪ〕*n.* 水銀
thermometer〔θəˈmɑmətɚ〕*n.* 溫度計

12. (**D**) 依句意，選 (D) ***a day***「一天」。
desert〔ˈdɛzɚt〕*n.* 沙漠
gram〔græm〕*n.* 克；公分
square〔skwɛr〕*adj.* 平方的　　yard〔jɑrd〕*n.* 碼

13. (**B**) 現在分詞修飾事物，過去分詞修飾人，故選 (B) ***excited***〔ɪkˈsaɪtɪd〕*adj.* 興奮的。而 (A) exciting「刺激的」，(C) excitement「刺激」，(D)「興奮地」，均不合。

14. (**C**) 原句爲：Before he went to…，而比過去動作早發生，須用「過去完成式」，選 (C) ***had learned***。

15. (**D**) 依句意，選 (D) ***so far***「到目前爲止」。而 (A) until now「直到現在」，(B) for now「暫時」，(C) ever「曾經」，均不合。

16. (**D**) 空格應塡一名詞子句，做 know 的受詞，又名詞子句中，主詞與動詞不須倒裝，故選 (D) ***what she does***。
free time 空閒時間

17. (**B**) ***consider A (to be) B*** 認爲A是B

(B) rude〔rud〕*adj.* 無禮的

consider〔kən'sɪdɚ〕*v.* 認爲

cell phone 手機　theater〔'θiətɚ〕*n.* 電影院

18. (**C**) 依句意，選(C) ***unlike***「不像」。而(D) unlikely「不可能的」，則不合句意。

silver〔'sɪlvɚ〕*n.* 銀　copper〔'kɑpɚ〕*n.* 銅

platinum〔'plætṇəm〕*n.* 白金

nugget〔'nʌgɪt〕*n.*（尤指天然貴金屬的）礦塊

pure〔pjʊr〕*adj.* 純粹的　iron〔'aɪɚn〕*n.* 鐵

rarely〔'rɛrlɪ〕*adv.* 很少

nature〔'netʃɚ〕*n.* 大自然；自然界

19. (**C**) 依句意，選(C) ***territorial marking***「標示地盤」。

territorial〔,tɛrə'torɪəl〕*adj.* 地盤性的

marking〔'mɑrkɪŋ〕*n.* 做標記；標示

odor〔'odɚ〕*n.* 氣味

identification〔aɪ,dɛntəfə'keʃən〕*n.* 身分確認

sexual〔'sɛkʃuəl〕*adj.* 性的

attraction〔ə'trækʃən〕*n.* 吸引力

alarm〔ə'lɑrm〕*n.* 警報；緊急訊號

variety of 各種；各式各樣的　purpose〔'pɝpəs〕*n.* 目的

20. (**A**) 依句意，「當地表冷卻」，選(A)。

temperature〔'tɛmprətʃɚ〕*n.* 溫度

inversion〔ɪn'vɝʃən〕*n.* 逆溫

earth〔ɝθ〕*n.* 地上；陸地

surface〔'sɝfɪs〕*n.* 表面　cool〔kul〕*v.* 冷卻

Ⅲ. 閱讀測驗：20%

21-25 題

【譯文】

「我的朋友都叫我『3M』，」Charlene Huang 說，她四十二歲，擁有三個碩士學位：一個是地震學，一個是台大新聞所，然後一個是加州柏克萊大學的土木工程所。這樣的學歷讓黃小姐成爲一名口譯員，主要負責與科技相關的工作。爲什麼黃小姐的工作對她這麼有吸引力呢？她半開玩笑地說，自己的工作很棒，因爲這份工作有三個優點，也就是台灣人對好工作的定義：錢多、事少、離家近。此外，口譯員還能有充分的休息，可以睡到自然醒。

「我以前是在台北的一個研究機構工作。而當那個機構搬到新竹之後，我早上六點半就必須從台北的家出門，然後要到晚上七點半之後才能到家。我必須要花四個小時，往來於台北和新的工作地點。當時，我兒子才七歲，所以我需要時間來照顧他。因此，我在 1991 年的時候，辭掉了那份工作，並找了另一份上班時間有彈性的工作。」

「對我來說，每一份工作都是一個新的挑戰，因爲它意味著新的演講者、新的題目，還有新的聽衆。你也知道，每個人的智力都是有限的。對口譯員來說，二十分鐘的工作就非常累人了。許多人在得知口譯員的薪水是多少時，他們的反應都是『哇！』，但是他們必須了解，那並不是一份簡單的工作。薪水的多少，要看這個機構是否了解這份工作有多費腦力。」

【答案】

21.（A）　22.（D）　23.（C）　24.（B）　25.（C）

【註】

master's degree 碩士學位
seismology〔saɪz'mɑlədʒɪ〕*n.* 地震學
journalism〔'dʒɝnḷ,ɪzəm〕*n.* 新聞學
NTU 台灣大學（= *National Taiwan University*）
geotechnical〔,dʒɪo'tɛknɪkḷ〕*adj.* 地理工程學的
engineering〔,ɛndʒə'nɪrɪŋ〕*n.* 工程（學）
educational〔,ɛdʒə'keʃənḷ〕*adj.* 教育的
background〔'bæk,graʊnd〕*n.* 背景
educational background 學歷
interpreter〔ɪn'tɝprɪtɚ〕*n.* 口譯員

primarily〔'praɪ,mɛrəlɪ〕*adv.* 主要地
technology〔tɛk'nɑlədʒɪ〕*n.* 科技
related〔rɪ'letɪd〕*adj.* 有關聯的
assignment〔ə'saɪnmənt〕*n.* 被分配之工作；職務
attractive〔ə'træktɪv〕*adj.* 有吸引力的
define〔dɪ'faɪn〕*v.* 爲～下定義
handsome〔'hænsəm〕*adj.*（金額）可觀的
pay〔pe〕*n.* 薪水　workload〔'wɝk,lod〕*n.* 工作量
workplace〔'wɝk,ples〕*n.* 工作場所　***wake up*** 起床

naturally〔'nætʃərəlɪ〕*adv.* 自然地　***used to*** 以前曾經
research〔'risɝtʃ〕*n.* 研究
institute〔'ɪnstə,tjut〕*n.* 研究機構
travel〔'trævḷ〕*v.* 行進　***take care of*** 照顧
as a result 因此　quit〔kwɪt〕*v.* 辭（職）
flexible〔'flɛksəbḷ〕*adj.* 有彈性的
hours〔aʊrz〕*n. pl.* 上班時間　challenge〔'tʃælɪndʒ〕*n.* 挑戰
audience〔'ɔdɪəns〕*n.* 聽衆；觀衆

mental〔 'mɛntḷ 〕*adj.* 智能的；智力的
limit〔 'lɪmɪt 〕*n.* 限度；限制　　rather〔 'ræðɚ 〕*adv.* 相當地
exhausting〔 ɪg'zɔstɪŋ 〕*adj.* 令人筋疲力盡的
organization〔 ,ɔrgənə'zeʃən 〕*n.* 機構
brain-taxing〔 'bren'tæksɪŋ 〕*adj.* 費腦力的
task〔 tæsk 〕*n.* 工作；任務
technical〔 'tɛknɪkḷ 〕*adj.* 工業的；技術上的
due to 由於　　training〔 'trenɪŋ 〕*n.* 訓練

technological〔 ,tɛknə'lɑdʒɪkḷ 〕*adj.* 科技的
term〔 tɝm 〕*n.* 名詞；用語　　receive〔 rɪ'siv 〕*v.* 獲得
payment〔 'pemənt 〕*n.* 報酬　　stable〔 'stebḷ 〕*adj.* 穩定的
chuckle〔 'tʃʌkḷ 〕*v.* 低聲輕笑；咯咯笑
partway〔 'pɑrt'we 〕*adv.* 在中途；到一半
sentence〔 'sɛntəns 〕*n.* 句子　　***make for*** 有助於；導致；促成
commuting〔 kə'mjutɪŋ 〕*adj.* 通勤的
indicate〔 'ɪndə,ket 〕*v.* 表示

consider〔 kən'sɪdɚ 〕*v.* 考慮；考量
deeply〔 'diplɪ 〕*adv.* 徹底地；深深地
compensation〔 ,kɑmpən'seʃən 〕*n.* 報酬；補償
extra〔 'ɛkstrə 〕*adj.* 額外的　　hidden〔 'hɪdṇ 〕*adj.* 隱藏的
anguish〔 'æŋgwɪʃ 〕*n.*（身心上的）苦悶；痛苦
a great deal of 大量的　　suitable〔 'sutəbḷ 〕*adj.* 合適的
intellectual〔 ,ɪntḷ'ɛktʃuəl 〕*n.* 知識份子

26-30 題

【譯文】

流行性感冒的病毒，是由好幾百萬個原子所組成的單一分子。雖然細菌也可以算是一種植物，它們會把有毒物質，藏進所侵襲的生物

體中，病毒，像是流感病毒，本身也是生物。我們可能會把它們看成是一般的化學分子，因爲它們擁有明確的原子結構；但另一方面，我們也必須把它們看成是活的，因爲它們可以繁殖出無限多個個體。

體內如果有流感病毒存在，那麼發作時，就會產生暫時性的免疫力，但不幸的是，這種防禦能力，只能對抗引起這次感冒的那種病毒。因爲這種疾病，可能是由三種病毒中的任何一種所引起的，也就是 A 型、B 型或 C 型，而且每一個類型又包含許多種病毒，對一種病毒免疫，將無法使你免於感染另一種病毒。

大約每十年，在全世界流行的流行性感冒，也叫做世界流行性感冒，就會發生一次。這些流行性病毒擴散得非常快，它們被認爲是由 A 型病毒的新品種所引起的，這些病毒感染了幾百萬人。以 A 型病毒來說，平均每兩年或三年就會爆發流行病，或是地區性的疾病，而 B 型病毒則是每四年或五年爆發一次。

【答案】

26.（**A**）　27.（**C**）　28.（**B**）　29.（**B**）　30.（**C**）

【註】

influenza〔ˌɪnfluˈɛnzə〕*n.* 流行性感冒（＝*flu*）
virus〔ˈvaɪrəs〕*n.* 病毒　　single〔ˈsɪŋgḷ〕*adj.* 單一的
molecule〔ˈmɑləˌkjul〕*n.* 分子
compose〔kəmˈpoz〕*v.* 組成　　million〔ˈmɪljən〕*n.* 百萬
individual〔ˌɪndəˈvɪdʒuəl〕*adj.* 個別的；單獨的
atom〔ˈætəm〕*n.* 原子　　bacteria〔bækˈtɪrɪə〕*n. pl.* 細菌
consider〔kənˈsɪdɚ〕*v.* 認爲　　secrete〔sɪˈkrit〕*v.* 隱藏
poisonous〔ˈpɔɪzṇəs〕*adj.* 有毒的

substance 〔 'sʌbstəns 〕 *n.* 物質
organism 〔 'ɔrgən,ɪzəm 〕 *n.* 有機體；生物
attack 〔 ə'tæk 〕 *v.* 侵襲　*n.* 發病；發作
regular 〔 'rɛgjələ˞ 〕 *adj.* 一般的；普通的
chemical 〔 'kɛmɪkḷ 〕 *adj.* 化學的
strictly 〔 'strɪktlɪ 〕 *adv.* 嚴格地；全然
defined 〔 dɪ'faɪnd 〕 *adj.* 清楚的
atomic 〔 ə'tɑmɪk 〕 *adj.* 原子的
structure 〔 'strʌktʃə˞ 〕 *n.* 結構　alive 〔 ə'laɪv 〕 *adj.* 活的

multiply 〔 'mʌltə,plaɪ 〕 *v.* 繁殖
unlimited 〔 ʌn'lɪmɪtɪd 〕 *adj.* 無限的
quantity 〔 'kwɑntətɪ 〕 *n.* 量　***bring on*** 導致；引起
presence 〔 'prɛzṇs 〕 *n.* 存在
temporary 〔 'tɛmpə,rɛrɪ 〕 *adj.* 暫時的；臨時的
immunity 〔 ɪ'mjunətɪ 〕 *n.* 免疫力
protection 〔 prə'tɛkʃən 〕 *n.* 保護；防禦
against 〔 ə'gɛnst 〕 *prep.* 對抗；抵抗
be referred to as 被稱為　strain 〔 stren 〕 *n.* 菌種；病毒
infection 〔 ɪn'fɛkʃən 〕 *n.* 感染
approximately 〔 ə'prɑksəmɪtlɪ 〕 *adv.* 大約

worldwide 〔 'wɝld'waɪd 〕 *adj.* 全世界的
epidemics 〔 ,ɛpə'dɛmɪks 〕 *n.* (傳染病的) 的流行
pandemic 〔 pæn'dɛmɪk 〕 *n.* 世界性的流行病
spread 〔 sprɛd 〕 *v.* 擴散；傳播
rapidly 〔 'ræpɪdlɪ 〕 *adv.* 迅速地　infect 〔 ɪn'fɛkt 〕 *v.* 感染
regional 〔 'ridʒənḷ 〕 *adj.* 區域性的；地方性的
outbreak 〔 'aʊt,brek 〕 *n.* 爆發

be concerned with 和～有關
complex〔'kɑmplɛks〕*adj.* 複雜的
variable〔'vɛrɪəbḷ〕*adj.* 易變的；變化不定的
analyze〔'ænḷ,aɪz〕*v.* 分析；解析
chemically〔'kɛmɪkḷɪ〕*adv.* 在化學上
react〔rɪ'ækt〕*v.* 反應

further〔'fɝðɚ〕*adj.* 更進一步的 invade〔ɪn'ved〕*v.* 入侵
immune〔ɪ'mjun〕*adj.* 免疫的
various〔'vɛrɪəs〕*adj.* 各種的
susceptible〔sə'sɛptəbḷ〕*adj.* 易受…影響的；罹患…
name〔nem〕*v.* 舉出
characteristic〔,kærɪktə'rɪstɪk〕*n.* 特性

Ⅳ. 翻譯：10%

Losing your temper occasionally is human nature. And letting your anger out orally can calm you down and even get rid of your temper. Knowledgeable parents will often use real examples to teach their children to use a direct but moderate way to express anger. They let them know that losing their temper is like a summer storm. After the rain, the air will be clear.

國立暨南國際大學九十三學年度
碩士班研究生入學考試英文試題

I. Vocabulary:(30 %)

Directions:

In Questions 1-30, each sentence has a word or phrase underlined. Choose the word or phrase which would best keep the meaning of the original sentence if it were substituted for the underlined part.

1. The repairman only comes around once in a while.
   (A) accidentally (B) on request
   (C) occasionally (D) initially

2. The Stewarts seldom buy books and magazines.
   (A) usually (B) never
   (C) often (D) hardly ever

3. The commissioner agrees to attend.
   (A) to be present (B) to be angry
   (C) to be polite (D) to be absent

4. In the dark room I took him for Joseph.
   (A) failed to notice (B) introduced him to
   (C) confused him with (D) brought him to

5. This section of the city is zoned for commercial buildings only.
   (A) business (B) high-rise
   (C) condemned (D) apartment

6. You have the option of saying yes or no.
   (A) preference for (B) choice of
   (C) habit of (D) knack for

7. To prevent scorching, select the iron temperature to suit the garment being ironed.
   (A) drying (B) steeling
   (C) hardening (D) burning the surface

8. Although Sam had seen the accident, he was reluctant to act as a witness.
   (A) ashamed (B) unwilling
   (C) eager (D) anxious

9. Mary crated all of her books so that she could send them home.
   (A) numbered (B) packed
   (C) cataloged (D) inventoried

10. Because of the many trees, the Allens' backyard was without sun most of the day.
   (A) misty (B) shady
   (C) balmy (D) windy

11. Please do not repeat the speech word for word; just give us the highlights.
   (A) details (B) summaries
   (C) main points (D) small allusions

12. The visitors decided to prolong their stay in the city.
   (A) promote (B) enjoy
   (C) extend (D) cancel

13. The dust particles released during volcanic eruptions disturb the earth's magnetic field and <u>interfere with</u> communications.
    (A) formulate　(B) increase
    (C) disrupt　(D) create

14. The biologist needed more <u>proof</u> before her theory could be accepted.
    (A) financing　(B) publications
    (C) evidence　(D) recognition

15. There were many <u>half-formed</u> plans for improving the northern waterway before 1792.
    (A) small-scale　(B) well supported
    (C) initial　(D) incomplete

16. <u>Vast</u> amounts of money are being invested in the local market.
    (A) Enormous　(B) Constant
    (C) Unknown　(D) Sufficient

17. The new ruler of the nation carefully <u>handpicked</u> his chief officials.
    (A) removed　(B) managed
    (C) instructed　(D) selected

18. He managed to keep <u>an earnest</u> expression on his face even though he wanted to smile.
    (A) a pleasant　(B) a neutral
    (C) a serious　(D) an annoyed

19. During the years before the American Civil War, differences between the North and the South gradually came to focus on the question of slavery.
    (A) angrily　(B) guiltily
    (C) actively　(D) slowly

20. The governor's aim is to increase state income.
    (A) promise　(B) duty
    (C) proposal　(D) goal

21. Living things consist of minute structures called cells.
    (A) numerous　(B) variable
    (C) diverse　(D) tiny

22. Glassmaking was apparently the first industry to be brought from Europe to the United States.
    (A) predictably　(B) regretfully
    (C) seemingly　(D) naturally

23. Bay laurel leaves are still an emblem of victory.
    (A) a symbol　(B) a result
    (C) a suggestion　(D) a spoil

24. X rays are basically a form of radiation.
    (A) fundamentally
    (B) definitely
    (C) probably
    (D) frequently

25. The future survival of the bald eagle is still an important American ecological concern.
(A) migration (B) population
(C) existence (D) evolution

26. One of the greatest breakthroughs for professional women came in 1973 when the field of banking opened up for them.
(A) serious disappointments
(B) significant advances
(C) abrupt declines
(D) crucial situations

27. The symptoms of influenza are fever, headache, and muscular pain.
(A) effects (B) delights
(C) forces (D) signs

28. Although a newspaper's primary function is to inform, special features are usually included for entertainment.
(A) jointly (B) cautiously
(C) commonly (D) intentionally

29. Acetate is one of the most important artificial fibers.
(A) insulating (B) synthetic
(C) unadorned (D) complex

30. One of the most widely discussed environmental effects of supersonic travel is the sonic boom.
(A) completely (B) distantly
(C) extensively (D) deliberately

II. Structure and Written Expression: (40 %)

A. Structure: (20 %)

Directions:

Questions 31-50 are incomplete sentences. Beneath each sentence you will see four words or expressions, marked (A), (B), (C), and (D). Choose the one word or phrase that best completes the sentence.

31. Certain layers of the atmosphere have special names ________.
    (A) which indicated their character properties
    (B) whose characteristic properties are indicating
    (C) what characterize their indicated properties
    (D) that indicate their characteristic properties

32. ________ adhesive force between gases and solids.
    (A) An　　(B) With an
    (C) Since an　　(D) There is an

33. Galaxies and clusters of galaxies are the largest units ________ the structures of the universe.
    (A) among　　(B) and
    (C) but　　(D) that

34. Lizards' tails may teach us how cells learn to specialize, how heart muscles grow, and even ________.
    (A) the cancer growth is arrested
    (B) how cancer growth is arrested
    (C) where is cancer growth arrested
    (D) to be arresting cancer growth

35. Legal tender is any type of money that must, ________, be accepted in payment of a debt.
    (A) law (B) by law
    (C) its law (D) which law

36. During an economic depression, those hurt include ________ workers and their families, but also the storekeepers who depend on their business.
    (A) when (B) both
    (C) not only (D) without them

37. Antibodies ________ by small, round cells called lymphocytes and plasma cells.
    (A) to be made (B) making
    (C) made (D) are made

38. Known for her caricatures of American society, ________.
    (A) Peggy Brown wrote and illustrated books for children
    (B) the writing and illustrating of books for children by Peggy Brown
    (C) children's books were written and illustrated by Peggy Brown
    (D) Peggy Brown's writing and illustrating of children's books.

39. ________ pure lead, the lead ore is mined, then smelted, and finally refined.
    (A) Obtaining (B) Being obtained
    (C) To obtain (D) It is obtained

40. Western Nebraska generally receives less snow than ________ eastern Nebraska.
(A) does (B) in
(C) it does in (D) in it does

41. Nobel prizes are the ________.
(A) height of world prestigious honors
(B) world's most prestigious honors
(C) honors of the world's highest prestige
(D) prestiges with the most honor in the world

42. ________ was not incorporated as a city until almost two centuries later, in 1834.
(A) Settling Brooklyn, the Dutch
(B) The Dutch settled Brooklyn
(C) Brooklyn was settled by the Dutch
(D) Settled by the Dutch, Brooklyn

43. ________ inclination to be a farmer, John Adams' schooling prepared him for college and a career in the ministry.
(A) His
(B) Although his
(C) Despite his
(D) Because of his

44. In the 1850's Harriet Beecher Stowe's "Uncle Tom's Cabin" became the best seller of the time, _______ a host of imitators.
(A) inspiring (B) inspired
(C) inspired by (D) to inspire

45. South of Gallup, New Mexico, ________, was one of the legendary Seven Cities of Cibola visited by Coronado in 1540.
   (A) where the ancient ruins of Hawikuh lie
   (B) the ancient ruins lie of Hawikuh
   (C) the ancient ruins of Hawikhu lie
   (D) like the ancient ruins of Hawikuh

46. ________ a baby turtle is hatched, it must be able to fend for itself.
   (A) Not sooner than　　(B) No sooner
   (C) So soon that　　(D) As soon as

47. Tungsten, a gray metal with the ________ is used to form the wires in electric light bulbs.
   (A) point at which it melts is the highest of any metal
   (B) melting point is the highest of any metal
   (C) highest melting point of any metal
   (D) metal's highest melting point of any

48. Rattan comes from ________ of different kinds of palms.
   (A) its reedy stems　　(B) the reedy stems
   (C) the stems are reedy　　(D) stems that are reedy

49. At thirteen ________ at a district school near her home, and when she was fifteen, she saw her first article in print.
   (A) the first teaching position that Mary Jane Hawes had
   (B) the teaching position was Mary Jane Hawes' first
   (C) when Mary Jane Hawes had her first teaching position
   (D) Mary Jane Hawes had her first teaching position

50. Vitamin C, discovered in 1932, ________ first vitamin for which the molecular structure was established.

(A) the　　(B) was the

(C) as the　　(D) being the

B. Written Expression: (20 %)

Directions:

In questions 51-70, each sentence has four underlined words or phrases marked (A), (B), (C), and (D). Identify the part that must be changed in order for the sentence to be grammatically correct.

51. In the United States, the individual (A) income tax is the governmental (B) largest source (C) of revenue (D).

52. The human body contains more than (A) six hundred muscles who (B) account for (C) approximately forty percent of body weight (D).

53. In order to (A) prevent disease on a worldwide (B) scale, nations (C) must to work (D) together.

54. The (A) Allegheny Mountain (B) range are (C) rich in (D) coal.

55. Some (A) trees have (B) distinctive features that (C) identify they (D) at first glance.

56. Every machine consume more energy than it creates.
A B C D

57. Compared about other areas, deserts are sparsely populated.
A B C D

58. The Cherokee writing system was invented 1821 by Sequoya,
A B C
a member of that American Indian nation.
D

59. Industrial designers try to make products attraction, efficient,
A B C D
and safe.

60. Chickens are raised for both meat or eggs, which makes
A B
them the most important domesticated birds in the world.
C D

61. Chalk, which is a softly mineral than limestone, consists of
A B C
minute marine shells.
D

62. The Earth travels at a high rate of speed around Sun.
A B C D

63. Financial problems beset many of the early museums in the
A B
United States and caused its closure.
C D

64. Pure cane sugar and pure beet sugar are (A) chemically identical (B) and do not different (C) in sweetness (D).

65. For (A) ancient people, myths were often attempts explanation (B) catastrophic events such as (C) volcanic eruptions (D).

66. Mineral prospectors use (A) their knowledge of (B) geophysics to locate (C) deposits of oil, uranium, and another (D) valuable minerals.

67. Spectrum (A) analysis led (B) to the discovery dramatic (C) of the element helium (D).

68. Alive (A) creatures are remarkably (B) diversified in their (C) sizes and shapes (D).

69. Dried (A) fruits are not costing (B) to produce and can be stored satisfactorily (C) for long periods of time (D).

70. The tides of the Indian Ocean vary (A) greatly, but (B) not too (C) much as those (D) of the Atlantic or Pacific.

III. Reading Comprehension: (30 %)

Directions:

Read each of the following two passages carefully. Select the best answer to each of the fifteen questions.

A. Questions 71-77

People appear to be born to compute. The numerical skills of children develop so early and so inexorably that it is easy to imagine an internal clock of mathematical maturity guiding their growth. Not long after learning to walk and talk, they can set the table with impressive accuracy — one plate, one knife, one spoon, one fork, for each of the five chairs. Soon they are capable of noting that they have placed five knives, spoons, and forks on the table and, a bit later, that this amounts to fifteen pieces of silverware. Having thus mastered addition, they move on to subtraction. It seems almost reasonable to expect that if a child were secluded on a desert island at birth and retrieved seven years later, he or she could enter a second-grade mathematics class without any serious problems of intellectual adjustment.

Of course, the truth is not so simple. This century, the work of cognitive psychologists has illuminated the subtle forms of daily learning on which intellectual progress depends. Children were observed as they slowly grasped — or, as the case might be, bumped into — concepts that adults take for granted, as they refused, for instance, to concede that quantity is unchanged as water pours from a short stout glass into a tall thin one. Psychologists have since demonstrated that young children, asked to count the pencils in a pile, readily report the number of blue or red pencils, but must be coaxed into finding the total. Such studies have suggested that the rudiments of mathematics are mastered gradually, and with effort. They have also suggested that the very concept of abstract numbers — the idea of a oneness, a twoness, a threeness that applies to any class of objects and is a prerequisite for doing anything more mathematically demanding than setting a table — is itself far from innate.

71. What does the passage mainly discuss?
    (A) Trends in teaching mathematics to children.
    (B) The use of mathematics in child psychology.
    (C) The development of mathematical ability in children.
    (D) The fundamental concepts of mathematics that children must learn.

72. It can be inferred from the passage that children normally learn simple counting ______________.
    (A) soon after they learn to talk
    (B) by looking at the clock
    (C) when they begin to be mathematically mature
    (D) after they reach second grade in school

73. The word "illuminated" in the second paragraph is closest in meaning to ______________.
    (A) illustrated
    (B) accepted
    (C) clarified
    (D) lighted

74. The author implies that most small children believe that the quantity of water changes when it is transferred to a container of a different ______________.
    (A) color (B) quality
    (C) weight (D) shape

75. According to the passage, when small children were asked to count a pile of red and blue pencils they ______________.
    (A) counted the number of pencils of each color
    (B) guessed at the total number of pencils
    (C) counted only the pencils of their favorite color
    (D) subtracted the number of red pencils from the number of blue pencils

76. The world "They" in the second paragraph refers to ______________.
    (A) mathematicians
    (B) children
    (C) pencils
    (D) studies

77. The word "prerequisite" in the second paragraph is closest in meaning to ______________.
    (A) reason (B) theory
    (C) requirement (D) technique

B. Questions 78-85

Botany, the study of plants, occupies a peculiar position in the history of human knowledge. For many thousands of years it was the one field of awareness about which humans had anything more than the vaguest of insights. It is impossible to know today just what our Stone Age ancestors knew about plants, but from what we can observe of preindustrial societies that still exist, a detailed learning of plants and their properties must be extremely ancient. This is logical. Plants are the basis of the food pyramid for all living things, even for other plants. They have always been enormously important to the welfare of people, not only as food, but also for clothing, weapons, tools, dyes, medicines, shelter, and a great many other purposes. Tribes living today in the jungles of the Amazon recognize literally hundreds of plants and know many properties of each. To them botany as such has no name and is probably not even recognized as a special branch of knowledge at all.

Unfortunately, the more industrialized we become the farther away we move from direct contact with plants, and the less distinct our knowledge of botany grows. Yet almost everyone unconsciously develops an amazing amount of botanical knowledge, and few people will fail to recognize a rose, an apple, or an orchid. When our Neolithic ancestors, living in the Middle East about 10,000 years ago, discovered that certain grasses could be harvested and their seeds planted for richer yields the next season, the first great step in a new association of plants and humans was taken. Grains were discovered and from them flowed the marvel of agriculture: cultivated crops. From then on, humans would increasingly take their living from the controlled production of a few plants, rather than getting a little here and a little there from the many varieties that grew wild — and the accumulated knowledge of tens of thousands of years of experience and intimacy with plants in the wild would begin to fade away.

78. Which of the following assumptions about early humans is expressed in the passage?
    (A) They probably had extensive knowledge of plants.
    (B) They divided knowledge into well-defined fields.
    (C) They did not enjoy the study of botany.
    (D) They placed great importance on ownership of property.

79. The word "peculiar" in line 1 is closest in meaning to ________.
    (A) clear (B) large
    (C) unusual (D) important

80. What does the comment "This is logical." in the first paragraph mean?
    (A) There is no clear way to determine the extent of our ancestors' knowledge of plants.
    (B) It is not surprising that early humans had a detailed knowledge of plants.
    (C) It is reasonable to assume that our ancestors behaved very much like people in preindustrial societies.
    (D) Human knowledge of plants is well organized and very detailed.

81. The phrase "properties of each" in paragraph one refers to each ________.
    (A) tribe (B) hundred
    (C) plant (D) purpose

82. According to the passage, why has general knowledge of botany declined?
    (A) People no longer value plants as a useful resource.
    (B) Botany is not recognized as a special branch of science.
    (C) Research is unable to keep up with the increasing number of plants.
    (D) People have direct contact with a smaller variety of plants.

83. In paragraph 2, what is the author's purpose in mentioning "a rose, an apple, or an orchid"?
(A) To make the passage more poetic.
(B) To cite examples of plants that are attractive.
(C) To give botanical examples that most readers will recognize.
(D) To illustrate the diversity of botanical life.

84. According to the passage, what was the first great step toward the practice of agriculture?
(A) The invention of agricultural implements and machinery.
(B) The development of a system of names for plants.
(C) The discovery of grasses that could be harvested and replanted.
(D) The changing diets of early humans.

85. The word "controlled" in paragraph 2, is closest in meaning to ________.
(A) abundant (B) managed
(C) required (D) advanced

國立暨南國際大學九十三學年度
碩士班研究生入學考試英文試題詳解

I. 字彙：30%

1. (**C**) ***once in a while*** 偶爾；有時候
   (A) accidentally〔ˌæksəˈdɛntḷɪ〕*adv.* 意外地
   (B) on request 一經請求
   (C) ***occasionally***〔əˈkeʒənlɪ〕*adv.* 偶爾；有時候
   (D) initially〔ɪˈnɪʃəlɪ〕*adv.* 起初
   repairman〔rɪˈpɛrmən〕*n.* 修理工人
   come around 過來

2. (**D**) seldom〔ˈsɛldəm〕*adv.* 很少
   (D) ***hardly ever*** 很少；幾乎不

3. (**A**) attend〔əˈtɛnd〕*v.* 出席
   (A) ***present***〔ˈprɛzṇt〕*adj.* 出席的
   (D) absent〔ˈæbsṇt〕*adj.* 缺席的
   commissioner〔kəˈmɪʃənɚ〕*n.* 首長；長官

4. (**C**) ***take*** A ***for*** B 把 A 誤認爲 B
   (A) ***fail to V.*** 無法　notice〔ˈnotɪs〕*v.* 注意到
   (B) introduce〔ˌɪntrəˈdjus〕*v.* 介紹
   (C) ***confuse*** A ***with*** B 把 A 和 B 弄混

5. (**A**) commercial〔kəˈmɝʃəl〕*adj.* 商業的
   (B) high-rise〔ˈhaɪˈraɪz〕*adj.* 高層的（大廈；公寓）
   (C) condemn〔kənˈdɛm〕*v.* 譴責
   section〔ˈsɛkʃən〕*n.* 區域　zone〔zon〕*v.* 劃分

6. (**B**) option〔ˈɑpʃən〕*n.* 選擇
  (A) preference〔ˈprɛfərəns〕*n.* 比較喜歡；偏好
  (D) knack〔næk〕*n.* 技巧；竅門

7. (**D**) scorch〔skɔrtʃ〕*v.* 燒焦
  (A) dry〔draɪ〕*v.* 使乾燥
  (B) steel〔stil〕*v.* 用鋼包起來；狠下（心）
  (C) harden〔ˈhɑrdn̩〕*v.* 使變硬
  (D) ***surface***〔ˈsɝfɪs〕*n.* 表面
  burn the surface 使表面燒焦
  iron〔ˈaɪɚn〕*n.* 熨斗；熨燙
  temperature〔ˈtempərətʃɚ〕*n.* 溫度
  suit〔sut〕*v.* 適合　garment〔ˈgɑrmənt〕*n.* 衣服

8. (**B**) reluctant〔rɪˈlʌktənt〕*adj.* 不情願的
  (A) ashamed〔əˈʃemd〕*adj.* 感到羞愧的
  (B) ***unwilling***〔ʌnˈwɪlɪŋ〕*adj.* 不願意的
  (C) eager〔ˈigɚ〕*adj.* 渴望的
  (D) anxious〔ˈæŋkʃəs〕*adj.* 焦急的；渴望的
  act as 擔任　witness〔ˈwɪtnɪs〕*n.* 目擊者；證人

9. (**B**) crate〔kret〕*v.* 把…裝進板條箱
  (A) number〔ˈnʌmbɚ〕*v.* 給…編號
  (B) ***pack***〔pæk〕*v.* 把…打包；把（東西）裝進（容器）
  (C) catalog〔ˈkætl̩ˌɔg〕*v.* 分類
  (D) inventory〔ˈɪnvənˌtorɪ〕*v.* 清點

10. (**B**) (A) misty〔ˈmɪstɪ〕*adj.* 有霧的
  (B) ***shady***〔ˈʃedɪ〕*adj.* 蔭涼的；多陰影的
  (C) balmy〔ˈbɑmɪ〕*adj.* 清爽的
  (D) windy〔ˈwɪndɪ〕*adj.* 多風的
  backyard〔ˈbækˈjɑrd〕*n.* 後院

11. (**C**) highlight (ˈhaɪ,laɪt) *n.* 最重要的部分
   (A) detail (ˈditel) *n.* 細節
   (B) summary (ˈsʌmərɪ) *n.* 摘要
   (C) ***main points*** 要點
   (D) allusion (əˈluʒən) *n.* 暗指；隱喻
   word for word 逐字地；一字一字地

12. (**C**) prolong (prəˈlɔŋ) *v.* 延長
   (A) promote (prəˈmot) *v.* 升遷
   (C) ***extend*** (ɪkˈstɛnd) *v.* 延長
   (D) cancel (ˈkænsḷ) *v.* 取消

13. (**C**) interfere (,ɪntəˈfɪr) *v.* 妨礙
   (A) formulate (ˈfɔrmjə,let) *v.* 有系統地表達（想法等）
   (C) ***disrupt*** (dɪsˈrʌpt) *v.* 使分裂；使中斷
   dust (dʌst) *n.* 灰塵　　particle (ˈpɑrtɪkḷ) *n.* 粒子
   release (rɪˈlis) *v.* 釋放
   volcanic (vɑlˈkænɪk) *adj.* 火山的
   eruption (ɪˈrʌpʃən) *n.* 爆發　　disturb (dɪˈstɝb) *v.* 擾亂
   magnetic (mægˈnɛtɪk) *adj.* 磁鐵的
   magnetic field 磁場
   communications (kə,mjunəˈkeʃənz) *n. pl.* 通信

14. (**C**) proof (pruf) *n.* 證據
   (A) finance (ˈfaɪnæns) *v.* 提供…資金
   (B) publication (,pʌblɪˈkeʃən) *n.* 出版；發行
   (C) ***evidence*** (ˈɛvədəns) *n.* 證據
   (D) recognition (,rɛkəgˈnɪʃən) *n.* 認可
   biologist (baɪˈɑlədʒɪst) *n.* 生物學家
   theory (ˈθiərɪ) *n.* 理論

15. (**D**) (A) small-scale〔'smɔl'skel〕*adj.* 小規模的
(B) support〔sə'port〕*v.* 支持
(C) initial〔ɪ'nɪʃəl〕*adj.* 最初的
(D) ***incomplete***〔,ɪnkəm'plit〕*adj.* 不完全的
northern〔'nɔrðən〕*adj.* 北部的
waterway〔'wɔtə,we〕*n.* 運河；排水道

16. (**A**) vast〔væst〕*adj.* 巨大的
(A) ***enormous***〔ɪ'nɔrməs〕*adj.* 巨大的
(B) constant〔'kɑnstənt〕*adj.* 不斷的
(C) unknown〔ʌn'non〕*adj.* 未知的
(D) sufficient〔sə'fɪʃənt〕*adj.* 足夠的
invest〔ɪn'vɛst〕*v.* 投資
local〔'lokḷ〕*adj.* 本地的；當地的

17. (**D**) handpick〔'hænd'pɪk〕*v.* 仔細挑選
(A) remove〔rɪ'muv〕*v.* 除去
(B) manage〔'mænɪdʒ〕*v.* 管理；設法
(C) instruct〔ɪn'strʌkt〕*v.* 教導；指示
ruler〔'rulə〕*n.* 統治者
chief〔tʃif〕*adj.* 首席的；主要的
official〔ə'fɪʃəl〕*n.* 官員

18. (**C**) earnest〔'ɝnɪst〕*adj.* 認眞的
(A) pleasant〔'plɛzṇt〕*adj.* 令人愉快的
(B) neutral〔'njutrəl〕*adj.* 中立的
(C) ***serious***〔'sɪrɪəs〕*adj.* 認眞的；嚴肅的
(D) annoyed〔ə'nɔɪd〕*adj.* 苦惱的
expression〔ɪk'sprɛʃən〕*n.* 表情

19. (**D**) (B) guiltily〔'gɪltəlɪ〕*adv.* 內疚地
(C) actively〔'æktɪvlɪ〕*adv.* 積極地
Civil War 南北戰爭　***come to*** 變得
focus〔'fokəs〕*v.* 集中於 <*on*>
slavery〔'slevərɪ〕*n.* 奴隸制度

20. (**D**) aim〔em〕*n.* 目標
(C) proposal〔prə'pozḷ〕*n.* 計劃；提案
(D) ***goal***〔gol〕*n.* 目標
governor〔'gʌvənɚ〕*n.* 州長

21. (**D**) minute〔mə'njut〕*adj.* 微小的
(A) numerous〔'njumərəs〕*adj.* 許多的
(B) variable〔'vɛrɪəbḷ〕*adj.* 易變的
(C) diverse〔daɪ'vɝs〕*adj.* 多種的；不同的
(D) ***tiny***〔'taɪnɪ〕*adj.* 微小的
living things 生物　***consist of*** 由…組成
structure〔'strʌktʃɚ〕*n.* 構造　cell〔sɛl〕*n.* 細胞

22. (**C**) apparently〔ə'pærəntlɪ〕*adv.* 似乎；明顯地
(A) predictably〔prɪ'dɪktəblɪ〕*adv.* 不出所料地
(B) regretfully〔rɪ'grɛtfəlɪ〕*adv.* 後悔地
(C) ***seemingly***〔'simɪŋlɪ〕*adv.* 表面上；似乎
(D) naturally〔'nætʃərəlɪ〕*adv.* 自然地
glassmaking〔'glæs,mekɪŋ〕*n.* 玻璃製造工業

23. (**A**) emblem〔'ɛmbləm〕*n.* 象徵
(A) ***symbol***〔'sɪmbḷ〕*n.* 象徵
(C) suggestion〔sə'dʒɛstʃən〕*n.* 建議
(D) spoil〔spɔɪl〕*n.* 戰利品　*v.* 破壞
bay〔be〕*n.* 月桂樹　laurel〔'lɔrəl〕*n.* 月桂冠
victory〔'vɪktrɪ〕*n.* 勝利

24.（**A**） basically〔 ′besɪkəlɪ 〕*adv.* 基本上

(A) ***fundamentally***〔 ˌfʌndəˈmɛntḷɪ 〕*adv.* 基本上

(B) definitely〔 ′dɛfənɪtlɪ 〕*adv.* 明確地

(C) probably〔 ′prɑbəblɪ 〕*adv.* 可能

(D) frequently〔 ′frikwəntlɪ 〕*adv.* 經常

X ray〔 ′ɛks′re 〕*n.* X光

radiation〔 ˌredɪ′eʃən 〕*n.* 放射線

25.（**C**） survival〔 sɚ′vaɪvḷ 〕*n.* 生存

(A) migration〔 maɪ′greʃən 〕*n.* 遷移

(B) population〔 ˌpɑpjə′leʃən 〕*n.* 人口

(C) ***existence***〔 ɪg′zɪstəns 〕*n.* 存在；生存

(D) evolution〔 ˌɛvə′luʃən 〕*n.* 進化

bald eagle 白頭鷹

ecological〔 ˌɛkə′lɑdʒɪkḷ 〕*adj.* 生態的

concern〔 kən′sɝn 〕*n.* 關心的事；重要的事

26.（**B**） breakthrough〔 ′brekˌθru 〕*n.* 突破

(A) serious〔 ′sɪrɪəs 〕*adj.* 嚴重的

disappointment〔 ˌdɪsə′pɔɪntmənt 〕*n.* 失望；挫敗

(B) ***significant***〔 sɪg′nɪfəkənt 〕*adj.* 重大的

advance〔 əd′væns 〕*n.* 進步

(C) abrupt〔 ə′brʌpt 〕*adj.* 突然的

decline〔 dɪ′klaɪn 〕*n.* 下降；減少

(D) crucial〔 ′kruʃəl 〕*adj.* 非常重要的；艱難的

professional〔 prə′fɛʃənḷ 〕*adj.* 職業的

field〔 fild 〕*n.* 領域

banking〔 ′bæŋkɪŋ 〕*n.* 銀行業

27. (**D**) symptom〔'sɪmptəm〕*n.* 症狀

(A) effect〔ɪ'fɛkt〕*n.* 影響

(B) delight〔dɪ'laɪt〕*n.* 欣喜

(C) force〔fors〕*n.* 力量

(D) ***sign***〔saɪn〕*n.* 跡象；（疾病的）徵兆

influenza〔,ɪnflu'ɛnzə〕*n.* 流行性感冒

fever〔'fivɚ〕*n.* 發燒

muscular〔'mʌskjəlɚ〕*adj.* 肌肉的

28. (**C**) (A) jointly〔'dʒɔɪntlɪ〕*adv.* 共同地

(B) cautiously〔'kɔʃəslɪ〕*adv.* 小心地

(C) ***commonly***〔'kɑmənlɪ〕*adv.* 一般地；通常

(D) intentionally〔ɪn'tɛnʃənḷɪ〕*adv.* 故意地

primary〔'praɪ,mɛrɪ〕*adj.* 主要的

function〔'fʌŋkʃən〕*n.* 功能

inform〔ɪn'fɔrm〕*v.* 告知；通知

feature〔'fitʃɚ〕*n.*（報紙、雜誌等的）特別報導

entertainment〔,ɛntɚ'tenmənt〕*n.* 娛樂

29. (**B**) artificial〔,ɑrtə'fɪʃəl〕*adj.* 人造的

(A) insulate〔'ɪnsə,let〕*v.* 使隔絕；使絕緣

(B) ***synthetic***〔sɪn'θɛtɪk〕*adj.* 合成的；人造的

(C) unadorned〔,ʌnə'dɔrnd〕*adj.* 未加修飾的

(D) complex〔kəm'plɛks ; 'kɑmplæks〕*adj.* 複雜的

acetate〔'æsə,tet〕*n.* 醋酸纖維

fiber〔'faɪbɚ〕*n.* 纖維

30.（**C**） widely〔ˈwaɪdlɪ〕*adv.* 廣泛地
(B) distantly〔ˈdɪstəntlɪ〕*adv.* 遙遠地
(C) ***extensively***〔ɪkˈstɛnsɪvlɪ〕*adv.* 廣泛地
(D) deliberately〔dɪˈlɪbərɪtlɪ〕*adv.* 故意地
environmental〔ɪn,vaɪrənˈmɛntḷ〕*adj.* 環境的
supersonic〔,supɚˈsɑnɪk〕*adj.* 超音速的
sonic boom （超音速飛行器的）聲震

Ⅱ. 結構與書面表達：40%

A. 結構：20%

31.（**D**） 空格應塡一形容詞子句，修飾先行詞 names，又依句意爲現在式，故 (A) 不合，選 (D)。
certain〔ˈsɜtṇ〕*adj.* 某些　　layer〔ˈleɚ〕*n.* 層
atmosphere〔ˈætməs,fɪr〕*n.* 大氣層
indicate〔ˈɪndə,ket〕*v.* 指出
characteristic〔,kærɪktəˈrɪstɪk〕*adj.* 有特質的；獨特的
property〔ˈprɑpɚtɪ〕*n.* 性質

32.（**D**） 本句缺乏動詞，又依句意，there is 表示「有」，故選 (D)。
adhesive〔ədˈhisɪv〕*adj.* 有黏性的
gas〔gæs〕*n.* 氣體　　solid〔ˈsɑlɪd〕*n.* 固體

33.（**A**） 表「在…之中」，介系詞用 among，選 (A)。
galaxy〔ˈgæləksɪ〕*n.* 銀河系
cluster〔ˈklʌstɚ〕*n.* 星團
unit〔ˈjunɪt〕*n.* 單位　　structure〔ˈstrʌktʃɚ〕*n.* 構造
universe〔ˈjunə,vɜs〕*n.* 宇宙

34. (**B**) and 爲對等連接詞，須連接文法地位相同的單字、片語或子句，前面兩個都是 how 引導的名詞子句，故選 (B)。
cancer〔ˈkænsɚ〕*n.* 癌症；腫瘤
arrest〔əˈrɛst〕*v.* 阻礙；抑制　lizard〔ˈlɪzɚd〕*n.* 蜥蜴
tail〔tel〕*n.* 尾巴　cell〔sɛl〕*n.* 細胞
specialize〔ˈspɛʃəl,aɪz〕*v.* 使以特殊方式演化
muscle〔ˈmʌsl̩〕*n.* 肌肉

35. (**B**) 空格應塡插入語，且依句意，選 (B) ***by law***「根據法律規定」。
legal tender 法定貨幣　payment〔ˈpemənt〕*n.* 支付
debt〔dɛt〕*n.* 債務

36. (**C**) ***not only…but also～*** 不僅…而且
depression〔dɪˈprɛʃən〕*n.* 蕭條；衰退
storekeeper〔ˈstor,kipɚ〕*n.* 店主

37. (**D**) 依句意爲被動語態，須用「be + p.p.」，故選 (D) ***are made***。
antibody〔ˈæntɪ,bɑdɪ〕*n.* 抗體
lymphocyte〔ˈlɪmfə,saɪt〕*n.* 淋巴球
plasma〔ˈplæzmə〕*n.* 血漿；淋巴液

38. (**A**) 由分詞構句 known for…可知，應是前後主詞相同，才省略副詞子句中的主詞，形成分詞構句。依句意，主詞應是 Peggy Brown，故選 (A)。
be known for 以～聞名
caricature〔ˈkærɪkətʃɚ〕*n.* 漫畫；諷刺畫
illustrate〔ˈɪləstret〕*v.* 加插畫於（書本等）

39. (**C**) 表目的，須用不定詞，選 (C) ***To obtain***「爲了要獲得」。
pure〔pjʊr〕*adj.* 純粹的　lead〔lɛd〕*n.* 鉛
ore〔or〕*n.* 礦石　mine〔maɪn〕*v.* 開採
smelt〔smɛlt〕*v.* 冶鍊　refine〔rɪˈfaɪn〕*v.* 精煉；琢磨

40.（**A**）空格應填動詞 receives，為了避免重複，可用助動詞 does 代替，且 does 可移至名詞前面，形成倒裝。
western〔ˈwɛstɚn〕*adj.* 西部的
Nebraska〔nəˈbræskə〕*n.* 內布拉斯加（美國中西部一州）
generally〔ˈdʒɛnərəlɪ〕*adv.* 通常
receive〔rɪˈsiv〕*v.* 得到；承接
eastern〔ˈistɚn〕*adj.* 東部的

41.（**B**）依句意，「諾貝爾獎是全世界最有聲望的榮譽」，故選 (B)。
Nobel prize 諾貝爾獎
height〔haɪt〕*n.* 極致
prestigious〔prɛsˈtɪdʒɪəs〕*adj.* 有聲望的
honor〔ˈɑnɚ〕*n.* 榮譽
prestige〔ˈprɛstɪdʒ〕*n.* 名聲；聲望

42.（**D**）依句意，「被荷蘭人殖民的布魯克林區，直到大約兩世紀後，也就是 1834 年，才被併入城市中」，故選 (D)。而 Settled by the Dutch 是由副詞子句簡化而來的分詞構句。
(A) settle〔ˈsɛtl̩〕*v.* 定居於；殖民於
Dutch〔dʌtʃ〕*n.* 荷蘭人
incorporate〔ɪnˈkɔrpəˌret〕*v.* 把…併入；把…編入
century〔ˈsɛntʃərɪ〕*n.* 世紀

43.（**C**）依句意，選 (C) ***Despite***「儘管」。而 (B) Although 是連接詞，須引導子句，在此用法不合。
inclination〔ˌɪnkləˈneʃən〕*n.* 愛好；想做…
schooling〔ˈskulɪŋ〕*n.* 學校教育
career〔kəˈrɪr〕*n.* 職業；生涯
ministry〔ˈmɪnɪstrɪ〕*n.* 神職人員的職務

44. (**A**) 空格前已有動詞 became，而兩動詞之間沒有連接詞，第二個動詞須改爲現在分詞，故選(A)。
inspire〔ɪn'spaɪr〕*v.* 鼓舞；激勵
cabin〔'kæbɪn〕*n.* 小屋　***best seller*** 暢銷書；暢銷商品
time〔taɪm〕*n.* 時代　host〔host〕*n.* 許多
imitator〔'ɪmə,tetɚ〕*n.* 模仿者

45. (**A**) 表地點，關係副詞須用 where，故選(A)。
ancient〔'enʃənt〕*adj.* 古老的；古代的
ruins〔'ruɪnz〕*n. pl.* 廢墟；遺跡　lie〔laɪ〕*v.* 在
legendary〔'lɛdʒənd,ɛrɪ〕*adj.* 傳奇性的；有名的

46. (**D**) (A)(B)「No sooner + S_1 + had + p.p. + than + S_2 + 過去式動詞」表「一～就…」。
(D) ***as soon as*** 一…就…
hatch〔hætʃ〕*v.* 孵化
***fend for** oneself* 自食其力；獨立生活

47. (**C**) 依句意，「在所有的金屬中，具有最高的熔點」，故選(C)。
melting point 熔點　tungsten〔'tʌŋstən〕*n.* 鎢
gray〔gre〕*adj.* 灰色的　metal〔'mɛtḷ〕*n.* 金屬
wire〔waɪr〕*n.* 電線　electric〔ɪ'lɛktrɪk〕*adj.* 電的
light bulb 燈泡

48. (**B**) rattan〔ræ'tæn〕*n.* 藤條
(B) reedy〔'ridɪ〕*adj.* 細長的　stem〔stɛm〕*n.* 莖
palm〔pɑm〕*n.* 棕櫚

49. (**D**) position〔pə'zɪʃən〕*n.* 工作；職位
district school（美國的）鄉村學校
article〔'ɑrtɪkḷ〕*n.* 文章　***in print*** 印好的；已出版的

50. (**B**) 本句缺少主要動詞，故選(B) ***was the***。
vitamin〔ˈvaɪtəmɪn〕*n.* 維他命
molecular〔məˈlɛkjələ˞〕*adj.* 分子的
structure〔ˈstrʌktʃə˞〕*n.* 結構
establish〔əˈstæblɪʃ〕*v.* 確立

B. 書面表達：20%

51. (**B**) *governmental* → ***government's***
individual〔ˌɪndəˈvɪdʒuəl〕*adj.* 個人的
income tax 所得稅　source〔sors〕*n.* 來源
revenue〔ˈrɛvəˌnju〕*n.*（國家的）歲入；收入

52. (**B**) *who* → ***which***
muscle〔ˈmʌsḷ〕*n.* 肌肉
account〔əˈkaʊnt〕*v.*（在數量、比例方面）佔 <*for*>
approximately〔əˈprɑksəmɪtlɪ〕*adv.* 大約

53. (**D**) *must to work* → ***must work***
disease〔dɪˈziz〕*n.* 疾病
worldwide〔ˈwɝldˈwaɪd〕*adj.* 世界性的
scale〔skel〕*n.* 規模

54. (**C**) *are* → ***is***
range〔rendʒ〕*n.*（一列）山脈
be rich in 盛產～　coal〔kol〕*n.* 煤

55. (**D**) *they* → ***them***
distinctive〔dɪˈstɪŋktɪv〕*adj.* 獨特的
feature〔ˈfitʃə˞〕*n.* 特徵　identify〔aɪˈdɛntəˌfaɪ〕*v.* 分辨
glance〔glæns〕*n.* 看一眼

56. (**B**) *consume* → ***consumes***

consume〔kən'sum〕*v.* 消耗

57. (**A**) *about* → ***with***

compared with 和～相比　　desert〔'dɛzɚt〕*n.* 沙漠

sparsely〔'spɑrslɪ〕*adv.* 稀少地

populate〔'pɑpjə,let〕*v.* 居住於

58. (**B**) *invented 1821* → ***invented in 1821***

Cherokee〔'tʃɛrə,ki〕*adj.* 徹羅基人的

invent〔ɪn'vɛnt〕*v.* 發明　　member〔'mɛmbɚ〕*n.* 成員

Indian〔'ɪndɪən〕*adj.* 印第安人的

59. (**C**) *attraction* → ***attractive***

industrial designer 工業產品設計師

efficient〔ə'fɪʃənt〕*adj.* 有效率的

60. (**A**) *or* → ***and***

raise〔rez〕*v.* 飼養　　meat〔mit〕*n.* 肉

domesticated〔də'mɛstə,ketɪd〕*adj.* 馴養的

61. (**A**) *softly* → ***softer***

chalk〔tʃɔk〕*n.* 白堊　　mineral〔'mɪnərəl〕*n.* 礦物

limestone〔'laɪm,ston〕*n.* 石灰石

minute〔mə'njut〕*adj.* 微小的

marine〔mə'rin〕*adj.* 海的；海產的

shell〔ʃɛl〕*n.* 貝殼

62. (**D**) *around Sun* → ***around the Sun***

rate〔ret〕*n.* 比率　　speed〔spid〕*n.* 速度；速率

63.（ **D** ） *its* → ***their***
financial〔fə'nænʃəl〕*adj.* 財務的
beset〔bɪ'sɛt〕*v.* 困擾
museum〔mju'ziəm〕*n.* 博物館
closure〔'kloʒɚ〕*n.* 關閉

64.（ **C** ） *different* → ***differ***
pure〔pjʊr〕*adj.* 純的
cane sugar 蔗糖　　***beet sugar*** 甜菜糖
chemically〔'kɛmɪklɪ〕*adv.* 化學上
identical〔aɪ'dɛntɪkl〕*adj.* 完全相同的
differ〔'dɪfɚ〕*v.* 不同
sweetness〔'switnɪs〕*n.* 甜度

65.（ **B** ） *explanation* → ***to explain***
ancient〔'enʃənt〕*adj.* 古代的
myth〔mɪθ〕*n.* 神話
attempt〔ə'tɛmpt〕*n.* 嘗試
catastrophic〔,kætə'strɑfɪk〕*adj.* 大災難的
volcanic〔vɑl'kænɪk〕*adj.* 火山的
eruption〔ɪ'rʌpʃən〕*n.* 爆發

66.（ **D** ） *another* → ***other***
mineral〔'mɪnərəl〕*n.* 礦物　*adj.* 礦物的
prospector〔prə'spɛktɚ〕*n.* 勘探者
geophysics〔,dʒio'fɪzɪks〕*n.* 地球物理學
locate〔lo'ket〕*v.* 查出…的位置
deposit〔dɪ'pɑzɪt〕*n.* 礦藏；礦床
uranium〔ju'renɪəm〕*n.* 鈾

67. (**C**) *discovery dramatic* → ***dramatic discovery***

spectrum〔ˈspɛktrəm〕*n.* 光譜　　***lead to*** 導致
dramatic〔drəˈmætɪk〕*adj.* 重大的；戲劇性的
discovery〔dɪˈskʌvərɪ〕*n.* 發現
element〔ˈɛləmənt〕*n.* 元素　　helium〔ˈhilɪəm〕*n.* 氦

68. (**A**) *Alive* → ***Living***

alive〔əˈlaɪv〕*adj.* 活著的（不可放在名詞之前）
living〔ˈlɪvɪŋ〕*adj.* 活的（置於名詞之前）
creature〔ˈkritʃɚ〕*n.* 生物
remarkably〔rɪˈmɑrkəblɪ〕*adv.* 顯著地
diversify〔daɪˈvɝsə,faɪ〕*v.* 使不同；多樣化
shape〔ʃep〕*n.* 形狀

69. (**B**) *costing* → ***costly***

dried〔draɪd〕*adj.* 乾燥的　　***dried fruit*** 水果乾；蜜餞
costly〔ˈkɔstlɪ〕*adj.* 昂貴的　　store〔stor〕*v.* 儲存
satisfactorily〔,sætɪsˈfæktərəlɪ〕*adv.* 令人滿意地

70. (**C**) *too* → ***as***

tide〔taɪd〕*n.* 潮水　　vary〔ˈvɛrɪ〕*v.* 變化；不同

Ⅲ. 閱讀測驗：30％

A. 71-77 題

【譯文】

人類似乎生來就會計算。小孩子的數字能力很早就開始發展，而且無法阻擋，所以我們不難想像，有一個代表數學成熟度的生理時鐘，正引導著他們成長。在學會走路和說話後不久，他們就能以令人印象

深刻的準確度，擺好餐具準備開飯——替五張椅子，每一張都擺上一個盤子、一把刀子、一支湯匙和一支叉子。很快他們就會注意到，他們擺了五把刀子、湯匙和叉子在桌上，然後再過一下子，他們就會發現總共是十五件銀製餐具。在精通加法之後，他們會繼續學習減法。看來我們幾乎可以合理地預期說，如果有個孩子，一出生就被隔離在荒島上，七年之後才把他找回來，那麼他或她可以直接就讀二年級的數學課程，而不會有什麼智力調整方面的重大問題。

事實當然沒這麼簡單。在本世紀，認知心理學家的研究中，把智力發展要靠每天學習的微妙方式說得很清楚。觀察孩童如何慢慢理解——或者，看情況，也可能是偶然發現——那些大人視爲理所當然的概念，舉例來說，當他們拒絕承認，水從一個矮胖的杯子倒進一個高瘦的杯子時，量並沒有改變時。心理學家從那時起，就已經說明，當小孩子被要求數一堆鉛筆時，他們可以輕易地說出藍色鉛筆或紅色鉛筆的數量，但卻必須要哄他們，他們才能算出總數。從這樣的研究可以知道，數學的基本原理是要逐漸掌握的，而且要靠努力才能辦到。從這些研究，我們還可以知道，就連抽象數字的概念也是如此——一、二、三的概念，可以被應用在任一種物體上，而且在做任何比準備餐具更需要數學的事時，它都是不可或缺的——這樣的概念絕不是與生俱來的。

【答案】

71. (**C**)　72. (**A**)　73. (**C**)　74. (**D**)　75. (**A**)
76. (**D**)　77. (**C**)

【註】

appear 〔ə'pɪr〕*v.* 似乎　born 〔bɔrn〕*adj.* 天生的
compute 〔kəm'pjut〕*v.* 計算
numerical 〔nju'mɛrɪkl̩〕*adj.* 數字的

inexorably〔ɪn'ɛksərəblɪ〕*adv.* 不容變更地；不可阻擋地
imagine〔ɪ'mædʒɪn〕*v.* 想像
internal〔ɪn'tɜnḷ〕*adj.* 體內的　***internal clock*** 生理時鐘
mathematical〔ˌmæθə'mætɪkḷ〕*adj.* 數學上的
maturity〔mə'tjʊrətɪ〕*n.* 成熟　guide〔gaɪd〕*v.* 引導
set the table 把餐具擺在桌上準備開飯
impressive〔ɪm'prɛsɪv〕*adj.* 令人印象深刻的
accuracy〔'ækjərəsɪ〕*n.* 正確
plate〔plet〕*n.* 盤子　knife〔naɪf〕*n.* 刀子
spoon〔spun〕*n.* 湯匙　fork〔fɔrk〕*n.* 叉子
note〔not〕*v.* 注意　bit〔bɪt〕*n.* 一會兒；片刻

amount to 總計；共計　piece〔pis〕*n.* 件
silverware〔'sɪlvɚˌwɛr〕*n.* 銀器；銀製餐具
master〔'mæstɚ〕*v.* 精通
addition〔ə'dɪʃən〕*n.* 加法　***move on*** 繼續前進
subtraction〔səb'trækʃən〕*n.* 減法
reasonable〔'riznəbḷ〕*adj.* 合理的
seclude〔sɪ'klud〕*v.* 隔離；隔絕
desert〔'dɛzɚt〕*adj.* 荒涼的；無人煙的　***at birth*** 一出生
retrieve〔rɪ'triv〕*v.* 尋回　grade〔gred〕*n.* 年級
serious〔'sɪrɪəs〕*adj.* 嚴重的

intellectual〔ˌɪntḷ'ɛktʃuəl〕*adj.* 智力的
adjustment〔ə'dʒʌstmənt〕*n.* 調整
century〔'sɛntʃərɪ〕*n.* 世紀　work〔wɜk〕*n.* 研究
cognitive〔'kɑgnətɪv〕*adj.* 認知的
psychologist〔saɪ'kɑlədʒɪst〕*n.* 心理學家
illuminate〔ɪ'luməˌnet〕*v.* 把…解釋清楚
subtle〔'sʌtḷ〕*adj.* 微妙的
progress〔'prɑgrɛs〕*n.* 發展；進步

observe〔əb'zɝv〕*v.* 觀察　grasp〔græsp〕*v.* 理解
as the case may be 看情況　***bump into*** 偶然遇到；意外碰到
concept〔'kɑnsɛpt〕*n.* 想法；概念
adult〔ə'dʌlt〕*n.* 成人
refuse〔rɪ'fjuz〕*v.* 拒絕　concede〔kən'sid〕*v.* 承認
pour〔por〕*v.* 傾倒　stout〔staut〕*adj.* 矮胖的
demonstrate〔'dɛmən,stret〕*v.* 說明；示範
pile〔paɪl〕*n.* 一堆　readily〔'rɛdɪlɪ〕*adv.* 輕易地
report〔rɪ'port〕*v.* 報告；說　coax〔koks〕*v.* 勸誘；哄
suggest〔sə'dʒɛst〕*v.* 顯示

rudiment〔'rudəmənt〕*n.* 基礎
gradually〔'grædʒuəlɪ〕*adv.* 逐漸地　very〔'vɛrɪ〕*adj.* 正是；就是
abstract〔'æbstrækt〕*adj.* 抽象的　apply〔ə'plaɪ〕*v.* 應用
class〔klæs〕*n.* 種類　object〔'ɑbdʒɪkt〕*n.* 物體
prerequisite〔pri'rɛkwəzɪt〕*n.* 先決條件
mathematically〔,mæθə'mætɪklɪ〕*adv.* 數學上
demanding〔dɪ'mændɪŋ〕*adj.* 要求多的
far from 完全不；一點也不
innate〔ɪ'net〕*adj.* 天賦的；與生俱來的
trend〔trɛnd〕*n.* 趨勢　psychology〔saɪ'kɑlədʒɪ〕*n.* 心理學

fundamental〔,fʌndə'mɛntl̩〕*adj.* 基本的　infer〔ɪn'fɝ〕*v.* 推論
normally〔'nɔrml̩ɪ〕*adv.* 通常　counting〔'kauntɪŋ〕*n.* 計數
mature〔mə'tjur〕*adj.* 成熟的　illustrate〔'ɪləstret〕*v.* 說明
clarify〔'klærə,faɪ〕*v.* 使清楚明白　light〔laɪt〕*v.* 點燃
imply〔ɪm'plaɪ〕*v.* 暗示　transfer〔træns'fɝ〕*v.* 轉移
container〔kən'tenɚ〕*n.* 容器　guess〔gɛs〕*v.* 猜
subtract〔səb'trækt〕*v.* 減　***refer to*** 是指
requirement〔rɪ'kwaɪrmənt〕*n.* 必備條件
technique〔tɛk'nik〕*n.* 技術

B. 71-77題

【譯文】

植物學，就是植物研究，它在人類知識的歷史上，佔據著一個獨特的位置。好幾千年來，它是人類唯一認識的領域，而且人類對它不只是模糊的瞭解。現在要知道我們石器時代的祖先，對植物有何瞭解是不可能的，但是我們可以從觀察現在仍然存在的未工業化社會中發現，他們很久以前就已經對植物和其特性有了詳盡的了解。這是很合理的。植物對所有生物，甚至是對其他植物而言，都是食物金字塔的基礎。它們對人類福祉來說，一直都非常重要，它們不但可以當作食物，還可以做成衣服、武器、工具、染料、藥物、住處，還有很多其他用途。現在住在亞馬遜叢林裡的部落，確實可以認出數百種植物，還有它們各自擁有的許多特性。對這些部落來說，植物本身沒有名字，而且他們可能一點也不認為那是一門專門的學問。

很不幸地，我們工業化的程度愈高，就愈不可能和植物有直接的接觸，而且對植物的瞭解，也比較沒有明顯的增長。但是幾乎每個人，都無意間對植物發展出驚人的認識，所以很少人會認不出一朵玫瑰、一顆蘋果，或是一株蘭花。大約一萬年前，當我們住在中東的新石器時代祖先，發現某些草可以被採收，而且栽種它們的種子，能為下一季帶來更豐富的收穫時，使植物和人類產生新關聯的第一大步，就由此展開了。他們發現了穀物，而且還因此產生了農業奇蹟：栽種農作物。從那時起，人們控制了某些植物的生產，並逐漸以此維生，而不再東採一點，西採一點野生的各種植物了——至於他們好幾萬年以來，由經驗所累積的知識，還有和野生植物的親密關係，也開始逐漸消失了。

【答案】

78. (A)　79. (C)　80. (B)　81. (C)　82. (D)
83. (C)　84. (C)　85. (B)

【註】

plant〔plænt〕*n.* 植物 *v.* 種植
botany〔ˈbɑtṇɪ〕*n.* 植物學 study〔ˈstʌdɪ〕*n.* 研究
occupy〔ˈɑkjəˌpaɪ〕*v.* 佔據
peculiar〔pɪˈkjuljɚ〕*adj.* 獨特的
field〔fild〕*n.* 領域 awareness〔əˈwɛrnɪs〕*n.* 意識；察覺
vague〔veg〕*adj.* 模糊的 insight〔ˈɪnˌsaɪt〕*n.* 深入了解
Stone Age 石器時代 ancestor〔ˈænsɛstɚ〕*n.* 祖先
observe〔əbˈzɝv〕*v.* 觀察
preindustrial〔ˌpriɪnˈdʌstrɪəl〕*adj.* 未工業化的

detailed〔dɪˈteld〕*adj.* 詳盡的
learning〔ˈlɝnɪŋ〕*n.* 學問；知識
property〔ˈprɑpɚtɪ〕*n.* 特性
extremely〔ɪkˈstrimlɪ〕*adv.* 非常
ancient〔ˈenʃənt〕*adj.* 古代的；年代久遠的
logical〔ˈlɑdʒɪkḷ〕*adj.* 邏輯上的；合理的
pyramid〔ˈpɪrəmɪd〕*n.* 金字塔 ***food pyramid*** 食物金字塔
enormously〔ɪˈnɔrməslɪ〕*adv.* 極大地
welfare〔ˈwɛlˌfɛr〕*n.* 福祉

dye〔daɪ〕*n.* 染料 shelter〔ˈʃɛltɚ〕*n.* 避難所；住處
purpose〔ˈpɝpəs〕*n.* 用途 tribe〔traɪb〕*n.* 部落
jungle〔ˈdʒʌŋgḷ〕*n.* 叢林
recognize〔ˈrɛkəgˌnaɪz〕*v.* 認出；認爲
literally〔ˈlɪtərəlɪ〕*adv.* 確實地 ***as such*** 本身
branch〔bræntʃ〕*n.* 部門；分科 ***at all*** 一點也（不）
unfortunately〔ʌnˈfɔrtʃənɪtlɪ〕*adv.* 不幸地
industrialized〔ɪnˈdʌstrɪəlˌaɪzd〕*adj.* 工業化的

farther〔'fɑrðɚ〕*adj.* 更遠的
contact〔'kɑntækt〕*n.* 接觸
distinct〔dɪ'stɪŋkt〕*adj.* 明顯的；清楚的
unconsciously〔ʌn'kɑnʃəslɪ〕*adv.* 無意間地
amazing〔ə'mezɪŋ〕*adj.* 驚人的
botanical〔bo'tænɪkḷ〕*adj.* 植物的
fail to V. 無法　　orchid〔'ɔrkɪd〕*n.* 蘭花
Neolithic〔ˌniə'lɪθɪk〕*adj.* 新石器時代的
grass〔græs〕*n.* 草　　harvest〔'hɑrvɪst〕*v.* 收割；採收
seed〔sid〕*n.* 種子

rich〔rɪtʃ〕*adj.* 豐富的　　yield〔jild〕*n.* 生產量
association〔əˌsosɪ'eʃən〕*n.* 關聯
grain〔gren〕*n.* 穀物　　flow〔flo〕*v.* 產生
marvel〔'mɑrvḷ〕*n.* 奇蹟
agriculture〔'ægrɪˌkʌltʃɚ〕*n.* 農業
cultivated〔'kʌltəˌvetɪd〕*adj.* 栽培的
crop〔krɑp〕*n.* 農作物
increasingly〔ɪn'krisɪŋlɪ〕*adv.* 逐漸地
controlled〔kən'trold〕*adj.* 受控制的
variety〔və'raɪətɪ〕*n.* 種類　　wild〔waɪld〕*adj.* 野生的

accumulated〔ə'kjumjəˌletɪd〕*adj.* 累積的
tens of thousands of 好幾萬的
intimacy〔'ɪntəməsɪ〕*n.* 親密關係；親近
in the wild 在野外　　fade〔fed〕*v.* 逐漸消失
assumption〔ə'sʌmpʃən〕*n.* 假設
extensive〔ɪk'stɛnsɪv〕*adj.* 廣泛的
divide〔də'vaɪd〕*v.* 分類；劃分
well-defined〔'wɛldɪ'faɪnd〕*adj.* 明確的

ownership (′onə͵ʃɪp) *n.* 所有權
comment (′kɑmɛnt) *n.* 評論
extent (ɪk′stɛnt) *n.* 程度；範圍
reasonable (′riznəbl) *adj.* 合理的
assume (ə′sjum) *v.* 假定　　behave (bɪ′hev) *v.* 行爲；表現
organized (′ɔrgən͵aɪzd) *adj.* 有組織的
phrase (frez) *n.* 片語
general (′dʒɛnərəl) *adj.* 一般的；全面的
decline (dɪ′klaɪn) *v.* 減少

no longer 不再　　value (′væljʊ) *v.* 評價；重視
resource (rɪ′sors) *n.* 資源　　research (rɪ′sɝtʃ) *n.* 研究
keep up with 趕上　　***a variety of*** 各種的
mention (′mɛnʃən) *v.* 提到
poetic (po′ɛtɪk) *adj.* 富有詩意的
cite (saɪt) *v.* 引用　　illustrate (′ɪləstret) *v.* 加插圖於
diversity (daɪ′vɝsətɪ) *n.* 差異；多樣性
practice (′præktɪs) *n.* 實行　　invention (ɪn′vɛnʃən) *n.* 發明

agricultural (͵ægrɪ′kʌltʃərəl) *adj.* 農業的
implement (′ɪmpləmənt) *n.* 用具
machinery (mə′ʃinərɪ) *n.* 機器
replant (ri′plænt) *v.* 再種植　　diet (′daɪət) *n.* 飲食
abundant (ə′bʌndənt) *adj.* 豐富的
manage (′mænɪdʒ) *v.* 管理
required (rɪ′kwaɪrd) *adj.* 必修的
advanced (əd′vænst) *adj.* 先進的

私立輔仁大學九十三學年度
碩士班研究生入學考試英文試題

I. Choose the best answer to complete each sentence.

1. The corporation ________ its prices temporarily until the board reviews the situation.
   (A) freeze (B) has frozen
   (C) freezing (D) had frozen

2. Stock prices ________ sharply last week after the strike was announced.
   (A) fell (B) have fallen
   (C) had fell (D) have been falling

3. The mayor ________ from the race for governor because of inadequate financial support.
   (A) had withdrawn (B) withdrawn
   (C) withdrawing (D) has drawn

4. The department managers in the home office ________ the most competitive products for the branch offices from several alternatives.
   (A) is choosing (B) choose
   (C) has chosen (D) were chosen

5. Ms. Jackson ________ more than 50,000 miles this year on company business.
   (A) was flying (B) got flown
   (C) must have flown (D) had been flown

6. I was annoyed ________ the loan officer when she postponed the meeting again.
   (A) for (B) on (C) to (D) with

7. The new assistant adapted readily ________ the demands of the job.
   (A) to (B) with (C) for (D) at

8. Why did the boss object ________ your decision about next year's budget?
   (A) with (B) at (C) to (D) for

9. This machine differs ________ the one you are using now.
   (A) with (B) by (C) from (D) to

10. Our textbook is the same ________ yours.
    (A) from (B) with (C) like (D) as

11. He often does ________ about the house.
    (A) works (B) jobs
    (C) homework (D) houseworks

12. The train ________ at a terrific speed.
    (A) passed (B) go by
    (C) past (D) speeds

13. He is ________ difficult child. He objects to everything.
    (A) so (B) such kind of a
    (C) so much a (D) such a

14. I'm not very good at chess. He always ________ me.
    (A) wins (B) won
    (C) beats (D) beated

15. I ________ swimming in cold water.
    (A) am used to (B) used to
    (C) usually (D) use to

16. Do you think it will ________ any difference?
    (A) do (B) make (C) be (D) let

17. He often lies, so I ________ he is not telling the truth now.
    (A) suspect (B) wonder
    (C) doubt (D) deny

18. She likes *The Lord of the Rings* so much that she has seen it ________ times.
    (A) for six (B) sixth
    (C) six (D) past six

19. Her teacher suggested ________ read extensively for pleasure.
    (A) she to (B) her for
    (C) her (D) that she

20. The ancient people who lived here long ago ________ farmers.
    (A) could be (B) should be
    (C) was (D) must have been

Ⅱ. Choose the answer which means the same as the model sentence.

21. I thought you did your banking at First Federal.
 (A) I think you do your banking at First Federal.
 (B) Don't you do your banking at First Federal?
 (C) I think you did your banking at First Federal.
 (D) I thought you should bank at First Federal.

22. My daughter graduates in a couple of days.
 (A) Will my daughter graduate in a couple of days?
 (B) My daughter's graduation was in a couple of days.
 (C) My daughter is graduating in a couple of days.
 (D) My daughter goes to graduate school in a couple of days.

23. They decided to take a bus around the city for a couple of hours.
 (A) Their decision on a bus around the city took them a couple of hours.
 (B) It took them a couple of hours around the city to decide on the bus.
 (C) Taking a bus around the city would take a couple of hours, they decided.
 (D) They decided to ride around the city on a bus for a couple of hours.

24. Do you mind if I ask what kind of grades you have?
 (A) Did I ask what kind of grades you have?
 (B) What kind of grades do you have?
 (C) I won't ask what kind of grades you have.
 (D) Do you want to know about your grades?

25. If you'll just wait here another few minutes....
    (A) If you waited here another few minutes....
    (B) Are you going to wait here another few minutes?
    (C) Have you been waiting here long?
    (D) Please wait here a few more minutes.

Ⅲ. In the following passage, some of the words have been left out. First, read over the entire passage and try to understand what it is about. Then, choose the answer that *best* fits in each blank from the choices offered after the passage.

The Personality of Man

Why does the idea of progress loom so large in the modern world? Surely because progress of a particular ___(26)___ is actually taking place around us ___(27)___ is becoming more and more manifest. ___(28)___ mankind has undergone no general improvement ___(29)___ intelligence or morality, it has made ___(30)___ progress in the accumulation of knowledge. ___(31)___ began to increase as soon as ___(32)___ thoughts of one individual could be ___(33)___ to another by means of speech. ___(34)___ the invention of writing, a great ___(35)___ was made, for knowledge could then ___(36)___ not only communicated but also stored. ___(37)___ made education possible, and education in ___(38)___ turn added to libraries: the growth ___(39)___ knowledge followed a kind of compound-interest ___(40)___, which was greatly enhanced by the ___(41)___ of printing. All this was comparatively ___(42)___ until, with the coming of science, the ___(43)___ was suddenly increased. Then knowledge ___(44)___ to be accumulated according to a ___(45)___ plan. The trickle became a stream; ___(46)___ stream has now become a torrent. ___(47)___, as soon as new knowledge is ___(48)___, it is now turned to practical ___(49)___. What is called "modern civilization" is ___(50)___ the result of a balanced development of all man's nature, but of accumulated knowledge applied to practical life. The problem now facing humanity is: What is going to be done with all this knowledge? As is so often pointed out, knowledge is a double-edged sword which can be used equally for good or evil. It is now being used indifferently for both. Could any spectacle, for instance, be more grimly whimsical than that of gunners using science to shatter men's bodies while, close at hand, surgeons use it to restore them? We have to ask ourselves very seriously what will happen if this twofold use of knowledge, with its ever-increasing power, continues.

26. (A) kind (B) age
(C) society (D) situation

27. (A) and (B) that
(C) but (D) which

28. (A) Even (B) Despite of
(C) Although (D) Despite that

29. (A) about (B) in
(C) on (D) with

30. (A) some (B) unanimous
(C) anonymous (D) extraordinary

31. (A) This (B) Progress
(C) Knowledge (D) Culture

32. (A) the (B) idiosyncratic
(C) unique (D) collective

33. (A) transmuted (B) changed
(C) accessible (D) communicated

34. (A) Having (B) Supported by
(C) Without (D) With

35. (A) tradition (B) advance
(C) impairment (D) civilization

36. (A) be (B) become
(C) get (D) make

37. (A) Acquisition (B) Knowledge
(C) Libraries (D) Schools

38. (A) a (B) the
(C) its (D) every

39. (A) with (B) for
(C) from (D) of

40. (A) account (B) route
(C) progress (D) law

41. (A) invention (B) inflection
(C) completion (D) system

42. (A) slow (B) regressive
(C) delayed (D) staggered

43. (A) trade (B) rate
(C) ratio (D) efficiency

44. (A) became (B) began
(C) got (D) was made

45. (A) systematic (B) compound
(C) complete (D) regressive

46. (A) a (B) and
(C) the (D) but the

47. (A) Whereas (B) Apparently
(C) Nevertheless (D) Moreover

48. (A) made (B) acquired
(C) communicating (D) accumulating

49. (A) value (B) science
(C) account (D) practice

50. (A) not only (B) nothing but
(C) not (D) by no mean

私立輔仁大學九十三學年度
碩士班研究生入學考試英文試題詳解

I. 選擇最適當的答案來完成每個句子

1. (**B**) 依句意爲現在完成式，故選 (B) ***has frozen***。
freeze〔friz〕*v.* 穩固（物價、工資）
corporation〔ˌkɔrpəˈreʃən〕*n.* 公司
temporarily〔ˈtɛmpəˌrɛrəlɪ〕*adv.* 暫時地
board〔bord〕*n.* 董事會
review〔rɪˈvju〕*v.* 再考量；觀察

2. (**A**) 依句意爲過去式，故選 (A) ***fell***「下跌」。
stock〔stɑk〕*n.* 股票
sharply〔ˈʃɑrplɪ〕*adv.* 劇烈地；急速地
strike〔straɪk〕*n.* 罷工　announce〔əˈnaʊns〕*v.* 宣佈

3. (**A**) 依句意爲過去完成式，選 (A) ***had withdrawn***。
withdraw〔wɪðˈdrɔ〕*v.* 退出
mayor〔ˈmeɚ〕*n.* 市長　race〔res〕*n.* 競賽；競選
governor〔ˈgʌvənɚ〕*n.* 州長
inadequate〔ɪnˈædəkwɪt〕*adj.* 不足的
financial〔fəˈnænʃəl〕*adj.* 財政的；財務的
support〔səˈport〕*n.* 支持；資助

4. (**B**) department〔dɪˈpɑrtmənt〕*n.* 部門
manager〔ˈmænɪdʒɚ〕*n.* 經理　***home office*** 總公司
competitive〔kəmˈpɛtətɪv〕*adj.* 經得起競爭的
branch〔bræntʃ〕*n.* 分公司；分店
alternative〔ɔlˈtɝnətɪv〕*n.* 可選擇的事物

5. (**C**) 依句意，選(C) ***must have flown***。

6. (**D**) annoy〔əˈnɔɪ〕*v.* 使生氣
be annoyed with 對～生氣　　loan〔lon〕*n.* 貸款
officer〔ˈɔfəsɚ〕*n.* 職員；官員
postpone〔postˈpon〕*v.* 延期

7. (**A**) assistant〔əˈsɪstənt〕*n.* 助理
adapt〔əˈdæpt〕*v.* 適應 < *to* >
readily〔ˈrɛdɪlɪ〕*adv.* 迅速地；輕易地
demand〔dɪˈmænd〕*n.* 要求；需求

8. (**C**) ***object to*** 反對
budget〔ˈbʌdʒɪt〕*n.* 預算

9. (**C**) ***differ from*** 和～不同

10. (**D**) textbook〔ˈtɛkst,bʊk〕*n.* 課本
be the same as 和～一樣

11. (**B**) (D) housework〔ˈhaʊs,wɝk〕*n.* 家事（爲不可數名詞）

12. (**A**) (B) go by 經過（須改成 went by）
(C) past〔pæst〕*prep.* 經過
(D) speed〔spid〕*n.* 速度　*v.* 加速
terrific〔təˈrɪfɪk〕*adj.* 極大的

13. (**D**) { such a difficult child
= so difficult a child

difficult〔ˈdɪfə,kʌlt〕*adj.* 麻煩的；難以取悅的
object〔əbˈdʒɛkt〕*v.* 討厭；反對 < *to* >

14. (**C**) (A) win〔wɪn〕*v.* 贏（其後只能接「比賽」、「獎品」，不可接人，故在此不合。）
(C) ***beat***〔bit〕*v.* 擊敗（三態變化爲：beat-beat-beat）
be good at 擅長
chess〔tʃɛs〕*n.* 西洋棋

15. (**A**) (A) ***be used to + V-ing*** 習慣於～
(B) used to + V. 以前常常

16. (**B**) ***make a difference*** 有影響；有差別

17. (**A**) (A) ***suspect***〔sə'spɛkt〕*v.* 相信（＝*believe*）；懷疑
(B) wonder〔'wʌndɚ〕*v.* 想知道
(C) doubt〔daʊt〕*v.* 不相信（＝*disbelieve*）；懷疑
(D) deny〔dɪ'naɪ〕*v.* 否認
lie〔laɪ〕*v.* 說謊

18. (**C**) six times「六次」雖是名詞片語，但在本句中當副詞用。
The Lord of the Rings 魔戒

19. (**D**) suggest（建議）爲慾望動詞，其後接 that 子句時，子句中的 should 可省略，故選 (D)。
extensively〔ɪk'stɛnsɪvlɪ〕*adv.* 廣泛地
pleasure〔'plɛʒɚ〕*n.* 樂趣

20. (**D**) 「must have + p.p.」表「對過去肯定的推測」，作「當時一定」解。
ancient〔'enʃənt〕*adj.* 古代的

Ⅱ. 選出和例句相同意思的答案：

21.（**B**）banking〔ˈbæŋkɪŋ〕*n.* 銀行業；銀行業務
federal〔ˈfɛdərəl〕*adj.* 聯邦的

22.（**C**）graduate〔ˈgrædʒʊˌet〕*v.* 畢業
in a couple of days 再過幾天
graduation〔ˌgrædʒʊˈeʃən〕*n.* 畢業；畢業典禮
graduate school 研究所

23.（**D**）

24.（**B**）grade〔gred〕*n.* 成績

25.（**D**）

Ⅲ. 克漏字

人類的特質

爲什麼現代社會充滿了進步的觀念？一定是因爲有某種進化過程正在我們周遭發生，而且它變得愈來愈明顯。雖然人類的智力或品德，沒有什麼全面性的進步，但在知識的累積方面，則有很大的進展。知識的增長，是從一個人的想法能夠經由言語傳達給另一個人就開始了。隨著書寫的發明，有了更大的進展，因爲知識不但能被傳遞，還能被記下來。圖書館使教育成爲可能，而教育也同樣使圖書館擴充：知識的增長遵循著一種複利法則，由於印刷術的發明，使知識的增長大有進展。但以上的發展都相當緩慢，直到科學的產生，才突然加速。然後知識開始遵循有系統的計劃累積。水滴變成河流；河流現在變成了急流。而且一旦獲得新知識，就會馬上把它變成實際的紀錄。所謂「現代文明」，不是由全人類本質上的均衡發展所造成的，而是由那些累積起來，並應用在日常生活中的知識所造成的。人類現在所面臨的問題是：接下來將利用這些知識做什麼？就像人們常說的，知識是一把雙刃劍，它可以同時被用來做好事或壞事。目前是有人運用知識來做好事，也有人用來做壞事。舉例來說，就在砲手運用科技把士兵的身體炸個粉碎時，附近的軍醫也正運用科技來使那些士兵恢復健康，有任何景觀比這個還要恐怖怪異嗎？我們必須很嚴肅地問自己，如果知識的雙重用途，力量不斷增強，那接下來會發生什麼事。

【註】

personality〔ˌpɝsn̩ˈæləti〕*n.* 特質；個性
progress〔ˈprɑgrɛs〕*n.* 進步；進化
loom〔lum〕*v.* 逐漸呈現；陰森地迫近
loom large 顯得突出；充滿
particular〔pɑrˈtɪkjələ˞〕*adj.* 某一的
actually〔ˈæktʃuəlɪ〕*adv.* 眞正地；實際上
take place 發生　　manifest〔ˈmænəˌfɛst〕*adj.* 明顯的

mankind〔mænˈkaɪnd〕*n.* 人類
undergo〔ˌʌndə˞ˈgo〕*v.* 經歷
general〔ˈdʒɛnərəl〕*adj.* 大體的；全面的
improvement〔ɪmˈpruvmənt〕*n.* 進步
intelligence〔ɪnˈtɛlədʒəns〕*n.* 智力
morality〔mɔˈræləti〕*n.* 品德
accumulation〔əˌkjumjəˈleʃən〕*n.* 累積

as soon as 一…就～　　individual〔ˌɪndəˈvɪdʒuəl〕*n.* 人；個人
by means of 藉由　　invention〔ɪnˈvɛnʃən〕*n.* 發明
not only…but also～ 不但…而且～
store〔stor〕*v.* 記存；儲存　　add〔æd〕*v.* 增加；擴大
growth〔groθ〕*n.* 增長　　***compound-interest*** 複利
enhance〔ɪnˈhæns〕*v.* 增長　　printing〔ˈprɪntɪŋ〕*n.* 印刷術
comparatively〔kəmˈpærətɪvlɪ〕*adv.* 相當地

suddenly〔ˈsʌdn̩lɪ〕*adv.* 突然
accumulate〔əˈkjumjəˌlet〕*v.* 累積
trickle〔ˈtrɪkl̩〕*n.* 水滴　stream〔strim〕*n.* 溪流
torrent〔ˈtɔrənt〕*n.* 急流　practical〔ˈpræktɪkl̩〕*adj.* 實際的
what is called 所謂的　civilization〔ˌsɪvl̩aɪˈzeʃən〕*n.* 文明
balanced〔ˈbælənst〕*adj.* 均衡的
nature〔ˈnetʃɚ〕*n.* 特質　apply〔əˈplaɪ〕*v.* 應用
humanity〔hjuˈmænətɪ〕*n.* 人類　***point out*** 指出

double-edged〔ˈdʌbl̩ˈɛdʒd〕*adj.* 雙刃的　sword〔sord〕*n.* 劍
equally〔ˈikwəlɪ〕*adv.* 同樣地　good〔gʊd〕*n.* 好事
evil〔ˈivl̩〕*n.* 惡事　indifferently〔ɪnˈdɪfərəntlɪ〕*adv.* 無差別地
spectacle〔ˈspɛktəkl̩〕*n.* 景象　***for instance*** 舉例來說
grimly〔ˈgrɪmlɪ〕*adv.* 恐怖地
whimsical〔ˈhwɪmzɪkl̩〕*adj.* 怪異的
gunner〔ˈgʌnɚ〕*n.* 砲手　shatter〔ˈʃætɚ〕*v.* 使粉碎

man〔mæn〕*n. pl.* 士兵　***close at hand*** 在近處
surgeon〔ˈsɝdʒən〕*n.* 外科醫生；軍醫
restore〔rɪˈstor〕*v.* 使恢復（健康的狀態等）
seriously〔ˈsɪrɪəslɪ〕*adv.* 嚴肅地
twofold〔ˈtuˈfold〕*adj.* 雙重的；兩倍的
ever-increasing〔ˈɛvɚɪnˈkrisɪŋ〕*adj.* 不斷增強的
continue〔kənˈtɪnju〕*v.* 持續

26.（**A**）依句意，選 (A) ***kind***「種類」。

27.（**A**）空格應填一連接詞，依句意，選 (A) ***and***。

28.（**C**）依句意，選 (C) ***Although***「雖然」。

29.（**B**）依句意，「在～方面」，介系詞用 ***in***。

30. (**D**) (B) unanimous〔juˈnænəməs〕*adj.* 全體一致的
(C) anonymous〔əˈnɑnəməs〕*adj.* 匿名的
(D) ***extraordinary***〔ɪkˈstrɔrdn̩ˌɛrɪ〕*adj.* 特別的；特大的

31. (**C**) 依句意，選 (C) ***Knowledge***「知識」。

32. (**A**) (B) idiosyncratic〔ˌɪdɪosɪnˈkrætɪk〕*adj.* 特異的
(C) unique〔juˈnik〕*adj.* 獨特的
(D) collective〔kəˈlɛktɪv〕*adj.* 集體的

33. (**D**) (A) transmute〔trænsˈmjut〕*v.* 將（性質、外觀等）改變成
(C) accessible〔ækˈsɛsəbl̩〕*adj.* 易接近的
(D) ***communicate***〔kəˈmjunəˌket〕*v.* 溝通；傳達

34. (**D**) 表「隨著～」，介系詞用 ***With***，選 (D)。

35. (**B**) (A) tradition〔trəˈdɪʃən〕*n.* 傳統
(B) ***advance***〔ədˈvæns〕*n.* 進步
(C) impairment〔ɪmˈpɛrmənt〕*n.* 損害
(D) civilization〔ˌsɪvl̩aɪˈzeʃən〕*n.* 文明

36. (**A**) 依句意爲被動語態，故選 (A) ***be***。

37. (**C**) 依句意，選 (C) ***Libraries***「圖書館」。而 (A) acquisition〔ˌækwəˈzɪʃən〕*n.* 獲得，則不合句意。

38. (**C**) ***in*** *one's* ***turn*** 自己也跟著；自己也一樣

39. (**D**) 依句意，知識「的」增長，選 (D) ***of***。

40. (**D**) (A) account〔əˈkaʊnt〕*n.* 帳戶
(B) route〔rut〕*n.* 路線
(D) ***law***〔lɔ〕*n.* 法則

41. (**A**) (A) ***invention*** [ɪn'vɛnʃən] *n.* 發明
(B) inflection [ɪn'flɛkʃən] *n.* (聲音的)抑揚聲調
(C) completion [kəm'pliʃən] *n.* 完成

42. (**A**) (A) ***slow*** [slo] *adj.* 緩慢的
(B) regressive [rɪ'grɛsɪv] *adj.* 後退的;逆行的
(C) delay [dɪ'le] *v.* 使延誤
(D) stagger ['stædʒɚ] *v.* 搖晃地走;蹣跚

43. (**B**) (A) trade [tred] *n.* 貿易
(B) ***rate*** [ret] *n.* 速度
(C) ratio ['reʃo] *n.* 比率
(D) efficiency [ə'fɪʃənsɪ] *n.* 效率

44. (**B**) 依句意,選 (B) ***began***「開始」。

45. (**A**) (A) ***systematic*** [ˌsɪstə'mætɪk] *adj.* 有系統的
(B) compound [kɑm'paʊnd] *adj.* 混合的
(D) regressive [rɪ'grɛsɪv] *adj.* 後退的;逆行的

46. (**C**) 指前面提過的那條溪流,須加定冠詞,選 (C) ***the***。

47. (**D**) (A) whereas [hwɛr'æz] *conj.* 然而
(B) apparently [ə'pærəntlɪ] *adv.* 顯然
(C) nevertheless [ˌnɛvəðə'lɛs] *adv.* 儘管如此
(D) ***moreover*** [mor'ovɚ] *adv.* 此外;而且

48. (**B**) 依句意,選 (B) ***acquire*** [ə'kwaɪr] *v.* 獲得。

49. (**C**) (C) ***account*** [ə'kaʊnt] *n.* 記述;記錄 (= *record*)
(D) practice ['præktɪs] *n.* 練習;實行

50. (**C**) ***not*** A ***but*** B 不是 A,而是 B
(B) nothing but 只是;不過是 (= *only*)

私立中原大學九十三學年度
碩士班研究生入學考試英文試題

第一部份 1～20 題為單選題，請選出最正確的答案，每題兩分 (40%)

1. The President of the United States appointed Powell to ________ the duty.
   (A) carried out　(B) help him carry out
   (C) carry away　(D) help him to carry

2. ________ I receive my paycheck, I can't pay my graduate school tuition.
   (A) When　(B) If
   (C) Unless　(D) Otherwise

3. Our research assistant is required to type at the ________ of 60 words per minute.
   (A) rank　(B) rating
   (C) rate　(D) ranking

4. ________ milk tea ________ jasmine tea is fine with me.
   (A) Neither…or　(B) Either…nor
   (C) Both…and　(D) Either…or

5. When the Wright brothers found something meaningful, they ________ everything and ________ it.
   (A) dropped…follows with　(B) dropped…went with
   (C) followed…dropped with　(D) left…went by

6. Professor Lee in the College of Engineering ________ his students work harder.
   (A) make (B) have made
   (C) made (D) made up

7. Thomas Edison, ________, held 1093 patents in 2001.
   (A) a great inventor (B) a great inventor whom
   (C) whom invented (D) who invented

8. Modern technology is closely ________ the basic needs of contemporary life.
   (A) assisted (B) associated
   (C) associated with (D) assisting with

9. As part of the young designer on an elite team, she is capable of designing artwork by ________.
   (A) himself (B) her own
   (C) his own (D) herself

10. ________ early retirement is popular among middle school teachers in Taiwan.
   (A) Taken (B) Doing
   (C) Taking (D) Done

11. ________ in the 20th century has provided a solid scientific basis in medical science.
   (A) Research (B) Researches
   (C) Researched (D) Researching

12. ________ students' demands, the Enrollment Center will announce the new schedule for enrollment much earlier than before.
   (A) Go with
   (B) Go hand in hand with
   (C) In response to
   (D) Due to the fact that

13. Art expresses the essential ________ of a period of time and provides a deeper understanding of a culture.
   (A) qualities (B) qualifications
   (C) qualifying (D) qualified

14. The churches of New York City are unique in American ________ for their revivalist style.
   (A) architect (B) architecture
   (C) whose architect (D) architecture where

15. Mark Twain's sense of humor was ________.
   (A) unlike most other people
   (B) unlike that of most other people
   (C) unlike another people
   (D) unlike that of other

In the new millennium, workaholism is still a fact of life for many working parents. The term "workaholic" describes people who are pretty much caught up in their work. They usually don't have time for leisure activities such as outings or family picnics.

Some workaholic parents work long hours because they fear being laid off or criticized for ineffectiveness. These people overwork but they don't really enjoy the job. As for other workaholic parents, they love their work and enjoy the success as well as high pay they earn from the job.

According to some well-known psychologists, workaholism is, in some ways, just like alcoholism; it is a compulsive disorder that slowly destroys the person's health, family relations, and interpersonal relationships.

However, many workaholic parents are afraid that they've raised youngsters just like themselves. Their work habits deeply affect the whole families. Children from a workaholic family tend to imitate their parents by working even harder.

Whether overwork is an addiction or a necessity in order to support the family, it does have a great impact on the family members, especially the little adults.

16. An important idea in this article is ________.
    (A) parental overwork is avoidable if they try
    (B) workaholic parents make time for family
    (C) workaholics often pass that on to the next generation
    (D) workaholic children are influential in the family

17. Workaholics are people who work long hours. They are ________.
    (A) sufferers of domestic violence
    (B) compulsory workers
    (C) compulsive workers
    (D) people with sadness and depression

In the future, students who are tired of paying a huge amount of money to heat their houses may have other options. Some claim that there is a trend to fuel a house by burning garbage.

Since the late 20th century, this alternative fuel source has been used by some innovators. They heat houses and shops by burning cubes of household garbage compressed by a trash compactor. The innovative heating units can handle tons of waste a day.

People who want to heat a house can purchase the alternative heating units, which cost over three thousand dollars, and a trash compactor, which also costs money. By using this alternative fuel source, these people probably can save up to $300 a year in heating costs.

Some professors have different views. They think that it might be meaningful from the energy-saving point of view, but doubt its popularity at present. After all, natural gas isn't that expensive.

Only time can tell if this alternative fuel source will be widely accepted by Americans in the future.

18. The main topic of this article is ________.
    (A) burning garbage would save our land
    (B) compacted waste may be a useful fuel in the future.
    (C) compacted waste is a trend
    (D) conserving energy is practical

19. Which of the following sentences is NOT true?
    (A) College professors think that this alternative fuel source is widely-accepted.
    (B) An alternative fuel source can conserve energy.
    (C) Future students may have a cheaper way to heat their houses.
    (D) An alternative fuel source will reduce the amount of waste usually placed in landfills.

20. Which of the following statements is true?
    (A) It's expensive to heat a house with natural gas.
    (B) This alternative fuel source is popular with college professors.
    (C) A user of this alternative fuel source can save $100 annually.
    (D) Burning garbage will reduce waste and conserve energy.

第二部份 英文作文 (10%)

Directions: Write about 100 words describing your future career plan.

國立中原大學九十三學年度
碩士班研究生入學考試英文試題詳解

第一部份　單選題：40%

1.（**B**）(B) ***help him carry out*** 幫助他執行
(C) carry away 帶走
appoint〔ə'pɔɪnt〕*v.* 指派　　duty〔'djutɪ〕*n.* 職務

2.（**C**）(C) ***unless***〔ən'lɛs〕*conj.* 除非
(D) otherwise〔'ʌðɚ,waɪz〕*adv.* 否則
paycheck〔'pe'tʃɛk〕*n.* 薪水支票
graduate school 研究所　　tuition〔tju'ɪʃən〕*n.* 學費

3.（**C**）(A) rank〔ræŋk〕*n.* 階級
(B) rating〔'retɪŋ〕*n.* 評價
(C) ***rate***〔ret〕*n.* 速度
(D) ranking〔'ræŋkɪŋ〕*n.* 名次；等級
research〔rɪ'sɝtʃ〕*n.* 研究
assistant〔ə'sɪstənt〕*n.* 助理
be required to 必須　　type〔taɪp〕*v.* 打字

4.（**D**）
either A or B「不是 A，就是 B；無論 A 或 B」
（動詞須與 B 一致）
neither A nor B「既不是 A，也不是 B；A 和 B 皆不」
（動詞須與 B 一致）
both A and B「A 和 B 兩者」
（其後須接複數動詞，在此不合）

依句意，選 (D)。
jasmine〔'dʒæsmɪn〕*n.* 茉莉　　***jasmine tea*** 茉莉花茶

5. (**B**) (A) drop〔drɑp〕*v.* 放下 follow with 依靠
(B) ***go with*** 跟著…走
(C) drop with 倒下
(D) go by 經過
meaningful〔ˈminɪŋfl̩〕*adj.* 有意義的

6. (**C**) 主詞為第三人稱單數，故 (A) (B) 不合，又依句意，「叫」他的學生更用功，須塡使役動詞，故選 (C) ***made***。而 (D) make up「組成」，則不合句意。
engineering〔ˌɛndʒəˈnɪrɪŋ〕*n.* 工程學

7. (**A**) a great inventor 是由 who was a great inventor 簡化而來。
hold〔hold〕*v.* 擁有
patent〔ˈpætn̩t〕*n.* 專利（權）

8. (**C**) (A) assist〔əˈsɪst〕*v.* 幫助
(C) ***be closely associated with*** 與…有密切關連
technology〔tɛkˈnɑlədʒɪ〕*n.* 科技
basic needs 基本的需求
contemporary〔kənˈtɛmpəˌrɛrɪ〕*adj.* 當代的；現代的

9. (**D**) (D) ***by herself*** 靠她自己（= *on her own*）
designer〔dɪˈzaɪnɚ〕*n.* 設計師
elite〔ɪˈlit〕*adj.* 最優秀的；精英的
artwork〔ˈɑrtˌwɝk〕*n.* 藝術品

10. (**C**) 空格應塡動名詞，才能做句子的主詞，又「退休」動詞須用 take，故選 (C) ***Taking***。
retirement〔rɪˈtaɪrmənt〕*n.* 退休
middle school 中學

11. (**A**) (A) ***research*** (rɪ'sɝtʃ) *n. v.* 研究
solid ('sɑlɪd) *adj.* 基礎穩固的；可靠的
scientific (,saɪən'tɪfɪk) *adj.* 科學的
medical science 醫學

12. (**C**) (A) go with 跟著…走
(B) go hand in hand with 與…步調一致
(C) ***in response to*** 爲了回應
(D) due to 由於
demand (dɪ'mænd) *n.* 需求
enrollment (ɪn'rolmənt) *n.* 入學
announce (ə'naʊns) *v.* 宣佈
schedule ('skɛdʒul) *n.* 時間表

13. (**A**) (A) ***quality*** ('kwɑlətɪ) *n.* 特質
(B) qualification (,kwɑləfə'keʃən) *n.* 資格
(C) qualifying ('kwɑlə,faɪɪŋ) *adj.* 給予資格的
(D) qualified ('kwɑlə,faɪd) *adj.* 有資格的
express (ɪk'sprɛs) *v.* 表達
essential (ə'sɛnʃəl) *adj.* 必要的；非常重要的

14. (**B**) (A) architect ('ɑrkə,tɛkt) *n.* 建築師
(B) ***architecture*** ('ɑrkə,tɛktʃɚ) *n.* 建築（學）
unique (ju'nik) *adj.* 獨特的
revivalist (rɪ'vaɪvḷɪst) *n.* 信仰復興運動者

15. (**B**) 爲避免重複前面提過的名詞，單數可用 that 代替。依句意，選 (B) ***unlike that of most other people*** (= *unlike the sense of humor of most other people*)。
sense of humor 幽默感

【譯文】

在這個新千禧年，工作狂仍是許多上班族父母無法改變的事實。「工作狂」這個名詞是用來形容非常熱中於工作的人。他們通常沒空從事像是郊遊或家庭野餐這種休閒活動。

有些有工作狂的父母長時間工作，因爲他們怕被暫時解僱，或是被批評說沒效率。這些人過度工作，但並不是眞的喜歡那份工作。至於其他有工作狂的父母，他們不但喜歡自己的工作和成就，而且也喜歡靠這份工作所賺得的高薪。

根據一些知名心理學家的說法，工作狂在某些方面，就像是酒精中毒一樣；它是一種強迫症，會慢慢破壞人們的健康、家庭關係和人際關係。

可是，許多有工作狂的父母，都怕看到自己的小孩長大之後會像他們一樣。他們的工作習慣深深影響了整個家庭。來自工作狂家庭的小孩，會學父母親，甚至工作得更賣力。

不管過度工作是一種上癮的現象，或是爲了養家而必須這麼做，它對於家庭成員的影響都很大，尤其是那些年輕人。

【答案】

16.（**C**）　　17.（**C**）

【註】

millennium（mə'lɛnɪəm）*n.* 千禧年
workaholism（'wɝkə,hɑlɪzm̩）*n.* 工作狂
a fact of life 無法改變的事實
term（tɝm）*n.* 名詞
workaholic（,wɝkə'hɑlɪk）*n.* 工作狂　*adj.* 醉心於工作的

be catch up in 熱中於　leisure〔'liʒɚ〕*adj.* 休閒的
outing〔'aʊtɪŋ〕*n.* 郊遊
lay off 暫時解僱　criticize〔'krɪtə,saɪz〕*v.* 批評
ineffectiveness〔,ɪnə'fɛktɪvnɪs〕*n.* 無效率
overwork〔'ovɚ'wɝk〕*n.* 工作過度　〔,ovɚ'wɝk〕*v.* 工作過度
as for 至於　***as well as*** 以及
pay〔pe〕*n.* 薪水　well-known〔'wɛl'non〕*adj.* 有名的
psychologist〔saɪ'kɑlədʒɪst〕*n.* 心理學家
alcoholism〔'ælkəhɔl,ɪzəm〕*n.* 酗酒；酒精中毒
compulsive〔kəm'pʌlsɪv〕*adj.* 強迫性的

disorder〔dɪs'ɔrdɚ〕*n.* 失調；病
destroy〔dɪ'strɔɪ〕*v.* 破壞
interpersonal〔,ɪntɚ'pɝsənḷ〕*adj.* 人與人之間的
raise〔rez〕*v.* 撫養　youngster〔'jʌŋstɚ〕*n.* 小孩子
tend to 易於；傾向於　imitate〔'ɪmə,tet〕*v.* 模仿
addiction〔ə'dɪkʃən〕*n.* 上癮
necessity〔nə'sɛsətɪ〕*n.* 必要；需要
support〔sə'port〕*v.* 扶養；支持
impact〔'ɪmpækt〕*n.* 影響　little〔'lɪtḷ〕*adj.* 年輕的
adult〔ə'dʌlt〕*n.* 成人　parental〔pə'rɛntḷ〕*adj.* 父母的
avoidable〔ə'vɔɪdəbḷ〕*adj.* 可避免的

make time 騰出時間　***pass…on to*** 將…傳給
generation〔,dʒɛnə'reʃən〕*n.* 一代
influential〔,ɪnflʊ'ɛnʃəl〕*adj.* 有影響力的
long hours 長時間　sufferer〔'sʌfərɚ〕*n.* 患者；受害者
domestic〔də'mɛstɪk〕*adj.* 家庭的
violence〔'vaɪələns〕*n.* 暴力
compulsory〔kəm'pʌlsərɪ〕*adj.* 強制的；義務的
depression〔dɪ'prɛʃən〕*n.* 沮喪；憂鬱

【譯文】

將來，厭煩支付高額費用，來使房子變溫暖的學生們，可能有其他選擇。有些人主張，以燃燒垃圾的方式來供給房子燃料，將成爲一種趨勢。

從二十世紀後期以來，有些創新的人已經開始使用替代性的燃料來源。他們燃燒經過垃圾壓縮機壓縮過後的塊狀家庭垃圾，來使房子或店面溫暖。這種新的暖氣裝置一天可以處理掉幾噸廢棄物。

想要讓屋子變溫暖的人，可以購買替代性的暖氣裝置，它的價格超過三千元，還要有一部垃圾壓縮機，那也要花錢買。那些使用替代性燃料來源的人，在暖氣費用上面，一年下來可能可以節省超過三百元。

有些教授有不同的看法。他們認爲，從節省能源的觀點來看，這或許是有意義的，但是卻對於它目前受歡迎的程度感到懷疑。畢竟，天然瓦斯也不是很貴。

只要再過一陣子，我們就會知道，替代性的燃料來源，將來會不會被美國人民廣泛地接受。

【答案】

18.（**B**）　19.（**A**）　20.（**D**）

【註】

heat〔hit〕*v.* 使溫暖　option〔ˈɑpʃən〕*n.* 選擇
claim〔klem〕*v.* 宣稱　trend〔trɛnd〕*n.* 趨勢
fuel〔ˈfjuəl〕*v.* 供給燃料　*n.* 燃料
garbage〔ˈgɑrbɪdʒ〕*n.* 垃圾
alternative〔ɔlˈtɝnətɪv〕*adj.* 選擇的；可供替代的

innovator〔ˈɪnə,vetɚ〕*n.* 改革者；創新者
cube〔kjub〕*n.* 立方體
household〔ˈhaʊs,hold〕*adj.* 家庭的
compress〔kəmˈprɛs〕*v.* 壓縮　　trash〔træʃ〕*n.* 垃圾
compactor〔kəmˈpæktɚ〕*n.* 壓縮機
innovative〔ˈɪnə,vetɪv〕*adj.* 創新的
heating〔ˈhitɪŋ〕*n.* 加熱作用；暖氣裝置
unit〔ˈjunɪt〕*n.* 裝置　　ton〔tʌn〕*n.* 噸

waste〔west〕*n.* 廢棄物　　***up to*** 多達
view〔vju〕*n.* 看法　　save〔sev〕*v.* 節省
point of view 觀點　　doubt〔daʊt〕*v.* 懷疑
popularity〔,pɑpjəˈlærətɪ〕*n.* 受歡迎　　***at present*** 目前
after all 畢竟　　conserve〔kənˈsɝv〕*v.* 節省
practical〔ˈpræktɪkl̩〕*adj.* 實際的
annually〔ˈænjʊəlɪ〕*adv.* 每年

第二部份　英文作文：10%

提示：請用 100 字來描述你未來的生涯規劃。

If someone asked you what you want to be in the future, would you know what to tell them? I would. I want to be a writer in the future. I will start by working as a reporter for a newspaper where I can learn writing skills. Then I want some international assignments so that I can get sent to other countries. After a few years as a journalist, I would like to write a book detailing my travels and my experience. After that, I want to write books full time and work as a freelancer for newspapers or magazines from time to time.

私立淡江大學九十三學年度
碩士班研究生入學考試英文試題

I. In each of the following sentences, there is a blank. Fill in each blank with the correct preposition to form a proper idiom. The words in italics at the end of each sentence are an equivalent of the idiom. 20%

1. Jocelyn is leaving Taipei ________ good. — *forever* —
   (A) in (B) on (C) at (D) for

2. Louis was going to the meeting ________ place of Mary, who had to work. — *instead of* —
   (A) in (B) on (C) of (D) for

3. This movie discusses, ________ the most part, the possibility of life on other planets. — *mainly* —
   (A) in (B) on (C) at (D) for

4. We were walking on the beach when, all ________ a sudden, we heard the sound of the gun. — *suddenly* —
   (A) in (B) of (C) at (D) for

5. It rained off and ________ all day last Saturday.
   — *intermittently* —
   (A) in (B) on (C) at (D) for

6. Because Sophia doesn't care ________ dark colors, she buys only brightly colored clothes. — *like* —
   (A) in (B) on (C) at (D) for

7. ________ times, it is difficult to understand him because he speaks too fast. — *occasionally* —
   (A) In (B) With (C) At (D) Through

8. Iris came along ________ her supervisor to the budget meeting. — *accompany* —
   (A) in (B) with (C) at (D) through

9. It is difficult to get ________ to someone who doesn't understand your language. — *manage to communicate* —
   (A) in (B) with (B) at (D) through

10. Because of the increase in problems created after the game, the principal of the school decided to do away ________ all the sports activities this week. — *eliminate; get rid of* —
   (A) in (B) with (C) at (D) through

II. Vocabulary: In each of the following (11 to 20) sentences, there is a word in bold face. Below each sentence are four other words or phrases. You are to choose the one word or phrase, (A), (B), (C), or (D), which would best keep the meaning of the original sentence if it were substituted for the bold-face word. 20%

11. She closes her eyes and **moistens** her lips.
   (A) makes dry (B) licks
   (C) makes wet (D) kisses

12. She **despises** the fact that everything went from bad to worse. She kissed her boyfriend good-bye.
    (A) respects (B) hates
    (C) admires (D) appreciates

13. She left behind everything that was secure — a regular paycheck, a pension, electricity, phones, cars and television — to become **a volunteer** teacher in various parts of the underdeveloped world.
    (A) helpful (B) hard-working
    (C) responsible (D) without pay

14. I won't **demean** myself by taking a bribe.
    (A) degrade (B) please
    (C) cheat (D) flatter

15. There is a lack of **consensus** among the inhabitants that their children should have a broad understanding of the world.
    (A) feeling (B) conflict
    (C) agreement (D) ignorance

16. Like many **celebrities**, she complained of being persecuted by the press.
    (A) ethnic minorities (B) underprivileged people
    (C) poor people (D) famous people

17. The referendum is a direct vote of the people **superseding** the legislature.
    (A) being passed by (B) replacing
    (C) being vetoed by (D) drafted by

18. Unwilling to accept their opponent's come-from-behind slim victory calmly, they asked to have the result **annulled**.
(A) challenged (B) changed
(C) announced (D) invalidated

19. The leaders have **initiated** legal proceedings against the newspaper.
(A) started (B) vetoed
(C) contested (D) stressed

20. We expected a more **accommodating** attitude during discussions.
(A) knowledgeable
(B) learned
(C) helpful
(D) unwilling to do what someone else wants

III. Structure and Written Expression: In the following (21-30) sentences, there are four words or phrases underlined. The four underlined parts of the sentences are marked (A), (B), (C), and (D). You are to identify the one underlined word or phrase that should be corrected or rewritten. Then, on your answer sheet, find the number of the problem and mark your answer. 20%

21. In spite of (A) impressions that bottled water is the healthier (B), there is little (C) difference between bottled water and tap water, apart from cost (D).

22. Bottled water is the fastest growth beverage industry in the
A
world, worth up to US $22 billion a year, according to the
B C D
World Wildlife Fund, a conservation group.

23. A study authorized by the World Wildlife Fund found that the "bottled water market is partly driven by concerns over
A B
the safety of municipal water and by the marketing of many
C
brands which describe themselves as being healthy than tap
D
water."

24. As I was carried here so swiftly across the continent by a jet airliner, it occurred to me that I will really on the way
A B C
after ten years, for it was that long ago that you first invited
D
me to come to Tamkang College.

25. Had I come ten years ago, I am not certain what I
A
have talked about. But as I have lived and learned, one
B
thing stands out in my mind as having such vast
C
importance that I want to discuss it with you now.
D

26. I wish to speak today of man's relation to nature and
A
more specifically of man's attitude toward nature. A
B
generation ago this perhaps have been an academic subject
C
of little interest to any but philosophers.
D

27. The word nature has many and varied connotations, but for
A B C
the present theme I like this definition: "Nature is the part of the world that man did not make."
D

28. You who have spent your undergraduate years at Tamkang
A B
College have been exceptionally fortunate, for you living in
C
the midst of beauty and comforts and conveniences that are
D
creations of man.

29. I would like to say that you always have the majestic and
A
beautiful mountains in the background to remind you of
B
a older and vaster world — a world that man did not make.
C D

30. Man has long talked somewhat arrogant about the conquest
(A: arrogant about)
of nature; now he has the power to achieve his boast. It may well be our final tragedy that this power has not been tempered with wisdom but has been marked by irresponsibility.
(B: final; C: has not been tempered; D: marked by irresponsibility)

IV. Translation: Translate the following sentences into English. 20%.

1. 如果沒有這個古拙的音樂盒子在身邊，祖母晚年會很驚惶空虛。
2. 早逝的祖父曾說那是一位金匠用"心之石 (elixir of the heart)"打造的。
3. 她也說它是天地結合時才有的產物，比魔戒還要美麗。
4. 祖父母相繼走後，從沒有人眞正知道他背後的秘密。
5. 後來我從祖母的日記得知，那是他年輕時送給她的定情物。

V. Composition: 20%. Write a short essay of 150 to 200 words on one of the following statements:

(1) Compassion, not passion, is what we need for the survival of our individual lives, our families, and our society.

(2) Economic growth is secondary to environmental protection for three reasons.

(3) There are three reasons that passengers should be allowed to drink mineral water on the MRT.

私立淡江大學九十三學年度
碩士班研究生入學考試英文試題詳解

I. 文法：20%

1.（**D**）***for good*** 永遠（= *forever*）

2.（**A**）***in place of*** 代替（= *instead of*）

3.（**D**）***for the most part*** 大體上；大部份
possibility〔ˌpɑsəˈbɪlətɪ〕*n.* 可能性
life〔laɪf〕*n.* 生物　planet〔ˈplænɪt〕*n.* 行星

4.（**B**）***all of the sudden*** 突然地（= *suddenly*）
gun〔gʌn〕*n.* 槍

5.（**B**）***off and on*** 斷斷續續地（= *on and off*）
intermittently〔ˌɪntɚˈmɪtn̩tlɪ〕*adv.* 斷斷續續地

6.（**D**）***care for*** 喜歡　dark〔dɑrk〕*adj.* 暗的；深的
brightly〔ˈbraɪtlɪ〕*adv.* 明亮地　***brightly colored*** 鮮豔的

7.（**C**）***at times*** 有時候
occasionally〔əˈkeʒənl̩ɪ〕*adv.* 偶爾；有時候

8.（**B**）***come along with*** 隨同；和～一起來
supervisor〔ˌsupɚˈvaɪzɚ〕*n.* 上司
budget〔ˈbʌdʒɪt〕*n.* 預算
accompany〔əˈkʌmpənɪ〕*v.* 陪同；與…一起來

9.（**D**）***get through to*** 使～瞭解
manage〔ˈmænɪdʒ〕*v.* 設法 <*to*>
communicate〔kəˈmjunəˌket〕*v.* 溝通；傳達

10.（B） ***do away with*** 取消；廢除
create〔krɪ'et〕*v.* 引起
principal〔'prɪnsəpḷ〕*n.* 校長
eliminate〔ɪ'lɪmə,net〕*v.* 消除；刪掉 ***get rid of*** 消除

Ⅱ. 字彙：20%

11.（C） moisten〔'mɔɪsṇ〕*v.* 使濕潤
(A) dry〔draɪ〕*adj.* 乾燥的
(B) lick〔lɪk〕*v.* 舔
(C) ***wet***〔wɛt〕*adj.* 濕的
moisten one's lips 舔濕嘴唇

12.（B） despise〔dɪ'spaɪz〕*v.* 討厭；不喜歡
(A) respect〔rɪ'spɛkt〕*v.* 尊敬
(B) ***hate***〔het〕*v.* 討厭
(C) admire〔əd'maɪr〕*v.* 欽佩
(D) appreciate〔ə'priʃɪ,et〕*v.* 欣賞
go from bad to worse 愈來愈壞；每下愈況

13.（D） volunteer〔,vɑlən'tɪr〕*adj.* 自願的
(B) hard-working〔'hɑrd,wɝkɪŋ〕*adj.* 勤勉的
(C) responsible〔rɪ'spɑnsəbḷ〕*adj.* 負責的
(D) ***without pay*** 沒有薪水的
leave behind 放棄
secure〔sɪ'kjʊr〕*adj.* 安定的；受到保障的
paycheck〔'pe'tʃɛk〕*n.* 薪水支票
pension〔'pɛnʃən〕*n.* 退休金
electricity〔ɪ,lɛk'trɪsətɪ〕*n.* 電力
various〔'vɛrɪəs〕*adj.* 各種不同的
underdeveloped〔,ʌndədɪ'vɛləpt〕*adj.* 低度開發的

14. (**A**) demean〔dɪ'min〕*v.* 貶抑；降低（品格）
  (A) ***degrade***〔dɪ'gred〕*v.* 降低人格
  (B) please〔pliz〕*v.* 取悅
  (C) cheat〔tʃit〕*v.* 欺騙
  (D) flatter〔'flætɚ〕*v.* 奉承；阿諛
  bribe〔braɪb〕*n.* 賄賂

15. (**C**) consensus〔kən'sɛnsəs〕*n.* 意見一致；共識
  (B) conflict〔'kɑnflɪkt〕*n.* 衝突
  (C) ***agreement***〔ə'grimənt〕*n.* 意見一致；同意
  (D) ignorance〔'ɪgnərəns〕*n.* 無知
  lack〔læk〕*n.* 缺乏　inhabitant〔ɪn'hæbətənt〕*n.* 居民
  broad〔brɔd〕*adj.* 廣博的；豐富的

16. (**D**) celebrity〔sə'lɛbrətɪ〕*n.* 名人
  (A) ethnic〔'ɛθnɪk〕*adj.* 民族的
  minority〔mə'nɔrətɪ〕*n.* 少數
  ethnic minority 少數民族集團
  (B) underprivileged〔'ʌndɚ'prɪvəlɪdʒd〕*adj.* 貧困的
  (D) ***famous***〔'feməs〕*adj.* 有名的
  complain〔kəm'plen〕*v.* 抱怨
  persecute〔'pɝsɪ,kjut〕*v.* 使困擾
  press〔prɛs〕*n.* 新聞記者；新聞界

17. (**B**) supersede〔,supɚ'sid〕*v.* 取代；接替
  (A) pass by 經過
  (B) ***replace***〔rɪ'ples〕*v.* 取代；接替
  (C) veto〔'vito〕*v.* 否決；嚴禁
  (D) draft〔dræft〕*v.* 徵召（入伍）
  referendum〔,rɛfə'rɛndəm〕*n.* 公民投票
  vote〔vot〕*n.* 投票；表決
  legislature〔'lɛdʒɪs,letʃɚ〕*n.* 立法院

18.（**D**）annul〔ə'nʌl〕*v.* 無效；取消
(A) challenge〔'tʃælɪŋdʒ〕*v.* 挑戰
(C) announce〔ə'naʊns〕*v.* 宣佈
(D) ***invalidate***〔ɪn'vælə,det〕*v.* 使無效
unwilling〔ʌn'wɪlɪŋ〕*adj.* 不願意的
opponent〔ə'ponənt〕*n.* 對手
come-from-behind 後來居上的
slim〔slɪm〕*adj.* 少的 victory〔'vɪktrɪ〕*n.* 勝利
calmly〔'kɑmlɪ〕*adv.* 冷靜地

19.（**A**）initiate〔ɪ'nɪʃɪ,et〕*v.* 開始；著手
(B) veto〔'vito〕*v.* 否決
(C) contest〔kən'tɛst〕*v.* 爭取；競爭
(D) stress〔strɛs〕*v.* 強調
legal〔'ligḷ〕*adj.* 法律的
proceeding〔prə'sidɪŋ〕*n.* 行動；行爲

20.（**C**）accommodating〔ə'kɑmə,detɪŋ〕*adj.* 肯幫忙的；樂於助人的
(A) knowledgeable〔'nɑlɪdʒəbḷ〕*adj.* 有知識的
(B) learned〔'lɝnɪd〕*adj.* 有學問的
(D) unwilling〔ʌn'wɪlɪŋ〕*adj.* 不願意的

Ⅲ. 結構與書面表達：20%

21.（**B**）*the healthier* → ***healthier***
in spite of 儘管
impression〔ɪm'prɛʃən〕*n.* 印象
bottled〔'bɑtḷd〕*adj.* 瓶裝的
tap〔tæp〕*n.* 水龍頭 ***tap water*** 自來水
apart from 除了…之外 cost〔kɔst〕*n.* 費用

22.（ A ） *the fastest growth* → ***the fastest growing***
beverage〔ˈbɛvərɪdʒ〕*n.* 飲料
worth〔wɝθ〕*adj.* 值…的
up to 高達　　billion〔ˈbɪljən〕*n.* 十億
wildlife〔ˈwaɪldˌlaɪf〕*n.* 野生生物
fund〔fʌnd〕*n.* 基金
conservation〔ˌkɑnsɚˈveʃən〕*n.*（資源的）保存；維護

23.（ D ） *being healthy* → ***being healthier***
authorize〔ˈɔθəˌraɪz〕*v.* 授權；認可
partly〔ˈpɑrtlɪ〕*adv.* 部分地；有些
drive〔draɪv〕*v.* 驅策；驅使
concern〔kənˈsɝn〕*n.* 關心；憂慮
municipal〔mjuˈnɪsəpl̩〕*adj.* 都市的
marketing〔ˈmɑrkɪtɪŋ〕*n.* 銷售；行銷
brand〔brænd〕*n.* 牌子
describe〔dɪˈskraɪb〕*v.* 敘述；說明

24.（ C ） *will really* → ***was really***
carry〔ˈkærɪ〕*v.* 載運
swiftly〔ˈswɪftlɪ〕*adv.* 迅速地
continent〔ˈkɑntənənt〕*n.* 大陸
jet〔dʒɛt〕*adj.* 噴射的
airliner〔ˈɛrˌlaɪnɚ〕*n.*（大型）客機；班機
occur to 使（某人）想起　　***on the way*** 來到；接近

25.（ B ） *have talked about* → ***would have talked about***
live and learn 活到老，學到老
stand out 浮現；突出
vast〔væst〕*adj.* 很大的

26. (**C**) *perhaps have been* → ***perhaps would have been***

man〔mæn〕*n.* 人類
specifically〔spɪ'sɪfɪkḷɪ〕*adv.* 具體地
generation〔,dʒɛnə'reʃən〕*n.* 一代
academic〔,ækə'dɛmɪk〕*adj.* 學術的
subject〔'sʌbdʒɪkt〕*n.* 主題；科目
philosopher〔fə'lɑsəfɚ〕*n.* 哲學家

27. (完全正確)

varied〔'vɛrɪd〕*adj.* 不同的
connotation〔,kɑnə'teʃən〕*n.* 涵義
present〔'prɛznṭ〕*adj.* 當前的；正在處理中的
theme〔θim〕*n.* 主題
definition〔,dɛfə'nɪʃən〕*n.* 定義

28. (**C**) *for you* → ***for your***

undergraduate〔,ʌndɚ'grædʒʊ,et〕*adj.* 大學生的
exceptionally〔ɪk'sɛpʃənḷɪ〕*adv.* 特別地；非常地
fortunate〔'fɔrtʃənɪt〕*adj.* 幸運的
midst〔mɪdst〕*n.* 中間
comfort〔'kʌmfɚt〕*n.* 舒適
convenience〔kən'vinjəns〕*n.* 便利
creation〔krɪ'eʃən〕*n.* 創作；產物

29. (**C**) *a older and vaster world* → ***an older and vaster world***

majestic〔mə'dʒɛstɪk〕*adj.* 雄偉的
background〔'bæk,graʊnd〕*n.* 背景
remind〔rɪ'maɪnd〕*v.* 使想起；使注意到
vast〔væst〕*adj.* 廣大的

30.（ **A** ） *arrogant about* → ***arrogantly about***

somewhat〔 'sʌm,hwɑt 〕*adv.* 略微；有點
arrogant〔 'ærəgənt 〕*adj.* 傲慢的；自大的
conquest〔 'kɑŋkwɛst 〕*n.* 征服
boast〔 bost 〕*n.* 自誇；引以爲傲的事
may well 也許；很可能　　tragedy〔 'trædʒədɪ 〕*n.* 悲劇
temper〔 'tɛmpɚ 〕*v.* 調和
wisdom〔 'wɪzdəm 〕*n.* 智慧
mark〔 mɑrk 〕*v.* 使具有…特徵
irresponsibility〔 ,ɪrɪ,spɑnsə'bɪlətɪ 〕*n.* 不負責任

IV. 中翻英：20%

1. If it wasn't for this antique music box, grandmother would have felt very lonely and scared in her later years.

2. Our late grandfather used to say the music box was made by a goldsmith using an "elixir of the heart."

3. Grandmother also said that the box was made from extremely rare materials, even more beautiful than the magical ring.

4. After my grandparents passed away, nobody really knew the secret behind the music box.

5. It was after I found out from my grandmother's diary, that the music box was a love token given to her by grandfather when he was young.

V. 作文：20%

根據下列敘述的其中一個，寫一篇150至200字的短文。

(1) 同情心才是我們個人生活、家庭和社會生存所必須的，而非熱情。

(2) 經濟成長次於環境保護，原因有三點。

(3) 乘客在搭乘捷運時，應該要被允許飲用礦泉水，有三個原因。

Economic growth has propelled and advanced humanity for the last century. Today, we enjoy unprecedented luxuries and comforts due in large part to improved trade and industry. But with any gains there are associated costs.

One of the biggest trade-offs is the environment. There are three reasons why we should now view economic growth as secondary to environmental protection. First, the earth's natural resources are running out. Soon, there will be no more oil to pump and no more coal to mine. Second, pollution is rapidly causing the earth's atmosphere to deteriorate while clean water supplies are declining rapidly. Third, we are driving many species of plants and animals to extinction by encroaching on their natural habitats.

These reasons are why environmental protection should now take precedence over economic growth. The price to be paid for this growth is far too high to bear.

93年度各校新增系所與考試科目

學校	新增系所	考試科目
台灣大學	法醫學研究所	甲組： 1. 法醫學（甲）（含公共衛生學） 2. 英文（A） 3. 內科學、口腔內科學【二擇一】 4. 病理學、口腔病理學【二擇一】 5. 解剖學、生物化學（一般生物化學）【二擇一】 乙組： 1. 法醫學（乙）（含公共衛生學） 2. 應用病理學 3. 解剖學及生物學（各佔50%） 4. 英文（A） 5. 生物化學（一般生物化學）、臨床生化學、內外科護理學、衛生行政學、物理治療學、職能治療學【六擇一】
	資訊網路與多媒體研究所	書面審核與口試
	科技整合法律學研究所	
政治大學	台灣史研究所	1. 台灣史 2. 台灣近代政治經濟史 3. 東亞近代史
	法律科技整合研究所班	1. 分析能力一（測驗題） 2. 分析能力二（申論題） 3. 英文
台灣師範大學	應用電子科技研究所	1. 國文 2. 英文 3. 電子學 4. 工程數學

學校	新 增 系 所	考 試 科 目
台北大學	通訊工程研究所	1. 台灣文學史 2. 中國文學史 3. 文學理論 4. 英文
彰化師範大學	生物技術研究所	1. 分子生物學 2. 英文
	翻譯研究所	甲組（筆譯組） 1. 英文（含作文、中譯英、英譯中） 乙組（口譯組） 1. 英文（含中譯英、英譯中） 2. 國文
	兒童英文研究所	1. 英文（含作文與翻譯） 2. 語言學概論（含兒童語言習得） 3. 英語教學概論（含兒童英語教學）
	資訊工程研究所	1. 資料結構與演算法 2. 離散數學及線性代數 3. 作業系統及計算機結構 4. 英文
	車輛與軌道技術研究所	1. 工程數學 2. 自動控制 3. 工程英文
	歷史學研究所	1. 中國史 2. 世界史 3. 史學概論 4. 英文
	政治學研究所	分為三組，考試科目相同：甲組（公共行政組）、乙組（比較政治組）、丙組（國際關係組） 1. 政治學 2. 英文 3. 國文 4. 行政學

學校	新增系所	考試科目
彰化師範大學	應用運動科學研究所	甲組（運動科學組） 1. 體育英文 2. 體育統計學 3. 運動科學（含運動生理學、運動生物力學、運動心理學） 乙組（運動教育組） 1. 體育英文 2. 體育統計學 3. 運動教育（含體育原理、體育行政、運動管理）
高雄師範大學	客家文化研究所	1. 客家族群研究　2. 人類學導論 3. 社會學（註：有參考書目，詳見網址：http://www.nknu.edu.tw/~hakka/）
	復健諮商研究所	1. 國文　2. 英文 3. 身心障礙者的生理與心理 4. 身心障礙者輔導理論與實務 5. 特殊教育研究與評量
	人力與知識管理研究所	A 類 1. 國文　2. 英文 3. 人力資源發展　4. 教育政策 5. 知識管理 B 類 1. 國文　2. 英文 3. 人力資源發展　4. 管理學 5. 知識管理
	體育系研究所	1. 運動心理學　2. 運動生理學 3. 運動社會學　4. 運動管理學
國立台北師範學院	特殊教育學系早期療育碩士班	1. 國文 2. 英文 3. 早期療育 4. 兒童發展 5. 教育研究法（含教育統計）

學校	新增系所	考試科目
國立台北師範學院	語文教育學系碩士班	1. 英文　2. 國語文能力 3. 語文科教材教法　4. 兒童文學
	資訊科學研究所	1. 英文 2. 計算機概論（含資料結構、物件導向程式設計） 3. 離散數學 4. 計算機系統（作業系統、計算機結構）
	生命教育與健康促進研究所	1. 英文 2. 社會科學研究法 3. 健康促進（含衛生教育、健康行為科學）、生命教育【二擇一】
中正大學	台灣文學研究所	1. 台灣文學史 2. 中國文學史 3. 文學理論 4. 英文
中興大學	電機工程學系丁組	1. 工程數學（含線性代數、微分方程） 2. 電子學 3. 積體電路設計、計算機組織【二擇一】
暨南國際大學	人類學研究所	1. 人類學概論 2. 台灣社會與文化 3. 英文
高雄大學	人類學研究所	一、光電組 1. 電磁學 2. 工程數學（微分方程與線性代數各佔 50%） 3. 近代物理 二、計算機組 1. 計算機概論（含程式設計、資料結構） 2. 計算機系統（含計算機組織、作業系統） 3. 工程數學（含線性代數、離散數學）

學校	新增系所	考試科目
高雄大學	電機工程學系碩士班	三、半導體組 1. 積體電路與系統 a. 微電子學 b. 工程數學（微分方程、線性代數） c. 計算機組織 2. 元件 a. 微電子學 b. 工程數學（微分方程、線性代數） c. 半導體元件物理（含電磁學 50%） 四、通訊組 1. 通訊系統 2. 工程數學（線性代數與機率各佔 50%） 3. 微電子學
高雄第一科技大學	光電工程研究所	1. 工程數學 2. 普通物理
台中師範學院	早期療育所	1. 國文 2. 英文 3. 幼兒發展 4. 教育研究法 5. 早期療育理論與實務
	教學科技所	1. 國文 2. 英文 3. 資訊科學概論 4. 多媒體概論
	課程與教學所	1. 專業英文 2. 教育學 3. 課程理論 4. 教學理論

研究所英文試題詳解④

主　　編 / 謝靜芳
發 行 所 / 學習出版有限公司　☎ (02) 2704-5525
郵撥帳號 / 0512727-2 學習出版社帳戶
登 記 證 / 局版台業 2179 號
印 刷 所 / 裕強彩色印刷有限公司
台北門市 / 台北市許昌街 10 號 2 F　☎ (02) 2331-4060・2331-9209
台中門市 / 台中市綠川東街 32 號 8 F 23 室　☎ (04) 2223-2838
台灣總經銷 / 紅螞蟻圖書有限公司　☎ (02) 2795-3656
美國總經銷 / Evergreen Book Store　☎ (818) 2813622
本公司網址　www.learnbook.com.tw
電子郵件　learnbook@learnbook.com.tw

售價：新台幣三百八十元正

2007 年 8 月 1 日新修訂

ISBN 957-519-796-8